MW00856313

THE BETRAYER'S BANE

By

Michael G. Manning

Cover by Amalia Chitulescu
Editing by Grace Bryan Butler
© 2016 by Michael G. Manning
All rights reserved.
ISBN: 978-1943481064

For more information about the Mageborn series check out the author's Facebook page:

https://www.facebook.com/MagebornAuthor

or visit the website:

http://www.magebornbooks.com/

FOREWORD

As I stare at this page, wondering what to say to you, Dear Reader, my first impulse is to say that perhaps this section should be titled, 'Forewarning'.

Presumably those of you reading these words have read the two books that come before, and there's a good chance you've also read the Mageborn series that referenced the story here as ancient history. If so, you should have some idea of what is to come.

This was a difficult book to write. I didn't expect that, though in hindsight, I should have. Tyrion began his journey as a relatable young man, one who endured some terrible things, sure, but he had many chances to change the path his life eventually took him down.

Don't expect that he'll turn it around now. This bus is heading down a steep slope, and nothing good waits at the end. I'm not even sure if this fits with what I personally think of as fantasy. It borders a realm normally reserved for horror, or non-fiction stories about terrible events in history.

Fantasy, at its best, highlights the strength of the human spirit, the things people can do when placed in extraordinary and extreme situations. It explores the characteristics of a hero or heroine, and no matter how dark, it shows us that people can overcome almost any challenge.

This is not that sort of book.

This is a story about failure, about the darkness that resides in all of us, and which, in this case, consumes the main character and those closest to him. Brace yourself, Dear Reader, for reading this book is to look into the void within. Be careful that you don't look too long, or you may find the void staring back at you.

My only consolation for you is that from the ashes left in this novel, will eventually rise the stories you find later in Mageborn.

PROLOGUE

Are you sure you want to hear the rest of this?" I asked them.

Matthew gave me a grim look, "I've been remembering it since you started telling. I know what to expect."

"Maybe we shouldn't hear the rest," put in Moira, glancing at her brother. "I had bad dreams last night."

"I want to hear the rest," said Lynaralla.

I sighed, "They're your parents after all. If anyone has a right to know, it would be you."

"They lived through it at least, right?" said Moira half-heartedly. "It can't be all bad."

Matthew and I looked at each other and I pressed my lips into a tight line. He looked at his sister, "Yeah, it is."

Moira groaned.

"I'll start with one of the nicer moments," I told her, "not long after Kate had given birth to her first child with Tyrion…"

CHAPTER 1

"Take her would you, Daniel?" asked Kate.

It wasn't really a request of course, as any husband or father knows. Nor was it truly a burden. Tyrion stepped closer immediately, grateful for the opportunity to hold little Inara. The babe had just finished her breakfast, and Kate wanted both hands to put the leftovers back under cover of her dress.

Leftovers was the nickname he had given her still lovely breasts when they were alone. The name was a joke of course, but it had annoyed her at first. He had made sure she didn't stay annoyed for long.

Right now his attention was occupied by the tiny life in his arms. Even the 'leftovers' couldn't distract his eyes from the baby for long.

She's so small, he thought. *So fragile, her life could be snuffed out in an instant.* As usual his protective instincts took a dark turn without warning, and his overly sharp imagination showed him an image of the child dead in his hands. *No!* His heart seemed to clench in his chest. With an act of deliberation, he banished the morbid vision and focused his eyes again on the beautiful creature he held.

Soft strawberry curls framed chubby cheeks and eyes that were still the blue of the recently born. Inara was only a month and a half old now and was the subject of a lot of attention. There were only two children in Albamarl at present, Inara and her half-brother, Layla's son Eldin. The two babes had been born only weeks apart.

3

Tyrion's grown children, particularly his daughters, competed to spend time with the infants which meant that Kate and Layla had no shortage of helpers to give them breaks. If anything they had too little time with their infants. As a result, Tyrion found himself feeling a bit jealous, not of the attention that the small ones received, but of his own time with them.

A sharp pain brought his mind back to the present, Inara was pulling on his beard again. He didn't fight the tug, instead he ducked his head closer to kiss her cheeks. She squirmed in his hands, for his whiskers tickled. She also forgot her grip on his beard, and he pulled his head back, smiling at her.

"Daniel, are you alright?" Kate was watching him with concern.

"Yeah," he replied. "Why?"

She touched his cheek, "You're crying."

He hadn't been fully aware of the fact until just then. "She was pulling my beard. It made my eyes water for a moment," he answered.

"Liar," said Kate, kissing his forehead. "I can take her now."

"Mind if I hold her for a while?" he said, not ready to give her back. "This is my first time to get to do this."

Kate frowned, "You were holding her just an hour ago. This isn't your first time."

"No, I mean the first time in my life. I've never been a father before, not a real one, not like this," he explained.

Her eyes softened, "That's a strange line from a man with eighteen children."

"Fifteen now, they took three from me," he responded, reminding her of the three that had been lost in the arena, *Haley, Gabriel, and Jack.* The names echoed once more in his mind. *Never forget.*

A surge of aythar outside the house caught his attention, and his magesight refocused on it, taking the foreground of his thoughts. Brigid was practicing again. Alone.

Her magic was razor sharp, flickering around her in blinding flashes, moving at the speed of thought. She remained perfectly still, her mind had nothing left to spare for physical movement. Small poles had been driven into the ground around her and stood at various heights, with lines marking them at specific places. Some of them were quite lengthy, towering over her, but they didn't remain that way for long.

With a clatter they fell around her in small sections. Some pieces were only inches in length and others were several feet, but without exception every cut had been made at a point marked by a black line. Her practice had lasted only a few seconds, but Brigid had sliced the thick wooden rods with near perfect precision. Each had been touched only at the places she had marked beforehand.

"What is it now?" asked Kate, bringing his attention back to the room they were in.

"Brigid is practicing again."

"That's nothing new," she commented. "I really worry about her."

He nodded, "We all do." *And most of the others are afraid of her,* he mentally added, *not that I blame them.* Brigid practiced fanatically, and always alone. None of the others wanted to take the risk of sparring with her anymore. She was too fierce, and she had shown a marked disregard for her partners' health and wellbeing.

The only thing she showed any interest in apart from honing her battle skills, was Tyrion. She followed him like a dark shadow and madness seemed to lurk in her eyes whenever one of her siblings made the mistake of meeting her gaze.

Tyrion knew he should have done something, tried to help her, to refocus her obsession on something less destructive, but he didn't. Secretly he found her deadly singlemindedness to be a balm; her passionate hatred comforted him. *At least I'm not the only one that is mad, and she is the finest blade I have ever produced.*

A sharp tug of his beard brought his attention back to Inara staring intently up at him. The stark contrast between his dark thoughts and the sweet bundle in his arms caused him a pang of guilt. Tyrion felt like two different people were living in his head, one he was afraid of, and another he could never hope to be again.

He kissed Inara once more before handing her back to Kate.

"I still think you should wait," said Kate once more. The wan morning light cast her hair in iridescent shades of copper.

"You worry too much," said Tyrion soothingly. "I'll be back before you know it."

Her eyes narrowed, "You aren't telling me everything."

He stared back at her seriously. Experience had taught him that looking away would only increase her suspicion. "It really isn't that big a deal, just a trip to Lincoln to talk to the stone masons there and then over to Sabortrea to pick out the next lucky people to join our free community here."

"Why so suddenly? Lyra tells us she's going to speak to the elders, and the minute she's gone you spring this on me. Your timing is odd. You never said anything about this last week."

"I've been talking about this with Ryan for weeks," soothed Tyrion. "I thought I had mentioned it to you before."

"That's a complete fabrication," she insisted.

Damn, she's too sharp. "Why would I lie?" he asked, feigning innocence. "Ask Ryan, he'll tell you."

"He'd say anything you told him to," snapped Kate.

"Ask Emma then…"

"Her too, she'd just say it more convincingly."

He sighed, "Now you're just talking crazy."

Kate's eyes lit with sudden anger, "Me!? I'm the only sane one in this weird collection you call a family. The others worship you. Who would tell me the truth if it went against your wishes?"

That was the plain truth, so he didn't bother trying to argue around it. Distraction might be a better tactic. Giving her a rare smile he deflected the question, "You think I'm off to meet a woman? Don't you trust me?"

"You're the only one I trust, but that doesn't mean you aren't a liar, Daniel Tennick. If I was worried about women I'd never have married you to begin with. You've fucked half the women in Colne and who knows what you did here before I came along. I'm more worried about you doing something stupid. Promise me this has nothing to do with your insane vendetta against the She'Har."

Tyrion's countenance went dark, "That's not something I'll give up, Kate, but it can wait for now. This is nothing more than what I've said."

"Then why is *she* going with you?" Kate's voice came out in a strained hiss.

"Ryan's too busy and Tad has his own projects to tend to now, and she wanted to come. Besides, your sister is the best bodyguard anyone could ask for if that's what you're worried about."

"Bodyguard?" Kate nearly laughed. "As if anyone would threaten you. I'd be more worried about you keeping her from hurting the people in Lincoln."

"Sabortrea is considerably more dangerous than Lincoln," he reminded.

"Then take one of the others, what about Abby?" she countered.

"She's busy with teaching."

"It could wait for a few weeks."

He clenched his jaw, "That's enough. I'm done debating with you." Turning, he started to leave the room. Brigid was already waiting outside with their horses.

Kate's expression changed, and her next words held a faint note of desperation, "Daniel, remember Inara, and Eldin. Come home safe. Please."

"I'd never forget any of my children, young or old," he returned. *This is all for them, and the generations to come,* he added silently. Then he closed the door and left.

She stared after him for a long minute before whispering, "Liar."

CHAPTER 2

Brigid rode quietly beside him, but there was something almost jovial about her mood. She kept her back straight and her black hair flowed out behind her in the wind. A stranger would never have seen it in her somber features, but Tyrion could see that she was brimming with excitement.

"What are you so happy about?" he groused.

The taciturn girl didn't answer for a while, but when she did it was a terse response, "Because it has finally begun."

He stared at her back, watching the tattoos move as her lean muscles rippled under her tawny skin. His daughter's body was athletic and mostly bare. While most of his children had happily resumed wearing clothes after becoming free, Brigid frequently ignored the custom. "You don't even know where we are going."

"It doesn't matter," she quipped back. "I can feel your resolve."

"Aren't you curious?" he asked.

"You would have told me if I needed to know. Since you haven't I can only assume it is best that I don't. Either way, it matters not to me, so long as there is blood at the end of the road."

Damn, she's cold enough to make a demon shiver. "You're going to be disappointed then. If all goes well, there'll be no blood on this trip." After a few seconds he added, "You should put a shirt on at least."

"I'm not naked, Father. I have breeches on, and I packed a dress for Lincoln. Do my breasts bother you?" she asked challengingly.

"If we meet anyone on the road they'll think you're mad, or a savage."

She smiled, "I am. I prefer to fight naked. If I had to use my tattoos the enchantments would ruin my clothes anyway."

"We won't be fighting," he told her. "Get off your horse."

Brigid tightened her reins and drew her horse to a stop. Dropping lightly to the ground, she immediately moved to remove her chain from where it was tied above her horse's saddlebags. The chain was particularly frightening to look at. Made of almost delicate iron links, it was razor sharp and covered in runes painstakingly etched along the entire length. It was her favorite weapon, and she never let it stray far from her hand.

Each end terminated in a sharp six-inch blade, and the enchantment worked into its metal ensured that no one but her dared to touch it. The magic in each link shifted between two states, one state sheathed the sharp edges to prevent injury, but only for Brigid herself. The other state was one of deadly sharpness. She never held the chain when using it anyway, she used her aythar to move it directly, whipping it through the air around her to lethal effect. It would cut through spells and spellweaving with equal facility, and it shed the touch of anyone else's magic much as a duck sheds water. It wouldn't be used against her.

"Leave that," he ordered. "This will only take a moment."

She pulled her hand away but didn't say anything, instead she watched him with quiet eyes.

Tyrion made no move as he listened to the voice that was ever present beneath them, the voice that only he and Emma had been able to hear. His eyes grew glassy and then brown, not the warm brown of human eyes, but that of flint, and even the whites vanished, consumed by a stony metamorphosis.

Brigid was astonished, but she held her peace. She would rather die before showing fear in front of him. She sensed no movement of aythar, but the earth between them began to shift and roil as though it had lost its solidity and become some strange fluid. After a moment, a shape appeared, and a box rose from the earthen pool, bobbing slowly to the surface and then resting there as the soil regained its former density.

Her father stared at it before bending down to scoop the small box into his hands. His eyes regained their normalcy as he straightened, but he watched her as though she were a puzzle for seconds afterward. Tyrion's expression was alien and despite herself Brigid felt unsettled.

Then he smiled, "We can go now—Brigid." The pause before her name was awkward, as though he had forgotten what to call her temporarily.

She mounted her horse nimbly and followed behind him for some time before she finally asked, "What was that?"

"So you do have some curiosity."

"There was no aythar, the earth moved as if it were possessed," she said softly.

Tyrion looked over his shoulder for a moment with a smile born of malevolence on his lips. It was an expression she treasured, and she knew then that he was still the man she loved. The man who would grant her desire for vengeance. He had hidden it so well over the past year that she had begun to harbor doubts. "We have more allies than just those in our family, Brigid. The earth itself will aid us, the earth and sky both. It isn't just us, this world is crying for blood, but first I need to learn more, so you'll need to be patient."

She felt a shiver run down her spine as he spoke. The words didn't really make sense, but she could feel something behind them. "I trust you, Father, but you sound like a lunatic."

He laughed, "That means a lot coming from you."

"What's in the box?"

"Knowledge, but it may drive me mad, or even kill me."

She frowned, "Is it worth the risk?"

"We can't win without it. What you've seen is just a hint of what's possible, but it isn't enough. I think I could create chaos, and we could destroy a lot of them, but it would mean nothing in the end. We would die, and they would recover. To win we need knowledge and cunning. We have to recover what humanity has lost and learn the weaknesses of our enemy. I don't know what I will learn, but it may require more patience than one lifetime."

Brigid growled. It was a deep guttural sound completely at odds with the delicate femininity of her throat. "I won't wait that long, Father."

"I hope you don't have to," he responded, *and I'll put you out of your misery myself, if it does take that long.*

"So what do you want me to do?"

"There's a fruit in this box, stolen from the She'Har. It contains a multitude of their secrets, and I think I can learn them if I eat it. I need you to watch over me. Lyra told me that it drives some of them mad, and I'm no She'Har. If things don't go right, you may have to kill me." *And if things go really wrong, I may kill you.*

"Why me?"

"I can tolerate a certain amount of madness, if it allows me to accomplish our goals, but you're the only one I trust to judge that."

Brigid scowled, "Because I'm the craziest one of the lot, right? That's what you meant isn't it?"

He nodded, stepping closer, "And if I do have to be put down, you, more than anyone, deserves the right to do it. Hell, you may be the only one who *could*."

She looked at the ground, "I won't kill you. I was mistaken before. If you go mad, I'll just join you until they put us both down." *You're the only one I love anymore.*

He put his arms around her, pulling her close, "Even if I turn into a She'Har, or a tree-lover?"

She tensed, and the chains on her horse's saddlebags shifted, clinking ominously. "That wouldn't be you. Maybe I could do it then. How long will this take?"

Tyrion released her and went to his horse, "Days for sure, weeks possibly, there's no way to know."

"I hope you have a quiet place in mind, then."

He grinned, "I already have it picked out."

They journeyed deep into the foothills, skirting Colne and making for the rocky hinterlands that lay beyond. The region was too rough for the She'Har's elders to grow, and even the beleaguered remnants of humanity had found it too difficult to eke out a living there. The ground was too hard for farming, and there wasn't enough water to subsist on.

For Tyrion it was perfect.

He didn't know the area, though. There were probably caves that would have been suitable places to find shelter, but he didn't know where they were. Rather than waste time hunting, he asked the earth to help and it followed his suggestion, creating a deep cool niche in the side of one of the stony hillsides. A small spring rose in the back, providing water and a cold pool to bathe in.

They had brought their own food, but if they had to stay too long, Brigid was an able hunter, although her cooking skills left a lot to be desired.

Once they had made the place somewhat comfortable, Tyrion arranged his pallet and stripped. He had no idea if he would sleep, dream, or simply rave. From what Lyralliantha had told him previously, he suspected he would be unconscious for some time, at least in the beginning.

The loshti was still the same deep purple brown when he opened the stasis box, exactly as it had been when he had stolen it a year earlier. Despite himself, he felt uncertain when he looked on it, uncertain and afraid. *What will it do to me?*

"How did you get it?" asked Brigid, watching him intently.

"It was meant for Lyralliantha, but I snuck into the grove and took it the night before she was meant to have it," he explained.

Her brows went up, "Just like that?"

"It was unguarded." He didn't bother describing the methods he had used to avoid detection, or the fact that he had had help from Emma and Ryan.

"That seems suspicious. Why would they leave something like that unprotected?"

"Hubris," Tyrion replied. "Lyra told me that they didn't need to guard it. Apparently no one has ever stolen from the Illeniel Grove before."

Brigid narrowed her eyes, "Because of their foresight. You shouldn't have been able to take it, not unless they meant for you to. Don't you think this might be a trap?"

"You couldn't sense anything when the earth moved, remember? I think my special ability is something they can't perceive."

"But you don't know that," she insisted. There was a hint of worried desperation behind her words.

Tyrion nodded, "You're right, I don't know. It could be a trap. It could be poison, or something worse, but if it's truly what Lyralliantha told me about, then I can't imagine they would have let me have it voluntarily. No one would be such a fool as to let something containing the knowledge of ages fall into the hands of his enemy. For that reason, if they had been able to see what I would do, I believe they would have stopped me."

"Don't do it," said Brigid, but her father was biting down on the fruit already.

It was sweet, far sweeter than ordinary Calmuth. Tyrion took a large bite and swallowed, gulping quickly. He wasn't sure how fast it would begin to affect him, and he wanted to get it all down before he lost his senses. He took another bite and then another.

"Stop Father! That's enough, you don't know what it will do…"

He wolfed it down, sparing none of it. There was no seed in the center of its juicy pulp, making it easy to finish. The taste seemed to radiate through his lips, across his tongue, and down his throat. He couldn't get enough.

His entire body seemed to tingle, and he stared in wonder at his daughter. "You are so beautiful, Brigid. Have I ever told you that?"

She bit her lip, "I don't think so. Do you feel alright?"

"I feel wonderful," he answered. "Do you see that?" He looked at the empty air above and behind her. "It's getting lighter in here. Are you making that light?"

It was dusk outside and the entrance was far enough away that it was fairly dim in their hideaway. "What light? Nothing has changed, Father."

Tyrion stared through her, watching the trees grow around them, great statuesque behemoths that seemed to reach for the stars. They were bathed in a gradually intensifying luminous glow, a warmth that fed and nurtured them. A light that was full of meaning and importance. Far below he could feel his roots expanding, touching his brothers and sisters and connecting him to the entire world. Pleasure seeped through him, into his very bones, and it grew stronger with each passing moment as the light grew brighter.

Soon he could no longer see at all, and the brilliance became a sort of reverse blindness that rather than obscuring sight, instead overwhelmed him with an unimpeded view of *everything.* The pleasure became so intense it was painful, and at its core he began to burn.

Brigid watched him as he stared blankly around himself. Her father's mouth had formed an 'o' of wonder, but his eyes were unsteady. She felt helpless and all she could do was help ease him into a prone position as his body went slack. His skin was hot. No sooner than she had gotten him down, but he began to writhe, alternating between a tense rigid state and a limp placid one.

She had no idea what to do as he began to babble incoherently, so she simply sat nearby, stroking his head with one hand. "Please don't die," she whispered. "You're all I have left."

CHAPTER 3

Lyralliantha had returned a month after Tyrion's departure, but she hadn't seemed very curious about his absence, which only made Kate more anxious.

In fact, none of them openly expressed any concern, despite Kate's pointed questions. It was now a full two months since he had left, and she had had enough. Albamarl had grown into a community of almost a hundred people over the past year, with the addition of the first batch of liberated slaves from Ellentrea and a few brave transplants from Colne, but tonight she had gathered the inner circle. Tyrion's twelve surviving adult children, along with Layla and Lyralliantha were gathered in the main room of his home.

"It's been two months with no word from him…" she began.

Fourteen pairs of eyes gazed back at her, but no one said anything.

"Someone has to know something," prodded Kate.

"Why?" That was Ian's voice. He stood with a small space around him, since none of the others particularly cared for him. "He never tells us anything," continued the young man.

"No one would talk to you anyway," noted Piper sarcastically from the back of the room.

Several of the others laughed and someone coughed, "Pervert."

Ian heard the remark, but he held his temper. He wasn't the brightest of Tyrion's children, but time and repeated 'lessons' had taught him the wisdom of not reacting to his siblings' provocations. Being in a room with almost all of them at once meant he was completely outnumbered.

Anthony spoke up, "He has a point, though. Whatever he's doing he wouldn't tell anyone if he didn't want to."

"He told me he was going to Lincoln and then on to Sabortrea," said Ryan, repeating what he had said several times over the past two months. "Maybe he got sidetracked."

"There are a lot of women in Sabortrea," put in David, glancing at Kate almost apologetically.

Emma was standing by Ryan, as usual, and she scowled at David, "You know he isn't interested in the slaves, not like that."

Ian broke in, "I heard he used to keep one of the nameless in Ellentrea as a sex-slave."

Piper sneered, "Speaking of which, shouldn't you be back in Ellentrea, raping the baratti?"

Ian's face colored instantly. Being unpopular with his siblings, he had been spending a lot of time with the slaves in Ellentrea. None of them had any real doubts about what he was probably doing there. "Shut your mouth, bitch!"

"Why? Don't you like girls who talk back? Or is it that this girl can whip your ass? You should go back to the slave camp and be with the other animals. You can be a big dog there where all the bitches are too weak to stand up to you," responded Piper angrily.

"Piper!" broke in Abby. "You shouldn't call them baratti, or animals. They're still people."

"Hardly," muttered Piper under her breath.

Ian was making his way to the door, "Fuck this."

"We aren't done yet," called Kate.

"Let him go," suggested David. "He wouldn't know anything anyway."

"At least one of you must know something," said Kate imploringly. She looked to Lyralliantha for support, but the She'Har woman merely stood by with a bored expression on her face.

Emma came forward, "Kate, I know it's hard to believe, but I really don't think we do. Ryan is the only one he discussed his plans with, and he's already told us what he knows. We just have to be patient…"

"What if he doesn't return? Aren't any of you the least bit worried?!" exclaimed Kate in frustration.

Lyralliantha put a graceful hand on her shoulder, "He will be back."

Kate frowned, "How can you know that? You weren't even here when he left. Do you know something?"

The She'Har woman sighed, "No, but the Elders told me to be patient. They trust him."

"Then they are fools," growled Kate. "Do they know something? What else did they tell you? Lyra, please, talk to me!"

The silver-haired Illeniel smiled sadly, "They tell me less than Tyrion tells us."

Emma Philips sat at her dressing table, trying vainly to brush the curls out of her soft brown hair. The curls weren't tight enough to be attractive, instead they fell loosely and gave her hair a ragged unkempt appearance. Ryan had reassured her that he thought her hair was quite lovely, but she knew he was lying. *He'd say anything to make me feel better.* That thought brought a faint smile to her lips.

Her room was guarded by an enchantment to protect her privacy, as most of their rooms were, but a soft sound outside her door made her turn her head. Rising swiftly, she opened the door before he could knock. Ryan slipped inside silently, and she closed it behind him.

"Did anyone see you?" she asked her half-brother.

He grinned roguishly at her, "No. Stop acting guilty. We're just talking. If you act guilty everyone will start getting ideas." Opening his arms, he embraced her.

She held onto him for a long moment, but he didn't complain. Emma listened to his strong heart beating, finding comfort there. Of all her siblings, Ryan was the only one she trusted fully. He was the only one who knew about the secret voices she heard. Almost unconsciously she drew a deep breath, inhaling his scent. Then she released him, embarrassed as she realized what she had done.

Ryan sat on the end of her bed, his cheeks slightly flushed. Glancing up at her, he said what they were both thinking, "He's been gone too long."

She nodded, "I thought Kate was going to snap tonight."

"I was more worried about Lyra," said Ryan, "but she didn't seem worried at all."

Emma watched the candlelight play on his straight sandy brown hair. "Do you think he told her something?"

Ryan shook his head, "No. He's in love with her, but he doesn't trust her. He doesn't trust any of the She'Har. Hell, he didn't even tell Kate, and he *does* trust her."

She bit her lip, "Then why is she so unconcerned?"

"You heard her, the Illeniel Elders told her to be patient. She also said he *will* be back," observed Ryan. "Not that he *probably* be back, or that he was *probably* alright, but that he *would* be back. Why do you suppose that is?"

"You still think they can see the future? It was just a turn of phrase. You're reading too much into it," argued Emma.

"You saw what their krytek did during the fight to protect us," reminded her brother.

"So they have a sixth sense or something. It doesn't necessarily follow that they're omniscient."

Ryan stood and paced the room, "Well they clearly know something."

"If they knew what his intentions were, they'd have killed us all by now," said Emma.

"That's the only thing that doesn't make sense," agreed Ryan. His eyes lit on her once more and he studied her for a moment, "Did you brush your hair?"

"Maybe."

His expression softened, "Em', we talked about this."

"No, you talked about it."

"It's wrong. You're my sister."

She scowled at him, "So I'm not supposed to love my brother?"

"Not like *that*. You need to find someone," he said firmly. "There are plenty of men in Ellentrea."

Emma laughed, "Please, some of them can barely speak! I might as well lie with a goat."

"I wouldn't say that in front of Layla," he opined.

She waved her hand in dismissal, "She's exceptional, and even she's not right in the head."

"Maybe someone from Colne will come along…"

"And you? Have you found a girl you fancy from among the villagers? Don't tell me you like one of those broken nosed sluts from Ellentrea." Her voice was dripping with disdain.

Ryan took a step back, "Well no, but I've resigned myself to living a simple life."

"How noble of you," said Emma bitterly. "And I suppose you look down on me for wanting some warmth and love in my life."

"I didn't say that."

"Is it so wrong to want someone to hold? That's all I really want, Ryan," she said emphatically.

He looked uncertain, "A hug maybe, but we kissed, Em'!"

"So! We didn't grow up together. We didn't even know we were related until recently. I liked you long before that."

He shook his head, "It's wrong."

She stalked toward him as though she might take a swing at him, but instead she threw her arms around him. Ryan tensed but after a moment he returned the embrace. "I love you, Ryan. Nothing will change that. If this is all we can have, then I'll gladly take it."

He buried his head in her hair, his lips close to her neck, "I know that Em'. But it isn't just you, it's me. This is dangerous. I'm not like you. I don't think I can do this without wanting more." His voice had become deeper. "That would definitely be wrong."

"Only if we had a baby," said Emma suddenly. "I've been talking to Layla. She told me that the slaves in Ellentrea do all sorts of things that don't result in children. We don't have to suffer, Ryan." She turned her head, putting her lips against his.

For a moment he returned the kiss, but then he pushed her away, "No." Before she could respond, he opened the door and darted out.

Ian was standing at the end of the hall, apparently about to enter his own room. He smirked knowingly when he saw Ryan, "And they call me a pervert..."

Ryan glared at him, "Shut up, bastard!"

Ian shrugged, holding his hands out, "We're all bastards together here in Albamarl, brother dearest."

Ryan's response was instantaneous, his will lashed out, flinging his brother against the wall. Moving forward, he put his face close to Ian's, "Not—another—word. Do you hear me?"

Ian smiled, "Careful brother. Remember what you told me? It's not about *this* anymore." He illustrated his words by grabbing his own crotch, then he tapped his temple, "It's about *this*." Then he ignited the enchantment tattooed along his right arm. "You startled me, what if I had accidently cut your pretty head off?" He dismissed the enchantment almost as soon as the blade of force around his arm appeared. He had made his point. Ryan had left himself wide open.

Cursing, Ryan turned away, heading for his own room.

Ian laughed as he withdrew, "Don't forget to use the sound proofing enchantment, brother. Privacy wards are only good if you use them." He kept laughing as Ryan slammed his door. Only then did he notice Emma staring at him from her doorway.

"If you ever hurt him, if I even *think* you've done something to him, I'll have your balls off before you even realize they're gone," she warned in a dark tone.

Another voice called out, Sarah had poked her head out at the far end of the hall, "What's going on?"

Emma said nothing, keeping Ian under a cold stare.

He smiled, "Nothing. Just a friendly late night discussion." He returned to his own room, but he continued chuckling softly under his breath.

Emma closed her own door before her sister could ask her anything else.

CHAPTER 4

Ages passed, and Tyrion watched, from the first world and its wild splendor, to the latest world and its myriad differences. The She'Har had evolved, and along the way they had lost much. The first world had been filled with a thousand different races, trees of every description and type, some intelligent and others less so.

For the trees the difference was less important, for they all *felt,* and the meaning contained within their worldwide community was deeper than mere thought.

They had conquered their first foes, disease and predators, but though they reshaped their world to better suit them, it never lost its intense beauty, just the danger. The five races that would later become what they now called the She'Har lived in harmony and the animals that became their kianthi were as much a part of them as their branches and roots.

Their science grew, and with it came knowledge of things far beyond their simple world. With knowledge came increased safety and prosperity, but it also brought its own dangers. As they learned of the greater universe beyond their small part of it they began to crave more, and none knew more than the Illeniels, for their minds saw farther than any of their kin.

Eventually they found the means to go beyond, and the universe was opened to them. They spread to new worlds and new places, though none ever matched their original home.

But opening the door proved to be a dangerous mistake. There were others in the void. Those they met at first proved peaceful, but others were not, and the She'Har learned to make war. Even at that they were successful, until the ANSIS found them. Machine-like beings, they had none of the weaknesses of the She'Har's previous foes, and slowly, inexorably, they began to lose.

Against other opponents, retreat might have been possible, but although the ANSIS had no aythar, they also had the key to traveling between dimensions. Non-living, they showed no remorse or respite to the She'Har. They hunted them, finding every hidden plane and quiet sanctuary. The ANSIS would not be satisfied until the She'Har were no more.

The She'Har fought, and lost, and grew cold in their desperate struggle for survival. When the first world was taken, they lost their kianthi, and with them, their heart. They had changed themselves many times to adapt to new worlds, but without the kianthi, existence became almost meaningless. To survive they became more like their enemy, but it was never enough.

A desperate plan was created to save the five groves and find a new world to use for their final refuge. The race that lived there was intelligent, but possessed no soul, no aythar or true awareness. They were more like the ANSIS than a true sapient species.

The Illeniels wrapped the new world in an artificial dimension, sustained by the immortal creations of the Centyr Grove, the Kionthara. The god-like kionthara would guard the new dimension, sealing it against any intrusion from beyond, and within it, their new world would be safe.

And then they made the new place their home.

The initial invasion went unnoticed while the She'Har quickly built their strength. Once they were discovered, it was already too late. The soul-dead animals that defended that world proved to be more powerful than expected, but their science was still new. The She'Har had tools and weapons at their disposal that were beyond the ability of the younger and mechanistic animals.

In particular, the She'Har were masters of genetics and biology. They grew their soldiers and modified them endlessly to meet the needs of any situation. The machines of the baratti were unable to keep up.

When the humans grew desperate, they began using weapons that would destroy their own world. They poisoned the land with chemicals and destroyed large regions with devastating bombs that left the land ruined by radiation.

The She'Har no longer had time for patience and slow warfare. Turning once more to their finest mastery, they fashioned a new type of krytek, a biological horror that would devour their flesh and bone opponents from within. A microscopic creature that could multiply on its own, their new weapon took the form of a parasitic disease that spread rapidly through their enemies.

Even the cold-hearted She'Har were dismayed by the result. Unable to respond rapidly to the tailor-made plague, the human resistance dissolved, but even the She'Har could not stop their new creation. The parasitic krytek devoured their hosts until there were none remaining, and then it finally starved.

When all was finally over, only a few isolated groups of humanity remained, but they were a shadow of their former selves. Their society devolved with a speed even the She'Har could hardly fathom, and within a short span of years most of their science and knowledge was lost.

The She'Har had won victory and discovered shame. In the course of the short war they had begun to doubt the soul-less nature of their enemy, but once it was over they could not face such a realization. Some experimented, trying to revive the intelligence their enemy had once displayed, but the humans who were left only grew more savage and primitive. Even giving them the ability to sense and manipulate aythar did nothing to alleviate their brutality and stupidity.

It was easier, morally and pragmatically, to assume that their first assumption had been correct. The humans were little more than biological machines, intelligent once, but not truly aware. Perhaps as a tribute to their fallen enemy, the She'Har gave their children human forms, although it might also have been because the humans somewhat resembled their long lost kianthi.

"But that was not all!" screamed Tyrion. He knew there was more, so much more. The indignities heaped upon humankind didn't end with the war.

He felt weak. It was hopeless, and he was starving, mentally and physically. The ground was hard and gave him no water, while the sun seemed to be completely absent. He was dying.

His roots, stunted by the rocky ground, could find no others to communicate with. He was alone and his leaves shriveled for lack of sun and water. Tyrion was a prisoner, trapped in a dead place that offered no hope of survival— just as the She'Har still were.

"The Illeniels knew!" he screamed again, but his roots could find no audience, no one could hear him.

"They foresaw it all. They knew the kionthara couldn't last forever. It would eventually come tumbling down around them." He saw it then, in a blaze of enlightenment. "They knew *I* was coming, long before I was born."

"Why? Why did they give me this?" he asked, for he knew for certain now what the loshti meant. No one could steal from the Illeniels, because they would know before anything could be stolen. Every decision they made was planned with thousands of years of foresight helping to inform their choice.

The knowledge would be there. It had to be. The decision to allow him to take the loshti, the reason behind it, must have been made long ago. He should already know the answer.

But he didn't.

It was simply blank. He found nothing regarding it in his memories. There could be only one explanation for that. They had removed it.

He had received the collected knowledge of ages of She'Har history and learning, but they had carefully edited out at least one thing, the reason for letting him acquire that knowledge. *What else might they have removed?*

That was something he had no way of knowing, but he had at least one hint regarding the thing he knew was hidden. If he was allowed to see why they had given him the loshti, it would affect his choices; by denying it they were helping to ensure he would do what they needed.

Reviewing what he had learned, that made some sense. The Illeniels couldn't truly see the future, their gift went beyond that, they had the ability to see the infinite and endlessly different realities that lay side by side with their own. That was how they had been able to use their magic to transport the She'Har to new worlds, and it was how they saw the most likely future for the reality they were living in.

They could never be sure, but they could be damn close, and what they relied on was the knowledge of what was *probable.* And the farther away it was, the more uncertain that probability was.

Tyrion was dry, parched. He could feel himself dying, ever so slowly.

He needed to see what the Illeniel elders had seen, but he didn't have their gift. *Perhaps I could gain it,* he thought suddenly. The special gifts of each grove were the product of elaborate genetic calculating mechanisms. *What did the humans call it? DNA computers. Hah! Little did they know, the She'Har took it to far greater heights than they ever imagined.*

The seed implanted in each of their children was the true She'Har offspring, like a second mind, living alongside that of their artificially created flesh host. It held the machinery required for spellweaving, but the intricate machinery required for the gifts that each grove gave to their children were housed in two places, both the seed and the host.

If I can create that within myself, I could gain the gift that the Illeniels use, and then I could see for myself.

But first he needed to know the code that was unique to constructing the Illeniel gift. And it wasn't there.

"Damn them!" Now he knew of two things they had hidden from him. The knowledge to create the gifts of the other groves were there, but not that of the Illeniels.

It's useless. I'm trying to outthink a thousand minds that have planned ahead for anything I might try long before I was even born. That thought brought another memory to the foreground of his mind.

The slaves of the Groves were effectively sterile. The safeguards the She'Har had employed to prevent their gifts escaping into the wild human population were more complex than he had ever guessed, going far beyond the spellwoven collars. The male children of the She'Har could produce human children, but they were genetically flawed. Along with the gift they inherited from their She'Har parent, they also received two lethal mutations. In the male children of the She'Har they were inactivated, in the human children of the She'Har both were active, but they canceled each other out. But if a slave and a wild human produced a child, it would receive only one of the lethal genes, and that no longer held true, such offspring would die very young, if they even survived to be born.

The coldly reasoned nature of their failsafe chilled him to the bone, but that lasted only a short while. After it had gone, he was filled with rage. The slaves of Ellentrea and the other camps would be useless to him. They could not help establish a new future for humanity, whether he civilized them or not.

They could only produce dead children with their wild counterparts. Even among themselves, half of every generation would certainly die. Mating with the children of the She'Har would only prolong the problem for one more generation, not that the She'Har would agree to even that.

Humankind was doomed, and even if he could keep the small population of free humans safe and growing, they would never share the special gifts of the She'Har.

It might be possible to produce viable offspring with the female children of the She'Har, but they were sterile, well, voluntarily sterile anyway. Female She'Har had their menstrual cycle suppressed. They had to deliberately activate it before they could ovulate.

"You are a rapist," Lyralliantha had once told him, and now it made him want to laugh at the irony. The She'Har had planned against even that, long before he had ever come along.

Tyrion could feel himself drying out. The sensation was so powerful that he at last began to turn his senses outward, to explore the world around him once more. He was still in the cave.

How had he forgotten that? An animal was nearby, a human. His physical eyesight was absent, but his magesight remained; by her aythar he could tell it was Brigid. She seemed distraught and the enchanted blade tattoos on her arms were active as she paced back and forth near his—*trunk?!*

The final realization struck home. *I'm a fucking tree. I really did turn into one of them!*

He watched Brigid with fresh concern, *and now my daughter is about to cut me down.* He tried to speak to her, to tell her to wait, but of course he had no mouth.

She was preparing to strike.

His aythar felt sluggish and slow to respond, not that it would do much good against her enchanted arm blades, only his enchanted tattoo defenses had any chance of deflecting their strikes.

But when he tried to activate them he failed. They were gone, along with his human skin.

Time slowed, or perhaps his mind sped up. He remembered his tattoos, every inch of them. They had cost him days of pain and blood. They were etched within his mind just as much as they had been on his hide. He focused on their memory, and he felt something within him let go.

The world snapped into focus and time sped up as they blazed up protectively inside his mind. They were *there!* Throwing his will and aythar into them he raised his defensive shield, and then he opened his eyes.

Brigid stood stock still in front of him, an expression of shock on her face. "Is this a trick?" Her former resolve had disappeared, and now her hands had begun to tremble, sending shivers through the magical force sheathing her arms. "Answer me!"

Raising his arms in a placating gesture he tried to speak, though his lips and tongue felt strange and unfamiliar, "Wait." *When did my arms come back?*

"Wait?! I've been waiting! It's been months! Are you still Tyrion? What have you become?" Her voice had risen, becoming strident.

"I am—I think. Give me a moment to adjust," he told her. Waving one hand around his head in a chaotic swirling motion he added, "It's all strange—in here. Let me think."

Her eyes narrowed, "Who was my mother?"

"The one who raped me," he said without pausing to think. "Brenda."

Brigid's mouth gaped slightly.

"You already knew that."

"But, you, you never said it, not like that," she replied. "You were always too proud, even after I figured it out."

"Proud?" he laughed. "Ashamed more like it, afraid to admit to my own weakness."

"You don't sound like yourself. You don't sound like my father," accused Brigid. "How do I know if I can trust you?"

Tyrion searched her face, thinking hard. Finally, he answered, "You don't, but you don't have any other choice. Killing me now would only bring an abrupt end to your dream, whether I've turned against you or not, assuming you could even manage it."

Her enchanted chains rustled where they lay a few feet away on the cave floor and Brigid's features grew more animated, as though the challenge excited her. "Perhaps I should try."

He gave her a feral grin, "I'd hate to lose such a fine weapon."

Tyrion was hungry, and thirsty. Thirstier than he could ever remember being. He drank all the water he could hold, not bothering to dip it from the pool at the back of the cave. Instead he put his face directly in the water and drank.

Later, after he had eaten, he felt better, but it was not enough. The dried meat and hard bread they had brought with them was thoroughly unsatisfying and did little to fill his belly. It was an effort of will to keep himself from eating everything that remained of their rations.

Glancing up at his daughter he voiced a question, "You said months, how long has it been?"

"Nine weeks."

"And I was like that, the entire time?"

Brigid shook her head, "No. You moved and babbled a lot the first few days, like a man having a nightmare, then you settled down and grew peaceful. The third morning I woke up and found you had transformed."

Tyrion stared at the ground, thinking hard. "It doesn't make sense. I don't have the Gaelyn gift. How did I change like that?"

She gave him a confused look and shrugged at the same time.

"I wasn't really asking you," he told her, but then he had another thought. "Wait, did you sense any aythar moving either time?"

"I was asleep the first time, but definitely not the second time. What does it mean?"

He gave her an empty stare, "I don't know."

"What should we do then?"

Tyrion stood, a calm resolve had replaced his earlier uncertainty, "We go home." A wave of dizziness threatened to take him from his feet, and the room began to spin. He sat abruptly to avoid falling, and then he eased himself to the floor. "After a good rest—I think…"

CHAPTER 5

Something has changed. The future is shifting.

The Illeniel elders were meeting, but that was nothing new. They were always meeting. Indeed the majority of their existences were spent in continual communion with one another. What was new was the sense of fear that had entered the conversation.

We knew this was a possibility, answered another.

But it was not the most likely, now it has risen to the second most probable outcome.

The third voice was calm, *We have always been prepared to accept it if necessary. Even if it is not our preferred outcome, at least we will survive. In every other scenario everything is lost.*

The most palatable resolution is still more likely.

The Illeniel Grove had been planning for a long time. Their vision extended over millennia, and while their predictions were more uncertain the farther out in time they extended, they had been forced to make a terrible gamble.

They had examined a thousand choices since coming to their new home, possibly their last home. In almost all of them they were eventually found. For one reason or another, the kionthara would fail, and the enemy would find them. Only one choice offered hope and even that had been slim. One mistake and disaster would find them much sooner, and even if they succeeded, there was a strong chance that their solution would be almost too dark even for them, cold and calculating She'Har to accept.

That darker hope had just become more likely.

It should not be shifting so soon, nothing has occurred. Could one of the other Groves have discovered our plan?

No, answered the first voice. *This can only be the result of some internal choice he has made.*

Perhaps he has decided to share information with one of the other Groves? suggested another.

Lyralliantha is here, we must instruct her carefully.

The first elder spoke then, *Agreed. Too much knowledge and she could upset the plan.*

A new mind entered their presence. Lyralliantha sent a silent feeling of inquiry outward.

He will return soon, daughter. You must guide him, advised the second elder.

Her confusion was immediately felt, *I don't know what is required.*

You must calm his heart. Tyrion must be anchored. He must understand our commitment to him, to his people, said one of the elders.

He does not trust the Grove, said Lyralliantha in dismay.

The first elder spoke once more, *Give him a child. He will understand the meaning of it now.*

Lyralliantha was shocked, *But it would have our gift. I understood that that was to be avoided at all cost.*

Until now, explained the elder. *It was always part of the plan.*

I wasn't told... she began to protest.

We share only what instructions are required, and only when they are required. More would jeopardize the future, the elder informed her.

Lyralliantha felt the beginnings of anger, which surprised her, *A child will not win his trust, he has many children, nor would I use such a thing against him. He is my kianthi, I love...*

The first elder interrupted again, *Love is all that is needed, all that will save us.*

Night had already fallen when Tyrion and Brigid returned. Ryan had completed the wall around the tiny community of Albamarl, but there was still no gate yet, nor anyone to man it, so they simply walked in.

A few of the recently liberated wardens from Ellentrea spotted them as they walked toward the main house, but none approached them. It was not their place. Even so, most of Tyrion's children and Kate had already gathered by the door to the house when they entered. One of them had obviously noticed his return and alerted the others.

"Father," said Abby, speaking first. "We have been worried."

Kate stood near her, but her aura was awash in much stronger emotions. Tyrion guessed that she didn't trust herself to speak yet, at least not in front of the others. Lyralliantha was there as well, calm as always, but he sensed a hint of expectation from her, as though she anticipated something from his arrival.

Ryan spoke next, "You don't look well. Did you have a hard journey?"

Tyrion fought to contain himself, "Everyone out, now. I will speak to you in the morning."

His children knew better than to argue, and they began filing out quickly, but Kate, Lyralliantha, and Layla waited. Layla had little Eldin against her breast, and as usual she failed to read his mood accurately.

"Your son has grown fat. Look at him, Tyrion!" Layla announced with pride.

Tyrion stared at her, and his eyes were drawn to the babe. *Poor thing, born to suffer, and for nothing.* Averting his eyes he warned her, "I said 'everyone'. That includes you, Layla."

The warden flinched slightly at his words but she gathered herself and went to her room.

Kate was already glaring, "That was incredibly rude…"

"We need to talk," he interrupted without meeting her gaze. He kept his eyes lowered, but there was an animalistic urgency in his expression. "Wait in our room."

Lyralliantha gave a sly smile, "Perhaps I should come too?"

"Get out," he told her, but his voice wavered. Staring at Lyralliantha, he felt a surge of lust, but his anger was stronger. "I don't want to see…," he couldn't finish the sentence. *I don't want to see you again.* "We will talk tomorrow."

The She'Har frowned, but she didn't argue. As she left he realized Brigid was still standing beside him.

Tyrion growled softly. *I've made it this far, only a little farther.* "Brigid, go. I need to be alone." Sweat was standing out on his brow. Without waiting for her response he headed for the bedroom.

Kate was already waiting, "What is wrong with you?!"

He closed the door behind him. His face felt hot, much like the rest of his body. Moving forward he began pushing her back, toward the bed.

"You said we needed to talk," she reminded him with a barely subdued undercurrent of anger in her tone.

He nodded, "After, this can't wait."

She frowned at his touch, "Your skin is hot. Are you feverish?" Then she felt him pressing against her. "What? You can't think I'm in the mood. We need to have a serious talk before you can even consider that!"

"It burns."

"Too fucking bad. At the moment I don't have the faintest interest in your whims. You should find Lyra, she seemed to be happy to see you," she responded sarcastically.

For a moment he drew back, as though he would turn for the door, but then he stopped, "No, it can't be her." He shoved Kate onto the bed.

The look on his face frightened her. "Daniel, what's going on?"

He was desperately pulling at his trousers already, "I'll tell you everything, but I can't wait any longer."

"Talk first," she said adamantly, "otherwise you can go satisfy yourself with Layla, she's always been a good *servant*."

"Won't work," he muttered. "She's a dead end, just like her son. It has to be you, or—or—Lyra." His voice had grown huskier.

"Then go to her," said Kate with growing irritation. "Seriously, Daniel, I am *not* in the mood, and your behavior isn't helping that one whit."

"No! That's what they want. No. Help me, Kate. It has to be you."

"Talk to me," she said, studying his features. There was a strangeness about him, a desperation she found completely unfamiliar.

"I stole the loshti," he said rapidly, his hands already tugging at her dress. Lacking her cooperation, the garment was proving to be a frustrating impediment. One of the seams tore as he tugged at it. Rather than stop, he ripped it the rest of the way.

39

Kate's eyes were wide, "The loshti? That thing that Lyra was supposed to have last year?"

"Yes," he said hoarsely. "I ate it…" The dress was ruined but Kate stubbornly resisted him still, as the fabric came away she twisted, rolling away from him across the bed.

"And what? It gave you a raging erection?!"

He scrambled toward her, "In a word, yes." His hand missed her wrist as she jumped up from the bed, but a hastily created shield prevented her from retreating farther. "It wants out."

"It? You really aren't instilling confidence with this, I hope you realize that," she told him.

"It doesn't like the risk of being lost. The first drive it instills is the urge to procreate. It wants to pass itself on to my next child," he explained. "Hold still!" Lunging at her he caught her at last.

Changing tactics, she pushed forward unexpectedly, causing him to lose his balance as his feet caught on the edge of the bed behind him. Falling backward he landed on the mattress and Kate sat on his chest. "Alright, fine, but give me a minute, otherwise this will hurt."

He nodded, "Whatever, just hurry."

Kate sighed, "You are such a romantic. What woman could resist you?" She began crawling over him. "Kiss me."

"I can't reach your face," he replied, her knees had him pinned to the bed.

"Not here, stupid—there."

"Oh!"

An unusually short time later, it was over. Tyrion collapsed and Kate propped herself up on one elbow, watching him. "That was it?"

He nodded.

"Huh. Well that was underwhelming," she declared. "The way you were acting when you came in here had me seriously worried."

"Blame the She'Har," he told her. "Trees make terrible lovers."

"I wouldn't say 'tree'," retorted Kate. "More like a 'twig'."

Tyrion was embarrassed, but he still managed to glower at her, "I haven't changed physically."

"I was referring to the duration of the event," said Kate dryly.

He frowned, but he couldn't argue the point, his ardor had been exceptionally brief for once. Leaning back, he decided to rest his eyes. Now that the loshti was no longer driving him his fatigue from the journey was catching up to him.

Kate shook his arm, "Hey! Talking, remember?"

"I shouldn't have told you. Now you're at risk too. No one must know what I've done," he cautioned without opening his eyes.

"Who else knows then?" she asked.

He made a short list, "Emma, Ryan, Brigid, and now you." He stopped for a second, his mind drifting, but another thought bubbled, up, "Oh and probably Lyra and almost certainly the entire Illeniel Grove."

She shook him again, "That's hardly a short list."

"It was a trap—I think. They knew I would do it, but I'm not sure what they think I will do, they cut that part out of it."

"But at the very least, if they know, then they can't blame you, right?"

Tyrion pulled on her arm, drawing her in and holding her tightly against his chest. "Maybe," he mumbled, "but the other groves don't know. If any of them find out, there's a chance they'll try to do something about it. They don't fully trust the Illeniels." He buried his head in her hair, letting it block the light from the lantern across the room.

"Are you falling asleep?" Kate tried to move, but he held her fast. A moment later she heard the beginning of a snore. He had pinned her so she couldn't shake him awake again, at least not easily.

With a sigh she snuggled closer to him for a while, but eventually the heat of his body made her sweat, so she carefully extricated herself. Rolling over, she stared at his sleeping face. Daniel was beautiful, even more so when he was unconscious.

When he was awake it was a different matter, the anger that festered in his soul often darkened his features. But over the past year she had seen glimmers of hope, especially when he was with Inara and Eldin. Daniel had never been a father before, not really, and she thought the experience was changing him for the better.

And then he does something like this. She had no idea what the consequences would be, but she doubted they would be good. Reaching over, she brushed the hair away from his face so she could see it more clearly, "Damn you. You finally tell me what you're hiding and then you pass out and leave me alone to worry. How am I supposed to sleep now?"

Morning arrived early, as was its wont, but Tyrion slept late, which was unusual. His dreams were strange and jumbled, as they had been every night since he had awakened from taking the loshti. Kate still slumbered beside him. That was unusual too, but he guessed that she had been missing a lot of rest while he was gone.

Inara had a regular schedule, and normally that meant that Kate had a very fragmented schedule since the two never really coincided. She probably hadn't been allowed to oversleep in a long time, but when he had turned everyone away and taken Kate to bed, that had put Inara in Layla's care.

Since Layla was also nursing that meant she was ideally suited for the task. In fact, the two women had frequently spelled one another when one needed a break, even before he had left on his journey. He started to check, but the enchantment guarding the privacy of his bedroom blocked his magesight.

He gave up with a sigh and returned his attention to Kate's sleeping face. *If I continue on the path I'm on now she will pay the price,* he thought somberly. Inara and Eldin also came to the fore of his mind, *and so will they.* He had never had so much to lose before.

And they know it.

He was surrounded by an entire village of hostages, his children, Kate, and even Layla, though he was reluctant to admit it. And the reason for it was understandable—the She'Har were doomed unless he could somehow save them, although he had not the faintest clue how he was supposed to do that. For all he knew it wasn't even something *he* would do, it might be his children that they needed. *Lyra was certainly glad to see me.*

His jaw clenched tightly at that thought. Had she been using him all along? Did she truly love him, or was she just another part of their plan? Did it matter? The She'Har had destroyed humanity. They had shown no compunction in doing whatever was necessary to assure their own survival. Even the morally superior Illeniels had been complicit in his own torture and slavery—all to further their mysterious plan.

They will pay for it, for all of it, no matter the cost.

Kate snorted, beginning a soft snore, and for some reason that brought Inara's soft face and chubby cheeks to his thoughts once more. *Am I willing to sacrifice my own flesh and blood for vengeance?*

Once again he remembered humanity's last days; men, women, and children, all dying as the krytek parasites devoured them from the inside out. It felt as though his head was going to explode. Taking a deep breath Tyrion tried to relax, the slow beat of the earth beneath him helped to soothe his own tortured heart—and then he understood.

Sitting up, he stared at Kate, "I can protect you. I can protect Inara, and all the others." He smiled, feeling a rush of energy, "And I can kill every last fucking one of them!"

His sudden excitement made him fully aware of the urgent state of his bladder, so he found the chamber pot and used it, still grinning like a mad fool. His newfound enthusiasm made it difficult to focus on his aim, and he began to chuckle as he missed the pot for a second.

Kate's eyes were on him, "If anyone saw you giggling and pissing on the floor they'd never take you seriously again."

Tyrion was startled, but he hid his surprise and after he had finished relieving himself he waved his happy instrument at her, "Luckily, they won't."

She took an exasperated breath, closing her eyes and hiding a smirk, when she opened them again she noted, "You seem to be in high spirits this morning."

He nodded, "Yes, I am. I was doing some thinking when I woke up and 'Twig' and I had a wonderful idea."

"Twig?"

He glanced down, "Isn't that the name you gave him last night?"

She put her hand over her face, "Really? I wouldn't think you'd want to keep that as a nickname." Standing up, she crossed the room, "If you're done, I need the pot." Glancing at the damp spots on the floor she added, "And you're cleaning that up, by the way."

When she had finished he was sitting on the edge of the bed. He patted it while giving her a meaningful glance.

"What?" she asked suspiciously.

Since she wasn't coming closer he went to her, and then to her surprise he dropped onto his knees, putting his arms around her hips and resting his head against her stomach, "I'm sorry." When he looked up she was staring at him with an expression of great concern.

"Daniel, I don't…"

He held up a hand, "Let me finish." Standing, he drew her to the bed and sat beside her. "I know you've been worried, and you have every right to be. I've kept things from you. When you came to live here, I told you that you were joining my tragedy, that I had no hope for the future, that I had merely sunk to the level that I was willing to risk your life along with my own. But things have changed since then…"

Her green eyes had begun to water, "Inara…"

Tyrion nodded, "Exactly, and Eldin, and so many other things too, but mainly *you*. You and our little girl have shown me a new life, a new life that I mean to preserve."

Kate was rubbing at her cheeks, "Are you saying what I think you are? Don't tease me, Daniel. I couldn't bear it if you weren't serious."

Leaning over, he kissed her forehead, "I'm saying that I am going to make sure that nothing happens to you, or Inara, or any of the others. I'm going to make you safe."

She caught his chin in her hands, "You're giving up on revenge, right?"

He smiled, "They need us, and I think they want peace, but I'm going to make sure that no matter what happens, you and the others will be safe."

"And you're giving up on punishing them?" she insisted.

"It was never about punishment, Cat," he assured her, *It was about a reckoning.* "I'm not going to assume they will hold to their end of the treaty, but I will work to reassure them. I will *also* make certain that if they renege on it, that you and the children will be safe."

Kate frowned, "You still don't trust them."

"I only trust you," he told her, "but I will work to make them trust me, and I'll build a better world for you and our children."

She could feel a half-truth behind his words, "You aren't being completely honest, Daniel. What are you hiding this time?"

He kissed her, "The details. I need you to trust me."

Kate growled.

"I'm going to build a secret stronghold, several actually. Places that I know can keep you and the others safe, even if they break the treaty," he explained, hoping it would be enough.

"But that isn't everything," she stressed.

Tyrion sighed, "No, and I won't tell you everything."

She tensed, "Why?"

Stay relaxed, keep your eyes on hers. "You'll be safer not knowing everything. Some things you might not agree with completely, but I won't be swayed. My primary goal is to keep you and the others safe, but I've learned a lot from the loshti, and some of my plans will be deterrents rather than true defenses," he said, as calmly as possible. *A lie wrapped in truth.*

Kate watched him carefully, and she felt her chest growing tighter as he spoke. *How did he get so far away?*

With every soft word Daniel spoke she could feel an empty hollowness. He had gotten much better at lying, even to her. She could no longer tell where the line was, between what was true, what was untrue, and what he had merely convinced himself of. *Inside it all, he's lost. He loves, he hates, and even he does not know what he will really do.*

Daniel's arms were around her. "What's wrong? Why are you crying?" he asked.

"I miss you, Daniel," she said softly, "and I don't know if I'll ever find you again."

"Huh?"

She looked up into icy blue eyes. Once she had believed in him. Once she had known him, better than he had known himself. She had watched him grow up, she had seen his kindness as a child, as a boy, and even as a man. She had always known what he really meant, no matter what he said. Truth or lies he had been an open book. Now he was a stranger, a stranger wearing her lover's face. "You're mad," she said at last.

Tyrion grinned, "Is that a problem? I thought you were a lunatic for a while."

Kate blinked, "When?"

"When we killed that warden, and you gave me a speech about killing chickens and dogs, or something like that," he said bluntly. "I had never seen that side of you, and frankly I wondered if you were a few cards shy of a full deck."

"I guess I was a little crazy then," she admitted. "I was young and full of passion, and you were all I thought about. The world seemed empty if it didn't have you in it. It's kind of embarrassing to think about it now."

"You were scary. You know what I did then, when I realized I didn't understand you? When I thought you might be insane?" he asked.

47

Kate almost chuckled, "Yeah, you stole the horse, ran off, and left me with a bloody mess to clean up."

Leaning over he kissed her ear, "That's true, but I meant after that. I spent the rest of my life loving you. I loved you when you were crazy, and later, when I discovered you were definitely a lot saner than I was, I kept loving you."

Despite herself Kate felt a warm flush rising as his lips and words touched her ears. "When did you decide I was saner than you?"

Teeth grazed her neck and a shiver went down her spine, but Tyrion answered between his nibbling, "When I returned, and you told me that you were a mother and that your responsibilities to your family were more important than what you felt for me. It was the saddest moment of my life, and yet I admired you, I loved you even more for it."

Kate gasped before turning her lips to find his. Her body was reacting, and she could feel the heat rising within her. *Damn him! We are supposed to be talking.* She ignored that thought and ran her hand down his spine, letting her nails lightly rake his skin. "I'm still going to be angry after this." Her hand had moved on to grasp the center of his pleasure.

He gasped, "I wasn't just trying to distract you. I wanted you to know that my priorities have changed."

She stopped. "What does that mean?"

"That my love for you, for Inara, for my children, that my duty to my family, is more important than my hatred for the She'Har."

She could still see the madness lurking behind his eyes, but she also felt the truth in his voice. *If nothing else is true, let that one thing be enough.* Daniel's strong hands pressed her down onto the bed, and she wrapped her legs around his waist. *It has to be enough.*

CHAPTER 6

Tyrion and Kate didn't emerge from the bedroom until almost noon, and when they did, the first order of business was food. Tyrion ate like a man who had been starving for months.

He had had food, of course, but his extended experience as a tree trapped in a rocky cave had left him feeling malnourished. He had finished most of the few remaining rations after he had returned to himself, but during the trip back he and Brigid had been forced to rely only on what they could hunt. That hadn't been a problem, meat was easy to get when you were a mage, but vegetables had been lacking.

Once that was taken care of, he sent Sarah out to find her siblings. Kate took Inara and Eldin from Layla, thanking her for the break, and Tyrion made a point of spending a short time playing with his small son before the others arrived.

Every time he looked at Eldin however, he could only think about the fact that the child was doomed to be childless. He was a genetic dead end, and ultimately so were all the humans in the slave camps of the She'Har. *They can let us have the slaves and laugh about it later, because they know that in the end we will be right back where we started—no magic, no power, and ultimately doomed.*

The only magic humanity would possess was that passed on by his own offspring, and none of them would have the special gifts that those from the groves had.

Unless I can find a way around that. He had an idea, but it was dangerous in the extreme, and he knew that Kate wouldn't approve. He wasn't even certain if some of his children would go along with it, and they were all committed to the cause.

Layla wouldn't have an issue with it, he thought to himself, *but she's a complete psychotic. Brigid would be fine with it as well, for similar reasons.* But he needed more than just those two. In particular he would need assistance from some of his sons. *And Emma, of course.* She would be absolutely necessary for almost everything he wanted to accomplish.

A half hour passed before they were all assembled in the common room, his thirteen nearly adult children and Layla. Tyrion activated the privacy enchantment built into the walls of the room, and then he turned to Layla, "Create a privacy screen if you would. Make sure no sounds enter or leave this room."

That elicited some odd looks from them, but Layla did it without question.

He stood and looked over them, "I'm sure you have some questions, but I'll address the first one on your minds. The reason I asked Layla to create a secondary screen within the enchantment was to make absolutely certain that no one could eavesdrop on this conversation. I've recently gained a lot of new information, and I want to make sure our enemy doesn't learn that.

"I would also bet that many of you are wondering where I've been, but you'll be disappointed. If you don't already know, I won't be discussing it. If you do know, you will not discuss it either. Nothing said here today is to leave this room. No one who isn't present at this moment is to be told anything I tell you today. Is that clear?"

Abby held up a hand, and when he nodded at her she spoke, "Except Kate, right?"

Tyrion's face was as hard as flint, "Did I say, 'except Kate'?"

"Well, no, I just thought…"

He stopped her there, "Since it isn't clear, I will explain. If anyone here talks to anyone outside of this room about this, I will kill them, and I don't give a rat's ass whether it's Kate, or Lyra, or your families back in Colne. *This* stays here!"

A long pause followed, and once that had sunk in he continued, "After this meeting I will give additional information to each of you, specific assignments, tasks, that sort of thing. You won't discuss that information with anyone else unless they are also present when I give you your instructions, nor will you ask your brothers or sisters about what their tasks are. Do any of you understand my purpose in giving you such strict rules?"

Anthony Long made a shrewd guess, "You're worried that one or more of us will eventually be questioned?"

Tyrion smiled, "Tortured, mind-raped, questioned, or otherwise forced to talk to the enemy, yes, that is exactly my thinking. What you don't know you can't divulge. Is there anyone here who isn't still committed to our purpose? Is there anyone who doesn't understand who our enemy is?"

No one spoke.

"I'm not going to punish you. If there's anyone here who doesn't feel strongly about destroying the She'Har, speak now. I'll let you leave, so long as you don't interfere or discuss our goals with the enemy."

He waited again, but there were no takers for his offer. Most of them showed a solid resolve on their faces and in their auras. Only Abby displayed any hint of doubt. *Dear Abby,* he thought, *always the tender hearted one.*

He didn't doubt her commitment to their cause, though. She was still feeling uncomfortable about keeping Kate in the dark. *I'll make sure her job is the easiest, and that whatever she learns is safe for Kate to know.*

He wouldn't tell her that, of course. Sometimes even people with an overly developed sense of compassion were useful.

"I am going to increase the intake of people from the slave camps. In fact, I intend to bring most of them here within a year, so our work is about to get a lot more frantic…"

"Sir!" said Ryan, standing up from his seat, "We aren't nearly ready for that many people. We won't be for years…

Tyrion held up a hand, "I know that, allow me to explain. We won't be bringing them here to educate them, or try to civilize them. We will be bringing them here as slaves, and slaves they will remain. The first groups will be used for labor to create lodgings and farms to support those who follow."

"Then they might a well stay where they are," objected Ryan. "Why are we wasting so much effort if we aren't going to free them?" Layla nodded agreement from where she sat.

"Because we need an army, we need laborers, and most importantly, we need weapons," said Tyrion coolly.

Violet looked confused, "You want to use them to make weapons?"

No, they will 'be' my weapons, thought Tyrion. He shook his head negatively, "They will serve in many capacities, but they will be tools. I need their unique gifts, and I need more manpower."

Layla spoke then, "So after all you have said before, you intend to keep my people as slaves. How does this make you different than the She'Har?"

"You will be in charge of them," said Tyrion, "and we will remove their collars." He could see the gears turning in Layla's head already, and he fought to contain a smirk. The female warden was a product of her upbringing, and power definitely appealed to her.

After a moment she spoke again, "We cannot control them without collars. There are too many, and some of them are stronger than I am. They only respond to strength." It was a surprising admission from the warden. Back in Ellentrea it would have been unthinkable to admit to any weakness.

"As I mentioned before," responded Tyrion, "I have come to learn a lot of new information. I now know exactly how the collars were constructed. I cannot duplicate them, but I can create an enchantment that will allow us to do many of the same things. We can mark them with it, and I will give each of you a matching command enchantment to make certain they obey."

That piqued Layla's interest, "What will the enchantment do?"

Death and pain should be enough, thought Tyrion, *best to keep it simple.* "We can discuss that later after I break you into groups. I have one main piece of information to share with all of you before that, though."

He had their full attention then.

"You already know the past. You know what they've forced us to do, the fighting and killing. I've told you about the war with humanity, when they first came. I've learned more about that, and I intend to return the favor, but more importantly, you need to know the truth of this treaty they've signed with us.

"When they told me that they'd free the slaves, allowing us to build a new community, I thought perhaps they were sincere. The She'Har are cruel, but usually in ignorance, or so I believed. What I have recently learned is that the people of Ellentrea, Sabortrea, Garoltrea, and Baratrea, have been poisoned, not in the common sense of the word, but genetically…"

Violet held up a hand, "Genet—what word is that?"

"It's a word I first heard from Thillmarius, though I didn't understand it then," began Tyrion. "It's a human term, one used by our ancestors to describe the way traits are passed down from parent to child." *And I understand it a damn sight better now,* he thought silently. "It's too much to explain now, but this is how what they've done works. Those sired by male children of the She'Har can have children of their own, but those children will give rise to only stillborn offspring."

He caught Layla's stare, "You were sired by a Prathion She'Har, were you not?"

Her eyes were wide, "I was raised in the pens. There was no way for me to know…"

"You were," said Tyrion, pressing on though he knew the words were more painful than daggers. "If not, you would never have given birth to Eldin. Your son will never have children of his own; if he tries they will miscarry or be stillborn. This is the 'gift' the She'Har have given us."

Tyrion turned his gaze back to the others, "The only humans who can reproduce successfully are those who are in Colne, Lincoln, and in this room, and only we can give magic to the future human race.

"What may be less obvious is what would happen if the people of Colne and Lincoln were allowed to mix with the people of the slave camps. By freeing them, the She'Har all but guaranteed our extinction. It would have taken at least a generation or two before the result of their genetic tinkering was evident. There are not many people left as it is, interbreeding with the slaves would have reduced our numbers several times over.

"Humanity would not have survived that final blow, and they *knew* it!" finished Tyrion.

"How did you learn all this?!" asked Piper suddenly.

"I stole their secrets," answered Tyrion, "but I won't share how. If they were to learn the slightest hint of that, they would wipe us out. The more important question is what we will do about it now that we know?"

Brigid activated the tattoos on her arms, showing the razor sharp aythar that sheathed her arms to the others. Her eyes were fever bright, and a feral grin was on her face.

"There aren't enough of us," reminded Abby cautiously.

"There are almost a hundred thousand mages living in the slave camps," countered Tyrion.

Anthony broke in then, "Even if we make all of them into soldiers, it still isn't enough, not to mention that we won't be able to protect the people of Colne and Lincoln. Assuming you're serious about preserving our race."

Anthony's statement surprised Tyrion. The boy was one of the quieter ones among his children, quiet and thoughtful. He took several steps forward, bringing himself closer. "You're right Anthony. It isn't enough, but I'm not going to make them soldiers, or at least, not *just* soldiers. That won't be your job, however. I intend to put you in charge of protecting those people you just mentioned."

"What I am about to show you is based on the spellweave that the She'Har use to preserve fallen victors in the arena, to keep them from dying before a healer can see to them," explained Tyrion. "I call it a stasis enchantment, and it has a lot of very handy uses." Four of his children stood around him attentively, Anthony Long, Ashley Morris, Violet Price, and Blake Cruz.

"It looks complicated," commented Ashley. "You want us to learn this?"

His gaze was flinty as he looked down on the stocky girl. Ashley had never been as quick to learn as most of his other children. He blamed that on her mother, Peggy. *That woman was so dense I probably needn't have bothered using magic to seduce her.*

Nonetheless, he still felt a certain fondness for the girl. She had a small upturned nose that was cute despite her overly wide cheekbones. Combined with a sprinkling of freckles, pale eyes, and blond hair, she was somehow adorable despite being the least attractive of his daughters.

His expression showed no hint of affection toward her, however, and she wilted under his stare. She mumbled an apology, "Sorry, Father."

"A dog could learn this, if it was shown enough times," he said bluntly. "I expect you to do far better. The pattern looks complicated, but if you look closely it repeats after this stretch *here*. Keep the geometry of the pattern in alignment, and you can adjust the number or repetitions to cover containers of almost any size."

Anthony spoke then, "Is that what we will be making, containers? And if so, what size?"

Tyrion stretched out his hand, and using a fine line of aythar he sketched a long rectangle in the dirt. "Most will need to be about six feet in length and three feet wide, but there will be some variation…"

"Like coffins?" put in Violet. She was the most artistic of his children, which was one reason he had chosen her for the job. She had a good eye for detail which made her a natural when it came to enchanting.

"Exactly like coffins," he agreed, "made of stone."

Everyone groaned then, for they knew it would mean frequent trips to the quarry. While magic made cutting and moving heavy slabs much easier than it was using traditional methods, it was still extremely tiring.

"You aren't planning to bury all of our enemies are you?" joked Blake.

Tyrion lifted one brow, "That would be impractical."

"So what will you store in them?" asked Anthony.

"Bodies."

Violet sighed, "So they are coffins?"

"No, they'll be alive. If you'll recall, I told Anthony earlier that he would be in charge of protecting the villagers," reminded Tyrion.

Four teenaged wizards stared at him with mouths agape. "That's several thousand people!" exclaimed Anthony after a second of reflection. "We can't make that many!"

"You'll have help."

"Even if all of us work on them, we couldn't make enough..." began Violet.

"Think about it a moment," said Tyrion.

The four of them looked at one another for almost a minute before Violet's face lit up, "Oh! I see."

"What?" asked Blake.

Anthony filled in the blank for him, "Slaves."

Most of the afternoon was taken up giving instructions to each group. After starting the stasis enchantment assignment, he moved on to assign Thaddeus and Sarah to convincing the villagers to relocate.

Of course, 'relocate' was a euphemism, and strictly speaking they had a considerable amount of time to get the villagers moving, a lot of preparations had to be finished before they could actually take them.

Layla and Ian would be tasked with managing the influx of slaves. Tyrion had made it especially clear that his son was to defer to Layla. Ian's cruel temperament would make him ideal for the job, but he lacked her sensibility.

Emma and Ryan, along with Piper and Blake would oversee the construction of the new living quarters and 'other' more sensitive locations. The biggest part of the job would be handled by Emma, under her brother, Ryan's watchful eye. However, the details and cleanup would require a lot of effort to finish after her part was done. Piper and Blake would handle the labor, with a lot of assistance from the newly rehomed slaves of the She'Har.

Once he had finished giving orders, Tyrion headed back to the main house and his shadow, Brigid, fell in beside him.

"You do not intend to use me?" she asked as they walked.

"Do you want to build boxes or dig holes?" he asked her.

The dark haired girl laughed, "No."

"You will stay with me. In a week I should be ready for our first foray. You'll be coming along, as will Ryan and Emma," he told her.

"You said nothing to them while discussing their building assignment."

"I will tell them when I'm ready," he said simply.

Brigid looked up at him expectantly, "Will there be blood?"

"That's why I'm taking you, dear child."

She smiled, and for a moment one might have been able to mistake Brigid for a normal young woman looking forward to some happy event. She radiated a sense of contentment.

Tyrion put a hand on her shoulder, "You must promise to control yourself."

"I won't hurt Emma or Ryan," she replied reassuringly. "I only cut what I intend to cut."

"Not just them," he explained, "I intend to bring some of our targets back alive. The fewer you kill or maim the better."

Brigid pursed her lips, "That doesn't sound very fun."

"Would you rather stay here?"

Her sullen stare spoke for itself, but she answered anyway, "No."

CHAPTER 7

When he entered the house, the first thing he noticed was that the privacy enchantment around his bedroom had been activated. Kate couldn't do that, and Lyralliantha would have created a fresh spellweave to accomplish the same effect, if she had felt a need for privacy, which was rare.

No one else should be in his room other than one of those two. Tyrion glanced at Brigid and she nodded, activating her tattooed defenses and lifting her deadly chain. She released it, and her aythar held it suspended, writhing like a snake through the air around her.

Tyrion's own senses sharpened as adrenaline made his heart speed up. He activated his own enchanted shield and sheathed his arms in deadly blades of pure force. For a second his perception focused on Brigid, peering deeply, and he caught a flicker of something unusual beneath her skin.

Her bones were inscribed with runes in almost the exact same fashion that his shin bone was. She had copied what he had done and extended it to include virtually every bone in her body. *She's insane!* he realized, not figuratively, not a little, but completely nuts. *The pain would have been unbearable and it would have taken months at the very least. How did she survive it?*

For a second he was seized by an urge to hug the wild dark haired psychopath beside him, though with their defenses active that wouldn't have been realistically possible. His new realization made him both proud and sad for her at the same time.

Pushing those thoughts aside, he approached the doorway to his bedroom. It opened before he could dismiss the enchantment along his left arm and put his hand to it. Kate stared at him wide eyed.

"Are you alright?" he asked immediately.

She nodded briskly, "Of course. I was just having a chat with Lyra."

Now that the door was open, he could sense the presence of the other woman. No one else seemed to be present, although a Prathion could have hidden from his magesight. Stepping in, he looked at Lyralliantha, "Did you activate the privacy enchantment?"

"Yes."

"Why?" he asked suspiciously.

The silver haired She'Har lifted one brow, "So we could talk privately. That is what you made it for, correct?"

"I don't recall teaching it to you," he responded curtly. Activating the enchantment required a working knowledge of what each rune he had devised symbolized, as well as knowing which part of the structure needed to be completed in order to bring it to life.

"I pay close attention, dearest," Lyra replied lightly, "and Abby was kind enough to answer my questions when I was curious."

Tyrion felt a surge of anger at her lighthearted answer. For a moment he considered giving Brigid the signal she was waiting for, his daughter was full of restrained tension, like an angry hound straining at its leash. Just a twitch of his finger and it would be over. He wouldn't even have to do the dirty work himself. He wouldn't have to be the one who killed the woman he had trusted despite everything her people had done to him over the years.

Kate might not even realize he had given the order.

The vein in his temple was throbbing as the moment drew out painfully, and Brigid's lethal chain, which had been sinuously moving until then, stopped. The deadly metal hung expectantly in the air, quivering almost imperceptibly. "Get out," he whispered, staring at Lyralliantha.

"Daniel!" snapped Kate. She had been watching him with concern the entire time. "You need to talk to her!"

There was no easy way out with Kate there. Consciously, he relaxed his shoulders as he turned to Brigid, "It's alright. Go back to your room."

Mysteriously, Kate followed her sister out. Her only words were to Lyralliantha as she left, "Remember what I said."

The She'Har nodded, and then Tyrion closed the door on the others. "Make it quick," he told her. "I don't want you here any longer than necessary."

"You are angry with me."

He snorted derisively, "Perceptive."

"Kate told me," she added.

"You lied to me."

She tilted her head, something she often did when she was confused. It had always reminded him of his long gone dog, Blue. "I am not aware of having done that."

"You knew what they did to the people of the slave camps. You never told me they couldn't have children!" he snapped.

She didn't bother denying it, "That is not lying."

His anger was draining away already, replaced by the exhaustion he often felt when trying to talk to Lyra, "It's a lie of omission, leaving out an important fact…"

"We have never spoken of this…"

"Don't give me that shit!" he snapped. "I have a son with Layla! If you truly cared, you should have shared that information with me."

She looked down, silver hair falling over her features, "You never asked…"

"You should have told me anyway! Not that it matters. Would you have answered if I had somehow known to ask?"

"I would have asked the Elders first," she admitted.

"Wrong answer," he said bitterly.

"Was there a right answer?" she asked suddenly. "I have not lied to you, Tyrion. I have kept your secrets. Since we first met I have wanted nothing but the best for you, I have wanted nothing for myself—but you." There were tears in her eyes.

Emotion was rare for her, but he had seen it displayed before. He no longer believed in it, though. Stalking forward, he took her by the shoulder, pressing her back against the wall, "They gave me the loshti."

Her eyes widened, but the surprise was short lived, "So that is what happened."

"I know almost everything now, so don't think your lies will be effective anymore," he growled.

"You know more than I do then."

"What does that mean?" he spat.

"Exactly what it sounds like! I know almost nothing! I'm just a pitiful pawn. Did you think I was given some special knowledge? I know my people, I know the Elders, but only what any of us are given to know when we are made. I never expected this, never expected *you.*" Her knees gave way, and she might have sunk to the floor but his grip tightened, holding her up. "What am I supposed to do now?"

"Whatever they told you to do, probably," he sneered.

Pale blue eyes caught his own, "They told me to make you happy."

"Is that what our relationship has been?" he asked. "An act?"

"No!" she gasped. "Never. I've never been given any instruction regarding you before, and this one made me glad, because it is all I wanted anyway. How can I make you see that?"

"Bleed for me." Reaching out with his aythar he pulled the wooden sword from its sheath across the room. The sword flew to his hand and he offered it to her, "Die for me."

She took the hilt with trembling fingers as she stared at him, "Will you believe me then? Will you love me if I prove it with my life?"

Something in her tone unnerved him. He hadn't expected this reaction, but he was too angry to back down. "Yes."

Reversing the weapon, she set the point against her abdomen, "I have nothing else."

Tyrion lifted her hand, redirecting the blade, aiming it at her heart, "The gut would take too long. You could heal yourself. There's no going back if you put it here." He put every bit of spite and vitriol he felt for the She'Har into his words, but as he looked into her eyes his stomach lurched.

When Tyrion had first met Lyralliantha, she had been unshakably calm, a true ice princess in word and manner, but over the years she had warmed. Love had changed her. She had become something more than just a child of the She'Har, she had become a woman. And for all of her intelligence and complexity, she was still an incredibly naïve woman at that.

Back then, she hadn't particularly cared about living or dying. She had had nothing to lose. For the She'Har the human part of their lives was essentially meaningless.

Her nostrils quivered and her pupils dilated as tears trickled freely down her cheeks. She inhaled sharply and tried to speak, but her throat had closed, the words wouldn't come out, with a gasping sob she jerked her wrist inward, driving the wooden blade straight for her heart.

Tyrion felt his heart break. "No!" Striking out he tried to bat the point away, but it had already been against her skin when she began the thrust, as fast as he was, he couldn't stop it from piercing her chest. His blow sent it slewing sideways, ripping a deep gouge through her skin and nearly severing her collarbone into two parts. At the same time the edge tore through his palm, severing tendons and bones there as well.

Blood was everywhere, but Lyra's heart still beat. The point had been diverted before it reached it. The sword fell, clattering hollowly to the ground, and she slid down the wall. Tyrion sank to his knees beside her, "I'm so stupid. Forgive me." Working as quickly as possible he sealed the damaged veins and skin in the cut across her chest. Despite the depth of the cut and the damaged bone, the wound wasn't life threatening, just incredibly messy.

"You shouldn't have done that," he continued, babbling as he corrected the damage. "I'm not worth it. What were you thinking?"

"That I would rather die being loved—than live with your spite," she whispered. "Your hand…" She caught his wrist and lifted his damaged appendage. A large portion of the hand and fingers dangled limply from the rest while blood pumped from severed arteries.

"I deserved it," he told her as she used her aythar to clamp down on the blood vessels and arrest the bleeding.

Lyra's eyes flickered to his and then back to his hand as she focused on healing it. The wound was far more serious than the one she had suffered, and the complexities of repairing the tendons, bones, and ligaments made it more difficult to fix. "I have not had much practice at this," she said apologetically as she worked.

She did the best she could and then sealed everything and used a spellweave to make permanent the nerve block that was preventing him from feeling the pain.

Tyrion examined it with his senses and tried to move it experimentally. All he got for his effort was a spastic twitch, but he felt nothing from the injury.

"We need to go to Ellentrea. The healers there are much better. Otherwise you will probably lose the use of it," she told him pragmatically.

He studied her face, and what he saw made him ashamed. Lyra's eyes were red and swollen while her normally flawless hair was tangled and stuck together in odd places where blood had gotten into it and dried. "I'm so sorry…," he began.

She nodded, uncertain how to respond, her expression haunted.

He kissed her then, and she returned the gesture with hungry lips. When he thought to pull away she caught his hair, pulling him back.

"More."

That he could do. His wrongdoings and trespasses he could not mend, but he would not deny her that. Their kissing grew more heated as the minutes passed, and eventually he lifted her from the floor, with one good hand and one clumsy one. As he laid her gently on the bed she opened her lips to speak.

"Wait. I have to tell you something."

He paused.

"The elders told me to give you a child," she finished.

He had already suspected that, but his heart had changed, "The elders can go fuck themselves. What do you want?"

"I want it too," she answered. "I have wanted it for a long while now."

"Can you?" he asked.

She nodded.

He kissed her again, and she didn't release him for some time after that.

CHAPTER 8

Golden eyes looked at Tyrion over steepled ebon fingers. Thillmarius paused briefly before smiling faintly, "Really, Tyrion, I thought we were past this."

Tyrion ground his teeth, "I didn't come here for snide commentary."

The Prathion lore-warden clucked his tongue, "Don't be so testy. I am not mocking you. You know my people better than that. I am merely curious as to how you gained such a singular injury."

Tyrion regretted coming to Ellentrea already. Lyralliantha had suggested he go to Byovar, one of the Illeniel lore-wardens, but he hadn't felt comfortable facing anyone from her grove. He knew that the She'Har cared little for injuries to their 'children', but he still worried at their reaction to discovering that he had nearly killed Lyra. It was irrational, of course, but to him it felt something akin to facing ones in-laws after hurting their daughter.

Aside from that, he knew that the trainers in Ellentrea had far more experience in healing battle wounds. He had benefited from their care more times than he could count.

He had also considered trying to use his bizarre ability to do things without aythar. He had once inadvertently restored his mangled ear while creating a storm, so he knew it was possible, but he wasn't sure he wanted to experiment on something as important as his hand. He had a vague idea of how to go about it, but then, everything about those abilities was vague.

So, in the end, he had come to Ellentrea.

"You could have gone to Koralltis," suggested Thillmarius, referring to the other Prathion trainer who managed the slave camp. "He has even more experience than I do."

I'll stick to the devil I know, thought Tyrion. "I am more familiar with you," he admitted.

The Prathion She'Har showed a flash of white teeth, "I am grateful that you came to me."

Tyrion frowned, suspicious, "Why?" Of all the She'Har that lived, Thillmarius still sent chills down his spine whenever he thought of him. He had conquered his fear long ago, but some traumas went too deep for courage to fully overcome. Thillmarius had been in charge of his 'care' when he first came to Ellentrea, and his body remembered the punishments he had received. Sitting across from his torturer was enough to make the bile rise in his throat and set his legs to quivering.

He would never admit as much, though. Since the treaty with the She'Har had been signed Thillmarius had expressed his regret for his actions on several occasions, and it was also true that the lore-warden had helped both him and Lyralliantha through difficult circumstances in the past. If Byovar was to be believed, Thillmarius had also been one of the most outspoken proponents of creating the treaty between his people and humankind.

"Because it gives me yet another small opportunity to make up for the harm that I once did to you, Tyrion," answered Thillmarius. "I know it will never be enough, but it matters to me."

As usual, Tyrion had no idea how to respond to the She'Har's sudden expression of sentiment, so he ignored it, "You can mend it then?" With an effort of will he extended his hand across the small table and stretched it out before the Prathion.

"Certainly." Examining the hand with his senses Thillmarius raised one brow, "Lyralliantha did this?"

"It was a training accident," he lied.

"Not the injury," said Thillmarius, pointing to the tiny spellweave that continued to block the sensory nerves in Tyrion's wrist. "This."

"Oh," said Tyrion, somewhat relieved, "Yes, she did the initial healing."

"Crudely," snorted the lore-warden, "but she is very young. You could have done better yourself."

He glared at the She'Har, angry at the way Lyra's effort had been dismissed, "I was rather distracted at the time."

"Really?" said Thillmarius, his eyes widening, "I have seen you heal yourself under very trying circumstances in the arena."

"It wouldn't have mattered," said Tyrion. "Even if I could have produced a marginal improvement, I knew I would need expert treatment in the end."

Thillmarius was already working on his hand and Tyrion was glad for the nerve block as he watched him severing tendons and realigning them before making new attachments. Though the work was delicate, Thillmarius continued to chat, "I don't think I can do much for the bruise on your face. Did you get that during the same accident?"

The lore-warden was referring to the black eye that Tyrion had received later. Two days after the fact it was now showing an impressive display of purple and blue hues. "Something like that," he answered reluctantly. The shiner had been a gift from Kate when she had seen the results of his 'talk' with Lyra. Tyrion had resisted the urge to shield himself, wanting to avoid hurting her hand, but if he had realized how powerful her punch would be, he might have reconsidered.

That redheaded monster really knows how to throw a punch, he thought ruefully.

It was late afternoon when he got back to Albamarl. The name had originally been applied just to his house, but at some point they had begun using it to refer generally to the entirety of their small village.

He intended to check on Ryan's efforts, but Anthony caught him in the yard as he approached the large building that his children lived in. "This is taking too long," said the young man without preamble.

"Which is why I have four of you working on it," he answered unsympathetically.

His son was undeterred, "You said you wanted fifteen boxes done by the end of the week, but we won't finish that many…"

Tyrion gave him a cold stare, "Why?"

Anthony took a deep breath, "It's the stone. If it were just the enchantment we could probably finish them in time. It takes each of us only half a day to complete the runework on one, but hauling the stone and shaping the boxes takes a lot of time and effort. We need more help, especially for the simple work, like moving the materials from the quarry."

"Where are the slaves? Ian and Layla should begin bringing them in soon."

The boy shook his head, "Ryan says the first living quarters won't be ready for a few weeks. Whatever you have him working on is taking most of his time, but I was thinking, why don't we leave them in Ellentrea? At least for now. We could bring them in during the day and send them back in the evening…"

"No one who works here is going back there. Who knows what they might see? Tell Layla to bring twenty tomorrow. Half of them can work on the housing, and the others can assist you with the stonework," ordered Tyrion.

"We have nowhere to keep them!"

"Let them sleep on the ground. It will give them more incentive to finish their work quickly."

Anthony opened his mouth but closed it again almost immediately. He could sense it would be futile arguing with his father.

Tyrion started to turn away, but then he paused, "Have you seen Ryan?"

"No, he disappears every morning—along with Emma," noted the young man with a tone of disapproval.

"I have them working on something together."

Anthony looked concerned, "Are you sure that's wise?"

"Wiser than questioning my decisions," answered Tyrion with a dangerous smile. "Blake is with them anyway."

"Blake came back an hour ago," observed his son.

Tyrion found them half an hour later, precisely where they were supposed to be, which of course was a location that none of the others had been told about, aside from Blake and Brigid.

The entrance was less than a quarter mile from Albamarl, in the direction of the foothills that stretched beyond the border of the Illeniel Grove. It was a good location because the ground was too hard there for the elders to put down roots. The doorway was built into one of the first rocky outcrops.

There was no door yet, but that didn't matter. It would be finished later. Within the darkened archway a cave sloped downward before turning back and dropping yet further. The first chamber was at least a hundred yards and almost directly below the entrance above. It stretched for fifty yards in every direction with small alcoves cut into the walls. But that was not where Emma and Ryan were, they were still farther down, where no magesight could detect them.

He walked across the chamber until he had reached the last alcove. It was not noticeably different from any of the others, but when he put his hand against it and closed his eyes, the stone wall melted away, revealing another tunnel. No one but Tyrion and Emma could open this door, and thus far none of his other children had even been able to sense the tunnel behind it. He had tested it by watching Anthony and Violet's reactions when they were first shown the chamber and directed them as to where the stasis boxes would be placed when they were finished.

To magesight, the earth presented a feeling of wholeness and solidity. Even Tyrion detected nothing out of the ordinary when he came near it. If he hadn't known it was there already, he would never have suspected its presence.

But the earth answered his call and opened the way when he spoke to it. The tunnel sealed itself behind him as he descended, protecting the secrets that lay below once more. Aside from Emma and Ryan, only Brigid knew of the existence of the hidden tunnel.

It led him deeper into the bowels of the earth, until he could no longer even sense the surface above, and there he found them.

Ryan cradled his sister beside a stone pool that filled with water from a spring nearby. The water exited the pool to run down a channel along one wall of the large room before passing into another opening. The spring was new, the day before the pool had been dry.

Emma lay quietly, her head resting in Ryan's lap while he stroked her hair. She appeared to be unconscious.

"Is she alright?" asked Tyrion as he approached them.

Ryan looked up with worried eyes, "I think so, maybe. It was close. I almost lost her this time."

"The water?"

Ryan nodded.

Tyrion frowned, "Water is chaotic, she shouldn't have risked it. Far easier to mold the earth and form the channels for it."

His son's eyes caught fire. "Then perhaps you should have done it yourself," he said bitterly.

Tyrion rarely responded well to a challenge, but he calculated his words carefully this time, "You might be right, but I can't do everything myself. She volunteered for this."

Ryan looked away, "She had her reasons."

Any excuse to be alone with you, thought Tyrion, but he knew better than to test his son by saying it. "You've made a lot of progress. Once Blake finishes the light stones, and you set the doors in here, it will be almost ready for use."

"You still haven't told us what you plan to use it for," noted Ryan. "Why do you need water in here?"

"You don't really want to know. You've probably figured some of it out already, based on the floorplan," observed Tyrion.

"You'll have to tell us. You're going to need help," said the younger man.

75

Tyrion sighed, "I know you're committed Ryan, but your heart is still too kind for this. When I need assistance, it will be others I ask to get their hands dirty here."

"I thought it might be a refuge at first," said Ryan in a low voice. "The water would have made sense then, but the doors for these smaller rooms made it clear. They aren't living quarters; they're cells for a prison."

Tyrion walked across the center area, stopping to examine the smooth walls of one of the cells. "That's one name for it," he answered.

"What do you think is going to happen to her?" asked Ryan suddenly, changing the subject.

"Hmm?"

His son was studying Emma's features, worry on his face, "If she keeps doing this, I mean. Every time is different. When she comes back, she's different, it's as if she forgets who she is, or even *what* she is. She forgets who I am, and yesterday it was several minutes before she could even talk. What do you think it's doing to her?"

Tyrion walked back to look down on the two of them. They made a beautiful picture together, a picture of young love, if only it weren't for the disconcerting nature of their kinship. "I don't know, Ryan, I honestly don't. It's like becoming something else, and when it's over it's hard to understand yourself. Sometimes it isn't so bad, if you just go a little way, but the more you want to do, the farther you have to go. It feels as if you could go too far, could actually *become* what you're working with, whether it's the wind or the earth. I think we could be lost if that happens. That's why I have you looking after her."

Ryan's hand left Emma's face, so that he wouldn't disturb her as his fist clenched, "But you still think it's worth risking her?"

"No, I don't," said Tyrion, "but I will risk everything for this. *She* thinks it's worth risking herself, and I won't be the one to deny her the choice. All I can say is, that if the two of you survive the coming challenges, I will do the best I can to give you a chance to see the new world that follows this bloody business, but there are no guarantees."

"Do we deserve that chance?" Ryan's voice had taken on a tone of regret.

"What does that mean?"

"Because of how we feel," answered the young man. "I know you must suspect us already. It isn't natural. It's wrong." Ryan paused, stroking Emma's hair once more. "I can't help it, though. I think we're damned."

"This whole fucking world is damned, boy, but I don't think your love is part of that. I wouldn't recommend having children, but I'm the last person to judge anyone for their sins, real or perceived."

Ryan looked up, "You really think that?"

"Yeah," said Tyrion, "and I think Emma already knows that as well. Don't you, girl?"

She opened her eyes. "I'm not as slow to learn as he is," she replied, putting her hand over Ryan's.

Her brother pulled his hand away quickly, as though he had been burned, "How long have you been awake?" Shifting his legs, he eased her off his lap and moved away.

"Almost as long as I've been here," said Tyrion. "You need to pay better attention to her aythar."

"You should have said something Em'," Ryan scolded.

Emma smiled, "I was enjoying the moment. You won't even touch my hand anymore, but you're terribly sweet when you think I'm asleep."

Ryan flushed, but no one could see it in the dark. Tyrion only knew by the change in his expression and the jump the boy's heart had made. "Now that you're both awake, we need to talk. This is a good start, but we need more."

"More what exactly?" asked Ryan suspiciously, glad for the distraction.

"More places like this, with more levels, hidden and otherwise," said their father. "This is just the beginning."

Emma frowned, "How much more?"

"Ryan will need to help us figure that out," said Tyrion. "He's better at those sorts of calculations, but I'm sure it will be many times more than this."

Tyrion's son was aghast, "You can't expect all that of her! You know how dangerous this is!"

Emma held up one hand placatingly, "Ryan, please. It isn't that bad. Whether it's a small room or a massive chamber, it's almost the same. I don't actually do the work myself, the earth does."

"Once they start bringing in the slaves you'll have many more helpers to manage the finishing touches," reassured Tyrion. "She only needs to do the big things that would take too long using just magic."

"How many people are you planning to house in these places?" asked Ryan.

Tyrion told him.

CHAPTER 9

Ailayana Prathion walked softly through the fallen leaves. The ground was damp beneath them, and it kept the fallen detritus soft as well, so her light footsteps were muffled, almost too quiet to hear. That was one reason she loved to walk after it had been raining, but she would have done so even if the weather had been dry.

She was grateful that she lived where she did, near the border the Prathion's shared with the Illeniel Grove, for that meant she was never too far from the edge of the foothills. It was only by emerging from the boundary line that she got to see so much of the sun, and the sun was her favorite thing.

The rain had cleared the day before, so the sky was a scattered masterpiece of clouds across a blue canvas so large it defied imagination. The sun teased her, hiding now and again behind errant clouds only to pop out and dazzle her while she waited for it. It caught in her gold hair and despite the fact that her eyes seemed to share its color she was always forced to squint and shield her eyes with her black skinned hands.

Ailayana was well over two hundred years old, and with the world fully populated by the elders it might be much longer before she was ever given space to put down roots of her own, but she didn't mind. A quiet life suited her, and she longed for nothing more than the warm feel of sunlight on her skin.

It was quite a shock to her when the light disappeared, replaced with an empty void. No, not empty, the lightless space was filled with three others, baratti, two women and a man. One of them must be from Ellentrea for she was creating the invisibility shield that surrounded the area Ailayana had wandered into.

She could see them with her magesight now, though there was no light inside that sphere. The man watched her without moving, while the other woman stepped toward her. Even so, she felt no alarm, only curiosity. "What are you do…"

Ailayana's world spun as she fell toward the dark earth beneath her. The woman had struck her without warning. She hadn't even used any aythar, she had merely thrust upward with her palm, snapping Ailayana's head back before she had realized the attack was coming. A second blow landed in her midsection, and the last kick targeted her head. The world vanished.

"How was that?" asked Brigid, addressing her father.

"Better," he returned, "At least you didn't kill this one."

"He surprised me," groused Brigid.

"Surprised you? You cut him into three pieces before he had even stepped into the bubble! Layla told you he was almost to us. How could you be surprised?"

"I was surprised how much I enjoyed it," replied the dark haired girl. "It's harder to restrain myself than I thought it would be."

"Well learn to do so," said Tyrion, "or I won't bring you next time. I brought you as a kindness, but if you keep killing them, they're of no use to me."

"Then why did you keep his head?" interjected Layla.

"I might learn something from it, but I certainly don't need any more bodies. Make sure you keep them in one piece from now on, Brigid." After she had dismembered the first one Tyrion had called on the earth to swallow the rest of the body, but he had saved the She'Har male's head. Dissecting it might provide some extra information he hoped. "Lift her up, Brigid. You'll be the one carrying her."

His daughter balked for a moment, "Why can't Layla do it?"

"I'd rather she kept her attention on making sure we stay hidden," he told her patiently. "We have a long walk back."

"I still don't understand why you want them alive," complained Brigid. "Can I play with her later?"

"No," barked Tyrion. "We aren't taking them for torture, that would be pointless, although I doubt they'll thank us for the kindness." He smiled to himself. What he planned wouldn't be torture, but he had no doubt it would be extremely unpleasant for his subjects.

"This was so easy," remarked Brigid. "I don't see why we can't just take a few more. We could take as many as you need, and I could play with the extra ones."

"I'm nowhere near ready for that yet. Besides, while the She'Har don't particularly worry about their children, if more than a few disappear, they are bound to start wondering what's going on," explained Tyrion. "I can't afford to make them suspicious at this point."

Brigid levitated the She'Har woman's body behind them as they traveled, and Tyrion kept a close watch on her mental state. When Ailayana began to rouse he used his power to force her mind into a deep slumber.

Layla navigated, allowing only a tiny aperture for light to pass through into her invisibility shield. The others followed her closely since she was the only one who could see, but even so the size of the shield she was generating was beginning to take its toll on her. The female warden didn't have the seemingly endless quantities of aythar that Tyrion and his children did.

Tyrion had insisted that she cloak their movement before they had even left Albamarl that morning. He hadn't wanted anyone to observe their coming or going. That had been hours ago. At that time the shield had been smaller as well, since the three of them could walk closely together, but with the addition of their unconscious captive the area around them she had to hide was greater. It wasn't long before Layla was made well aware of the fact that even a small increase in the diameter of her shield meant a much larger increase in the power required to maintain it.

Though the air was relatively cool, she had begun to sweat, and it felt as if her heart was fluttering in her chest, but at the rate they were moving it would be hours more before they reached Albamarl.

"Damnitt, Layla! Keep the shield stable!" spat Tyrion. Ripples had begun to appear in the invisibility bubble, and faint waves of light and aythar had started passing through.

"I'm trying," she answered and renewed her effort. "I don't think I can cover an area this size much longer."

"Let that shield drop and I'll whip you blind!" he threatened.

They continued onward, but Layla knew she couldn't keep it up much longer. "Tyrion, I can't keep this up."

"Godsdamnitt! Are you a child Layla? You should know your limits by now. You said you could manage a shield for at least half a day! It's only been a few hours."

"I've never made one this large," she gasped. Her breathing was rapid and shallow. It felt as though she couldn't get enough air into her lungs.

"If there's no one near, we don't need the shield anyway," suggested Brigid.

"We are too close to the trees," countered Tyrion. "They see much farther than you realize."

"They're probably asleep," his daughter replied.

"They don't sleep, and they don't forget," said Tyrion. "It might be a week before they do anything. They think slowly, but don't ever make the mistake of believing they aren't paying attention." He put a hand on Layla's shoulder, her skin was cold and damp. "Stand still. Give me a few minutes more, and I'll let you rest."

She nodded, not trusting herself to speak.

Tyrion closed his eyes and opened his mind, casting his attention downward, letting his heart feel the rhythm of the earth. The coolness of dirt and stone enveloped him, and his boundaries expanded. The soil beneath their feet shifted, and they began to sink into the ground.

It was a disconcerting sensation for both Layla and Brigid, but they kept their silence as they sank, dirt and soil flowing around them like a strange fluid that never seemed to truly touch them or get them wet. When it finally stopped, they were at least twenty feet beneath the surface in a large pocket of air about ten feet across.

"You can release the shield," Tyrion notified Layla. His voice sounded strange with discordant inflections.

She did, but she still worried, "We aren't far down. They will be able to sense us."

"We are nothing but stones," replied Tyrion, his words seemed to have regained some of their normal timbre.

"He's right," said Brigid. "If you could move away and look back, your magesight would only find solid ground. He's done this before."

The warden didn't understand, but she was used to that, so she did what she normally did, moved on to pragmatic issues, "What next then?"

"You rest," answered Tyrion. "Take as long as you need. When you're ready, we'll go back up and finish making our way back."

"It could take a while if you want me strong enough to get us all the way. That larger shield tires me out much faster than I expected. I used up practically everything I had getting us this far. I'm exhausted. Might be hours before I'm ready," explained Layla.

"We can wait," he answered, leaning back and getting comfortable on one side of their subterranean bubble.

"What about air?" asked Layla.

His eyes were closed, "I'll exchange it when it gets stale."

"Don't go to sleep then," she cautioned. "I don't want to wake up dead."

Tyrion smiled, "Don't worry, when you start to suffocate your heart speeds up. You'll wake up well before the dead part."

"How do you know that?"

The question gave him pause. He had felt his heart pounding before, when he was being suffocated in some of his early arena fights, but he hadn't known how it worked exactly, now he did. The concentration of carbon dioxide in the blood stimulated a brain center that then increased heart rate and activated the adrenal response. The more he thought about it, the farther his knowledge went, tracing through the vast information the She'Har had collected over the ages.

Having the information was one thing, but understanding and using it was another. Doing that would take time and thought. He needed to ponder the knowledge he had gained in order to know the correct questions to find the answers he needed. His mind had become a labyrinth, and the only way to tame it would be spending time walking the maze until it had become familiar.

Putting his thoughts aside, he answered, "Don't worry about that, just rest up." They stopped talking after that, but despite closing his eyes, he didn't sleep. He did what he had been doing almost every idle moment since he had returned from somehow becoming a tree, he walked the maze.

His mind was different since taking the loshti, so much so that it frightened him at times. His recall was near perfect now; whatever mechanism preserved the information of the She'Har in the loshti, now worked to do the same with everything he experienced. He could remember breakfast, not just this morning's breakfast, but every breakfast he had had since eating the strange She'Har fruit.

His mental focus was altered as well, sharpened in ways he had never considered. With so much information at his disposal it would have been easy to get lost, but his mind's eye never wavered, he could follow a chain of thoughts or memories from one end to another without losing his course, no matter how many tangents presented themselves along the way.

What really worried him, though, were the changes in his personality. In the beginning it had been subtle, the core of his being was still the same, all the information he had gained was simply that, information. Most of it sat on dark shelves at the back of his brain, dusty and unused, but as he sorted through it, during idle moments, that knowledge filtered into the center of his being.

It was like living in a library. The knowledge of the loshti was like an endless supply of books. Those books sat dormant, quiescent, until he examined them, but once he had, they comingled with his personality. The process was fast, far faster than reading a real book, or learning from a teacher, for he didn't have to memorize anything. That part was done already, he simply had to think about what he was learning and discover how to fit it into the other things he had learned. It wasn't instantaneous, but it was too rapid for him to be comfortable with it, and worse, it seemed to be speeding up.

The more knowledge he integrated, the easier it was to add more since each new piece had more things to connect to. It frightened him, and at times he almost wished he could go back to being a tree. The existence that the She'Har elders experienced was far slower, nothing was rushed. It had felt impossible to be overwhelmed by mere information then.

The farther he progressed, the more distant and unimportant his passions became, and the less important the people around him seemed. They were ephemeral compared to the eons that lay within his mind. The only emotion that seemed truly significant, was his desire to repay the She'Har for what they had done to his world— and perhaps the love he felt for Kate, Lyra, and his children, although that was something that grew more difficult to hold onto with each passing day.

Hatred was easier. It burned hotter and was harder to forget than his softer emotions.

What am I becoming?

In his mind's eye there were two options beckoning; one was that of a cool passionless creature of pure intellect, while the other was an intellect ruled by the only desire hot enough to survive the deluge of information, the fire of revenge. *Wooden man, or passionate avenger, which will it be?* Neither would preserve his gentler emotions, neither would save his sanity, but one was infinitely more human. *And at least one has a goal, a purpose, while the other is nothing short of dying...*

But was it real? Was a choice truly necessary? It felt that way, but perhaps the whirlwind of changes he was experiencing hid the possibility of remaining a moderately decent human being. With time he might adjust, might find peace, might become a good man. Daniel Tennick still existed somewhere, trapped inside a lifetime of violence, and now beset by an avalanche of alien knowledge. Could that man find a way to coexist with the present, to forge a future without the need for retribution?

I can decide later, he realized. Nothing he was doing was irrevocable, so long as they weren't discovered. Let Tyrion continue with the planning and preparing, and if peace was possible, and if he wanted it, then perhaps in the future he could make that choice. For now, he would prepare for the worst. *And if it comes I will watch the world burn.*

Either way, he would never allow himself to become the wooden man.

His heartbeat had increased dramatically, and he noticed he was hyperventilating. It was time to refresh their air supply.

Roughly three hours passed before Layla felt able to continue their journey, but despite her extended rest she wasn't able to get them all the way before she needed to stop again. They were forced to repeat their tactic of hiding beneath the earth.

The time and difficulty of their expedition was not lost on Tyrion, and he resolved to improve things for their next excursion. He felt certain he would need many more test subjects, and doing it the way they had was simply too time consuming. He needed a Mordan mage.

The first batch of slaves coming from Ellentrea might have one, but it was unlikely. Most of the slaves in Ellentrea were Prathions. Fewer than one in ten were trades from other grove with differing gifts. He could send Ian and Layla to collect slaves from Sabortrea, where the majority were Mordan mages, but he worried that that might give away his hand.

A better option might be to make sure they chose carefully to get one of the few Mordan mages present in Ellentrea when they went.

Once they had reached the hidden entrance to the underground retreat, he dismissed Layla. Exhausted, she was only too glad to be sent home. Brigid followed him down, with their unconscious captive floating behind her.

When they at last reached the 'prison', he directed her to position the She'Har woman in the long box he had set up in the center chamber.

"You're going to put her in a stasis box?" asked Brigid, surprised.

Tyrion nodded absently, "Of course, it's the best way to keep them fresh. There's also the added benefit of not having to worry about escape attempts while she's in it. I can't afford to keep one of them outside the box for very long unattended. They may not be as strong as we are, but spellweaving could provide any number of ways for one of them to escape, or worse, signal their grove."

"Fresh," mumbled Brigid, turning the word over in her mind.

He smiled at her, "Exactly. I'll use the cells when I need to age them, but only after I've rendered them safe for storage outside the stasis box."

Brigid was mystified, but she was unwilling to admit it in front of her father. Instead she asked, "What do you mean by safe? If you are going to kill her, please allow me to assist…"

Tyrion shook his head, "No, I'm not going to kill her. I'm going to remove her ability to spellweave. Once that is done she, won't be able to escape, assuming she survives the procedure."

She stared at him open-mouthed, "Is that possible?!"

He smiled, "It might be, though I'm sure it won't be pleasant, and I may need a lot more subjects to test my idea on before I get it right. And of course, even after I come up with a workable method, we will need more subjects for what comes after. I hope you're prepared to work hard Brigid. This laboratory is going to be even larger later, and I will need you to keep it fully stocked."

"Laboratory?" She had never heard that word before. "What will you do after you remove their spellweaving abilities?"

"Now, now, Brigid," he tutted, "let's not get ahead of ourselves. We don't want to spoil the surprise." *Besides,* he added silently, *even you might think me mad if I told you what I plan.*

"Will they suffer?" asked his daughter with an aura of intensity.

Tyrion's eyes met hers, "Suffering is not my intention here, but I believe it will be unavoidable for most of them. Is that sufficient?"

"As long as I can watch," she answered.

Her father nodded, "Most of the time, certainly, except when I have other tasks for you."

CHAPTER 10

They left the Prathion woman in the stasis box, and Tyrion left the She'Har man's head on one of the laboratory's two tables. He didn't have a second box to keep it in yet. There were others in the chambers above, but they were built for full bodies, and he didn't feel like moving one just then. He doubted the head would decompose too much overnight so he dismissed it.

Then he and Brigid began the walk home. When the laboratory was finished there would be a second exit, one that would emerge in his bedroom, but it hadn't been completed yet.

Tyrion was surprised to see a wagon in the yard. Wagon's weren't that unusual, but all of their wagons were kept in a long shed Ryan had designed. This one belonged to someone else, and it had been parked near the front door.

"Looks as though we have guests," he commented.

Brigid's chain rustled as it lifted into the air around her.

"No need for that," he reassured her. "It's probably someone from Colne, not a threat."

They found Tom and Alice Hayes in the main room with Kate and Layla. Their son Tad stood nearby with Sarah. It appeared as though they had entered during a rather intense conversation. Every head turned to track him as Tyrion entered the room, but their attention didn't remain on him. A second later they all focused on Brigid, nearly naked and surrounded by serpentine chains that floated sinuously around her.

Tyrion smirked as he considered what sort of impact a sight like that must be having on the visitors from Colne. "Good evening," he intoned formally.

Alice Hayes stared at Brigid for a moment and then checked her husband Tom's gaze, annoyance flickering across her features as she noted his eyes fixated on the girl's nubile body.

Kate put one hand over her mouth, to cover her own expression of humor, while Layla seemed clueless regarding the reactions of their visitors. Sarah was the first to intervene, "Brigid, why don't you go change into something?"

"Father said I could do as I liked."

"Except when we visit the town," reminded Sarah.

"We are not in Colne…"

Sarah broke in, "But Colne has come to us, be mindful of our visitors."

It was Brigid's turn to be annoyed then, but when her questioning eyes turned to her father, he gestured toward the door, "I won't need guarding, Brigid. You may retire. If you want to rejoin us, be sure to wear clothes." His voice was firm and unyielding.

She lowered her eyes sullenly and turned away. Tom Hayes watched her backside with keen interest as she left, until Alice punched him in the arm.

Tyrion ignored Tom's sudden embarrassment, "Let's move to the dining hall. I don't think we have enough chairs in here for everyone to talk comfortably."

The dining hall had been added over the past year. It opened from the kitchen on the right side of the house and held a large trestle table capable of seating thirty, although they had only enough chairs for ten. One side was still serviced by a long bench, but Kate planned to replace it once they had a full complement of chairs. That might be a long time off, however, since Violet had been the only one interested in making such furniture, and she was now tasked with other things.

Ten chairs were more than sufficient for their guests at the moment, though. Tyrion moved to the head of the table and gestured toward the elegant seats, "Please, make yourselves comfortable."

Sarah and Tad sat on the bench across from the newcomers who were encouraged to sit in the chairs closest to Tyrion. Kate and Layla took the seats beside them.

Sarah took the initiative, "Thaddeus' parents are here to discuss the offer we presented to them a few days ago."

Tom Hayes looked distinctly uncomfortable sitting so close to the man who had once cuckolded him and then later kidnapped his son. It was a testament to the progress they had made over the past year that he had been willing to sit there at all. His wife, Alice, seemed even more awkward, and she avoided looking directly at Tyrion.

"I'm sure Sarah and Tad explained it to you fully, did they not?" asked Tyrion.

Tom coughed, "They did, but to be frank, it was hard to credit their words. Do you truly intend to build a new city?"

"I would not make such a statement in jest," announced Tyrion. "You know me better than that."

Taking a deep breath Tom continued, "But where will you get the resources? You don't have enough people. Such a thing will take time…"

"People?" interrupted Tyrion, "I thought that was clear. Colne and Lincoln will be my people."

"Your people?" said Alice incredulously. "The people of Colne have profited from our trading, but they fear you too much to move for you. Those in Lincoln hardly know you at all."

Tyrion leaned back, bringing his hands together in front of his face and making a steeple with his fingers, "Do you remember when I came to Colne and took the children?"

Tom and Alice were already nervous, but their faces flushed at that memory.

He smiled, "Of course you do. I took your son hostage and forced the two of you to gather the others for me under false pretenses. It was an unpleasant event I am certain, but you have come to understand the necessity of what I did then, even if you didn't appreciate my efforts at the time."

Tom reached for the cup of water that had been placed in front of him. His hand shook, and when he got it to his lips he almost choked on the first sip. Alice kept her hands in her lap, clenching the fabric of her skirt.

"This time is different, however," continued Tyrion. "There is no urgent necessity. Now that we have found peace, I want to use the gifts we have to provide for the prosperity of all mankind. Would you want to be an obstacle to my kindness? This goes beyond our old grievances."

"My lord," interrupted Tad, "There's no need to frighten them. The benefits will be more than enough incentive." Turning his attention to Tom and Alice he added, "Dad, look at this house. Imagine having a home like this one, and not just you and mother, but everyone. We intend to build an entire city of homes like this— houses, shops, everything."

Sarah was nodding, "In the past all of mankind lived in such places. We want to make it happen again. We *can* make it happen again. Even farmers and shepherds will have homes to make the finest citizen in Lincoln today envious.

"The peace brokered with the She'Har makes all of that possible, that and more. The people no longer need to struggle to survive in the hills. The soil is better here, closer to the Groves. The land is smoother and easier to till. The magic we possess can heal most injuries and allow us to produce wealth that was unthinkable before. This will be the start of a new age of prosperity, and *you* will be at the forefront of it."

Tyrion was surprised and pleased with Sarah's eloquence and enthusiasm. He hadn't realized how much she had taken his idea to heart. *She was a good choice. Her passion is infectious.* He had chosen Tad for this task because of his connection to Tom and Alice, but now he suspected that Sarah might be the most important piece in making his plan work.

Alice responded first, "We can understand what you're offering, but people resist change. Many will not wish to leave their homes. This all sounds wonderful, and if anyone can make such a thing happen, it would be you, and your brothers and sisters. I just don't think there's any way to convince two whole towns to pick up and move."

"They don't have to come all at once!" declared Sarah. "They can come a few at a time. They can see what we build for them and tell their friends and neighbors. It doesn't have to be sudden."

Damnitt, thought Tyrion. *That's not what I told her.* But the damage was done. Thinking furiously, he revised his plan. The more he considered it, the more he realized his previous idea had been unreasonable. The people couldn't be moved all at once. It would have to be done in stages. Even working cautiously there would be stragglers and holdouts at the end, but they could capture them afterward, provided there weren't too many to round up.

In other words, they would have to keep up the deception, and the longer they could manage that, the fewer they would have to capture by force afterward. *What a pain in the ass.*

Tom appeared uncertain, but Tyrion spoke up, "Sarah is absolutely correct. We don't want anyone who truly doesn't want to come, but they must see it before they decide against it. There is no possibility of a true choice unless they are allowed to see what they are accepting or rejecting first."

"What is it you want us to do, exactly?" asked Tom hesitantly.

Tyrion could feel the other man's capitulation already. Tom Hayes had given up, although he hadn't really had any other options to begin with. He smiled, "Just share the news. Talk to your neighbors. Gather a group of Colne's more successful citizens, and convince them to come see what we have to offer. Afterward they can return and share what they've seen with everyone else. People will be flocking to move to our new city after that."

"How soon do you want them to visit?" added Alice.

"In a year," announced Tyrion. "We need time to build our perfect city first."

Tom frowned, "That's still a long time away. You could have waited to share this with us until you were nearly ready."

"There would be no point in investing our time and energy in such a thing if you didn't think it was a good idea, Mr. Hayes," said Tyrion politely. "Surely you didn't think I would try to force you into this if you were opposed?"

"Of c—course not!" stammered Tom. "You've shown your true intentions since that time."

Liar, thought Tyrion. *You were ready to piss your pants in fear. But now you're a more perfect tool than I*

could have hoped for, thanks to Sarah's quick thinking.
He caught his daughter's eye for a moment, wondering if she could see his admiration for her clever words.

"Thank you, Mr. Hayes," said Tyrion. "I appreciate that. I assume since it is already late that you'll be staying with us tonight?"

"If that's alright," answered Tom.

Tyrion looked further down the table. "Do we have enough prepared to accommodate our guests, Kate?" he asked, deferring to her judgment.

She raised one coppery hued brow, "We practically feed an army every day now, two more will be no trouble, quite the opposite. It will be a delight to have some civilized company." She gave Alice a welcoming grin.

Tad leaned toward his mother, "Wait until you hear his playing. Tyrion is a genius with the cittern…"

Dinner went well. As usual Kate sat on one side of him, and Lyra sat on the other, while his nearly grown children sat scattered up and down both sides of the table. Alice sat next to Lyra, between the alien She'Har woman and her husband Tom. He seemed to have trouble not staring at her.

Tyrion could hardly blame him. Lyralliantha was beautiful, certainly, but there was no shortage of beauty in the room. It was her exotic coloring that made it difficult for both Tom and Alice to keep their eyes off of her. Vivid blue eyes and hair that shone like spun silver were a novelty not to be underestimated.

It wasn't their first time to Albamarl, but they had never spent any considerable amount of time there, nor had they ever been seated so close to one of the She'Har.

Tyrion couldn't help but wonder what their reaction might have been if there had been some of the more bizarrely colored She'Har in the room, like the Mordan with their blue skin, or the Prathions with their black skin and golden hair.

Once the food was finished Kate rose from her seat with a mysterious smile and left the room before returning a moment later carrying Tyrion's cittern. The sight of the stringed instrument brought audible sounds of approval from most of the people in the room. She handed it to him before retaking her seat and leaning toward Alice, "You'll enjoy this."

Tyrion pulled his seat away from the table, creating some space between himself and his audience. It had been several months since he had played for them. Normally he played every evening, but he had been gone for a while, and after returning from his secretive journey he hadn't resumed his usual habits.

The instrument felt strange in his hands.

Idly he strummed it, and then began to tune it, making sure it was ready. It was an old ritual for him, but it seemed almost foreign to him now.

The people of Ellentrea had never heard music until he had arrived. The She'Har, despite their ancient history had never indulged in it either. He hadn't understood that at the time, but now it made sense. The Elders had no ears, and their children had little in the way of culture or a desire to find ways to entertain one another.

The true society of the She'Har was a silent one. A rich world full of complex minds connected through the root systems of the god-trees. He had felt it first-hand, so he understood its beauty. A lifetime of sun and wind and shared thoughts, but it was missing one thing that was fundamental to human beings, music.

Warming his fingers with a few chords he started into a lively rendition of 'The Merry Widow'. It was a favorite tune of his, and it never failed to arouse smiles, but today it felt off. His timing was good, his execution without mistakes, but it didn't ring true, somehow the melody had lost its humor.

When he finished everyone clapped politely, but their eyes didn't give the impression that they had enjoyed it. Kate was frowning at him, as if confused by something.

Undeterred, he launched into an improvisational piece. During his years in Ellentrea he had been without much to do other than play, aside from brief moments of forced combat. As a result, he had composed long melodies with no names, tunes that frequently changed with his whims and moods. These days it was his favorite way of playing, for it allowed him to express his heart directly, changing the tempo, style, and feel of his music to match his inner world.

'The Merry Widow' simply hadn't suited his inclinations. Letting his fingers find their own desire seemed to work better, and he picked his way through a meticulous series of notes and chords unlike anything he had played before. It was a harmonious structure built of symmetry and balance, with sharp edges and well defined patterns.

His song spoke of order and precision, and it was filled with cold intelligence. It went on for fifteen minutes before he realized that it had no heart. It was a dead thing, sterile and alien, much like the interior of his soul. The looks on the faces of those around the table mirrored that judgement. Some of them looked bored, while others seemed almost imperceptibly disturbed.

Irritated with himself, Tyrion struggled to infuse the notes with life, but the only emotion that answered his call was anger. Rather than give up, he embraced it, letting the fire inside him burn away the calculated geometry of his playing, replacing it with the rage that grew ever greater as he fed it fuel.

That garnered a better response. Brigid and some of his other children looked as though they were enjoying it, even Tom and Alice had warmed to it, their feet tapping in time with the savage tempo.

Kate didn't like it, however. Once he had finished, she rose and apologized for retiring early. "I'll take the private room tonight, Lyra." The two women had a simple system for their sleeping arrangements. When they were both home, they alternated sleeping alone and sleeping with Tyrion, but frequently if one or the other felt the need for privacy they would simply volunteer for the smaller room.

Lyralliantha frowned but nodded, "If that is what you wish…"

Kate was already on her way. As soon as she had closed the door behind her she sat on the bed and cradled her head in her hands. Tyrion's playing had upset her more than she had realized. The first song had been clumsy, disorganized; and while the second had been meticulous, it hadn't been her husband playing. It felt as though a stranger had taken his place, a man with a stone in the place where his heart belonged.

The latter part had been more human, at least, but the violence of the melody disturbed her even more. *I'm losing him,* she thought. *If there was even anything left of him when he returned…* In her mind she saw a vision of Tyrion, skin stretched over a stiff wooden manikin.

A small knock made her look up to see Lyra peeking around the edge of the door, "Are you all right Catherine?"

Kate rubbed her face, surprised to find tears on her cheeks, "Yes, I'm fine. I just wasn't feeling well."

Lyra shut the door behind her and sat on the bed beside her, "You said we should be honest with each other."

Kate stared at the She'Har woman for a moment, startled, "I suppose you're right."

"Will you share it with me?"

"What did you think of the music?" asked Kate.

Lyralliantha's expression became thoughtful, "I liked it."

"Did it sound like Tyrion playing?"

Lyra's face was quizzical, "Who else would it have been?"

Kate sighed, "I mean, did it sound the same as his playing in the past? Did you notice a difference?"

"It was unlike the music he has made in the past, but I enjoyed it. I have never heard anyone else play music, so I can't compare it other than that," said the She'Har woman, picking her words carefully.

"He sounded like a stranger," declared Kate. "It worries me."

"It will be fine," stated Lyra firmly.

"How do you know that?"

"His heart cannot change," she replied, placing her hand on the left side of Kate's chest. "His heart is here, in you. It cannot change without you. If he is losing his way, we will help him hear its beat." Leaning over she kissed her human friend softly on the cheek.

Kate hugged her tightly. *For such a strange person, Lyra is sometimes the kindest one of us all.*

Chapter 11

The head was missing.

Tyrion stared at the flat wooden table he had left it on. A table in the center of a stone chamber hundreds of feet below ground. A chamber with enchanted doors that would only open when given the proper command. To reach those doors someone would first have to go through other doors that were not even properly doors, but special creations of the earth that only responded to someone with the special abilities that thus far only he and Emma had displayed.

It couldn't be gone, but it was.

With a thought he activated the enchanted light-globes that hung from the ceiling, giving his purely mundane eyes a better view of what his magesight wasn't seeing. They still didn't see the head either. It had vanished from the long worktable in the middle of the laboratory and was simply not there.

He was about to step forward, to walk around the table, when he noticed something else. He activated his shield tattoos and leapt backward, moving him fully away from the doorway. Something struck his shield as he moved, sending him into a spin and knocking him sideways into the wall.

Only his instincts had saved him, and now that his adrenaline was pumping Tyrion's rational mind had shifted into the background, making plenty of room for the beast that had kept him alive for so many years in the arena. Light flared as his arm blades slashed outward, cutting through the invisible spellweaving that had nearly caught him head on a moment before.

As he destroyed it his magesight saw a flicker within the room itself, revealing a spindly sapling beside the table. It vanished again almost as fast as thought, but the beast within him didn't need to think. It existed in a place beyond thought, a place where life and death stood side by side, and only pure action and reaction separated the two. Leaping forward he used his aythar to push himself through the air like an arrow leaving a bow.

His arms moved as he flew, slicing through the second attack as his opponent responded to his entry. The leap carried him thirty feet in, over the traps that he assumed were lying in wait on the ground by the doorway and taking him completely over the table. He turned in midair to let his shoulder and back take the hit when he struck the opposite wall, trusting in his shield to protect him from serious injury and hoping that there wasn't a trap waiting there as well.

Tyrion's luck held. The force of his collision with the stone wall sent him bouncing back, off balance and falling, but it was just a plain wall. As he stumbled he lengthened his armblades and swept them across in front of himself in a scissoring motion. He felt the resistance when they met in the air beside the table, and then his foe became visible.

The small tree fell into two parts, cut cleanly through the middle.

Wasting no time, Tyrion followed that attack with several more and quickly cut the spindly roots and branches away from the two trunk sections. He considered cutting the two long truck pieces apart as well, but his rational mind had begun making itself felt once more. The She'Har elder was dead already. He would save the two larger pieces for a trophy of some sort later.

Taking a deep breath, he let his heart rate slow down and surveyed the room. Using his arm blades he carefully destroyed the spellwoven traps that surrounded the entrance to the chamber. They were visible now that the Prathion who had been hiding them was dead.

I was a fool, thought Tyrion, *and I almost paid for it with my life.* He should have realized that the seed within the Prathion She'Har's head would germinate. Even without soil or light it could survive on the flesh of its human host. The head wasn't large enough to allow it to grow very large, but it had been enough.

Left alone in the lightless chamber, it would have shriveled and died eventually, but that might have taken a week or longer. He knew from personal experience that She'Har god-trees could last for long periods without much in the way of sustenance.

The fact that it had been a Prathion also made it exceptionally dangerous. Their ability to become invisible, coupled with their skill with illusions made for a deadly combination when it came to ambushes.

He spent half an hour cleaning the chamber and disposing of the ruined and desiccated remains of the skull that had nourished the She'Har elder. He paused before cleaning the table, though, studying the blood stains that remained. That had been the clue that tipped him off to the illusion hiding the true contents of the room.

No thief would have bothered cleaning the surface of the table after taking the decapitated head, but when he had looked into the room it had appeared completely smooth and unblemished.

Tyrion took the leaves, branches, and roots to the surface and incinerated them. The two long pieces of the trunk, he stored. Once they had dried he could make something out of them, just for spite. The thought made him smile.

Returning below, he opened the cell that held the stasis box that contained his sole prisoner. His encounter had cost him almost two hours, but he had all day.

The She'Har woman had been asleep when he had placed her in the box, and she remained so when he removed her and used his aythar to lift and carry her over to the table. He felt her consciousness begin to stir, but he used a quick spell to force it back down into the darkness. It wouldn't do for her to wake up before he was ready.

He removed the thin garments she wore and used the leather straps he had brought with him to secure her to the table. As an added precaution the leather had been enchanted to make it exceedingly difficult to break or cut, although he had no doubt that if she were left alone and conscious, she could probably create a spellweaving that would free her. But he had no intention of allowing the woman that much free time.

Tyrion already knew of several spellweavings that would have made her imprisonment much easier; ways to draw away her aythar, or to seal her mind up within an internal prison, but he couldn't create them on his own. He would have to design enchantments to do the same thing. Figuring out how to convert the knowledge he had gained of those spellweaves into his system of enchanting would take time.

Fortunately, he wouldn't have to worry about her being able to escape for very long.

Keeping a tight grip on her mind, he released the sleep spell and roused her to consciousness. Her eyes opened slowly and then focused blearily on his features. She tried to raise one hand, possibly to rub her face, but the straps prevented it. Alarmed, she quickly realized she was bound.

Tyrion could see the panic spreading through her heart as her magesight reported her surroundings to her. Waking up bound and trussed on a table in an underground chamber would probably be a disconcerting experience for almost anyone. "Relax," he told her, speaking in soothing tones.

"Where am I?"

He ignored the question as he leaned over her, "I apologize for waking you. It would have been much less stressful for you if I had left you asleep, but I'm afraid I need you awake."

She remained silent for a moment, thinking hard. She thought she recognized the man looking down on her, but she wasn't certain, "Who are you?"

Tyrion put one hand on her forehead, brushing the hair back gently. "You already know the answer to that. A better question is, who are you?"

A surge of aythar answered his question as the woman tried to spellweave, but he was ready for that. He clamped down on her mind before she could begin. He had done the same in the past with human mages. With them it was purely a matter of strength once he was past their defenses, but with a She'Har it was more complicated. The children of the She'Har produced aythar in the same way a human did, but when they were spellweaving the energy was routed to the seed-mind where it was organized and formed into complex structures.

To stop her he had to keep a firm grip at all times. If enough aythar reached her seed-mind, and a spellweave began to emerge he might be unable to counter it without withdrawing and using his tattoos. That would effectively end his experimentation and probably produce a dead opponent rather than a test subject.

She fought hard. Even though the children of the She'Har considered themselves effectively expendable, they still had the same instinct for survival that every human is born with. Fear and desperation made her stronger than normal, and for a moment Tyrion almost lost control. Snarling he drove his fist into the bound woman's midsection. Air exploded from her lungs, and her concentration abruptly disappeared as she fought to draw breath.

"Being unable to breathe can make magic difficult," Tyrion commented. "When you manage to get enough air, answer the question. What is your name?"

Her eyes were watering as she wheezed, but she nodded, and a minute or two later she choked out her response, "Ailayana."

He complimented her, "That's a nice name. I only ask because you're the first. If things go well, you'll be the first of many. If things don't go well—in that case I suppose you'll still be the first of many. I will just have to keep working at it until I get it right."

Ailayana was still panting, trying to catch her breath, but she managed another question, "Working at what?"

"I'm going to disable your ability to spellweave," he answered reasonably. "If possible I will kill your seed-mind while leaving you unharmed. In essence, I'm trying to make you purely human, although there's no helping your strange upbringing."

Her body lurched upward, but the restraints arrested her movement while Tyrion's will fought hers once more. Her resistance ended as he punched her in the belly again, harder this time.

"You're probably asking yourself, 'why?' Why would I want to do something like that? The answer is right here," he caressed the smooth skin just beneath where her belly button would have been if she had been born in the normal fashion. "Your womb is what I need. Since your elders decided to make their male children a genetic dead end, you, and the other She'Har children of your gender, are the only road I have to gaining the special gifts of the various groves. Unfortunately, your seed-mind is a real problem, since it not only makes it very difficult to keep you a prisoner, but it also suppresses your menstrual cycle.

"Please don't struggle further. If I have to keep hitting you, it might damage your internal organs, and that's just what I'm trying to avoid, right?" he added.

She was close to breathing normally again, so he began, focusing his aythar and burning a tiny portion of the seed-mind nestled inside her brain. Ailayana's body arched as all the muscles in her body contracted at once and then she went limp, but her eyes were still open.

"How do you feel?" he asked clinically.

She attempted to spellweave again, and he was forced to subdue her once more. Then he cauterized another spot in her seed-mind. This time she screamed, a hoarse piercing cry that seemed as though it would never end. With his magesight Tyrion could see Ailayana's aura was lit up with an overwhelming indicator of pain.

That was unexpected, since the knowledge he had gained with the loshti indicated that the human brain was incapable of feeling pain when damaged directly. *But I suppose that doesn't necessarily apply to the seed-mind that the She'Har have added.* It appeared as though the alien tissue was sending a variety of scrambled signals outward now that it was injured, causing her intense discomfort.

Perhaps I should try cauterizing the points of connection first next time? he wondered. The seed-mind was supposed to be a largely dormant organ normally.

From the loshti he understood its primary function to be recording sensory stimuli and storing memories of the host's experiences until their death. At that point the human brain would die, and the seed would germinate, becoming an elder She'Har with full recall of the memories of its human incubator. The only real 'active' function of the seed-mind was producing spellweavings, and that only when the mind of its host sent the appropriate signals to it.

Obviously, though, the seed-mind could have more direct effects on its host. *Which I should have guessed,* thought Tyrion, *since I already knew it was affecting the menstrual cycle.*

Ailayana's screaming ended, and she attempted to spellweave again, interrupting his thoughts. It was a clumsy effort, however, and he easily suppressed it without needing to hit her again. He cauterized another spot within the seed-mind, observing carefully to see how it affected her.

Ailayana's body was covered in sweat, and she twitched uncontrollably. She continued screaming for another half an hour as he experimented, until her voice gave out completely, leaving her unable to do anything other than make rasping inarticulate wheezes.

Eventually, she died.

"That's no good," noted Tyrion, his nose wrinkling at the smell of feces and urine. Her body had voided itself even before she had died. He would have to consider improving his lab design. He hadn't given much thought to body disposal. Incinerating a corpse in an enclosed chamber deep underground was a bad idea, if you liked breathing that is. Transporting bodies to the surface repeatedly would also be a chore if he had to keep doing this.

Perhaps I can devise an enchantment to pulverize the bodies. Then I could let the water take the remains away. He might need to enlarge the waterway leading out of the chamber. The only other option he could see would be transporting the bodies above ground and then composting them. *They would probably make excellent fertilizer.*

Either way, he was going to need a lot more test subjects.

CHAPTER 12

"Where are we?" asked Layla.

"In the Gaelyn grove, across the western ocean," replied Brangor. "This is the only spot I know here."

"So you don't know where we are," she stated acerbically. Layla looked to Tyrion, "We could be anywhere. This fool knows nothing."

Brangor growled, but Tyrion held up his hand, "Just because he doesn't know exactly where this place is, doesn't mean that it isn't across the ocean." He addressed Jordan, the other Mordan mage that had accompanied them, "Can you find this place now?"

The blond man nodded, "I can go anywhere once I have been there once."

"Even though you don't know where we are now either?" asked Layla skeptically.

Jordan nodded.

The expression on her face was almost a sneer. Layla didn't trust the Mordan mages. Apparently she had had a bad experience with Brangor in the past, back when she had still been a slave in Ellentrea. "If I discover you have lied to me, I will have your balls."

Brangor spat on the ground defiantly. A second later he began screaming when Layla activated the tattoo on his neck. Seconds went by, but she didn't release him from his pain.

"We aren't shielded for sound, Layla," cautioned Tyrion.

Her face was casual as she answered, "I altered the screen to stop sound when I activated his tattoo."

Brangor was still writhing. "Let him go," ordered Tyrion. "Keep that up for too long and he will be useless."

She dipped her head, "Very well, my lord." With a word she canceled the pain, and the blond Mordan went mostly silent, gasping and sweating as he tried to recover his composure.

"You learned your lesson, didn't you?" asked Tyrion amicably.

Eyeing Layla fearfully the man panted, "Yes, my lord."

Ryan spoke up then, "How will we find a good location, Father? I can sense nothing through Layla's shield. We're effectively blind, and the region is completely unknown to us." While they could see each other with their magesight within the shield, it was pitch black to normal vision, and the outside world was completely blocked from their senses, arcane and otherwise.

"I will handle that," answered Tyrion. "Emma can do the same if necessary. Let me have a few minutes and I'll know more." Sitting down he began to listen.

"Wait," said Emma. "Someone needs to keep a watch on you. Let me help."

"I'll do it," offered Brigid, placing her hands on Tyrion's shoulders.

Tyrion felt the tentative touch of her mind on his. She had never done such a thing with him before, but he felt more comfortable having her watch him than Emma. Of all his children, Brigid was the wildest, the most aggressive, and certainly the most violent. Whatever she might see lurking in the darkness of his heart, she was the least likely to be repulsed by it.

Letting go of his concerns, he started listening once more, forgetting the six people around him and focusing on the slow beat of the earth. His awareness expanded, and his body grew larger. Well, his human body didn't change; he just wasn't defined by its boundaries any longer. He was the soil, the stone, and he stretched outward into the distance.

The land became his body, and he felt the roots of the trees growing into him for miles in every direction. Over one portion of him ran a great line of water, meandering along a curving course. In another place he rose to greater heights where the stone had thrust itself skyward forming a massive stone outcrop. Scattered across him were places where small things moved, their feet sending tiny vibrations through his skin.

To the east he dipped low, and a great body of water lapped over him, the beginning of the ocean. The trees were few there, but a large number of animals gathered there, some running into the water and others lying quietly on the soft sandy shores.

He felt an insistent tug on his mind. *That's enough, Father. Come back.* He resisted the pull for a moment, but it felt familiar. Collapsing, he began to shrink into himself, letting the other awareness guide him.

When he opened his eyes again it was to darkness, but his magesight showed him six figures gathered around the small body that seemed to contain him. The one that had been calling him was closest, a female, with her arms around his shoulders, clutching him tightly.

"Is he back?" asked a masculine voice.

"Yes," answered a feminine voice. *That's Emma,* supplied his brain as it began to function more normally.

Two men were watching him with expressions of disgust on their faces. *Brangor and Jordan,* he realized. *They are uncomfortable seeing people touch one another.* Brigid still had her arms around him. "That's enough," he told Brigid, shrugging free of her and retaking his feet.

"Did you find a suitable place?" asked Ryan.

"Yes. The ocean is to the east of us. There's a group of She'Har there, sunbathing and enjoying the waves. The grove stops a mile short of the shoreline, so we won't have too much trouble remaining unobserved," he told them.

"How many?" asked Brigid.

"Thirty or forty."

"We only have enough boxes for twenty-five," observed Ryan.

Tyrion shook his head. "Boxes for twenty-three," he reminded. "Two have already been allocated."

"Sorry," said Ryan. "I forgot. So what will we do if we get more than twenty-three?"

"Those are mine," announced Brigid, grinning evilly.

"Try to kill the males rather than the females," ordered Tyrion. "If necessary I can use them, but I'd prefer the women. Once I find my answer, they will be the foundation of the next stage."

They spent the rest of the day trekking across the landscape, heading eastward. They rested every couple of hours, when Layla could no longer keep her invisibility shield up. It made the journey slow, but she was buoyed by the fact that once they arrived she wouldn't have to do the same for their return trip.

When they finally reached the ocean, Layla risked making a small opening in the shield to survey the surrounding area more directly, but she was unable to spot the She'Har children that Tyrion had mentioned before. "I don't sense anyone."

Emma was beside her, "Almost a mile north of us. They're almost too far for me to detect."

Layla nodded. She already knew that Emma and Tyrion had a far greater range for their magesight. "We need to get closer then."

They marched north, following the shoreline. Except for Layla, who strained to keep her invisibility shield up, the rest of them enjoyed the walk. They had removed their boots, and the wet sand was pleasant sensation for tired feet.

They moved carefully when they got closer to the group of She'Har lounging on the beach. When they were within a hundred yards, Tyrion shifted the sand beneath them and they sank into the ground. From there they slowly made their way through the earth until they were directly underneath their prey. Twenty feet above them the She'Har rested, unaware of the threat below them.

"You can release your shield now," Ryan told Layla. "Emma has us concealed."

"You're certain it will work?" asked Layla. "They are very close."

"Trust her," answered Ryan.

Layla's shield vanished and suddenly their magesight began reporting the world around them. They were surrounded by waterlogged sand, for while they were under the beach, they were below the sea level. Above the She'Har sat and lounged, enjoying the sunset to the west and the appearance of the stars on the eastern horizon.

"Forty-one," counted Brigid.

"Add five more to that," said Tyrion. "There are a few stragglers coming in from the water."

Ryan frowned, "There's no one there. Wait—oh they've transformed into some sort of big fish."

"Dolphins," supplied Tyrion as the unfamiliar word came to his lips. "That's what the ancient humans called them. They aren't fish, they're a type of seagoing mammal."

"Well, they look like fish," said Layla.

Tyrion tapped Emma on the shoulder, "Go ahead and start working on the weather. You need to work slowly. I want this to look natural."

"There's nothing natural about a wind that can tear down trees and rip up stone," replied his daughter.

"It happens quite often in some parts of the world," her father informed her. "Just because you've never seen one, doesn't make it unnatural. You remember the picture I showed you?"

"Yes," said Emma, sitting down and getting comfortable. Ryan sat beside her, holding her hand.

"Can she still hide us and do this?" asked Layla worriedly.

Tyrion nodded, "The earth will continue to do as she has bidden it. She won't have to waste her attention on that."

"What if the storm scares them away?" asked Brigid.

"They are confident in their power. They will probably just create a spellweaving to shield them and enjoy the show," said Tyrion. "If they do start to move, Ryan will notify Emma and we will start sooner."

"You're sure no one will see us?" asked Layla.

Tyrion smiled, "Their parents are too far from here to observe us. We simply have to make sure none escape."

"Parents?"

"The god-trees," he responded. Turning to Jordan, he commanded, "Go. Tell the others we are ready. Bring them here."

Ste'lar watched as clouds rolled in from the ocean, bringing darkness even sooner than the setting sun might have. The wind was picking up, and there was every indication that a truly spectacular storm was brewing.

Eal'estea strode toward him from the waves, her long red hair whipping wildly in the fierce breeze. Water rolled down her smooth brown skin. Having just transformed, she was naked, but the air didn't bother her. Modesty was unknown among the children of the She'Har. "Perhaps we should return," she suggested, looking up at the sky.

Ste'lar smiled, "We would miss the show. Imagine what the storm will look like from here, rolling over the horizon and across the sky. Between the lightning and the waves I cannot believe we will see something so majestic any time soon."

Apia laughed, her red eyes shining, "He's right. Let us build a shelter and watch the show."

The others agreed, and within a minute two of them had created a spellwoven shelter, a transparent dome to stop lightning and rain, with openings along the sides to allow the wind and smells to enter. The entire group gathered beneath it to lie on their backs, facing the sky. Most of them did, anyway. Four paired off into couples to pursue more sensual pleasures while the storm passed over.

Of the five groves, the children of the Gaelyn Grove were the most given to indulging in sexual activity. Possibly because of their gift for transformation. Their time in the bodies of animals made them more aware of the primal instincts.

The wind built steadily, until the force of it began lifting small pieces of driftwood from the beach and sending them tumbling across the sand. "Is this a hurricane?" asked Eal'estea.

"Impossible," replied Ste'lar. "The Elders would have warned us if such a thing were approaching."

"Perhaps we should return after all," she suggested.

"Wait, look at that!" said one of the others, surprise and awe in his voice. Over the water, beyond the range of their magesight, loomed a dark shape rising from the water. It towered into the sky, a black column that went too far to see. A roiling, twisting, mountain of water approached, a waterspout.

"Should we run? We can't fly in this," said Apia.

Ste'lar shook his head negatively, "We'd never make it. Our best hope is to wait here. It will probably miss us. We can strengthen the spellweave to protect us."

They waited and watched as the massive waterspout moved past them to the south. It changed as it came inland, dumping its water and beginning to roar. It grew ever more powerful and without knowing exactly how close it was they couldn't gauge its true dimensions, but it was huge.

It moved directly for the closest of the elders.

"Will it damage them?" wondered Apia.

No one answered. They were all watching, awestruck at the size of the tornado. The elders could defend themselves from most weather events, but something that powerful—there could be no doubt that any of the massive trees in its path would be torn down.

And then the ground fell away beneath them.

Startled, most of them fell. Only Ste'lar reacted quickly enough to transform, taking the form of a gull and beating his wings to keep from falling. His body exploded as a flash of serpentine metal flicked upward from the hole to slice through his feathered torso.

Eal'estea screamed as she saw him die. There were figures all around her, moving through the darkness. The sudden change in lighting made it difficult to see properly, and her magesight was confused by the chaos around her. Many of her companions were already lying limply, unconscious. Others were creating defensive spellweaves to protect themselves.

Apia rose to her feet beside her and began a spellweave of her own. Eal'estea started to follow her example when she saw her friend's head explode. A sudden burst of raw aythar had struck before Apia's defense had materialized.

Eal'estea managed to finish her own when a human male rushed her, aythar blazing around his body and forearms. Trusting to her defense she began working on her offense when his armblade ripped through her shield and impaled her right shoulder. Shock and pain ran through her, draining her concentration as she fell back.

"Damnitt, Sarah! I told you to try and take the females alive!" shouted the man that had just impaled her. He followed her to the ground, and before she could recover he cut away her remaining defenses. His bare hand was coming down over her face.

She felt a surge of power smothering her will as he pushed her onto the ground, but her magesight still showed her the fight raging around her. She could see there were only ten humans, possibly a few more, but half of the She'Har were dead already and most of the others were unconscious.

Four of her kin had formed a small defensive square, but before they could unify their efforts a small woman charged toward them, black hair flying behind her. A metal snake floated around her, and her arms were covered with the same lethal magic that had probably killed Eal'estea. The metal whipped outward, cutting through magic and flesh with equal ease and Eal'estea's companions were dead before the woman even reached them with her armblades.

Not that the furious woman seemed to care. She cut into them even as they fell, slicing them into ever smaller pieces. Seconds later she stopped. The woman was panting, her blood covered chest heaving for air even as she smiled. "That's the last of them, Father!"

Eal'estea's consciousness faded, but she could still hear the man holding her down speaking in Barathion, "How many did we get? I can probably save this one if we don't have twenty-three but I don't want to waste the effort if we already have our quota."

"We did well," said Ryan, "eighteen females and five males."

"I would have preferred all females," said Tyrion sourly.

"It was difficult to be precise," commented Layla. "Too much caution and we might have let one escape or worse, injure one of us; too little and we might have killed them all."

Tyrion nodded, "It probably doesn't matter. I can start testing with the males and hopefully by the time I finish with them I will be able to complete the process without killing the females."

They were back in Albamarl, or more accurately, near Albamarl, in the upper chamber he had hidden underground there. The two Mordan mages had worked for several minutes to transport them all back. It had taken quite a few trips since neither of them could easily bring more than four or five people with them with each teleportation.

"Line them up on the floor over there," instructed Tyrion, "and make sure to refresh the sleep spells. I don't want any of them to wake until I have them safely tucked away. Once you've done that you can all leave. Go home, and don't let anyone see you until you have the blood cleaned off of yourselves."

All of Tyrion's children had participated in the raid, as well as Layla and the two Mordan mages. One by one they began to leave, talking quietly among themselves. Most of them seemed energized by their successful foray, but a few were subdued. Abby in particular, was notably quiet.

"Emma, Ryan, Brigid, and you two," he ordered, pointing at Brangor and Jordan, "stay. I still have need of you."

When the others had left he looked at the two Mordan mages and then pointed at the only two stasis boxes in the chamber, "These are for you."

"What?!" asked Jordan, startled.

"Today's raid must remain a secret. I trust the others, but you two are outsiders. To make certain of your silence, I only have two options," explained Tyrion. "This option allows you to keep living. Eventually, when everything is over, you will be able to return to a normal life. I also intend to see that you are well rewarded for your service.

"I'm sure I don't need to tell you what the other option is," he finished.

The two men were still, not the normal sort of stillness, but the absolute motionless of men contemplating sudden action. It was something Tyrion was well acquainted with.

Brangor made his decision first, and his body twitched slightly before he fell back screaming. Blood spurted from the stump of his left arm. It had been neatly removed just below the shoulder. Tyrion used his will to clamp down on the artery immediately, stanching the flow of blood. The vessels in that part of the arm were large enough that unconsciousness and death could follow within seconds of such a cut.

His eyes flickered upward to glance at Jordan. The other mage hadn't moved, his muscles were slack, relaxed in a way that indicated he had no intention of following his comrade's mistake. Brigid stood close behind him, a look of disappointment on her face.

Kneeling over his victim, Tyrion dismissed his armblade and began talking as he worked to seal the wound, "If you had managed to teleport I would have been forced to activate your tattoo. That would have killed you, no matter how far you went, but then I would have had to worry about someone finding your body and asking difficult questions.

"You should have thought about your decision more carefully. If you had, you might have realized that

I would prefer to keep you alive so that I don't have to keep recruiting new Mordan mages. You might also have considered that I don't really need you to keep your arms and legs to do this job."

Brangor's eyes rolled in his head, but the man was still conscious. Tyrion had sealed the wound quickly enough to prevent the loss of any serious amount of blood. His eyes focused on Tyrion's face, fear showing in them.

Tyrion stood and then used his aythar to lift the injured man and carry him to one of the stasis boxes. He lowered him into the box. "The box isn't anything to fear, you know. I will close the lid, and from your perspective I will be opening it again a second later. No time will pass for you. When you see my face again I will need you for the next raid, and you'll have to do it while feeling faint from an injury that only happened a minute before, for you. Once you understand that, you will realize how stupid your action was."

Jordan had already walked over to his own box and was climbing inside without a word.

Tyrion smiled at him, "I thought you were the smart one when I first met the two of you. It's good to see I was right."

Once the two of them had been sealed inside, Tyrion, Ryan, and Emma began moving the sleeping She'Har to the lower, more secret chamber. Brigid started to assist, but Tyrion stopped her, "Clean up the blood. I don't want to start attracting flies in here. You can help after that, if we haven't finished yet."

She pouted for a second, but then complied. It had been a good day. Who was she to complain?

CHAPTER 13

The sun had not yet made its way over the horizon when Abby heard a soft knock at her door. She had a privacy ward around her room, so she couldn't see who it was with her magesight, but it was unusual for someone to come to her room so early.

Her eyes were swollen, and her face was bound to be unseemly. She had been crying for half the night. Abby disabled the audible portion of the privacy screen and asked, "Who is it?"

"It's me, Sarah," announced a voice from the other side. "May I come in?"

She rubbed her face quickly with a small hand towel, though she knew it wouldn't do much good. "I'm not really presentable yet," she told her half-sister through the door.

"I couldn't sleep last night," said Sarah. Her voice sounded shaky. "Please, can we talk?"

Abby opened the door. Sarah Wilson stood in front of her, and she looked much like Abby imagined herself to look just then. Dark circles were beneath Sarah's eyes, and her hair was disheveled. The other girl entered, and Abby closed the door while simultaneously restoring the auditory portion of her privacy screen. "You look like I feel," she said bluntly.

Sarah's eyes filled with tears without warning.

"I'm sorry!" said Abby in a rush. "I didn't mean it like that. I was referring to myself, I must look terrible…" She stopped, that didn't sound any better.

"That's not it," said Sarah in a half-sob. "I can't stop thinking about it, about yesterday. I keep seeing them."

Abby embraced her then, while Sarah let her anguish have its way for a minute or two. She hadn't expected so much remorse from Sarah. The other girl always seemed to have her emotions under firm control, and she had certainly shown no sign of hesitation during their brief battle the day before.

She knew everyone thought of her as the most 'sensitive' of Tyrion's children. Abby took no offense at the label. In truth she considered herself the most stable, or perhaps the most balanced. She didn't hide from her emotions, and consequently she thought she was probably the most adept at dealing with them. Even so, yesterday had shaken her far more than she had expected.

Abby had been committed to their cause, despite the violence of their mission. She knew it was a necessary evil. No, that wasn't true. She told herself it was necessary, but without knowing their father's full plan, she couldn't truly judge that. Abby had resigned herself to closing her eyes and putting her faith in Tyrion's design.

No matter what, the She'Har had a lot to answer for. *But was that slaughter truly justified?*

Sarah's tears made her more uncertain.

"Thank you," whispered the other girl.

Abby hugged her tighter, "For what?"

"I couldn't bear it if I were the only one."

"The only one?"

Sarah sniffed, "That was upset. I know we're all related, but sometimes I feel so alone. Everyone seems so sure, so certain, as if they have no doubts. It's like the blood doesn't bother them at all."

Abby's stomach clenched as the word 'blood' brought an unpleasant memory from the day before into her mind, but she took a deep breath and mastered herself. "No, you are not the only one. In fact, before now, I thought maybe I was."

"You think the others might feel this way too then?" suggested Sarah hopefully. Disentangling herself from Abby's arms, she took a seat on the edge of the bed.

Abby nodded, "I'd be surprised if they didn't." Pouring a cup of water from a pitcher, she handed it to her sister. "Probably everyone is dealing with the same thing to one degree or another."

"They were practically defenseless," mumbled Sarah, her voice monotone. Most of the emotion had drained out of her. "We just cut them to pieces, except for the ones we took, and who knows what Father is doing to them now?"

Abby clenched her teeth, "Most likely some of the same things they did to him when he was first taken."

"Does that make it right?" asked Sarah.

"None of it is right," replied Abby. "We live in a world full of nothing but wrongs, wrongs and evil. My only consolation is that he thinks he can make some sort of future for those who come after us."

"What if he can't? What if he's lying, or mistaken, or just homicidal? You've seen his eyes. You know he's gone mad."

Abby sighed, "He isn't the only one. I still struggle with rage and self-loathing when I think about everything that has happened. What they did to Haley, what they did to us, what they made *us* do. Tyrion's madness didn't happen on its own. He may not even be the worst of us in that regard."

"Brigid."

Abby nodded.

"She was like a beast," said Sarah. "Did you see her, naked and covered in blood? But she reveled in it, she would have killed them all if he had let her. I've never seen anything so disturbing in my life. Seeing her was worse than looking at the dead. She looked like a greedy child eating candy, or as if she was having…" She couldn't finish her sentence.

"I wonder if I might have turned out like that," admitted Abby, "if I had been forced to do what she did. Haley was her best friend."

"It was a mercy then."

"What was?"

"Killing Haley," answered Sarah. "She had already had to do the same to Gabe. Think what it would have been like for her if she had killed Brigid instead? Or the rest of us? If it broke Brigid's mind, what would all that have done to her?"

Abby suppressed a shudder at the thought, "Be glad that Brigid is on our side at least."

"She's on Father's side and no one else's," said Sarah firmly. "If she had the slightest doubt about one of us, we wouldn't live another breath."

Abby gave a sad smile, "Good thing we are all on his side then, right?"

"Are you, Abby? You're the only one of us with a real heart anymore. The only one who understands kindness. Can you go on with this?"

Her chest tightened. "Sarah, you think too highly of me. I'm not as kind or pure as you think me. I just don't hide my sadness, or my compassion as well as some of the others do. The only thing I'm good at, is hiding my anger. I don't think what we're doing is right, but when I think of Haley, or Gabriel, or Jack, I'm so filled with hatred that I feel like I'm dying.

"Remembering yesterday isn't any better, though. Thinking of it makes me want to vomit. I'm not suited for violence, but I won't give up what he's trying to do.

What's the difference between murdering a few people in person, or abstaining from it, when he's planning to try and wipe out all of them? And I'm helping him with that."

"How?" gasped Sarah. "He never said that. You think he has a real plan to do that? It's impossible."

"I'm guessing," said Abby. "But I've watched him. He's mad, but he's no fool, and he doesn't think small. If I believed this was just a small plan for petty revenge, I would have nothing to do with it. He wants to kill them all, and if he can do that, then maybe it's worth it. What is right and wrong compared to that? Who will be left to argue the point?

Abby laughed, "See? I'm just as evil as he is. We all are. Every single one of us is helping, and it doesn't matter whether we feel remorse, or guilt, or sick at the sight of blood. Feeling bad doesn't make us better.

"But I do love you," added Abby. "I just hope we can finish what we start." *And that he really does have a plan to create a better world for humanity after this is done.*

But in her heart, Abby wasn't sure. *He may kill them and all of us as well. If he had to sacrifice every single human being to make certain the She'Har died, he might well do it, and never blink at the price.*

Eldin sat in the dirt in front of his home. To be fair, there was some grass too, but the regular traffic in the yard had reduced it to just a few straggling bits of green here and there. But Eldin liked the dirt better anyway.

He was covered in it, but he wasn't really aware of the fact. At the moment he was crawling along in pursuit of something moving in one of the isolated clumps of grass. It was definitely a bug of some sort.

At least he hoped so.

It never occurred to him to worry about what sort of bug it might be. The world was perfectly safe, and while his mother wasn't near, he knew his father was watching, a massive looming presence in the background. Nothing could hurt him if Dadda was around.

That didn't stop him from looking back over his shoulder, to see if the big man was still there. His eyes spotted the silent man, still in the same place he had been a minute before, sitting on a large log under the eaves of the house. He didn't seem to be paying close attention.

Eldin crawled farther away, testing the boundary. His father wasn't usually the one watching him, and the big man seemed to have different ideas about how far he could go before he needed to be captured and brought back. His mother and the others were far more restrictive, more than ten feet, and they would haul him back.

Dadda was different. He often let him manage twice that distance, and right now he wasn't watching. Eldin moved forward, he could probably make it to the clump where the bug was hiding.

The grass twitched slightly, moved by the creature hiding within. Eldin reached out and pushed it to one side with a clumsy hand. He was rewarded with a good look at his target.

The bug seemed to glow in the afternoon sun, reflecting the light. Bright yellow separated by bands of deepest black adorned the strange insect. Wings were neatly folded along its back, but it hadn't flown away— yet. Eldin could catch it.

His other hand came down hard, pinning it to the earth, and he could feel it squirming beneath his palm, trying to escape. Closing his fingers, he trapped it within his fist and turned his hand over. Slowly he opened his fingers to get a look at his prize.

A sharp pain blossomed as the wasp drove its sharp stinger into his skin. Eldin's mouth opened, but a full second passed as he tried to comprehend the magnitude of his injury. The pain was unbearable and as soon as his lungs had filled Eldin began to shriek, the ear piercing cry of one who had discovered the ultimate agony.

Tyrion's eyes snapped into focus as the scream activated the most primal and instinctive parts of his nervous system. Adrenaline flooded his bloodstream, and he forgot whatever he had been thinking of. Rushing forward, he snatched Eldin up from the ground and spotted the wasp in the same timeless moment. He crushed it underfoot and examined the boy's tiny hand. It was red and swollen already.

The pain was probably intense, at least by Eldin's standards, but Tyrion knew rationally that it would fade soon. The toddler's cry did not diminish, however. It gained in volume and pitch as the small child strove to extinguish the horror of his pain with the loudness of his voice.

Tyrion scraped at the wound with a fingernail, making certain that the stinger hadn't been left behind, but that only served to send Eldin's scream to a new octave. He held his son close, probably in much the same way his father had once held him, long ago, but his heart continued to pound.

He felt a tremor in his hand, and his stomach flipped. Tyrion's heart felt as though it might pound free of his chest.

"Give him to me," said Layla firmly, emerging from the house. Despite her new maternal instincts she had a distinctly harsher attitude toward parenting than anyone else in Albamarl. Probably because of her own childhood experiences. "Coddling him will only make him weak. The lessons of pain are for everyone to learn."

Tyrion handed him over, but his symptoms did not subside. With every shriek from the young boy he heard a different voice, Ailayana's. Her torment echoed through his mind, her voice sounding the same cry of agony. She had died in terrible pain, and now he felt it in his bones.

It was the same horror he had felt once at Thillmarius' hand, when he had been punished for rebelling. Eldin yelled and Ailayana screamed simultaneously in his heart, but it was the pain of his own tortures that burned through his nerves. Tyrion was shaking uncontrollably now. Bending over, he began to vomit before eventually dropping to his knees beside the dead wasp.

He emptied his stomach, but his belly continued to heave until it ached from the strain on his abdominal muscles. When it finally relaxed, he fell to one side, staring sideways at the crushed insect beside him. Alien eyes, dead and devoid of emotion stared back at him, and the world grew dark.

It was death returning his gaze, and it was coming for him.

Sweating, he closed his eyes, but he could still feel it there, watching him. His evil had called it, his actions, his guilt had summoned it, and it would kill them all. Everyone would pay the price for what he had done.

Eldin's screams were all he could hear as the cold world faded away.

CHAPTER 14

He awoke in darkness, but he knew immediately it was his own bed, though he didn't remember lying down.

Tyrion was naked, which wasn't unusual when he slept, but his magesight had already noted that his leathers weren't hanging from their usual peg on the wall. Kate lay beside him, asleep.

Was I dreaming?

As the sleep fog faded he was certain that wasn't the case. They must have brought him to his room after he collapsed. He tried not to think of the moments before that, his hand started shaking once more as he recalled Eldin's cry.

Why is this affecting me like this? He couldn't remember having a reaction like this before. It was similar to how he felt whenever he thought about his 'punishments' under Thillmarius' instruction, which was something he made a point to never think about. Normally those memories didn't bother him, except in dreams, or during the rare occasions he was forced to meet with the Prathion lore-warden.

His mind had betrayed him. He was breaking down. *Another consequence of the loshti?* he wondered, *or was it really because of what I did to that She'Har woman?* That thought brought a new wave of nausea to him.

Goddamn it! I can't afford to be weak!

He was strong. He knew that. No one survived years in the arena without becoming accustomed to blood and violence. He had done things no sane man would consider, and done them with aplomb. Whatever weakness existed in him should have died a slow death years ago.

Even I know that I am mad.

But perhaps madness did not preclude suffering. *More likely it insures it,* he thought.

"Daniel?" whispered Kate. "Are you awake?"

"I think so," he answered wryly. "What did you do with my leathers?"

"You rolled into the vomit after you passed out," she explained. "I cleaned them. They're hanging outside."

"Thank you."

"What happened?"

He realized he was holding his breath, and he let it out slowly, "I'm not sure. What did you tell the others?"

Kate stroked the side of his head gently with her hand, pulling it close and setting her cheek beside his, "That you were sick. I didn't know what else to say."

Sliding his arm around her shoulder, he pulled her close, but the warmth of her didn't seem to penetrate the cold emptiness of his solitude. His body was still, but within he felt his soul shivering, as though a chill lived inside his heart. "That's close enough to the truth," he said after a moment.

"You were crying earlier," she added.

He could feel her eyes on him although he knew she couldn't really see him in the dark. "I don't remember that. Did they see me?"

"It was after I had you put in bed," she reassured him. "Do you know why you were crying?"

"I don't remember anything after I passed out, but when you consider the life I've lived I'm sure there are plenty of things I could have been dreaming about," he said, dissembling.

"You kept mumbling things. You said a name several times…," added Kate, "…a woman's name."

He tried to laugh, but it wasn't very convincing, "Which one?" His brow felt cold and clammy. Had he been dreaming of Ailayana?

"Amarah."

Tyrion felt two things at once when she said that, a faint rush of relief and the dull throb of an old hurt. "I told you about her."

"Not much," said Kate. "You said she was a slave when you lived in Ellentrea, that you cared for her, and that she died. You never told me much more than that."

"That was the gist of it," he said bluntly. "Are you jealous?"

Kate chuffed, "You know me better than that, but I think you should tell me the story."

"Why?"

"You collapsed today. You need to talk to someone. Is there anyone else you can talk to?" There was an edge to her last question.

Kate might not be jealous of his past dalliances, but she would be hurt if he dodged her question by claiming he would bare his pain to someone else. And in truth, there wasn't. Lyra would listen, but she wouldn't understand, not fully. He sighed, "You have me there."

"Did she die in the arena?" asked Kate. "You weren't forced to…"

"No," he interrupted. "It wasn't like what happened to Brigid. She was one of the nameless, a servant. She never had to fight in the arena."

"A nameless with a name?"

"I gave it to her," he replied. His voice was growing thick. He hadn't expected to react to the memory so quickly. "I tormented her at first, pretending to name her. She brought my food every day, but she wouldn't talk to me. I was desperate for conversation back then. I was being kept in complete isolation. Sometimes she was the only other human being I would see for a week or more, and that for only a few minutes each day."

"And then?"

"Eventually we became lovers."

He wanted to stop there, but Kate's soft voice prodded him in the dark, "Just lovers, or were you in love?"

"I was in love, although at first I just considered it a product of my desperation and loneliness. She was the only light I had during that dark time, but I didn't believe she was capable of feeling love herself."

"You've always said love is almost impossible for the people in the slave camps," agreed Kate. "You've remarked the same about Layla numerous times, but I'm sure she feels it. She dotes on her son in her own rough way, and I've seen the light in her eyes when she looks at you. Do you think Amarah loved you too?"

"She never said so," he answered, keeping his words short as the tears ran down his cheeks in the darkness. "One of the She'Har trainers killed her, one of the Gaelyn Grove. She tried to cover me, to protect me. She thanked me for her name before she died."

Kate's hand was on his cheek, "She did love you, and you avenged her death."

He shook his head, "No. No, I didn't. I killed Syllerond, but I didn't avenge her. She died protecting me, not the other way around. Syllerond was a villain that day, but he wasn't the problem. It was everything the She'Har did to humanity, long before Syllerond showed up. She won't be avenged until I've corrected that."

"You're just one man, Daniel."

"No, I'm not. I have power that would have been beyond my belief when we were young. I have knowledge that will lead to even more, and I have children who will carry the standard forward even if I fall. I will reshape this rotten world, or die trying," he said defiantly.

"Or *we* will die trying," Kate corrected. "Don't forget that. The consequences of your actions will fall on all of us."

"I haven't forgotten."

"Is peace so impossible?" she asked. "Isn't it possible to find a way beyond the hatred and wrongs of the past? I think we could coexist with them. Think about Lyra."

"It will be on our terms this time," growled Tyrion. "Not because they've *granted* us the right to exist, but because they have no choice but to work with us, if they wish to survive."

Kate sighed, "That doesn't sound very diplomatic. What about the Illeniels? They have done nothing but help you. You said yourself that the loshti couldn't have been stolen. They never kept slaves either. Will you lump them into the same boat with the other groves?"

"They carry more blame than the other four groves put together," he said bitterly. "They *knew* what they were doing. They were not ignorant. *That* is why they didn't keep slaves. They knew it was wrong. They had already seen the outcome, yet they did nothing to educate the other groves. Their silence was their sin.

"And it goes beyond silence too. *They* brought the She'Har to this world. They couldn't see the outcome until they arrived, but once they were here, they pushed forward with the others in destroying our civilization. They did it knowing what would happen. None of the other groves understood, but they did, and they did it anyway. Their refusal to keep slaves was an empty gesture to assuage their guilty conscience.

"The only reason they have helped me, is because they want me to do something. They will do anything to survive, and for some reason I am key to that. Otherwise they would have wiped us out long ago. Never forget that. All of this was the result of cold calculation. Don't make the mistake of ascribing their actions to some ideal of noble responsibility."

Kate nodded in the dark, "Then what hope do you have of defeating such knowledge. If they already know everything, they will have accounted for anything you may do. Wouldn't it be wiser to work with them? At least you could benefit our people, since they need you so much."

"They don't know everything," said Tyrion. "You may be right. I may not be able to subvert their plan, but I can make sure it costs them more than they hoped. If the She'Har survive, I will do everything possible to make sure it is at the *feet* of humanity, and if that is not acceptable to them I will see them all damned!" He was getting worked up, and his last words were nearly a shout.

"And that is why you collapsed when you saw your son crying?" asked Kate softly. "Is that why you dreamt of a woman who died trying to help you? I know you better than that. A fight wouldn't unsettle you like this. What are you doing that could have disturbed you that much?"

"Sacrifices have to be made," he growled.

"How many of us are you willing to sacrifice?" she asked pointedly.

"As many as necessary," he admitted, "but I intend to make sure most of the sacrifices are theirs."

Suelynna and Taylok were forced to breathe deeply to get enough air into their lungs. The altitude was such that their hike was much more difficult than it might otherwise have been, but that was why they had done it, for the challenge.

Plus, there was a lake near the upper portion of the mountain that was a delight to see. They and several others went there occasionally to enjoy the view. Of course, they could have simply teleported, since they were members of the Mordan Grove, but that would have defeated the point of the trip.

The journey was half the reward, despite the strenuous demands of walking up the mountain.

"Look at these flowers, Suelynna!" said Taylok, having spotted some purple blossoms he hadn't noticed before, but he got no response.

Suelynna was gone, vanished, and he could find her with neither his eyes nor his magesight. Taylok straightened up and looked around, puzzled. Vanishing was not unusual for his people, but he hadn't felt any aythar moving, nor could he imagine why she had teleported without saying something to him first.

He expanded his senses, searching for predators. The only reason he could imagine that she might have teleported suddenly was if they had been at risk of sudden attack.

Not that a big cat or a bear would have been a real threat to them, but Suelynna preferred not to harm wildlife. She would avoid a confrontation rather than hurt a baratt. Still, they could have merely protected themselves. Nothing here was so dangerous that she would have to teleport.

He searched farther with his mind, hoping to spot her farther down the trail, or above, but he found nothing. Taylok took several steps, walking up the trail. *Any moment now and she'll pop back and ask me why I didn't follow her,* he thought. *She probably said something about where she was going and didn't realize I wasn't listening.*

With his next step the world vanished, and he found himself within a small bubble of darkness, cut off from the outside. There were people there, and for a split second he saw Suelynna lying on the ground. Then he was falling, and as he fell the world faded. It was with a shock that he realized his torso was no longer connected to his lower body, and then he was gone.

Brigid's chain returned, coiling in the air around her body, close but not quite touching her flesh. Blood dripped from the metal that seemed to refuse its presence. In just seconds the metal was clean again, although the dead She'Har's corpse remained on the ground next to her.

"Too bad that one was male," said Tyrion. "I had hoped to get another female."

"We can come back tomorrow," advised Layla. "I doubt the elders will notice their absence for several days."

Tyrion nodded, "I'd like to get a few more before we burn our bridges here."

"Bridges?" asked Layla, unsure what his statement meant.

"Once we get our quota, a volcanic event will occur," he explained. "That should cover any possible suspicion regarding the missing She'Har." Turning to Brangor, he ordered, "Take us back, but take the corpse first. We'll clean up the blood by the time you get back."

"Yes, my lord," said the one-armed mage, and a second later he, the She'Har woman, and Brigid were gone.

CHAPTER 15

"What do you think of the bread?" asked Thillmarius, leaning forward.

Tyrion's stomach clenched again at the sound of his former tormentor's voice, but he hid the reaction. In truth he couldn't appreciate any gustatory pleasures in the presence of his old trainer, but he lied anyway, "It's decent. Where did you get it? I've never seen your people eat anything other than Calmuth and simple vegetables."

The Prathion She'Har smiled, "Lyralliantha told me about your people's culinary prowess last year, and it sparked my curiosity. I did some preliminary research, but all my efforts still proved to be failures. Eventually it was with the kind help of a lady in the town you call Lincoln, that I was able to learn the art of making it."

Tyrion's brows shot up, "You made this yourself?"

"A friend, Tyvar, helped me, but most of the effort was my own," replied the lore-warden with barely concealed pride. "I have made it several times now, and it has become very popular among the Prathions."

The look on Tyrion's face said it all.

"You didn't think I could do something like this?" observed Thillmarius quizzically.

Tyrion nodded, "I don't mean to offend, but no. I would have assumed that you had servants do such things, if you were interested in them."

"We have no servants."

"You used to have slaves."

Thillmarius grimaced, "We did, but even then we would not have used them for something like this. You remember my old profession, but we never used the people of Ellentrea for anything other than the arena and patrolling. Even if I had had such an interest then, I would have done this myself. The people of Ellentrea were not very—delicate."

"But they did prepare food," noted Tyrion.

"Only for each other, not for us," explained the She'Har.

Because it tasted awful, thought Tyrion. It didn't take him long to summon memories of the terrible fare he had endured while a slave in Ellentrea. "Surely there were other She'Har you could have enlisted to take on a task like this for you," he suggested.

"Among the children of the She'Har status means little, and we have never made an occupation of food preparation the way your people have," said Thillmarius. "I am thinking of creating a social club here, for others of my kind who are interested in making foods like this. I believe your people would have called such a thing a 'restaurant'."

From slave master to cook, thought Tyrion. *This world never ceases to amaze me.*

They spoke for a while longer about human culture, particularly with regard to food, but the entire while Tyrion wondered at the Prathion's true purpose in calling him out. They were high atop one of the trees in the Prathion Grove, on a platform that he could only assume was Thillmarius' home. As always, being near the lore-warden was a profoundly uncomfortable experience for him.

He had come at Thillmarius' invitation, but he doubted that the true reason was just to try the man's baked goods.

"Tyrion?"

He had lost track of the conversation. "I'm sorry. I got lost in my thoughts. What were you saying?"

"I asked if you had heard about the disaster."

Tyrion's pulse sped up, but he controlled his breathing. It felt as though he was about to be interrogated again. Images of the table that Thillmarius had once restrained him on appeared in his mind. "Disaster?"

"There was a volcanic eruption. Part of the Mordan Grove was destroyed last month," said Thillmarius, watching him intently.

He feigned surprise, "Here?"

"No, across the ocean, an area they control on another continent," explained his host.

"Lyralliantha mentioned something about it, but she had to help me with the geography. Before that I didn't realize there were other lands beyond the ocean," lied Tyrion. "How bad was this eruption?"

Thillmarius looked away for a moment, "Thousands of Mordan Elders died. It has been a long time since we lost so many at once."

"Wasn't there another disaster recently, a storm that damaged the Gaelyn Grove?" asked Tyrion, dissembling.

The lore-warden nodded, "Yes, but it was nowhere near as bad as this. Less than a hundred were killed during it."

A hundred trees, he noted mentally. As usual the She'Har did not count the loss of their children. Seeds were easily replaced. "Why was this so much worse?" asked Tyrion.

"Storms are easier to deal with," said Thillmarius. "With a little preparation our elders can create defenses to protect themselves from wind, or from most natural events for that matter. Even earthquakes are only a minor nuisance in most cases, but volcanic eruptions are damaging on multiple levels. They are often sudden and unexpected. Burning ash can cause fires, and lava flows are certain death. For that reason, we rarely put down roots in areas that are likely to experience volcanic activity."

Tyrion shrugged, "I don't know much about geology."

Thillmarius smiled, "I was surprised you didn't ask me what I meant by a 'volcanic eruption', but you must know a few things, otherwise you wouldn't even know the Barion word for the study of the earth."

A cold shock passed through him as he realized his mistake, "Lyralliantha mentioned the topic last week, but I didn't understand her interest in it until now."

"It was probably the first time she had heard of such things herself, though I'm guessing someone else was required to give her the information she wanted to know," said Thillmarius condescendingly.

"Byovar, perhaps," agreed Tyrion with a sense of relief.

"It seems likely," said the Prathion. "Let's talk about something else. I'm sure you've been wondering if I had some ulterior motive to ask you over, beyond the bread, of course."

"It had crossed my mind," Tyrion replied, glad to change the subject.

"The bread was actually my primary reason," laughed Thillmarius, "but I am curious about all the activity near your new home."

"Have you been spying on us?"

"No more than usual," said the lore-warden enigmatically. He watched Tyrion, waiting, until the conversation stretched into an awkward pause, then he sighed, "That was a joke."

"Oh," he managed, at a loss for words.

"I see I still need to work on it," responded Thillmarius, picking up a piece of fruit from the table and taking a bite. "Honestly, though, it's all anyone can talk about. Even the humans in Ellentrea are whispering rumors from what I'm told. What are you doing, if you don't mind my asking?"

"Building a new settlement," said Tyrion plainly. "We will have to do much more before we can handle all the people of the slave camps."

"Some of the structures appear to be very specialized. Do you think the freed people of Ellentrea can become traders and craftsmen so easily?"

"It will be a long road."

"Is that why you have been seeking the advice of so many from the wildling towns? Pardon me, I should have said, the 'human towns'."

"Of course," he answered. "I hope to convince many of the people there to relocate as well. We will need their help if we are to civilize those who were raised in the pens."

"You have undertaken a truly gargantuan task," commented Thillmarius. "You have my admiration, though I worry for the safety of the townsfolk. You are well acquainted with how dangerous the people from the camps are."

"And how they became that way," added Tyrion, letting his irritation show. "I have no doubt it will be a task that will take generations." *Not that the slaves can survive for generations, though I'm sure you have no qualms about letting me believe they can.*

His former trainer stood and walked away from the table. There was something about his body language that spoke of anxiety, or perhaps agitation. "Regarding that, Tyrion, there is something you should know."

Tyrion watched him, suddenly curious, "Oh?"

"I shouldn't be telling you this. My Elders have decreed that this information should be withheld, but my conscience won't let me remain silent." Thillmarius stopped at the other end of the table, leaning on it with both hands, "You shouldn't interbreed with those from the slave camps."

"Why not?"

"They're a dead end, genetically speaking," said the lore-warden. "Any children they produce will not last beyond one or two generations. If your people, particularly your women, waste their energy and resources rearing their children, it could seriously deplete your population. Humankind might even go extinct."

Tyrion was surprised at his honesty, too surprised to even remember his anger for a moment. Standing as well, he stared at the She'Har, "If that is true, why would you tell me?"

Thillmarius' posture was rigid with barely contained emotions, "Because I believe in our accord, not just as a matter of maneuvering for advantage, but in its spirit. What we did in the past was wrong. I cannot atone for that, but I can't sit idly by and watch your people destroyed by my inaction, even if my elders have no problem with it."

"Clarify something for me. Are you saying that your elders want my kind to die out?"

The lore-warden shook his head, "No, they are not so malicious as that, but they would not cry over it. It might even be a relief to them, a guilt easily forgotten when those who were wronged no longer exist."

"Won't you be punished if they discover you told me this?" asked Tyrion, shocked at the normally unflappable She'Har's evident passion.

"There is no way for them to know how you learned this," said Thillmarius, "but I would tell you either way. Some things are too important to ignore."

Tyrion struggled with his own emotions. Faced with such genuine concern from one he considered his mortal enemy, he had no idea how to react. He turned toward the door, "I see. I need to return home."

Thillmarius stepped closer, "Tyrion, wait. I know you cannot forgive me, but believe me when I say that I would be a friend to your people."

"You are right," answered Tyrion, staring at the doorway, "I can't forgive you, but I do believe you." *Damn you!* He took two more steps before pausing, "Thank you." He left the room then, but a fresh thought took him back.

Looking through the doorway he spoke again, "Butter."

The lore-warden seemed confused.

"It goes well with bread. Ask the villagers how to make it, or Kate. I think you'll like it," and then Tyrion left.

The Prathion lore-warden stared after him for several minutes, pondering his parting words and wondering if they were a gift or some sort of mockery. It was only later that he wondered about the human's lack of questions regarding the genetic sabotage of the people of the slave camps. *It was almost as if he already knew,* thought Thillmarius.

Eal'estea sat in darkness. The only light came from beneath the ironbound wooden door of her stone cell. She was cold and miserable in such unnatural surroundings. Her memories of the sun felt like dreams to her now.

"Balewgraa," she uttered, trying to say 'sun' in Erollith.

She closed her mouth again, despair washing over her. She could hear the word in her mind, the way it should sound, but her lips only produced random noises when she attempted to voice it.

Her magesight was gone as well, which made the dim light her only source of comfort. Eal'estea had no idea how long she had been in the cell, her sense of time had become distorted with no way to see the sun.

Her days were marked only by the delivery of calmuth to satisfy her hunger.

Her captor clearly understood that without the fruit she would begin to take root, not that such a thing would do her any good in the hard darkness of her prison.

She shivered and once again tried to create a spellweave to warm herself, but she was only rewarded with pain. Spellweaving was beyond her reach now, she could not even touch aythar, much less direct it to her seed-mind.

Eal'estea wasn't even sure she still had a seed within her. It wasn't something she had ever been conscious of before, but now it felt as though she had a hole in her mind, an empty dead place. Without magesight the world had lost its vitality, as if the color had gone out of it, not that she could see color in the dim room anyway.

Her life was only endless shades of gray now. It lacked even the adrenaline that had come with her torturer. Tyrion had not visited her in days or perhaps weeks.

She had begun having cramps some time before, though she wasn't sure why. Unless the madman had damaged her body as well as her brain. There was no way to be sure, the pain had been so great the last time that she had passed out. Anything might have happened after that.

Her stomach felt better today, but she still had an uncomfortable sensation of being bloated. She needed to pee too. Standing up, she moved to the corner where a depression in the floor had been created. A trickle of water ran from a place in the wall and entered the bowl like area before draining away.

Once she was done, she returned to the stone bench where she had been sitting, but her hand felt something cold and unpleasant there. Raising her fingers to her nose, she smelled blood.

"Urkle!" she exclaimed holding her hand away from herself and searching for something to wipe her fingers on. Of course, she already knew there was nothing. She would have to use the wall or floor, or the water that trickled in above her sanitation bowl.

The door opened as she washed her hands.

"Good morning, G-1," said her captor.

"Blaba gee morno!" she spat back angrily. *My name is Eal'estea!*

Tyrion stood half a head taller, and he looked down on her with a mad smile, "Still trying to talk? You'll just frustrate yourself."

She glared at him as she moved away, trying to find the farthest corner of the cell from him.

"You should be proud; you were my first success. No more of your people had to die after my work with you. I've refined my technique since then as well. It is still painful, but not nearly as bad."

Eal'estea tried to curse him, but it emerged as nothing more than an unintelligible scream.

"Your voice won't return," he told her. "I had to destroy that part of your brain. It was interesting to discover that the area that controls speech is so intimately connected with the portion that controls the flow of aythar.

"I suppose it makes sense. It explains several things. I now understand why using the spoken word enhances spellcasting. Unfortunately, I had to destroy one to stop the other."

"Umu?!" she bleated.

"Why?" he asked. "I couldn't cauterize the seed-mind without stopping the flow of aythar to it first. Several of your predecessors died because of that. The seed-mind does all sorts of nasty things if it isn't deprived of aythar before I begin cauterizing it. It was also what caused much of the pain and discomfort you experienced. Now I destroy the speech centers first, which starves it of aythar. That's the only uncomfortable part of the procedure these days.

"The latest ones scream very little before I am finished," added Tyrion. "Your sacrifice has made it much better for your kin, G-2 through G-14. The 'G' stands for Gaelyn, in case you were wondering," he paused, his eyes traveling over her. They stopped somewhere below her abdomen, and then he glanced at the stone bench.

Tyrion took a deep breath and felt a sense of relief at the sight of her blood. *It worked.* "Don't be afraid," he told his captive. "I was worried that it might not work, that your pain might have been a pointless torment, but it appears I was correct. This is your menarche if I am not mistaken, since I doubt you have ever experienced a menstrual cycle before.

"You will be the mother of a new generation of humanity. The future rulers of this world will emerge from your womb."

Eal'estea could see the light of madness in his eyes. She wanted to back away further, but the hard stones behind her made that impossible. All she could do was shake her head in denial.

"Don't be like that, G-1. You're human now, after all. Our future is your future as well."

CHAPTER 16

Tyrion stood next to Ryan looking down on the layout of their new city. It was still a work in progress, but it was shaping up quickly.

They were on a wooden platform, at the top of a temporary tower built from logs. Its primary purpose was to provide just such a view. Ryan used it frequently to make sure the new construction fit within his overall plan. People moved below them, mages from Ellentrea primarily, along with a few from Sabortrea as well. None of them walked slowly; Ryan's workers moved as if they were in a hurry.

Ian had made certain of that. Those who didn't move with alacrity didn't last long.

The outlines of future streets could be seen from the tower, marked with lines of string and stretching out around the central plaza like the spokes of a wheel. Only a small section of the city had been built, several dozen stone buildings. They varied in size and purpose, but most of them were residences.

The slaves from the camps were building their new homes, but there were still far too few. They had almost a thousand mages working there now and despite the increase in manpower they had only managed to house a few hundred of them so far.

"What you have looks good, but it needs to look *grand*," said Tyrion. "It has to impress the villagers when they see it."

"It has to be functional," argued Ryan. "We have hundreds sleeping in the field every night."

"You need more manpower then," suggested Tyrion.

Ryan shook his head, "I have too much now. I can hardly use them. Half of what they do has to be torn down and remade. It takes more time to train them than I have to spare. More would just increase the overcrowding."

"Don't try to complete the city, Ryan," cautioned Tyrion. "We just need a small piece of it, a piece that looks grand and will appeal to the villagers when they come to see it. No one will actually live in it."

His son stared at him in frustration, "Then why did you ask me to plan the entire thing? Why did we survey all those streets? I've been wasting my time!"

"All those lines speak of the promise of the future," said Tyrion. "When they see the beauty you have already made; the strings will show them the magnitude of your vision. Their imaginations will fill the empty field with more streets and grand constructions, so long as the part that is already there is impressive."

Ryan rubbed his face before staring at the setting sun. He was sweating from the afternoon warmth, and it made the stubble on his cheeks itch. "It would help if you revealed the rest of your plan. You say no one will live in it? I already have several hundred people from the slave camps sleeping in those buildings."

Tyrion frowned, "That won't do. I don't want them dirtying up the site."

"They're human beings," protested Ryan. "You can't make them sleep on the ground forever!"

"If you have more than you can use, start them on stasis boxes for the vault," said Tyrion. "And stop thinking of them as human beings. They're little more than animals. Baratti is an accurate word for them."

Ryan looked away, uncomfortable with the turn of the conversation. "Even as slow as they are, if we train them to make stasis boxes, they'll be able to produce thousands in a short span of time. That work won't hold them for long."

"I need a *lot* of the boxes," responded Tyrion.

"How many?" asked Ryan.

"Enough for all the villagers, and when that is done, enough for almost all of the people from the slave camps," said Tyrion grimly. "They won't be sleeping in this farce of a city when they're done."

His son stared at him, "The vault won't hold a hundred thousand people, even if you're planning to box them all up."

"The vault is just for people. We will put the slaves in other places—for a while anyway."

"None of it makes sense," muttered Ryan. "If you're planning to use them as soldiers, they won't do you any good in suspended animation. Why don't we just build the city? It doesn't have to be a fake. I know I've been pessimistic, but if we train them, eventually we'll have a work force large enough to make it a reality."

"No."

Ryan gripped the handrail until his knuckles turned white, "Why not? Give it a few years and this could be a real city. From everything you've told me, the She'Har seem to be holding to their end of the accord. At least we could build our strength before whatever you're planning."

Tyrion stared at his son, "Look at me." He waited until Ryan had met his eyes before continuing, "A hundred thousand, even mages, is not enough to unseat the She'Har from their grip on this world. It would take many times that. And that number will never grow, those people are a dead end. Their children will all be dead within two generations. I can't afford to leave them roaming freely, mingling with the people of the villages. Any unions between them will only decrease the chances of humanity's survival.

"Those slaves, those *gifts* from the ever kind She'Har, are poison. Even if they were loyal, they would be insufficient for a war. They won't be my soldiers. Instead, I will take the poison that the She'Har have given us, and use it to destroy them."

"But how?" asked Ryan in exasperation. "Or do I even want to know? Will they be sacrifices for our goals?"

"You don't want to know," agreed Tyrion, "but sacrifice is an appropriate term."

Kate made a clean cut, removing the top of the onion before turning it down and cutting it in half, bisecting it through the root. She peeled the two halves before cutting a crosshatch pattern. It took her very little time, for her deft fingers were well practiced at the task.

The speed meant she didn't have to deal with the eye watering consequences, but today the smell was more pungent than usual. Before her eyes could even begin to water her stomach twisted, rebelling. Gagging she turned away and rushed from the kitchen.

She thought that would be the end of it, but she still lost her breakfast. *Am I sick?* she wondered. Normally her she had a strong stomach, and onions certainly never bothered her. The thought of the onion made her heave again. *What's wrong with me?*

Then she realized what it must be.

"Kate?"

It was Lyralliantha. She hadn't been in the kitchen. They had discovered long before that she should never be allowed to prepare food. She must have seen Kate run past the front room.

"Are you alright?"

Kate nodded, "I'm fine." She wiped her mouth with a kitchen rag. "This is normal." She gave Lyra a weak smile.

Lyra frowned, "Normal? I wasn't aware that nausea could be normal. I understood it to be a signal of illness."

"Or pregnancy," said Kate, voicing her suspicion. "I may have a third child on the way."

"I have not detected a child," said the She'Har woman. "Let me look deeper." Her eyes became distant for a while, and then she smiled. "It's small still, I wouldn't have noticed if you had not said something."

"Nausea happens early on," explained Kate. "It should get better later, but don't tell anyone."

Lyra frowned, "You do not wish to share your news?"

"Not yet," said Kate. "Let me tell him myself."

Lyralliantha looked thoughtful, "This will be a secret then. Should I do the same?"

Now Kate was confused, "What do you mean?"

"I was almost sick this morning, but I didn't understand why, until you explained your reason. It appears we are both going to bear young," said Lyra.

Kate was flabbergasted, "Are you sure?"

"I checked myself right after I checked you."

That's a handy skill, thought Kate somewhat jealously. "I thought you couldn't have children…"

"Not by accident," replied Lyralliantha. "I was given permission."

Kate was filled with a torrent of emotions, happiness predominated, but there was a slight undercurrent of jealousy as well. She would not be the only one to give Tyrion a new child. She suppressed that feeling however, for she knew it was uncharitable. Spreading her arms she embraced the other woman, "This is wonderful. You'll be a mother. Our children will be siblings."

Lyralliantha returned the hug and then stepped away, looking down as if uncertain, "I have been confused. I do not know how I should feel."

Kate straightened, "Do you love him?"

"Yes."

"Then you should be happy. Don't overthink it."

"The She'Har do not have children, not like this," explained Lyralliantha. "I do not know what to do."

"Eat, get plenty of rest," laughed Kate. "This is the easy part. Later you won't be able to wait to be done with it."

Lyralliantha's eyes were watering, "You don't understand. I know the process. That is not what I mean. I am not human, but this child will be. I do not know how to be a 'mother'."

"Nobody does in the beginning," Kate said reassuringly. "You'll learn, and I'll be there to help you."

"Will that work?" asked Lyra, a hint of desperation in her voice.

Kate studied the other woman carefully, trying to figure out what had her so worried. Whatever it was went beyond the normal fear that any new mother would have. With someone as strange as Lyra though, the only way to find out was to be direct, "What are you afraid of, Lyra?"

"Tyrion has told me about the slaves in the camps, about why they are so savage, compared to your people. He said it was because they had no mothers or fathers to raise them. I do not know how to be a mother. Will a father be enough?"

Kate laughed, but the seriousness in Lyra's tone struck her to the core, and midway her laughter turned to tears. She felt sad for her, for the fact that Lyra had never had a mother of her own. She hugged Lyra again. "It will be alright. You will be a wonderful mother. We'll help each other. Your baby will grow up healthy and happy." *You'll be a much better mother than I had.*

"None of my grove have ever done this before," said Lyra.

"I've seen you with Inara and Eldin," responded Kate. "You will do fine. You just have to love them."

"That's it?" Lyra seemed incredulous.

Kate smirked, "No, but that's how it starts. There's much more, but you get to learn as you go."

"You will teach me?"

"Of course. Can you cut onions?"

Lyra frowned, "I was told to stay out of the kitchen."

"If I have to smell that onion again, I'll be back out here heaving. I think it will be safe for you to do something as simple as that, unless the smell makes you nauseous too."

Lyralliantha reached out, touching Kate's temple, "Hold still."

A cool feeling passed through Kate. Her nausea faded, and her stomach relaxed. "Oh, that's wonderful. I didn't know you could do that. Thank you."

Lyra smiled, "I've had a lot of practice the past few days."

"I guess I had better get back to the kitchen then," said Kate ruefully.

Lyra put a hand on her shoulder, "Let me. You can supervise."

Kate laughed, "Fine. I won't turn down an offer like that. Keep it up and I may fall in love with you."

Lyra led the way back to the kitchen, "You said we would help each other."

CHAPTER 17

Craig Roe was an uncommonly tall man, standing nearly six and a half feet in height. His hair was dark, falling in tight curls against his dusky skin. His wife, Laura, had a similarly imposing stature and dark complexion.

Sarah found their coloring interesting. She had heard that many of the people of Lincoln tended to be darker, but she had expected something more like a heavy tan. Of course, she had seen far more exotic colorings among the She'Har; the Prathions for example, were so dark they appeared to be almost as black as coal, and that was mundane compared to the blue skinned Mordan, or the green haired Centyr.

She wondered if perhaps humanity had once had as many different colorations as the She'Har. Mrs. Roe would have stood eye to eye with Tyrion, if he were present, and Mr. Roe would have been half a head taller. *It will be interesting seeing them side by side later,* thought Sarah.

"Welcome to Albamarl," said Sarah.

"Is that to be the name of this new city?" asked Laura Roe. She had a deep yet feminine voice, and she presented herself with an air of confidence and authority. The mayor of Lincoln's wife was no shrinking violet.

Sarah smiled, "It was originally the name of our home, but we've decided to extend it to the entire city. It means 'white stone'."

"It seems premature to call it a city," said Craig, "when there is no one living there yet."

"Some of my people are there already," offered Layla, "but we hope once you see it, you will want to be among the first of its new citizens." Layla wore an elegant dress, but it did little to hide her warrior's bearing. She did not quite meet their visitor's height, despite being tall herself, but her musculature left little doubt about which of the three would win in a plain brawl.

At just a little over five feet, Sarah felt positively diminutive among them. She watched Layla with concern. *It was a mistake to have her here. She is no diplomat.* Unfortunately, they needed her skills for the tour.

Despite her crude upbringing, Layla was still far more skilled with illusions than any of Tyrion's children. In fact, her dress itself was a magical fabrication. The female warden was nearly naked beneath it. No amount of talking would persuade her to put on one of the fancy garments that Kate had recommended. This had been her compromise.

Sarah couldn't complain, though. Layla's illusory wardrobe was more impressive than the dress that Kate had tried to get her to wear, and Sarah could see Mrs. Roe watching the other woman with admiration, or perhaps jealousy.

"It you will follow me, we can show you how much we have already constructed," said Sarah courteously, leading them down the small paved road that stretched from their complex of buildings to the edge of the new city.

Layla took her cue. Gesturing ahead she spoke, "You can already see the tower from here."

"Tower?" asked Laura. "Is that what that is?"

Sarah nodded, "It's not complete yet, so we can't give you a tour of it, but when it's finished you will be able to see the entire city and the surrounding countryside from its pinnacle."

"What do you need a tower for?" said Mr. Roe. "It seems impractical, especially building it before the city is done."

"Albamarl is meant to be an inspiration," explained Sarah. "Lord Tyrion intends to resurrect humanity's greatness from the ashes of the past. The tower will sit above the city hall as a symbol to everyone living there. He intends to keep it open for the use of the citizens, allowing us to look out upon the world and provide a beacon of hope to those traveling to the city at the same time."

The tour lasted for nearly an hour while Sarah and Layla walked their two guests from Lincoln through the few buildings in Albamarl that had been finished. The questions were endless, and Layla's skillful illusions were so effective that it was difficult to draw the pair away once they had been shown what they were intended to see.

Layla hid the fact, but the effort of maintaining so much illusory imagery for that length of time was nearly too much for her. The tower didn't exist at all, and while the few buildings that they took their visitors into were real, most of the construction that was showcased in the distance was a complete fabrication.

When they returned to the main house, Layla made her excuses and left, presumably to attend to other duties, but in actuality she was heading to her room to rest.

Her part was done. Now it was Tyrion and Kate's turn to charm them.

The dinner was one of the best they had had in Albamarl, even though Kate had had no hand in making this one. Tonight's meal was a product of Abby's hard work and a lot of practice under Kate's tutelage.

Sarah led the two guests into the dining hall, but she was surprised before they reached it. Her magesight told her there was one additional person within, one that none of them had expected, a She'Har.

Not knowing what else to do, she took them inside and showed them to their seats. Byovar, one of the Illeniel lore-wardens, sat near Tyrion at the table.

Mr. and Mrs. Roe pulled up in surprise when they saw the silver-haired man sitting at the table before them.

Tyrion and Byovar stood as they entered. "You must be Craig and Laura Roe I presume?" said Tyrion. "May I introduce another guest who has come to dine with us this evening?"

They nodded quickly, and he went on, "This is Byovar, of the Illeniel Grove. Byovar, I would like you to meet Mr. and Mrs. Roe of Lincoln."

The Illeniel bowed respectfully, "Well met."

Unused to such things the two from Lincoln were quick to copy his example.

"They've come to see our work on the new city," explained Tyrion.

"It was most impressive," said Craig. He tried to avoid staring, but the otherworldly grace and beauty that was so evident in Byovar was hard to ignore for those who had never met any of the She'Har before.

Kate entered then, followed by Abby, Emily, and Ryan, all carrying plates and platters. To avoid unnerving their guests, they did everything manually. When the table was laid, another round of introductions was made and then they all sat to eat.

Lyralliantha entered a minute later followed by the rest of Tyrion's children, except for Inara and Eldin, who were under Layla's tired care for the duration of the meal.

It was a crowded room, and while the table still had room, there were only just enough seats for everyone. Craig and Laura seemed suitably impressed, and Byovar's presence probably helped that, but Tyrion couldn't help but wonder at the lore-warden's reason for coming. They hadn't had a chance to speak in private before Sarah had returned.

As soon as the meal was finished Tyrion stood, "If you'll forgive me, I need to step out for a minute. I'll return shortly." He nodded at Byovar, and the two left and walked outdoors.

"You came on a busy day," began Tyrion.

"I hope I wasn't intruding, Tyrion, but I have important news for you." The lore-warden's face was somber.

"I'm listening."

"The Centyr will be visiting you next week," said Byovar.

Tyrion frowned, "A peaceful visit I assume?"

The Illeniel She'Har nodded, "Yes, but caution is always advised when dealing with the Centyr, especially this one."

"What do you mean?" he asked.

"The visit is purely a formality, but given their particular talents, you must be careful not to let any disturbing information be discovered...," suggested the lore-warden, letting his sentence trail off meaningfully.

"Their talents?" said Tyrion dismissively. Spellbeasts might be handy, in battle but he couldn't see much threat in that gift during an information gathering visit. Perhaps Byovar worried that they might leave a tiny spy behind, but it would be hard to conceal a creature of magic from so many mages.

"They will send one of their lore-wardens, Ceylendor," added Byovar. "You must make sure that everyone keeps their minds firmly shielded at all times."

Tyrion felt a stirring in the back of his mind, more information from the loshti, things he hadn't examined yet. Why was Byovar so worried? "Why?" he asked.

Byovar sighed, "I forget you are new to the loshti. You must think about the Centyr, examine what you have learned about them. They are the most dangerous of the She'Har to you at this point."

Tyrion felt a cold shock run through him at the mention of the loshti. He knew from a practical standpoint that the Illeniels had known it was him that took it. Indeed, they had all but arranged for him to receive it, without telling him, but hearing Byovar say it so bluntly surprised him. He hadn't known if the Elders had been the only ones to know or not.

Byovar attempted to smile reassuringly, although his expression actually had the opposite result. "Relax, Tyrion. Only my Elders know, and whoever you have told. I was only informed today, before bringing you this message."

"And your message, it comes from your elders?" asked Tyrion.

The lore-warden nodded, "It does, and they wish you to know that your secret is theirs as well. We cannot allow the Centyr, or any of the other groves to learn about your acquisition of the loshti." Byovar leaned forward, "And that goes double for the matter of Lyralliantha's pregnancy."

All the cards were on the table. Lyra hadn't told Tyrion that she was pregnant yet, but he had been watching her carefully. Now Byovar had practically admitted that she was important to his Elders' secret plan. He glared at the She'Har sitting across from him, "I was already aware that your people had deliberately left certain information out of the loshti, but now you've all but admitted that you're using me. What are the Illeniels planning?"

"Survival," replied Byovar.

"But how?"

"If I could discuss that, the Elders wouldn't have gone to the trouble of omitting it from the knowledge you received," said the lore-warden.

"It doesn't make sense," said Tyrion. "With all your power, why would you need us? What can I, or Lyra's child do that the Illeniel Grove could not do for itself?"

Byovar looked pained. Pursing his lips, he remained silent for several seconds before speaking, "Tyrion, please, do not get caught up in speculation about the past. They've given you all the knowledge they can, without altering the important choices you will make. Those choices are what you must concentrate on now. Our people will be great allies in a future far too distant for you or me to see, but what happens now, in the present, will make a large difference in how we get to that future. There are several important cusps coming, moments of choice that could result in enormous suffering for both your people and mine.

"For your children's sake, don't let yourself be blinded by your anger. We have wronged you, we freely admit that, but if you can find your way past that, there is hope for all of us," finished the lore-warden.

The She'Har's plea sent fire through his veins, "Tell that to the billions your people murdered. Tell that to Brigid, after you forced her to kill her own sister. I'm *sick* of hearing your excuses for evils done based on some miraculous future that is yet to come."

"Tyrion..."

"Shut up," he barked. "Tell me what it is you want me to do and be gone!"

The lore-warden lowered his head, "The Centyr are dangerous. Keeping secrets from them is more difficult than with any of the other groves. Make sure that when Ceylendor comes, he finds no open minds to inspect. If he discovers what we have done, I am not sure we can protect you."

Tyrion took in every word, and then he gestured toward the massive trees in the distance, "Thank you for the warning. Now it is time for you to leave."

He watched the She'Har leave, staring into the night long after Byovar had vanished from sight. His arcane senses followed the man even longer, but his mind was occupied with thoughts about the warning. *How do they know the Centyr are coming? Did they receive a message from them, or was this yet another example of their magical foresight?*

Those questions were important. He knew from the loshti that they should only learn of things that somehow impacted them directly in the future. They weren't omniscient. If their knowledge came from their gift, then it meant that Ceylendor's visit would trigger events that would affect them, a chain of events that would inform them of its cause. But what would those events be?

Would the Centyr attempt to kill him? That would explain their warning, since presumably, if he died it would derail their plan for survival.

In any case, he could not ignore the warning, even if it made him painfully aware of the fact that he was still a puppet of the Illeniel She'Har.

He turned his attention to what he knew of the Centyr She'Har, letting his questions lead him down the paths of memory. Images, words, and thoughts assailed him as he explored new regions within his recently gained knowledge. The Centyr had been instrumental in the destruction of humanity, and not because of their spellbeasts.

The spellbeasts were merely an offshoot of their true gift, manipulating minds. Because of that they were the most feared among the different groves, aside from the Illeniels. Their abilities had turned entire armies against one another.

But even that had not been enough, otherwise the She'Har would not have used their final option, the plague of self-replicating krytek that had devoured humanity in a horrifying display of biotechnological mastery. He let his mind dwell on that once more.

Those krytek had been based upon a creature that had once plagued the She'Har. They had recreated it and modified it to feed upon human flesh rather than their own. It was a feat of precise control over the design of their warrior servants, one that Tyrion could never have reproduced on his own, but there had been one flaw.

Their design retained the original genes, those that gave the creature the ability to subsist on the She'Har elders themselves. They had silenced those traits, but the blocks that they had created could easily be omitted. If that were done the resulting krytek would feed upon humans and She'Har trees alike.

A second plague would wipe out humanity, but what would it do to the She'Har? They no longer had the kianthi that had saved them once long ago, but they covered the entire earth. As advanced as they were, it was quite possible they could stop the parasite, given time to react. They were so numerous it was unlikely they wouldn't find a solution before they were all gone.

It was a moot point anyway. Tyrion had no way to recreate the krytek they had used. The ancient scientists of humankind might have been able to, but while he possessed some of their knowledge now, he didn't have the tools, much less the skills to make any use of that information.

The only ones capable of it would be the father-trees. *I can't risk that,* he thought, *not yet.*

And besides, he was sure it wouldn't be enough. He would have to think of something else.

Or in addition to, he realized, a dark smile spreading across his face. *Geology, such an interesting word. Too bad the She'Har didn't know half as much about it as the people they butchered did.*

CHAPTER 18

Three days passed before they received their 'surprise' visit. Since they hadn't known exactly when it would occur Tyrion had forced everyone to stay home. As a result, most of his projects had been put on temporary hold. Ryan hadn't minded much, though, since it gave him a respite and an opportunity to work on some of the smaller improvements he had long planned.

Lyralliantha was the one exception. After hearing the warning she had volunteered to return to her place in the Illeniel Grove for a while. Protecting her mind wouldn't have been an issue for her, but hiding the secret within her womb would have been impossible.

Everyone else was under strict instruction to shield their minds as tightly as possible. Kate and the younger children were the only ones who wouldn't be able to do so, but the children didn't know anything anyway. Kate on the other hand, didn't know anything specific about her husband's plans, but she might know enough to get them in trouble.

Tyrion couldn't be entirely sure. At the very least he worried that a stray thought on her part might give away the fact that he had eaten the loshti, so he cautioned her to stay inside their bedroom for the duration of Ceylendor's visit. The privacy ward around it should be enough to keep her thoughts safe. *If I can't even sense whether someone is inside the room, I doubt he could read anyone's mind in there,* reasoned Tyrion.

The problem, of course, was not knowing when the Centyr lore-warden would arrive.

As fate would have it, Brigid was on watch when their unannounced guest arrived. Their original enclave had a stone wall around it now, enclosing a large yard. Inside it were the two main houses; Tyrion's and the dormitory his older children lived in, as well as a number of outbuildings, primarily storehouses and workshops.

Brigid was on the small platform next to the main entrance when she spotted Ceylendor's approach. She ignored the ladder and dropped lightly to the ground and jogged toward her father's house. Along the way she passed Violet and Blake. "He's coming," she told them. Those words were enough, everyone had been told to expect their visitor.

Word passed quickly among them, but Tyrion wasn't in the house. Brigid had known that, though. She went inside and entered his bedroom, closing the door behind her. In one corner stood an enchanted stone. It had been a small river rock originally, but now it was covered in runes and looked as though it had been split in two. Picking it up she spoke the command word and watched as it began to glow.

Its counterpart in Tyrion's deepest lab would be glowing similarly, letting her father know it was time to return.

She might have gone to fetch him herself. The bedroom held a secret entrance that led directly to it, but she couldn't open the door. It was one of the special doors he had made, and though she knew it was there, she couldn't sense it, much less open it. Only Tyrion and Emily could do that.

Brigid waited impatiently. An impartial observer might have called it 'fretting', but no observer that liked remaining in only one piece would have dared make such a remark to her. She paced back and forth. Outside the room she could hear voices. The others had come in, and she suspected the Centyr She'Har was with them.

Unsure what else to do she activated the privacy screen around the bedroom. "Hurry up, damnitt," she muttered. She had no idea what excuses to make for their guest if Tyrion didn't appear.

The stones in the corner of the room opened abruptly, sliding silently apart to reveal a long stairway descending into the ground. Tyrion marched briskly up them. "He's here?" he asked immediately.

Brigid nodded, "Yes, I believe he's in the dining hall already."

"Where's Kate?!" he asked in sudden alarm. "She's supposed to be in here!"

His daughter's eyes went wide, "I passed the word along. Someone should have told her. She should be here already."

"Find her," ordered Tyrion. Brigid started to run from the room, but he grabbed her shoulder, "Walk. I don't want to give him anything to wonder about." With that he released her and she proceeded to open the door at a more casual pace. He followed her out.

His eyes lit upon their visitor the moment he entered the dining hall.

Ceylendor was of average height, a little under six feet, but he had a commanding presence. Like all of his kind he had green hair, a subtle color reminiscent of oak leaves in the middle of summer rather than the bright colors of spring. It was his eyes that caught the beholder's attention. They were a vivid viridian, like emeralds under the noonday sun.

Kate's green eyes were a more humble, human shade, and seemed drab by comparison. That observation aroused an irrational hatred in Tyrion's heart that had nothing to do with the man's species.

Ceylendor's gaze was on him the moment he stepped out, and while the She'Har's stare should have seemed challenging, instead it felt warm. The man radiated a warm charisma that was impossible to deny. "You must be the man I've heard so much about," said the lore-warden.

Tyrion knew he was being influenced, much as everyone else in the room was. The flows of aythar that emanated from the Centyr She'Har were subtle, natural, almost impossible to identify as deliberate. It took an act of will to tighten the shield around his mind, which helped a bit, but their visitor's charm still seemed to seep into him.

He felt an odd urge to hug the stranger.

"I would appreciate it if you wouldn't do that," said Tyrion sternly. The words were hard to say, for he knew they were rude, and the last thing he wanted to do was offend their new guest. Fortunately, he had had years of practice at being cruel, even toward people he cared much more for than some unknown She'Har.

Ceylendor's brows went up in innocent surprise, "I'm sorry, did I do something to offend?"

For a second Tyrion felt chagrin and deep embarrassment for being so rude, but then Ceylendor's tone and expression brought a memory up from the past. The insouciance of his facial expression, the honesty in his tone, it reminded him of Thillmarius, and thinking of his former trainer brought with it the old panic and fear that had been ingrained in his soul.

With fear came adrenaline, and then anger. "I think you know damn well what I mean," ground out Tyrion. "Are you here for an honest meeting, or do you just want to mind-fuck everyone in the room?"

His words brought looks of shock and consternation from his children. Most of them, with the exception of perhaps Brigid, had already begun to relax under the waves of charisma emanating from the Centyr ambassador.

Tyrion's challenge shocked them, and they began tightening their own mental defenses.

The atmosphere in the room cooled abruptly. It was a sensation akin to sudden darkness when the light has vanished. Ceylendor made a quick half-bow, "My apologies. I have been so long among my own kind, I have forgotten my manners. Please do not judge the Centyr by my sloppy habits."

As if I believe that, thought Tyrion. *The man is a viper! Nothing he does is anything but calculated.* He controlled his anger when he replied, "I prefer to have conversations in which I can be sure that my emotions are my own. The accord between your people and mine is still new, let's not sully it with a bad start. Are you thirsty?"

Ceylendor watched him for a moment before replying, "I was sincere in my apology."

He felt my anger, thought Tyrion. *Despite my careful shielding.* Having someone answer his mood rather than his words was disconcerting to say the least. "If you would show your sincerity, then stick to the conversation at hand, rather than my perceived mood."

The lore-warden nodded, "Understood, and yes, I am thirsty."

Brigid had almost made it to the front door when it opened of its own accord. Kate stood on the other side. Everyone's eyes fell on her as she entered.

"Hello?" she said into the awkward silence.

Abby spoke first, "We have a surprise visitor, from the Centyr Grove."

Kate's face grew wary, but she covered the expression quickly, "Oh, it's nice to meet you. I'm Catherine—Tyrion's wife."

Ceylendor had already crossed the distance before anyone else could move. Stretching out his hand he took hers and dipped his head politely, "It is a pleasure to meet you, Catherine."

The instant their hands touched Tyrion felt something pass between them, something so small and quiet it was almost impossible to sense. Rushing forward he pushed them apart, glaring at Ceylendor. "Your actions belie your recent apology, Centyr." Without turning to face her he spoke to Kate, "Inara needs you in the bedroom."

Confused, and possibly charmed, Kate began to object, "But she's with, Lay…"

"Let me help you, sister," said Brigid, guiding her toward the bedroom.

Ceylendor appeared upset, "I meant no offense toward you or your concubine, Tyrion, please forgive…"

"Wife," corrected Tyrion. "The proper word is wife."

"Pardon me," said Ceylendor quickly. "It seems my Barion is not up to par. I have done nothing but commit one offense after another."

"Let's adjourn to the front room," said Tyrion, ignoring the apology. "It's more comfortable there, and more private." He glanced at the others, "Return to your rooms. We can have dinner later."

No one argued.

Ceylendor followed him without comment, taking a seat in one of the modestly cushioned chairs that Ryan had designed. "That really wasn't necessary."

Tyrion stared at him, holding onto his cold rage, "Wasn't it?"

His guest sighed, running a hand through soft green hair, "Perhaps it was a mistake for me to come here."

"Your mistake was in treating us like books to be rummaged through," replied Tyrion.

Ceylendor gazed at him appraisingly. The stare was unnerving. Tyrion felt a sudden sensation of uncertainty, something akin to the feeling a lamb might feel when it discovers it has been trapped in a pen with a hungry wolf.

But Tyrion was no stranger to fear. He and his fear had become old friends over the years. Rather than let it control him he used it instead to inform his actions. He had been holding his breath, but he released it slowly now. It was already apparent that no amount of mental shielding would keep Ceylendor entirely out of his thoughts, so he changed course. Listening carefully, he felt the firm beat of the earth. It called to him, but he didn't allow himself to be consumed by it.

Instead he touched it gently, letting it infuse his thoughts and permeate his body. He expanded slightly, becoming more than he had been, but only to a mild degree. His senses changed, and his boundaries shifted. He was the sum of everything around him, with one exception.

Ceylendor was foreign to him, like a splinter beneath his skin.

Balancing lightly on the edge between being human and embracing his strange ability more fully, he listened to the other man's words, registering them without feeling. The She'Har looked different now, less like a man and more like a predatory beast; his teeth were sharp, and his fingers ended in claws. He was almost reptilian, with hard scales where his skin should have been.

Tyrion's vision wasn't reality, at least not physical reality, but it held something truer than that within it. His perceptions made little sense, but he was in a place beyond reason and sense, in a place where things simply *were*.

"Have you considered that perhaps it wasn't a mistake? Isn't it possible I goaded you into driving everyone else away? Being alone with me might not be entirely wise…," Ceylendor was saying, but then his expression changed, and his words trailed off. Confusion flickered across his features. "What have you done?"

Tyrion's mind was stone, and Ceylendor was trapped within him, much like a fly in amber. "Nothing," he answered. "At the moment I'm debating whether I should kill you or continue attempting a civilized conversation. Which would you rather I do?"

The lore-warden's forehead was damp with sweat as he tried to sense something, *anything*, but his perception was dead. He still had his power, he still had his magesight, but he felt blind, for beyond his physical sight he could feel nothing whatsoever, not from the man standing apart from him or from anyone within the house itself. It was as though he was alone, talking to a stone made to resemble a man.

"I would prefer to talk," said the Centyr She'Har at last.

"Let's start with the purpose of your visit," suggested Tyrion mildly.

"My grove sent me to gather information," said Ceylendor. "I'm sure you can understand that. Our intentions are peaceful, however."

"Your intentions and your actions don't seem to coincide," he observed. "Peaceful might not be the correct word. Information gathering seems rational, but I would guess that your actions in regard to it are conditional upon what you find."

"We hope for peace then," corrected the lore-warden. "Surely any sentient being would defend itself if it found itself faced with a threat."

"We are no threat to the Centyr," said Tyrion flatly. "That's what the accord was about after all. If you came to reaffirm that, then you've done a poor job. Let me simplify it for you. Leave me and mine alone, and the Centyr have nothing to worry about."

Ceylendor bowed his head, "That is more than enough. Please forgive my insults to you and your family today."

"Stay away from us," warned Tyrion. "That goes for you and the rest of the children of the Centyr Grove. Do that and no mistakes will be made."

The lore-warden began again, "Tyrion if you…"

"Farewell, Ceylendor. I hope we don't meet again," interrupted Tyrion. He kept his face blank and said nothing more.

Ceylendor accepted his dismissal with as much grace as he could muster. He left, but his mind was spinning with the chaos and turmoil of his brief visit.

They were exactly what I expected, until he showed up. A little more complex than the humans in Baratrea, more powerful, but ordinary otherwise. Given an hour or two and Ceylendor would have known everything he could have possibly cared to know. They clearly weren't a danger to the She'Har, but meeting Tyrion changed his mind in that regard.

Of even more concern was what he had learned from the human's mate, Catherine. His brief contact with her unprotected psyche had been illuminating. She was pregnant. He had seen that immediately, but it was where her thoughts went from there that surprised him. *She was thinking of Lyralliantha. The Illeniels have allowed one of their own to bear a child—for Tyrion.*

That changed everything. The Elders of the Centyr Grove would want to consider that information carefully.

CHAPTER 19

Tyrion stared at the cell door for a long time, consumed with trepidation. Hesitation was something he thought he had conquered long ago, but now it had reappeared. He had known what his plan would entail all along, but now that the moment was here, he found himself reluctant.

Growling to himself he thrust his hand forward and opened the door. Within G-1 sat listlessly on the long stone pallet that served her as both bed and bench. It was covered with a bedroll now, as well as several extra blankets and pillows. At Emma's recommendation he had also had a cup and bowl provided for each of his 'guests', so that they would no longer have to collect water in their hands to drink.

It was still far from civilized, but it was better than it had been.

They will only have to suffer it for a matter of months and then it will be over, thought Tyrion. *Then begins the sleep, and when they wake it will be a different world.* He had repeated that to himself a dozen times over, but it still did little to relieve his guilt.

Recognizing his shame for what it was he became angry once more. *I owe the She'Har nothing! Not them, or their children, innocent or otherwise!* The anger helped more than excuses when it came to pushing aside his remorse.

"Stand up and turn around," he ordered. When G-1 had fearfully complied he added, "Bend over and put your hands on the bed."

Eal'estea's eyes widened as she realized what he meant to do. She shook her head in negation, "Nealoora!"

The word made no sense, but Tyrion recognized defiance when he saw it. His hand came up, as if he would strike her, but then he regained his composure. Applying his will and aythar, he trapped her in bands of force, bending and turning them to force her body into the position he desired. He tried to be gentle, but her struggling still resulted in marks and what would probably be bruises later.

In less than half a minute she was bent over before him, and since she was naked already, he could see his goal.

Tyrion unfastened his trousers, but he found his body unwilling. For a moment he felt something, a twitch, an urge, but then the sound of his captive's weeping broke his resolve. Decision made or not, he was limp.

You are a rapist, Lyralliantha had once told him, back before he had faced the reality of what he had actually done to the women in Colne. She had been right, but in the present, faced with the cold calculated decision to be just that, he found himself impotent.

"Damnitt!" he swore as he released her. He slammed the door closed as he left.

An hour later he had returned, this time with his son, Ryan. The boy and his sister had been busy working on another of the secret chambers, but he had pulled him away from the task with no explanation.

"What is it you need, Father?" asked the younger man. "Why didn't you just tell Emma we were coming here?"

"I didn't want to upset her," answered Tyrion. "I need you to do something."

Ryan waited patiently.

He gestured at the cell doors, "My work in cauterizing their seed-minds has been successful, and some of them are…," his words trailed off. *How the hell do I say this?*

"Are what?" asked Ryan.

"They're coming into season," stated Tyrion.

"Season?" Ryan stared at him in confusion but after a few seconds his cheeks colored. "Wait, what… you don't mean you want me…?"

"Someone has to," said Tyrion. "That's the whole point of this. Humanity will need their gifts in the future, and this is the only way to get them."

Ryan gaped at him. "That won't enable me to steal their gifts. You know that! What are you talking about?"

Tyrion closed his eyes, "Not you, their children. Any offspring will be human, but coming from the females they won't have the same genetic traps that the She'Har built into their male children."

"I still don't fully understand this 'genetic' thing you keep talking about," said Ryan, hoping to reroute the conversation.

"Their children will be able reproduce, and they'll have the same special abilities that their mothers have," said Tyrion. "But first, someone has to impregnate them."

"Someone?"

Tyrion nodded, "Three are ready now, but the rest will start soon."

"Three?!"

"I don't expect you to do it all in a single day," added Tyrion.

A long argument ensued, but eventually he convinced Ryan with a combination of threats and intimidation. There was no appealing to better nature in this case.

Ryan entered the cell under protest, but after a few minutes he reemerged, his head was down and his face in shadow.

"Well?" asked Tyrion. He had kept his magesight focused in other directions.

"I couldn't do it," mumbled Ryan.

"What?!"

"I couldn't do it!" shouted the young man.

Tyrion couldn't find his anger. *He's too young, too kind, and of course there's...* "Emma," he said at last.

It was a single word but it made Ryan's blood boil. "Shut up! I don't ever want to hear her name on your lips, not at a time like, like...," his words ran into an unintelligible growl. He cursed and swore, but eventually he ran out of steam. "Find someone else. I can't do this."

Tyrion stared at the wall and neither spoke for a long while. *Almost any one of the men from the slave camps would have no trouble, but of course, that would negate the entire purpose. All of them carry the lethal traits,* he thought. *It has to be one of us...*

Eventually the inevitable conclusion arrived. He didn't look at his son as he ordered, "Go find Ian."

That afternoon he had a small meeting with the small group that would be making the next clandestine attack.

They gathered in the front room of the main house, with the privacy screens active. Emma and Ryan stood to one side, looking particularly out of sorts, while the two Mordan mages, Brangor and Jordan stood on the other. Layla was opposite Tyrion and as usual, Brigid was close by his side.

"The Centyr are next," said Tyrion without preamble, "but since I'm sure most of you remember Ceylendor's recent visit they present some specific difficulties, the first being the location of the attack."

Jordan spoke up, "Neither myself nor Brangor have ever been to any part of the Centyr Grove."

"Which means that we need to take one of them there and pick our spot before we can do anything else," finished Tyrion.

Layla looked concerned, "The journey is much too far if you plan to have me conceal you."

Tyrion nodded, "Don't worry, that had already occurred to me. The easiest course would be to bring one of them with me on a trip to survey Baratrea, ostensibly in preparation for the next batch of slaves.

"However, I have some reservations," he continued. "As you recall, Ceylendor seemed quite capable of influencing us to some degree, even with our minds tightly shielded. Baratrea will be teeming with others of his kind. The biggest danger is that they might discern our motives while we are there."

Emma broke in, "Then the obvious conclusion is to keep the number of people on this visit to a minimum."

"Exactly," said Tyrion. "That's why I plan to take only Jordan with me. I believe I can protect both of us using the same technique that worked for me when Ceylendor came."

Brigid started, "But Father, if you're only taking one, it should be me…"

"You aren't a Mordan mage, Brigid," he said, stopping her before she could go on.

Emma looked worried too, "This is the 'stone mind' technique you described to me the other day?"

He nodded.

"It's too dangerous," she responded immediately. "You might have to maintain it for hours. If you make a mistake, lose control, there won't be anyone there to help you." Emma made a point of looking directly at Jordan.

Tyrion understood her meaning. If he accidentally went too far, he would need someone he trusted to help pull him back. Jordan was unsuitable for the task for more than one reason. For one, the man didn't understand the nature of Emma and Tyrion's special talent, and for another they couldn't trust him completely.

He wanted to dismiss her concern, but it was valid. Finally, he nodded, "You make a fair point. It will be the three of us then."

"If you're both going, then you can take me as well," suggested Brigid. "You can shield Jordan and Emma can protect me."

"Either of us could do all three, or four," explained Tyrion. "Only one of us will handle it at a time. The other will be there in case something goes wrong, or if we have to split up for some reason."

"You still haven't said how you will travel," reminded Layla. "On horseback Baratrea is more than a week away."

"Dormon," he answered. The dormon were massive winged plant creatures created by the father-trees for the primary purpose of transportation. They were grown in much the same way that the krytek were, and similarly had only a short lifespan, measured in months. The Illeniel Grove rarely needed them, but the Prathion Grove was much larger and still had the slave camp of Ellentrea, so they were in the habit of keeping several on hand.

Tyrion smiled, "Thillmarius has kindly offered to let us use one of the Prathion Grove's dormon."

"Father, are you sure?" asked Emma as they landed in an open area set aside for just such purposes in Baratrea. "You could damage your mind."

"Observe and learn, Emma," he responded. "It is easier than what you have done before, and less dangerous, so long as you don't allow yourself to slip too deeply. You may need to do the same at some point before we leave here."

She frowned, "I can't imagine trying to listen to the earth and continue walking around, much less talking."

"It's a balancing act, just watch for now, but if we have to separate for any reason I want you to do the same. I don't know if Ceylendor was an exception, or the rule, but if there are others here with his skill, ordinary mental defenses won't protect you for long. Do you understand?"

She nodded, placing her hand on his arm, establishing a direct link between their minds. It wasn't quite as easy as it was with Ryan, where his mind was an orderly place of ideas and constructions layered with almost hidden affection, her father's was a land of cold steel and sharp edges. On the surface Tyrion's mind was structured, sane, but beneath that she could feel a maelstrom of madness, barely contained.

Emma wondered that he could survive there. She was merely a visitor, but he had to live with himself. Did he see the interior of his mind the same way, or was he numb to it? Faintly she could hear a woman's voice, wailing, and somewhere beyond that a boy crying. Her father radiated despair, and she could feel it seeping into her bones. Unbidden, a tear rolled down her cheek.

From the emptiness, her father's voice spoke, *Steady Emma, when you stare too long into the darkness, the darkness stares back.*

She felt him looking at her, seeing her in much the same way that she now saw him. Something must have pleased him, for the cold receded slightly as a faint warmth appeared. *Is that a father's love?* she wondered.

What little I have, he answered. *Forgive me for whatever you find here, Emma. While you may have traded me some of your warmth, I fear you will only come away stained with my darkness.*

Tyrion's mind began to change then. It had opened, expanding and becoming something different, something foreign. From personal experience she recognized the shift as his 'self' grew to encompass some of the world around them, most particularly the ground beneath their feet.

The link between them was tenuous now, for it was difficult to maintain a connection between a purely human consciousness and the inhuman awareness of the earth. For a moment she began to follow him, to listen as well, matching her state to his, but then she mastered herself. Doing so would only put them both at risk, and make her effort to provide an anchor for him pointless.

Perhaps it is a poor idea to have one person with this ability try to safeguard another, she noted mentally. *It might be better to have a normal mage perform the task.*

The world took on a strange appearance. Her magesight was still functioning, but it presented something completely different to her than what her eyes did. She still stood beside her father and Jordan, but her magesight was reporting nothing but stone, solid unyielding stone. It extended outward some ten feet in every direction and within it they didn't exist, they were dead stone statues walking within stone air.

Beyond the edge of the stone her magesight still showed her a world that reflected what her eyes provided.

"That's very clever," she observed.

"Indeed," said Tyrion in a voice devoid of inflection.

Jordan, however, had broken into a sweat. "I know you warned me about this, but I think I may be claustrophobic."

"Try not to think too hard about what your magical senses are telling you," she advised the Mordan mage.

Jordan swallowed, "I'll do my best, but I have to tell you, this illusion, or whatever it is, works too well. I can't feel my position."

"What do you mean?" asked Tyrion tonelessly.

"I don't think I could teleport right now," explained the other mage. "Nor can I learn where we are now to return later. If I am to impress this place on my mind, I will have to step outside of your protection at some point, at whatever place it is you wish to come back to."

Tyrion nodded, "Very well. Stay inside me. I'll let you know later on when I want you to memorize a place."

Jordan shuddered at the thought of remaining locked inside the strange rock, but then he reflected on Tyrion's words, "Inside you?"

"He means inside the phantom stone," explained Emma.

Together the three of them walked away from the dormon and toward the edge of the landing area where a woman awaited them.

CHAPTER 20

Flashes of viridian framed by frowning brows. That was Tyrion's first impression of the She'Har woman who stood waiting to greet them.

"Greetings," said the Centyr She'Har. "My name is Serrelia."

Silence reigned for an awkward moment before Tyrion realized a response was expected. He could still think, but the 'stone-mind' was interfering with his ability to process social cues. "I am Tyrion. Will you be escorting us in Baratrea?"

The woman bowed slightly, "Yes, if that is agreeable with you. The elders have asked me to walk with you and answer any questions you may have. What would you like to see first?"

"The living areas," answered Tyrion. "I am here to see about bringing some of your former slaves to Albamarl."

"Of course," answered Serrelia. "I assumed that would be the case. If you will follow me...," she gestured with one hand as she began walking slightly ahead of them, leading them to where the buildings were clustered more thickly.

As they went she continued talking, "Ceylendor told me you were unusual. I think I see what he meant now."

Tyrion ignored her remark.

"If you don't mind me asking, what type of magic is that which you are using?"

"I do," said Tyrion curtly.

Serrelia looked confused, "You do what?"

189

"I do mind," he clarified.

"Oh." Walking so close to them brought her well within his 'stone-mind' which had to be doing odd things to her perceptions, but Serrelia did her best to hide her discomfort. As they went she drifted closer to Tyrion, as though she might walk beside him, but Emma already had his arm occupied.

Serrelia sent a sidelong glance at Emma who merely smiled in return. "Go ahead," said Emma.

"Pardon me?" asked the She'Har woman.

"Touch him if you wish," she challenged. "It won't help you find his psyche."

Serrelia looked unhappy, "I had nothing of the sort in mind. Ceylendor told me about his encounter. I was cautioned to be a perfect ambassador today."

Emma nodded, "That's good then," but she made no attempt to apologize for her directness.

They reached a large thoroughfare that passed between the buildings and found a large crowd of people standing there expectantly. Much like the other camps, the humans here were of a wide variety of sizes, shapes, and descriptions, but what made the scene eerie was their utter silence.

The scene made Emma uncomfortable, but if Tyrion noticed the strangeness, he gave no sign of it.

"Do you intend to take many back today?" asked Serrelia politely.

"No," said Tyrion flatly. "I only plan to choose twenty today. You can send them to us next week."

Serrelia dipped her head in acquiescence, "As you wish, although it will take a long time to empty Baratrea at that rate."

"We will increase the numbers as new housing is constructed," said Tyrion. After a moment he began walking along the front line of the crowd, forcing Emma and Jordan to stay close to him. It might have made their tiny group seem odd, the way they stayed so close together, but they were already a strange sight for everyone with magesight. The 'stone-mind' around them was a bizarrely jarring sight, since it was completely at odds with what normal vision showed.

The people they passed were beautiful, men and women both. As at most of the slave camps they were predominantly young, for the arena had kept most from reaching advanced age, but there was something else about them. Apart from the She'Har, and perhaps the people of Colne, they were the healthiest and most attractive looking group of humans Tyrion had seen.

If he had been in a normal frame of mind, it might have made him suspicious, but as he was, it only presented as an interesting puzzle to him. After a brief bit of consideration, he selected his twenty at random. "I think we have seen enough today," he told their guide.

Serrelia seemed disappointed, "You have only just arrived. Are you certain there is nothing else you would like to see?"

Emma spoke up, "Are all of these people Centyr?"

Their host frowned, "They are all property of the Centyr. Pardon, I mean they *were* all property of the Centyr."

Tyrion's daughter shook her head, "No, I mean are they all a product of your grove? How many come from other groves?"

"Oh, I think I understand," said Serrelia. "No, these humans all have the Centyr gift. We have never kept many humans from the other groves."

"But you do have some?" probed Emma.

"A few...," answered Serrelia, somewhat reluctantly.

"Where are they?" she asked.

"We keep them in another place, separate from the rest," admitted the She'Har. "They do not do well if we mingle them with our main stock."

"Why not?" asked Emma pointedly.

Serrelia pursed her lips, "You know how they tend to fight. We find it keeps such things to a minimum if we separate them."

"Can we see them?" said Emma curiously.

"We have seen enough," interrupted Tyrion.

His daughter sighed, but said nothing more. A quarter of an hour later they were back on the dormon and winging their way back toward home.

As soon as they were off the ground Tyrion released the stone-mind. Emma had maintained her hold on his arm, and she felt the change as his mind retreated back into itself. Once she was sure he had regained himself, she felt the pain and turmoil that seemed to constitute 'normal' for Tyrion. She withdrew her hand, but for a fleeting moment before she broke contact, she felt his reluctance. *Don't leave me alo…*

She started to put her hand back, but her father shrugged her off, "That's not necessary now."

Emma felt a mixture of emotions, but the primary one was relief. She hadn't been sure if she could handle any more of the biting cold that burned through his soul. That feeling was followed immediately after by a sense of guilt. She felt bad for him, but she couldn't bear to stay any longer than necessary.

"Why didn't you want to see the slaves from the other groves?" she asked, shifting her mind away from uncomfortable lines of thought.

"We have others with their gifts. It may be that they have been abused, but that isn't my concern. It was apparent that we wouldn't have any time alone there, so rather than waste any more time, I thought we should leave," he answered succinctly.

"At one time you were concerned about freeing all the remaining people…," she began.

"Before I understood they had no hope of being part of the future!" he interrupted, stopping her short. "I only have so much energy to spare. I can't afford to spare it on the living dead."

"By that logic our entire trip here has been a waste then."

Arguing was a far more comfortable mode of conversation for him. Glancing over his shoulder disdainfully he replied, "We will land just beyond their grove. Jordan can fix a location there. We will be back within a week to pick up C-1 and the others."

"C-1?" said Emma, mystified.

Tyrion smiled, "I name the test subjects according to their grove of origin. The first Centyr we capture will be C-1, the second will be C-2, and so on."

Emma thought about the She'Har women imprisoned near Albamarl, in a prison she had constructed. Suppressing a shudder she put that thought aside. "How are your experiments going?" she asked.

Tyrion's eyes shot a warning to her before darting toward Jordan. Reaching out, he took Emma's hand, and she felt his mind connecting to hers. *Oh no,* she thought as the cold washed over her.

They are going well, Tyrion told her, *but I don't want to risk talking about it in front of him.*

Have you succeeded? she asked.

He nodded, but kept his face neutral, *Yes.*

She had known he meant to find a way to neutralize the seed mind, but she wasn't entirely sure what he expected to do after that. *What's next?* she asked.

For a split second she heard the wailing of a woman's voice again in her mind and then her father withdrew his hand.

"What?" she asked aloud.

"The less you know, the less you will feel responsible for later," he replied.

"What does that mean?" she demanded, but he refused to respond.

The rest of their trip was silent and uneventful, other than a brief stop at the edge of the Centyr Grove. Emma spent much of it studying the back of her father's head. *So much pain, so much guilt.*

Thillmarius was waiting for them when they landed.

"Tyrion!" said the lore-warden with some excitement.

Tyrion was somewhat less enthused. He had been hoping to avoid another meeting with his old trainer. Glancing at Jordan he ordered, "Go ahead and take Emma back with you. I'll be along as soon as I deal with this."

"If you don't mind," interrupted his daughter, "I'll stay with you."

Tyrion looked at her and then Jordan, "Stay then, both of you." He left unspoken the fact that he expected one of them to remain with the Mordan mage, to make certain he was put back in 'storage' until he was needed again.

"I took your advice," said Thillmarius, ignoring their exchange. "Come and see."

Tyrion fought down an involuntary surge of nausea as the Prathion drew closer. "See what? I don't remember giving you any advice."

Thillmarius waved at the three of them, "Follow me." He refused to say more until they had done as he asked. They walked for several minutes until they reached an open area near the building that had once served as the lore-warden's training center for those who would be blooded before entering the arena.

Emma noticed the extra tension in her father's shoulders as they crossed the open space. She knew he didn't like the Prathion lore-warden, but she didn't know what had once happened there.

Tyrion still remembered the thin red-headed girl he had choked the life from. She had been the first, and while he might have forgotten many of those who came after, he never forgot that day.

Today, however, the small training arena held a very different occupant.

"Isn't she beautiful?" remarked Thillmarius.

Tyrion stared blankly at the lore-warden, "It's a cow."

Thillmarius nodded, "Yes. Do you think she is a good one?"

He didn't know nearly as much about cattle as he did sheep, but from what Tyrion could see the cow looked healthy. What he didn't understand was why the She'Har had it in the former training yard. "I'm no expert on cows, but I think so."

"I went back to Lincoln, to acquire more flour," explained Thillmarius, "and while I was there I took your advice."

"I advised you to buy a cow?"

"Butter!" said the lore-warden. "I tried it while I was in Lincoln, and I was so impressed that I found someone to show me how it was made. After that I simply had to have a cow of my own. I understand it is best when fresh and in any case it only stays good for a few days."

Emma struggled to contain a sudden giggle.

"You plan on making your own?" said Tyrion, still in shock.

Thillmarius looked proud, "Indeed. Mistress Waycomb was kind enough to show me how to milk her, how to let the milk sit until the cream had risen, and how to work a churn." The She'Har's eyes were twinkling. In a conspiratorial whisper he added, "I made my own butter churn as well. I have it stored in the building over there. I should be able to try it tomorrow."

Tyrion tried to imagine the somber She'Har trainer churning butter, but his mind came up blank. "Show me," he said at last.

Thillmarius nodded, "Just you, though. I think your daughter is laughing at me already."

Emma had her hand over her mouth.

Tyrion followed his past torturer to the small building, and sure enough there was a wooden churn within. It lacked the carpentry joins such a device would have, probably because Thillmarius had had it grown rather than manufactured. Otherwise it looked eminently functional. "That is a churn," he said noncommittally.

"When I finish my first batch I want you to try it," said Thillmarius.

He said nothing, but he did give a slight nod of acceptance. *A powerful She'Har, gifted with near endless knowledge and power, and he intends to spend his leisure time making butter,* he thought to himself.

"Some of my fellows think I've gone a little mad," confessed Thillmarius.

"They lack your vision," said Tyrion dryly.

"Well, as you know, most of my people eschew eating the flesh of animals, so the thought of purifying milk fat and spreading it on bread seems odd to them, but I am confident they will see the light."

For some reason that statement reminded Tyrion of the dead squirrel Lyralliantha had once brought him to eat when he had first been captured. "I am sure they will learn from your example." He turned away, preparing to walk back to Emma and Jordan.

"Tyrion," said Thillmarius suddenly. "Before you go back. I wanted to give you some advice as well."

The seriousness in his tone sent fresh chills down his spine. No matter how friendly he became, Tyrion's body would never forget the fear, not after what he had endured. Working hard to keep his breathing steady he turned back, "About what?"

"You're planning to bring some of the humans from Baratrea back, is that correct?" asked Thillmarius.

He nodded.

"Don't leave them alone with the others in Albamarl. In fact, I would advise you to keep them entirely separate," said the lore-warden.

Once again Tyrion felt awkward. The last person he wanted help or advice from was Thillmarius Prathion, and yet there it was. He kept his tone neutral when he replied, "Why do you say that?"

Thillmarius stared at him seriously with the gold eyes that so often haunted his nightmares, "I think we both know that you have some knowledge of the Centyr abilities, perhaps more than most would expect. Trust that information. Of the five groves, they are the most feared."

Aside from the Illeniels, Tyrion almost added. "I fought many Centyr mages in the arena as you should recall. I think I have a good measure of them."

"The slaves you fought never had the subtlety to develop their most dangerous skills," argued Thillmarius. "And besides, the Centyr are most dangerous at peace, not war. You met Ceylendor."

He shrugged, "So long as they do not have his level of ability I believe I can keep them under control."

The lore-warden shook his head, "Violence is simple, Tyrion, but control is far more difficult. Even stunted examples of the Centyr, like these humans you are adopting, they will have many more tools at their disposal than you will. Do not underestimate them."

"Why are you so concerned?" asked Tyrion at last. "Why do you want to help me so much?"

"I have told you before," said the Prathion. "I am not proud of what my people have done, nor what I have done. I do believe we can create a better world together."

"What do we have to offer the She'Har?"

Thillmarius arched one of his golden brows, "Bread and butter alone would have been worth it. We have much more to learn from your people than can be seen yet."

CHAPTER 21

He sat on the edge of the bed, turning the cittern over in his hands. It was the same instrument he had created himself during his captivity years ago. He had considered making another over the years, but he couldn't find the energy for the task.

It probably wouldn't be as good anyway. When he had made this one, he had been desperate for something to do to occupy his time. Despite a lack of proper tools or materials he had spent weeks and weeks building this one. Boredom and loneliness had driven him to expend every effort in making it as good as it could possibly be.

He simply couldn't devote the time to do such a thing again.

Tyrion plucked the strings idly and then took up a proper melody. He played alone today. In the past his family had requested, no demanded, that he play for them every evening, but that was no longer the case. Since he had eaten the loshti they had gradually lost enthusiasm for his music.

It had been gradual. At first a few of his children would drift out once dinner was done, having other things to occupy them, but over time more and more of them had had other things to attend to. Eventually it had been obvious to him. When he picked it up, everyone scattered, and no one ever *asked* him to play.

He could tell his music was different, but he couldn't put his finger on what was wrong. So he played alone to save the others from being forced to smile and pretend they enjoyed it.

The door opened, and Kate stepped in, her eyes falling to his instrument.

Tyrion stood and moved to set it aside. "It's alright, I can do this later…," he began.

A flash of guilt flittered across her features, but then she stopped him, "Actually, I'd like you to play for me."

"You don't have to pretend, Cat. I know no one enjoys my playing anymore," he told her.

She opened her mouth, about to deny it, but then she closed it again. After a moment she spoke apologetically, "It's different, but it isn't bad."

He sighed.

"Play for me anyway," she prodded.

"Why?"

"There's something I want to hear," she said tenderly. "Do you remember that tune you played for me on the mountain when we were just teenagers?"

Tyrion frowned, "You'll have to be more specific."

"The day I brought you lunch," she reminded. "The *first* time I ever brought you lunch. You were playing when I came up the hillside, and when I got there you just kept playing as if I wasn't there. Do you remember that?"

He smiled, "And you started dancing a jig." It was a pleasant memory. Glancing up, he could see her looking at him, no—watching him, with the expression that had first bewitched him so long ago. Her green eyes seemed to sparkle with either a question, or amusement, he never knew which.

It was the same look she had held on her face that day when she danced on the mountainside.

"Will you play it for me?" she asked.

For a moment he forgot the present, forgot the intervening years and all the horror he had been forced to live. All he wanted was to play for her.

And it simply wasn't there. Despite his yearning, he had no memory of the music he played that day. He could relive the moment with crystal clarity, remember every word they had shared, the way the light had set her hair on fire, but the music that had flowed from his fingers was nothing more than a hazy feeling.

"It wasn't a tune that I learned, Cat. It was something I made up as I went along. I did a lot of that back then, to fill the time while I watched father's sheep," he apologized with a shrug.

She smiled, refusing to give up, "It doesn't have to be the same exact melody, just play the feeling for me. Play what was in your heart that day."

For an average musician, that was a ridiculous request. Music was structure and harmony, trying to create it without a plan generally produced something disjointed or unpleasant. But Tyrion knew he had been able to do just exactly what she had asked for. He had spent so much time playing that he had been able to forget the structure and let his feelings lead him away.

But he hadn't been able to do such a thing since he had eaten the loshti. When he did, something strange happened and his music turned odd, rigid—cold. Even when he played songs that he knew by heart, somehow they were tainted by the unforgiving rules that seemed built into his mind now.

"I can't."

"You can. Just remember how you felt," she insisted.

He remembered how he had felt. He simply couldn't remember the music he had played. Everything else about that day, about every day, in all honesty, was sharp and clear. Only the music was fuzzy, as though time had made the memory blurry.

Since he had eaten the loshti his mind had changed in a number of ways. One of the most striking was his memory, and not just the memories he had gained, but his own memories. He forgot nothing. Oh, he could be forgetful, but anytime he *tried* to recall a specific event, or anything else, it came to him perfectly. Whatever the loshti had done when it implanted the memories of the She'Har in him, it had also given him perfect recall. Perfect recall of everything, except for music.

Why only that?

Because the She'Har never had music, he realized. The She'Har elders couldn't hear at all. Music had always been foreign to them.

The loshti had improved the way his brain stored information, but however it did that, it had done nothing for his ability to recall music. The perfect, crystal clarity of everything else made his knowledge of music seem dim and obscure.

They had given him the knowledge of ages and stolen his very heart. Glancing up at Kate he saw her still watching him intently, and the frustration made him want to cry.

"I don't know what you're thinking, Daniel, but forget whatever it is and just play for *me*," she told him earnestly.

That's it! He blinked, looking at her with sudden hope. "I'll try. Don't say anything, just let me play. No matter how it sounds."

She nodded and he closed his eyes.

Remembering that day on the hill didn't help, it was too bright, too clear. Instead he attempted to think of nothing at all. Beneath everything else, his feelings still resided, quietly smothered by a mountain of knowledge, information, and recollection. He held on to the *feeling* of that spring day and tried to block out all the actual memories of it, and at the same time, he tried to play without remembering all the minutia that surrounded his playing.

His finger plucked a string, letting a single note fill the air. He focused on that note, a single pure thing that existed outside of himself. When it began to die away he picked another note and listened to it, ignoring everything else.

Something was stirring within him. Something hazy and indistinct, yet still powerful. More notes followed, simple and innocent, as though a child had picked up his cittern and was experimenting with the pure joy of making sounds.

He was no child, however, and his fingers knew more, his *heart* knew more. He found himself strumming chords and then a melody formed. He almost stumbled a few times as memories intruded, making his fingers trip over the strings, but as he relaxed and kept his mind blank his hands found their rhythm.

The air in the room became taut with emotion as his soul tore free from the chains his brain had woven around it. His skin felt hot, and sweat began to bead on his brow, soon his entire body was damp. It was as though his hands had taken on a life of their own and were playing with a desperation he hadn't suspected existed.

The music triggered new memories, but if he let them take the forefront, his hands would begin to trip up again, so he fought to keep his mind clear. But clarity did not equal empty. The music pouring from the cittern carried with it all the things that had been hiding within him; sorrow, sadness, anger, rage, and overlaying everything else, horror. Horror at what he had become, what he had done, what he was doing, and most of all, horror at what he intended to do. Guilt threaded through it as well, along with the fear and uncertainty that hid from his waking mind.

Did the end justify the means?

No, that wasn't the right question. The end he had planned couldn't justify anything. Did the terrible injustices of the past justify destroying the present and possibly the future as well?

He played until he was empty, and the notes drew out, dying away into near silence, and then he filled the emptiness with his desire. For a moment he saw Eldin and Inara playing once more, and his fingers faltered, but he did not stop. Taking a deep breath, he fought on and refused to let the images in his head throw him off. Thoughts of his children filled his heart and behind it all, there was a hint of coppery red hair and sparkling eyes.

The music rose like a phoenix from the ashes of his desolate soul and despite everything that had come before it still bore a hint of hope.

And then it ended.

Opening his eyes, he found Kate staring at him. Her cheeks were damp, but the tears had already stopped. He felt ashamed, both of the music and what it had represented, and the fact that he had inflicted his suffering upon her, "I'm sorry."

"No! Don't be, not for that," she told him instantly. Her hand was on his cheek, "Don't be sorry. That's the first time I've seen the true Daniel in a long while."

He gave her a weak smile, "You aren't dancing a jig."

"Who could dance to that!? It was as if you ripped my heart out and set fire to it. I wouldn't know where to begin!" Pushing the instrument out of his lap she put her arms around him. "But it was beautiful, Daniel, and the ending felt as though the sun had come out from behind the clouds after a storm."

"The storm is yet to come, Cat, and I'm not sure there will be anything left of me for the sun to shine upon once it has passed."

She squeezed him tighter, "Don't be so gloomy. We are both coming through this, together until the end. History can judge the rest."

"History will not look kindly on me. The best I can hope for is that somehow it will forget me."

"Shut up, idiot," she said gently. "Keep playing like that and you will find a way to make the hope at the end of that song true for both of us."

Tyrion knew that was impossible, but he kept his silence. *In two days we will take our next subjects from the Centyr.* There was no turning back, and no amount of music would change that.

A presence on the other side of the bedroom door made him aware that he hadn't activated the privacy screen around the room. Turning his attention to his magesight he discovered Sarah, Layla and Blake were standing outside, leaning close to listen through the door. Standing up he crossed the distance and threw it open before they could retreat.

Their faces were an open book. Sarah appeared to be in shock, Layla seemed as though she might be near tears, and Blake seemed happy for some reason.

"Did you need to talk to me?" asked Tyrion.

Sarah stepped back, embarrassed and shaking her head, but Blake answered, "Glad you're back."

"Why are we waiting?" complained Layla. "The longer we are here the greater the risk of discovery."

"I need to do some investigating," said Tyrion, repeating his response from earlier. "And you know better than anyone that no one could find us behind your concealment."

"Maybe this looks easy to you, but it gets tiring after a while," she replied.

"Please, Layla, let him have some peace. The sooner he can focus, the sooner we can find our targets and be away from here," soothed Emma.

Tyrion linked hands with his daughter and let his awareness drift downward as he listened to the earth. His self expanded, and Emma felt the transition as he shifted from human to *other*. It was difficult to maintain the link with him, especially while she felt the urge to follow, but she kept her mind fully within the bounds of her own skull.

Minutes crept by but before an hour had passed he returned. Layla could see it in the change in his posture even before Emma let out a sigh of relief and released her father's hand. "Did you find whatever it was you were looking for?"

Tyrion blinked, still not entirely himself, "Yes. It's vast, and very close here."

"What is?" questioned the former warden.

"The blood of the earth," said Tyrion. "A sea of magma so vast it could drown this part of the world."

Layla frowned, "Mamga…?"

"Magma," corrected Emma.

She stared at the younger woman, "That still doesn't tell me what it is."

"Molten rock," explained Tyrion, "so hot it has become a fiery liquid. It's everywhere, if you go deep enough, but in some parts of the world it comes particularly close to the surface. According to the surveys of the ancients there was a super volcano here, but I needed to confirm it for myself."

"Now you're just making up words," said Layla with a combination of confusion and disgust. She held up a hand when he started to explain, "No, just tell me why you care. This place is miles from where the Centyr Grove begins. The land is too hard here for the She'Har elders. How does this super magma of yours help you?"

Emma stepped in, "It will make it easier to create a disaster to cover our abductions."

Tyrion shook his head, "No, it's too dangerous. We will have to make a storm instead. See for yourself." He reached out for Emma's hand.

Taking a deep breath, she linked herself with him and then let her own mind expand. Reaching down into the earth, she explored her new body and what she found would have amazed her, if she had still been capable of such a feeling. When she returned to herself she stared at her father, "How could such a thing exist?"

As her humanity returned Emma felt small and insignificant. With her special gift that was not a new feeling for her, but this time something new came with it—fear. She was keenly aware that they stood on a thin skin of earth that barely contained what was the geological equivalent of a massive bomb. She simply couldn't imagine what would happen if it were to be released.

"We should leave," said Emma. "It isn't safe here!"

"Relax," said Tyrion. "According to the ancients these things don't erupt often. It probably won't do anything for tens of thousands of years."

"Things?!" said Emma. "There are more than one? How are we alive? How is anyone alive?"

Her father smiled, "Because life endures, and while one of these going off might blacken the sky and kill off untold amounts of plants and animals, the world recovers."

"How many are there?" asked his daughter, struggling to suppress her fear.

"They knew of at least seven large ones," he told her, "scattered around the world." He glanced at Layla, "Come on. Let's find our targets. I've seen what I wanted to see here."

CHAPTER 22

The first place they chose to wait turned out to be a waste of time. By necessity they had to pick a place beyond the edge of the grove, and not within another grove since they didn't dare risk being near any of the elders when they made their move. For the portion of the Centyr Grove that they knew how to get to the only region remotely like that was the area with volcanic activity. The She'Har elders had chosen not to put down roots there, for obvious reasons.

Unfortunately, the area was also unlikely to draw many visitors. Scalding calderas and noxious gases plagued much of the region. They wasted an entire day waiting in one spot that was reasonably hospitable without ever sensing the presence of one of the She'Har.

The next day they scouted the region more thoroughly, until by chance they found a hot spring located within a grotto. The water was hot but pleasant, and it was shallow enough for wading. The entire thing was surrounded by thick brush and small trees, giving it an oasis-like feeling. It was much farther from the edge of the grove than the place they had waited at before, but there were already a number of the Centyr present when they found it.

Rather than try attacking them then and there, they left and returned in the small hours of the morning, before the sun had yet risen. An ambush would give them the best chance of success.

They were hoping for a small group. The day before they had detected only four or five relaxing in the spring, so they set their trap there, keeping their own numbers small to make hiding themselves easier.

Tyrion created one of his special cavities in the rocky ground beside the spring, enlisting the earth's assistance to make it undetectable to magesight. It wasn't the same as invisibility, but until he opened it and dropped their unsuspecting quarry into it with them they wouldn't be noticed. He waited there, with Bangor, Ryan, and Emma. As an extra precaution Layla, Jordan, and Brigid hid near the trail that lead into the grotto, using Layla's talent for invisibility.

If things went well, they wouldn't be needed. If they didn't, it would be their task to make certain that no one escaped to report what had happened. Needless to say, Brigid wasn't happy about being on reserve duty, but she did what she was told, after a certain amount of arguing.

It didn't help that they had to wait until midday before anyone appeared to enjoy a hot bath in the scenic spot.

Three men and two women came tumbling down when the ground opened beneath them. One of them was quick enough to react that she managed to create a spellweave to cushion their landing, but none of them could have expected the humans lying in wait for them.

Emma performed her role with surgical precision, identifying the males and drilling rapid-fire holes through their skulls before they could recover their bearings. Two of them were dead and the third just beginning to open his mouth in surprise when her final attack tore through his brain.

Over the course of the last few assaults it was a role that she had naturally fallen into. While Brigid was unabashedly lethal, she was not very discerning. Emma could pick her targets rapidly, and her lance-like attacks were precise.

Ryan watched without acting, ready to support her if necessary, or to assist his father if his own job proved to be too much for him. Bangor also held back. The Mordan mage was only to act if necessary. His job made him too valuable to risk in combat, and he wasn't especially skilled if it came to that anyway.

Tyrion's job was one perfectly suited to him, subduing the ones they would take captive. It was a task that frequently took brute force to accomplish, as well as the ability to restrain himself once the target was suppressed.

Tyrion swept the two women across the small rocky chamber with a broad stroke of power, slamming them against the wall with bruising force. His attack was anything but focused, it took the already dead bodies of the males along as well, not that they were capable of noticing anything now.

Stepping forward, he wrapped both of their throats in bands of force, choking them with calculated malice. It was enough that the women reacted instinctively, attempting to protect their ability to breathe rather than having time to think or strike back.

"Ryan," said Tyrion calmly, waving his hand at the woman to his left. His son immediately moved to assist, taking over her restraint and crushing her mind inward before she could attempt to spellweave.

Tyrion did the same with the one on the right, but he took it a step further. Trusting Ryan, he focused his attention and as soon as he had his target subdued he drove inward. The Centyr She'Har proved to be exceptionally resistant to his usual attempt at forcing a captive into unconsciousness. Despite his greater strength it was impossible to pin her mind down, it continually slipped away from his grasp. Instead of continuing the mental struggle he pinpointed the area he wanted and before she could gain the upper hand he cauterized it.

His victim slumped to the ground, twitching.

Turning back, he found Ryan struggling. His captive was beginning to turn the tables around. If it had been a normal fight, the young man would have had no trouble, but attempting to keep the woman alive put Ryan at a serious handicap. While he tried to keep her will trapped, she kept slipping past his assault and attempted to get into his mind.

"Wait," barked Tyrion, directing his command to Emma, who was already preparing to kill the She'Har woman to protect her brother. Stepping closer he slammed his fist into the woman's jaw, stunning her and allowing Ryan a moment to recover.

While she staggered, he took the opportunity to do the same thing he had done to the other, cauterizing the part of her brain that fed aythar to her seed-mind.

The fight was over.

Emma leaned over the two women, "What did you do to them?"

"It's part of what I've been working on," answered Tyrion. "I cauterized part of the speech center, that's what controls the flow of aythar to the seed-mind. She won't be able to spellweave now. It also disrupts their ability to talk."

Bangor chuckled, "An added bonus…"

Tyrion and both Emma and Ryan glared at the former warden. He closed his mouth and then Ryan resumed the conversation, ignoring the comment, "That's all you need to do?"

"That's the first thing," clarified Tyrion. "They can still sense and use aythar at this point, or they would, if they weren't in shock. Once we get them back I will finish by cauterizing another place to nullify their purely human abilities."

"Why didn't you do that part first?" asked Ryan.

"Can't," answered Tyrion, "The seed-mind starts causing all sorts of problems if it isn't deprived of aythar. Eventually it kills them, and quite painfully too." Glancing at Bangor he gave an order, "Take them back, and put them in stasis before you return."

The Mordan mage was sullen as he put a hand on each of the She'Har women's shoulders and promptly vanished.

"Father!" shouted Emma. Her warning ended the conversation as they all became aware that they were no longer alone. Twelve more She'Har had arrived while they were distracted and were now encircling their hiding place. They had already seen the end of the combat, and they wouldn't be taken by surprise.

Apparently more than one group had come to enjoy the hot springs.

"Shit!" swore Ryan.

Tyrion was already moving. Channeling his power downward, he leapt straight into the air as he shouted, "Shield yourselves!" He sailed skyward through the hole above them and landed several feet to one side. His jump had been carefully controlled to avoid sailing too high and making himself a target.

Despite his quick reaction their foes were already prepared for him; two glowing spellbeasts flew at him from either side. Others were heading into the hole after Ryan and Emma.

The magical constructs were four-legged and cat-like in form, and equipped with long claws and teeth, but they still couldn't penetrate Tyrion's enchanted body shield. His arm blades were out and slicing even as they reached him, but he couldn't prevent the sheer speed of their rush from bowling him over as he cut through them.

A long line of spellwoven power shot toward him with the speed of a striking snake, wrapping itself around his torso before he could recover. A split second later it was followed by several more. The She'Har had been ready for him.

Ryan started to come to his aid, but Emma caught his shoulder, her mind reaching for his as their skin made contact. They had practiced fighting while linked many times in the past, and he accepted the familiar contact instinctively.

They communicated on a level deeper than words, and in that timeless moment of adrenaline, Ryan realized he had been about to commit a terrible mistake. The other spellbeasts were already blocking his path, and he would be caught just as quickly as Tyrion had been.

Their eyes met, and their hearts beat once more before the world exploded around them. Emma sent the rock and stone that encased their small chamber flying outward in a stunning display of force. She was not the strongest of Tyrion's children, but her power was not to be dismissed lightly.

The flying stone shards and other debris might have killed the She'Har, but they were already prepared with spellwoven shields. The chaos and dust did serve to distract them however, as four different copies of Ryan raced out of the hole amidst the confusion.

Spotting the difference between an illusion and reality was something most survivors of the arena learned quickly, or else they didn't survive for long. For the children of the She'Har who faced them, the rush of combat made it difficult to react appropriately.

Two of the lines holding Tyrion vanished as their wielders tried to avoid the sudden appearance of Ryan's illusory clones. It wasn't quite enough to free him, because his arms were still tightly bound by two others, until the real Ryan cut through one of them.

The spellbeasts were on him immediately afterward, however. Ryan ignored them, knowing they likely couldn't penetrate his defenses, but their physical presence was a problem anyway. He was knocked to the ground and savaged fiercely.

Tyrion had cut his way free now and charged toward the She'Har closest to him. He almost made it before another spellbeast knocked him aside, and then his intended victim focused directly on him. A focused spellweave, shaped as a spear, caught him on the ground before he could recover his feet. Unable to dodge, the alien magic tore through his defense and impaled him, punching straight through his abdomen.

Three others had corralled Ryan and were close to taking him down when a gout of superheated steam rose from the nearby spring and blasted through the She'Har, neatly avoiding the area where Tyrion lay on the ground. It swept over Ryan who had already prepared an impromptu shield to keep the hot gas from entering his personal space. It also caught most of the She'Har.

Emma had hoped that their enemies hadn't prepared their shields to deflect gases, and she had been correct. Spellweaving was too slow to react to such an unexpected attack, and most of them screamed as the steam flash cooked their eyes and the outer layers of their skin. Four saved themselves by using raw aythar to direct the air around themselves.

The pain and loss of normal vision stunned the She'Har for a moment, but it wouldn't last long. Mages didn't need eyes to see, and adrenaline would probably enable some of them to resume their attacks within a moment, despite the physical agony. Of course, the four that had protected themselves were still perfectly able to fight, and they were redirecting their attention to the girl at the bottom of the pit.

Emma glared defiantly up at them, but her mind was blank as she searched for some solution. *Four still active, Father's down, Ryan struggling to escape the spellbeasts...,* her mind sorted through her options rapidly, but she couldn't see how she would save her brother and escape their opponents in time to make a difference.

And then five more She'Har appeared, running toward them to give support to their brethren.

Without thinking, Emma sent her aythar outward, ripping at the earth to create a wall between them and their new attackers. Tons of earth rose in a massive wave, but she knew immediately that she had made a terrible mistake; she had over-extended her power, leaving herself with nothing left. Her body was already trembling in reaction as her strength left her.

The surging earth made everyone pause for a moment, and Ryan found himself momentarily free of the attentions of the spellbeasts. Rolling to one side, he stood, but before he could do more, a spellwoven blast of focused power tore through the earthen wall. It was a wild shot, the sort that almost certainly should have missed, but in combat sometimes the worst luck was the only luck to be found. It tore through Ryan's enchanted shield as he unwittingly took to his feet in exactly the wrong place.

Emma felt his pain and shock through their link briefly before he collapsed. She saw his body topple, his left arm gone and blood pouring from both his shoulder and one side of his face. Her mouth was open, as if she might scream, but no sound emerged. One of the burned She'Har dropped into the pit and moved toward her, wrapped in a shield and holding a deadly looking sword of spellwoven aythar.

She tried to raise her power to defend herself, but nothing happened. She was empty, and her death was bearing down on her. Emma snarled in impotent fury, but deep down she was no longer sure if she cared.

A scream echoed from the direction of the She'Har's reinforcements, and Emma's antagonist paused, turning his head as he focused his attention for a moment on the area outside the pit.

Emma simply didn't care. Drawing again on her aythar, she focused what little strength she could summon into one hand, activated her tattoos and drove her enchanted hand through the She'Har's chest. Heat enveloped her wrist as her opponent died and Emma staggered, falling to her knees as he fell onto her, grasping weakly at her shoulders.

She shoved him aside, trying to disentangle herself. Some of the hot water from her earlier attack had gotten into the pit, turning the soil at the bottom into mud. Before she could rise another of the spellbeasts dropped down, crushing her into the muck. Her strength was returning, bit by bit, but it was all she could do to activate her defensive tattoos before it landed on her.

The claws on its massive, glowing paw failed to pierce her shield, so instead it pressed down, forcing her face beneath the surface of the mud.

She didn't have the strength or the will to fight anymore. She struggled weakly, mainly from panic, but her resolve was gone. *Ryan's dead.* The light vanished as her head went completely under. Her shield kept it out of her mouth and nose, but there was only a small amount of air between it and her skin. It wouldn't take long before she began to suffocate.

Relaxing her muscles, she gave in and decided to use her remaining time to watch what was going on above.

Tyrion was still conscious, but his wound was probably fatal. Ryan was gone. Emma could find no sign of him, other than the large splash of blood where he had fallen. *Did they take his body?* she wondered.

It didn't look as though they had the time to do anything as mundane as move a body. Brigid had arrived. The loincloth she had worn was gone, and she ran among the She'Har utterly unshielded. Blood had coated her from head to toe. Emma was sure if she had looked on her with her eyes, she would have been dyed in scarlet.

Brigid danced among her enemies heedless of their attacks. The enchanted chain whipped and wove around her as though it were possessed of a life of its own. It deflected, and generally destroyed, any spellweaving that came close to her, but that was not its primary purpose. When it wasn't busy defending its user, it was constantly flicking outward, making almost casual strikes at the She'Har who were now trying to escape her.

The first to face her were the lucky ones, Brigid killed those quickly. A light strike could easily remove an arm, a leg, or more likely, a head. The She'Har didn't recognize their peril immediately. They confidently attacked her from several sides at once, but with each failed assault another of them fell.

It almost appeared accidental at first, as though luck had blessed her during the course of defending herself, but it soon became apparent that that was anything but the case. Most of the spellbeasts were shredded as they came to the aid of their creators, and when there were only four of the She'Har left, they turned to flee.

Or rather, they tried.

Brigid killed one, and hamstrung the others in the space of a heartbeat. She could have removed their legs just as easily, but she chose to wound her remaining prey rather than end her pleasure too soon.

And she's been wide open the entire time, noted Emma, but she knew that the She'Har had never had a chance, not using spellweaving anyway. It was too slow, and weapons made purely of magic fell apart when they came into contact with the enchanted steel.

That was the advantage of the raw magic humans used. It was as quick as thought. Ordinarily the superior nature of spellweaving easily overcame that advantage, but Brigid's enchanted chain completely unbalanced the old equation.

The only person here who might have stood a chance against her would have been me, Emma realized. Her signature attack, a rapid-fire lance of pure force was the only thing that might have gotten past Brigid's chain. *And even that would be useless if she bothered to use her defensive shield.* She felt a moment's pride for her psychotic sister.

Emma's heartrate had increased dramatically during the fighting, but not from adrenaline. She was suffocating, and her heart was desperately trying to compensate for the lack of fresh air.

Brigid tormented her near helpless enemies now, making shallow slashes that left them bleeding without killing them. Oblivious to Emma's plight as she toyed with them, Brigid laughed as she sent bits of flesh flying. She had never been happier.

I guess I'm going to die anyway, thought Emma. The observation didn't bother her. She had already lost the one thing she had left to live for. Her heart fluttered like a bird's, completely unlike the slow thrumming of the earth beneath her.

Emma opened her mind. If she were going to die, she might as well do it right. Brigid would die too, but she knew her sister wouldn't mind if it meant that a far greater number of the She'Har would die as well.

This is for you, Ryan. And then Emma exploded outward, losing her humanity and becoming something far different.

There was no immediate physical sign. Her body continued to die, but it was a tiny thing compared to what she had become. Emma reached down and began unbinding the ties that held her molten rage at bay. She began, not where she had been, but on the side of her that would send her fury most directly against the Centyr Grove.

The ground jumped, making Brigid stumble and miss her latest strike. Her last plaything died instead of merely losing more skin. Seconds later a booming rumble found her ears, and she saw smoke rising in the distance, in the direction of the Centyr Grove.

Layla appeared, crouching over Ryan's unconscious form as she lost control of her invisibility. Jordan stood beside her, fear written on his face as he felt the earth lurch again. He released the man he had been dragging, and Tyrion slumped to the ground.

"Brigid!" shouted Layla. "We have to go!"

Brigid stared at them, struggling to make sense of the world as her bloodlust slowly faded. "Emma! We have to get her first." Leaping into the pit her chain made short work of the spellbeast holding her sister down in the mud. Pulling against the sucking force of the mud, Brigid lifted the other girl from the ground.

Emma's skin was grey, and she seemed to weigh far more than she should, but Brigid used her will to lift her sister up and out of the pit before settling her gently beside the others. She climbed out then, reaching out to join her hand with Jordan's to make it easier for him to teleport all of them together.

The ground shook once more, and a strange smell filled the air, a choking stench that made it difficult to draw breath.

"Wait," said a weak voice.

Everyone stared at Tyrion in confusion as they realized he was speaking.

"Not yet," he told them. "This is too soon."

"This place is coming apart," insisted Brigid urgently. She looked at Jordan, "Take us home."

Tyrion growled and waved a hand at Emma's body, "Move her and she's dead."

"She's still breathing, Tyrion," said Layla. "He's delirious," she told the others.

Jordan moved to obey, but Brigid was watching her father carefully. She knew better than to doubt him. "Wait," she commanded. "What do you think we should do, Father?"

"Let me try to stop this," he answered, struggling to find breath.

"He's dying," said Jordan bluntly. "I'm taking us back." He reached out to put his hand on Emma.

Brigid was not a woman to hesitate. She had already made her decision. The decision she always made. "Touch her and you die," she warned. "We let him do what he can." Razor sharp steel had already encircled the Mordan mage, hovering dangerously close to his throat.

"He can't do anything in the state he is in. If we wait, we'll all die," argued Layla.

The fist that caught her jaw came almost too quickly to see. Layla fell back, stunned.

Brigid loomed over her with the light of madness in her eyes. Her hair hung heavy with sweat and blood, and her skin was covered in dirt and gore. She pointed at her dying father, "You live to serve him. If he asks it, then we die. Would you rather die now, or wait a little while?" Even while her attention was fully occupied with the female warden, Brigid's chain never wavered as it hung close to Jordan's throat.

Layla nodded, casting her eyes downward in submission.

Brigid looked at Jordan, "Put a defensive shield around us while we wait." Then she addressed Layla again, "I see you already stopped most of the bleeding. Hide us while he works."

CHAPTER 23

Just a few more small shifts and the last restraints would be gone. Emma might have smiled if she could remember what facial expressions were, or represented.

All she had left was a goal. Accomplish that, and then she could rest. Vaguely she remembered pain and loss, but that was fading quickly. One more release and it would be over.

But part of her was refusing to respond.

Another presence was there. It was smaller, stranger, and less like her, but its will was strong. It held on to the key she needed, frustrating her attempt to destroy the things growing above her.

No, came its voice. *You must not do this, not yet, not now.*

The words were alien, but the meaning behind them reached her somehow. She ignored them, trying instead to envelop the thing that resisted her.

You'll kill many, but not all. Save your rage, and we can finish them entirely, but not now.

The concepts assailed her mind, forcing her to think in ways she wanted to forget. She wanted to reject them, but to do so she needed her own words. Her 'self' contracted as she searched for a means to express her denial.

Death! That was her answer, but she shrank further as she found the word.

Patience.

No.

Return with me, Emma.

She tried to argue, but she couldn't find the way. Annoyed, she continued to shrink, until finally she opened her mouth and screamed.

"Water," said Tyrion. Once again his mouth was impossibly dry. His body felt both hot and cold at once.

A hand lifted his head, and a cup was pressed to his lips. Greedily he slurped at the cool liquid within, but before he could get his fill the cup was withdrawn.

"More."

"Slowly," said Kate. "You can't have too much at once."

"I'm thirsty…"

"Your stomach can't handle it," she answered patiently.

"How long…?"

"They brought you back yesterday. We've had this conversation twice before already. You have a fever…," Kate's voice cut off abruptly. She sounded upset.

Tyrion turned his senses inward, examining his injury. What he found should have alarmed him, but he didn't have the energy for that. His heart beat rapidly, fluttering weakly in his chest. That and the thirst meant he had lost a lot of blood, but what shocked him was what he found in his belly.

Everything was inflamed. A large portion of his stomach was missing, and his intestines looked as though they had been torn apart and crudely put back together.

He knew from his time in the arena how serious gut wounds were. Even relatively minor injuries sometimes led to death days after a battle, but what he hadn't understood then was *why*. Thanks to the loshti he knew now, but the knowledge did little to comfort him.

The contents of his stomach and intestines had spilled into his abdominal cavity and the fever Kate mentioned was the product of a raging infection. Without expert treatment he would be dead within a day or two.

Even the best She'Har healers had a poor rate of success when dealing with a septic abdominal injury. Normally, if someone in the arena survived an injury like his, they could deal with it by immediately cleansing the peritoneal cavity.

He was already far beyond such strategies.

The ancient humans had once had chemicals that could have given him a decent chance, but the She'Har had only learned enough of their medical treatments to tease him with knowledge that there was a way—a way that was far beyond his reach.

"Emma?" he asked.

Kate brushed his hair back from his forehead, "She's with Ryan."

"He survived?"

She nodded, "Barely, but he is in worse shape than you, and his face…"

If the boy had made it this far, he had a decent chance, assuming his wound didn't go bad. On the outside he might look worse, but Tyrion guessed it was the opposite. "And Brigid?"

"She's just outside the door, with that wicked looking chain of hers," said Kate.

That made him want to chuckle, but all he got for his trouble was a painful choking cough. Kate watched him anxiously as a full minute passed before the agony subsided enough for him to talk again. "None of us would have made it back if it hadn't been for her and that chain."

"Layla told me she threatened to kill anyone who tried to move you."

"I'm surprised we aren't still there. I don't think I ever woke up to tell them we could leave," he observed.

"You would be, if Emma hadn't woken up and told them it was alright," explained Kate. "I'm worried about her, Daniel. We already knew about her problem, with Ryan, but now that he's hurt—I've never seen her like this."

"Like what?" he asked.

Kate paused, pursing her lips before continuing, "To be frank, like you. She's angry and intense. She won't leave his room, not even to sleep. We already have enough psychotic people around here."

"She'll be fine, if he lives."

"You say that, but I'm not so sure. I almost think it would have been better, for both of them, if he hadn't. He's disfigured. Half his jaw is gone, and his left arm, he'll never be the same. The only thing she cares about right now is him, and every time she looks at him you can almost see the anger building up inside her."

"Ahhh," said Tyrion, "to be young and in love."

Kate was aghast, "How can you joke like that? It's horrible."

He looked up at her with bloodshot eyes, "Because I'm just the same, only I'm disfigured on the inside. Now I get to watch my children turn into twisted younger versions of myself."

"And that makes you happy?"

"No, but I think if I started crying right now it might finish me," he told her honestly. "Is that Inara over there?" he asked, referring to the infant in her cradle nearby.

"She's sleeping."

"I want to hold her."

Kate protested, "You'll wake her. It took me forever to get her down."

"I don't think I'm going to get many more chances, Cat. Please…"

She stood up, turning her face away, but his magesight showed him the sudden tears that were filling her eyes. "Don't say that," she said, rebuking him, but she went to the cradle anyway. Kate knew as well as he did that he was probably right. Leaning over the crib, she gently lifted her daughter and brought her over to nestle her against his shoulder, inside the crook of his right arm.

By some miracle Inara hardly stirred, drifting back into deep slumber almost as soon as she was settled. Tyrion couldn't move much so he contented himself with watching her and listening to her tiny heartbeat. Inara's innocent breathing was the very antithesis of almost his entire life. *What have I ever done to deserve even this brief moment?* he wondered.

"You should rest too," suggested Kate after a while.

"I'm not sleepy," he countered. *Just dying.*

Kate frowned, "Then would you mind talking to Brigid?"

"About what?"

"First, tell her to stop glaring at everyone who tries to come in, but most importantly, she needs to take a bath."

That piqued his interest, "A bath?"

She sighed, "She came back covered in blood, and while she did rinse most of it off she still needs a proper bath. She won't leave the doorway, and she smells atrocious."

Pain seized him as he fought to keep his chest muscles relaxed. The urge to laugh was almost irresistible. When he had finally regained control he answered, "Actually I need to talk to her. I'll mention a bath while I'm at it."

"I don't think she should come in here until *after* the bath," said Kate firmly.

"I can't exactly get up and walk to her," said Tyrion. "I'll be quick."

She couldn't argue that point. Rising, Kate crossed the room and exited, wrinkling her nose when she passed the threshold. He couldn't hear what she said, but a moment later Brigid was standing by the bed, looking down on him and the sleeping infant.

"I knew you wouldn't die," she said bluntly.

The smell caught him a second later, assaulting his nose. The scent was like old meat, starting to turn bad. He couldn't see any visible stains on her, but her hair hung dull and heavy and there was no denying the olfactory evidence. It was made worse by the fact that there was no possible way for him to retreat.

"I will before long," he told her, "but I have too much to do to waste time. I need to speak with Emma."

"She won't leave Ryan."

"Tell her she doesn't have a choice," he said firmly. "She will want to hear this. After you speak to her take a bath, then I want you to get Jordan and bring him to me. I'll need some of the smaller stasis boxes as well."

Brigid stared at him for a moment, quietly processing his words. "Jordan is already in storage again, and I don't know where the boxes are kept."

"Emma should, and if she doesn't, she can ask Ryan. You'll have to get Jordan out of his box. I need him."

"Why?"

"I can't stay here. There are things that must be done."

His daughter became very still and didn't respond immediately. She looked like some strange statue as she considered her response. "Abby says you'll die if you move."

"I'm dying anyway. I have a day, maybe two. This can't wait."

Brigid stared at him with eyes that were like stone, "Then I should skip the bath."

Tyrion sighed, "No, you take the bath. Otherwise I won't be able to stand being near you. You'll have time. I need to talk to Emma. Send Abby and any of the others you see, but don't waste time hunting for them all, a few will do. Once you're clean, fetch Jordan and a couple of the boxes."

"How big should they be?"

He held up his hands, indicating something roughly a foot across. Brigid nodded, and without another word she left. Tyrion leaned his head back and relaxed. He took one more look at Inara before closing his eyes. He didn't feel like sleeping, but just breathing felt like a chore.

"Father."

A hand was on his shoulder, and Tyrion looked up to discover Emma leaning over him. She looked like a pale wraith. Her eyes were sunken and had dark circles beneath them. "You look terrible," he told her.

Her impatience was written large across her face, "You're dying." Unspoken was another implication, he would soon be irrelevant.

"That's likely," he admitted, "but I can't leave things unfinished. You have to be ready to take my place."

"I don't even know what you have been doing, or what you plan to do."

"Let me show you," he said, reaching for her hand.

She pulled away as though he might burn her. "It's too late. I'll find my own way."

"You'll fail," he said bluntly.

"You already have," she accused, covering her face with her palms. "Ryan is paying the price for that."

"Not yet. There's still time—if you help me. Otherwise his sacrifice will have been for nothing." He glared up at her with all the vehemence in his face that a dying man could muster. Everything that had happened was his responsibility, but he was defiant still. "Curse me if you wish, but you want what I want. I can see it in your eyes."

Emma's hands were balled into fists, but eventually she opened one and thrust it toward him, "Show me then, and I will judge, and if I think you wasted Ryan's future on pure folly I'll choke the life from you right here."

He took her hand and after a moment's resistance their minds linked. Emma no longer felt like the same person he had met mind to mind only a day ago. Gone was the warmth, replaced by a dark turmoil that echoed his own. She was practically his soul's twin now, filled with a towering rage. She hated him, almost, but not quite as much as she hated the She'Har.

Opening his memories, he showed her the weapon he would create. He felt her confusion at first, for the memories were not his own, but those of the She'Har, and the weapon was not easily identifiable as one at first. Her awe washed over him when she realized what it would do, followed by her recoil from the images of what it had done once before.

This is why you wouldn't tell us...

Mentally he agreed with her, *none of you would have gone along with this. You didn't hate them enough. Only you, Emma, only you have the hatred and conviction to see this done, if I fall.*

And Brigid, she corrected.

But she doesn't have the means, and she can't lead the others.

This will be the end of us, of all of us, she responded. *You can't mean to do this.*

Think! he commanded. *The stasis boxes, the women we've taken, let me show you the rest.* And he did, finally sharing the reason for the kidnappings, and revealing Ian's role. For a moment, he feared she would recoil, but her malicious glee surprised him.

Her evil had become greater than his own. Where Tyrion had lacked empathy, Emma did not, but instead her personal pain had been transmuted into a desire to inflict the same suffering on their enemies.

With this we can survive, she realized with sudden understanding. *Some of us, at least.*

He broke contact. Emma was staring down at him with a look of malign admiration.

"What do you need?" she asked.

"Keep my disappearance a secret. Brigid will return with what you need, assuming I don't die before I can create it. If I die, you will have to continue without me. No matter what, you must make sure the others don't try to find me, if I don't return."

"I can do that," she answered grimly. "But you're too sick. You can't do it."

"You were nearly helpless when you tried to destroy the Centyr Grove," he countered. "I don't need strength for this. Our special gift doesn't need power, we *become* the power we need."

When Kate returned, she found Emma in their bedroom, gently rocking Inara in her arms. The bed was empty. "Where is he?" she asked in alarm.

"Gone," answered Emma quietly.

"Where?! He's sick! Why would you let him get out of the bed?"

Emma's visage was serene, "He was dying anyway. I wouldn't dream of trying to stop him doing what he wants. Brigid's gone with him." Standing, she held out the infant, forestalling Kate's impending tirade.

Kate took Inara, and while furious, she still lowered her voice, "She's mad, as are you if you let him leave like this. What will we do if something happens?"

"The same as always," said Emma. "He's left me in charge. I need to talk to the others." And with that she left the room.

CHAPTER 24

The probabilities have collapsed, stated the First among the Illeniel Elders. *We face the worst outcome.*

Not the worst, said another. *The worst is complete annihilation.*

We should give up this course, said one of the youngest, an elder barely five hundred years old. *There is time to find another solution.*

You are naïve, objected the most senior.

Two millennia, that is a long time. We cannot be sure there is no other answer, continued the optimist.

Only to you, scoffed a new voice. *We might prosper for two thousand years, but it will be for naught once the enemy finds us again.*

Perhaps we can shift things once more. The better possibilities might resurface if we interfere.

And our last chance for survival might disappear completely, cautioned another.

Enough, said the First. *Our doom fell when Ceylendor was permitted to examine the humans. We must accept our fate.*

Even though we all perish? asked the youngest.

Our survival in the present means nothing, if our kind become completely extinct two thousand years from now, rebuked one of them.

We must protect his child.

Which, the one with our gift or the one who bears our wisdom?

They were supposed to be the same.

But they are not, we must deal with what is, not what might have been.

Can we not save both?

That is unclear, pronounced the First. *We can try, but the one bearing our wisdom must be the priority. We can more easily replace the one with the gift.*

There is little time.

Another has been prepared already. It sleeps. If the need arises we can insure it awakes at the proper time, stated the First.

Why were we not told before?

Because I hoped it would not be necessary, admitted the First.

Surely we could prepare our children in the same fashion?

Humanity's grudge will not allow it. We must fade from their memories, or they will destroy our hope, said the First with a hint of sadness.

Tyrion's belly felt as though it was on fire, yet he felt cold. Holding up one hand he stared at it. It was grotesquely swollen and he could not remember the last time he had felt the need to empty his bladder. His body was filling with fluid, and yet he still felt an unquenchable thirst.

My kidneys have shut down, and possibly my liver as well, he noted fuzzily. *Madness cannot be far behind.* The toxins in his blood would drown his sanity soon, not that he held much stock in the worth of sanity.

"I think this is the place," said Brigid. It had been a long time since she had been so near home. As a child, she had not thought to try and memorize the place, but she was reasonably certain that the small cottage on the sloping hillside above them was that of Helen and Alan Tennick, Tyrion's parents. "There are two people inside."

He tried to focus his magesight, to see them once more, but while he could recognize their aythar he couldn't see them clearly. "You found it," he affirmed.

Brigid looked troubled, "Do you wish to visit them?"

"No, that would only create more trouble," he said. "Take me beyond the house, up the hill to the right. Over the rise you'll find a sloping pasture looking down on another hill. You can see Kate's house from there. I'm sure you'll recognize it."

"Why there?"

Because it could be my grave! He wanted to shout it at her, but he didn't have the strength, and she wouldn't have understood the sentiment anyway. "The soil is better there," he announced, making a pretense of having some rationale. *But it's still too shallow for proper growth. Even the strong roots of the She'Har would take forever to grow deeply there.* "Thankfully, I don't have to worry about growing for long."

They proceeded as they had for most of the journey. Tyrion couldn't walk, his daughter kept him suspended lightly with her aythar. It was rather like reclining on a bed of air. Jordan teleported them in short steps, taking them as far as he could see, a few hundred yards at a time.

It was an odd way to travel, but it allowed them to cover ground faster than a man on a horse, or even someone flying on a dormon. The only downside was that teleporting so many times since leaving Albamarl had pushed Jordan to the brink of exhaustion.

Tyrion couldn't have cared less.

When they found the place he sought, it was much as he remembered. It hadn't been so many years after all, since he had sat there, playing his cittern and watching her home, hoping for a glimpse of coppery hair.

"Give it to me," he commanded, directing his words to Brigid.

They had brought little with them, so his meaning was clear. She unslung the instrument she had over her shoulder and handed it to him. The cittern he had crafted while being kept as a slave. It was still strung with the strings his mother had given him. He stroked the body with rough hands, appreciating its feel one last time.

Brigid used her power to shape the ground, making it rise gently so he could recline without straining before she lowered him.

A cool breeze stroked his cheek while he looked down the hill, watching the house Kate had grown up in. Smoke still rose from the chimney, presumably because Seth and their son still lived there. In his heart, he wished for nothing more than to go back in time, to be young again, with nothing but the hope of seeing Kate to motivate him.

His fingers brushed the strings, and the music she had wanted came to life. A lively tune that had nothing in common with the occasion, but his heart didn't care. He played for several minutes, his swollen fingers tripping clumsily through a song too intricate for them to reproduce.

Then he handed the cittern to Brigid, "I won't need this anymore."

"What should I do with it?" she asked.

"Give it to my mother. She might find a use for it," he answered. Motioning them back, he shielded his body against heat and then he ignited the grass around him. It was already dry and within seconds he had a lively blaze going. He burned everything within ten yards of where he lay, grass, brush, and a couple of unfortunate stubby trees. Once he was satisfied, he extinguished the flames.

Fire was easy, it fed itself, but controlling it was more effort. By the time he had put the fire out he was breathing heavily, a fact made worse by the smoke lingering in the air. A deep racking cough sent shivers of agony through his fevered body.

Brigid was thoughtful enough to send a strong gust of air once the flames were gone, clearing the air around him as she walked back. "What was the point of that?" she asked bluntly.

"Got rid of the weeds, and the ash will feed the soil," he told her, still gasping. "Can you break the ground up for me? Turn it over and work the ash and cinders into it."

She frowned, "It's mostly rock, once you get past the first few inches."

"I don't think I have the strength," he responded. "Just do the best you can."

Her face was a picture of disgust as she stared down at the feeble man who was her father, but it softened as her expression shifted from pity to something approaching a kind sadness. "I will do more than that—for you," she pronounced. "Watch."

Jordan teleported twenty yards back as he felt the aythar begin to twist around her. The intensity of it sent adrenaline shooting through his bloodstream. The woman in front of him radiated danger.

Stretching one arm skyward, Brigid lifted her father softly into the air. The chain that was always near her went with him, circling him protectively as she directed her attention and her power downward. The aythar that surrounded her hardened into adamantine scythes before dipping into the earth and ripping through it.

The shallow soil yielded immediately, and the small rocks and gravel beneath that surrendered almost as quickly. The heavier boulders resisted for a moment but her power would not relent. A series of snapping cracks shook the air as they shattered and broke.

Down her power went, ever further, tearing and breaking as she ground the very bedrock to gravel with her will. The earth rippled and churned around her, as though she stood in the center of a watery maelstrom, untouched amid the chaos.

Tyrion watched her as she worked, marveling at her smooth features as she bent the entirety of her power to the task. Brigid had always been strong, that had never been in doubt. She was one of the strongest of his children, but her focus had become harder than steel, unforgiving and perfect. Her face betrayed no hint of the strain that dealing with so much aythar at once must be putting on her. To look upon her one might think she was merely enjoying the afternoon sunshine, except for the destructive storm of rock and soil that roiled just beneath her feet.

Brigid smiled, and then the ground slowed before coming to a stop. A faint sheen of sweat covered her cheeks and brow, but if her labor had been tiresome, there was no other sign of it.

So beautiful, he thought as she lowered him to the shattered earth, *and without an ounce of mercy in her, the perfect child of my vengeance.*

"Jordan!" he called. When the Mordan mage had approached, he went on, "You cannot return to Albamarl."

The other man's brow furrowed, "What would you have me do then?"

"Come closer," said Tyrion softly, "I have one more task for you."

The mage leaned close and hardly twitched as a flicker of Tyrion's aythar ignited one armblade. It slipped through Jordan's chest and out between his shoulder blades as though his body were made of air. He fell across the older man as his life's blood spilled frantically from his chest, covering both men. His heart ruined, his eyes dimmed quickly as Tyrion said a few more words in his ears, "The She'Har grow best when they have a body to consume during their germination."

Brigid had a look of annoyance on her face as she looked down on them, "I'll have to walk back. Was that really necessary, Father?"

Tyrion fought the urge to laugh, not only would it have been painful, but the man across his chest already made it hard for him to breathe. "You're staying here," he wheezed. "I couldn't risk sending him back alone. Besides, I don't know that I have the strength for this. His body may well make the difference."

"How long will I have to remain?"

He sighed, "Most She'Har elders don't attempt to produce krytek for years after they take root, but this is small, so I hope to be able within a few weeks, but I can't be sure. You will have to be patient."

Brigid nodded, "How will I know when it is ready?"

"I think I will be able to communicate with you," he said, struggling to breathe. "If not, when the fruit falls to the ground. Be watchful, it won't remain in its casing for more than a day after that. You must seal them in the stasis boxes before that, otherwise…"

"Are they that dangerous?"

"They wiped out billions of people in a matter of weeks," he replied.

"It's trees we're after," she reminded him.

"The She'Har are resourceful. They may find a way—if given the chance. We must not allow that. That's why it's important that they are contained until the proper time. If I don't return, you must obey your sister."

Brigid wasn't happy with that answer, "Why?"

"Emma is the only one who can create the proper time. Obey her as you do me, in everything. Make certain that the others do so as well," he said firmly.

"From what you said, I may not be going back for some time. You think she can control them that long?"

Tyrion smiled, "You were the only one I worried about."

Brigid knelt on the ground beside him and looked at the dead man across his chest. Reaching out she dipped the first two fingers of her right hand in the warm blood and wiped them across her lips. "You were right to worry. There's only one thing I love more than blood, Father, and that is you." She kissed him lightly. "I love you more than the others, more than Kate or Lyralliantha.

"They love you for what you *were*. I love you for what you *are*, for your hatred and spite. You are something purer than they could ever understand."

He grimaced, tasting the blood she had left on his mouth, *she's completely insane, and brutally honest.* "I don't have much time…"

"You *will* return from this," insisted Brigid.

"If possible. My body is almost done. I'm not sure how that…," he began.

"You *will*!" she interrupted, "Or I'll cut your tree down and give it to grandmother for firewood."

Tyrion smiled, "That would…" His voice failed him. *That would probably be fitting.* There was no more time. Focusing his mind, he tried to relax as he sought the memory of the trees. The earth's drum beat solidly beneath him but he shut it out, he needed something different. He had to become again what he had once become by accident.

Roots and sunshine… The world faded away, replaced by a comforting darkness.

A knock at the door drew Helen Tennick away from the trousers she was trying to mend for what was probably the hundredth time. They had been patched so often they were composed more of patches than the original material. Alan worked hard, and it showed in his clothing.

The young woman at the door was both familiar and frightening. She had long dark hair and seemed clean, in a haphazard manner, as though she had taken a dip in a stream and simply let herself dry. She wore a simple tunic that reached to her thighs but there was no evidence of clothing beneath that. A dark smudge around her lips hinted at something feral and reminded Helen of a cat that had just eaten.

It was her eyes that frightened Helen. They were calm but hinted at horrors unspoken.

"Good afternoon, Grandmother," said the young woman, before she could ask.

Helen studied her face closely. Her vision was no longer sharp, but it was good enough, and she knew that voice. "Brigid? Is that you? I haven't seen you in so long."

"It's me," said the dark-haired teen. She stood several inches taller than her grandmother. "May I come in? I brought you something." Stretching out her hands she held the cittern in front of her.

"A cittern?" asked Helen in confusion. "Isn't that Daniel's? What happened? Oh, no! Don't tell me he…"

"It's alright," said Brigid soothingly. "He's fine. He's taking a long trip. I'm to wait here for him, and he thought you might take better care of it."

Helen's heart had jumped in her chest, and now it was beating fast. She breathed deeply to try to calm her nerves. "A trip? Of course, you can stay with us, but there isn't very much room. Are you sure he is alright?"

"Well, no one is ever sure of that…"

"Especially when it concerns him," finished Helen wryly. "Will you tell me what he is doing?"

Brigid shook her head, "I'm afraid not, Grandmother."

Helen didn't like the answer, but something cautioned her not to pursue a better one. She had given up on understanding her son years ago, and the strange air about Brigid made her wary. There was something seriously odd about the girl. It felt like being in the same room as a big cat, one that might turn on her at any moment.

She changed subjects, "How long do you think you'll be staying?"

"Several weeks at least," answered Brigid promptly, "possibly months."

"Oh my," said Helen. "What a pleasant surprise." In another life, it might have been. In truth though, she felt only dread.

CHAPTER 25

"No," said Emma firmly. "Your work is finished."

Ian smirked, "What does it matter? They can't even speak, surely you wouldn't begrudge me a little fun..."

Tyrion had been gone for months, seven to be exact. There had been no word from him or Brigid. Not long after he had left, she had taken it on herself to finish the task, collecting another five She'Har women from the Mordan Grove.

Ian had been disturbingly enthusiastic about his particular 'task', but all of their captives were now well into their pregnancies. Emma had cut off his access to the women as soon as she was certain they were all with child.

And yet he never missed an opportunity to beg for another visit to them.

"You're done," she growled. Despite her hatred for the She'Har she had never been able to reconcile her conscience to her brother's *job*. Emma had been tempted to kill him after seeing the bruises after his last visit.

"But surely..."

Emma snapped, and Ian fell back, screaming in pain and clutching at his thigh. Fresh blood trickled down his leg, staining the leg of his trousers. It had happened so quickly he hadn't had a chance to register her gathering her will.

"What the fuck!? You crazy bitch!" he shouted as he regained his capacity for words.

"One more word, Ian, just one more," said Emma softly. "The next hole will be through that empty head."

He clamped his mouth shut, but she could see him weighing his options, considering whether to raise a defensive shield. If he could get the shield up, it would be an ugly fight, but Emma almost relished the possibility.

She leaned closer, "You are laboring under a great misapprehension, brother *dear.* For some reason, you think I won't kill you, but what you have failed to appreciate, is that *you* are no longer needed. If I were you, I'd spend less time thinking about your dick and more time figuring out how to be useful."

He stared back at her, hatred burning in his eyes.

"Do it," she challenged. "Please, give me a reason."

Ian lowered his gaze.

"Not as stupid as I thought," said Emma with some disappointment. "Get back to work. I don't want to see you again for at least a week. Just the sight of you makes me sick. I might do something rash." She turned her back and continued on her way.

Her destination was the newly finished council hall. It stood halfway between the first buildings, Tyrion's home and their dormitory, and the new city construction. Just looking at it filled her with pride. It was Ryan's most beautiful project yet.

Built under his guidance, with the aid of several thousand slave-mages, it rose nearly a hundred feet into the air, but it was no tower. It was the heart of a fortress, composed of an uncountable number of enchanted blocks of granite. Someday, if Ryan's plan was ever finished it might serve as the heart of the city, though Emma doubted that day would ever come.

At its heart lay the council chamber, although it looked more like a throne room. It was a large circular area, elevated on one end to hold a massive stone chair, delicately carved. That was Violet's work; using her keen eye and her aythar to sculpt the hard stone as though it was a softer material like wood or marble.

They called it 'Tyrion's Seat', but it was Emma's place for now, and it loomed over the large round table in the center of the chamber.

The room was already full when she entered, except for two seats, Brigid's and Ian's. She smiled at Ian's empty chair. One advantage of having lost her temper was that she wouldn't have to look at him for a while.

"Good evening everyone," she addressed them as she entered.

Her siblings stood, nodding at her and issuing a mixed chorus of greetings, chief among them being 'First', for that was the title they had agreed upon. Ryan was 'Second', and the rest merely went by their names or a simple, 'brother' or 'sister'.

Ryan was silent, of course, with most of his jaw gone speech was impossible for him. He remained standing even after the others had resumed their places, waiting for her to take Tyrion's Seat before he sat. *Sister,* he announced mentally. He had become skilled at projecting his thoughts to multiple people at one time, since it was now his primary means of communicating.

The reminder of their relationship irritated her, as it always did. He never referred to her as 'Em' anymore and only rarely used her title as First.

"Second," she responded, nodding at his silent figure as she passed.

Once she was seated Ryan lowered himself into his own chair. Of the eleven siblings in the council room, he was the strangest to look upon. A shining silver mask covered his features, another gift from Violet, lovingly crafted to reflect the visage he had once possessed, but no amount of artistry could overcome the cold hard nature of even a beautiful metal. His left arm was metal now as well, black iron in contrast to the silver of his mask and chased with gold runework.

The arm was purely his own work and while it lacked the smooth beauty of the mask, it was smoothly jointed and entirely functional. He had taken his inspiration from Brigid's chain, enchanting it to resist any aythar but his own. It wasn't actually attached to his body of course, but a harness and the enchantment itself held it firmly in place. He had become skilled at using his aythar to manipulate it as though it were his own hand.

Some of the others had silently questioned his need to create the prosthetic limb, since as a mage it did nothing for him that his own power could not do already. Sufficient skill in magic could perform any function a hand might otherwise do. None of them had dared voice that opinion however, even the normally crass Ian had kept his thoughts to himself on the subject.

"We will start with reports on the various projects," announced Emma. She addressed Ryan first, "Second, what is the status of our building projects?"

His words echoed in their minds, *The repositories are complete, as you already know. We have sufficient space for all of Colne and Lincoln's citizens. The city is still a work in progress, other than this building and a few other key buildings. We have enough housing for most of the current slaves, but no more.*

"How many slaves are living there now?" she probed.

Slightly more than five thousand, he answered promptly. *You will need to ask Ian or Layla if you desire a more exact figure. We will have room for five hundred more in a week's time.*

"Where is Ian?" asked David. "He should be here."

"He isn't feeling well," she informed them.

246

"If Layla were here, she could update us," David reminded.

Emma frowned, "No. You know our rule. Only blood in this room."

"I think we can trust her," argued David, "Father did, and any rule that puts Ian in here and excludes her is obviously flawed."

"We have already been over this," she responded. "I don't intend to go over it again.

"But…"

Emma stood, "Do you think me unfit to lead?"

"No," answered David immediately, "But some decisions should be reconsidered."

"This is not a committee. Do you wish to challenge me?" Emma let her eyes roam across each person's face, "Does anyone?"

No one spoke, and most averted their gaze, but after a moment Abby raised her hand, "Sister, no one here disputes your right to lead us. But there are things we need to talk about." She kept her tone demur.

"Such as?" asked Emma.

"Father has not returned, neither has Brigid. We should examine the possibility that they may never return. We need an alternative plan," replied Abby calmly.

"We can't do this if he doesn't come back," agreed Blake.

Everyone stared expectantly at Emma, and she could see that the issue could no longer be avoided. "I think it is too soon for this, but very well. What alternatives would you propose?"

"We may have to figure out how to live with the She'Har, rather than destroying ourselves with a hopeless war," said Abby, jumping straight to the point. Several gasps could be heard. No one had expected her to be so direct, although many of them had been thinking the very same thing.

Emma fought to control her anger. Abby was probably the closest one to her, aside from Ryan, or had been. They had grown more distant over the past year. "That is not an option," she ground out between clenched teeth.

"Then what would you have us do if he doesn't come back?" asked Abby softly. "You know yourself that we need his weapon. There are too many for us to fight in any conventional sense, even if they are weakened first."

"If it comes to that, we will find another way," said Emma.

"How?" replied Abby directly. "We don't have the information he did. He had the loshti, we do not."

Emma had, in fact, been considering that very thing, but she didn't like being forced to reveal her hand so soon, "We can take the knowledge we need. The She'Har have many lore-wardens."

"We don't have any way to…," started Abby.

Emma cut her off, "We have Centyr mages and we've proven time and again that we can take their people without getting caught. We simply have to be more selective about our target."

"The Centyr slaves that you put in storage?" interjected Blake incredulously. "The ones that are too dangerous to allow them to mingle with the other slaves?"

"The same," she confirmed. "If we release only one, and work together to keep him or her closely controlled, I think it can be done safely."

"It's too dangerous…," began Blake, but Ryan lifted his iron hand to forestall his objection.

It is risky, but it can be done. We would only do this if Tyrion does not return, he said in his silent voice.

Sarah spoke up, "I would rather take a chance than give up, but we also have to worry about the schedule. In a few months the villagers are expecting to begin moving here. If we change our plan it will likely take us much longer to find a solution. What will the She'Har think when they notice that all the 'wild' humans have vanished?"

"We may have to change our timetable," said Emma, "but we have months before we need to consider these options. For now, we stick to the original plan. Tyrion may yet return."

Abby nodded her head in acceptance and the tension at the table eased. After a moment Emma went on, "We can return to this in a month, let's return to the matters at hand. How close are we to finishing the stasis boxes we need?"

Ashley and Anthony looked at one another, silently deciding which of them should answer, then Anthony spoke, "We are done. The slaves have already produced a surplus."

Emma raised one brow, "So soon? That is good news."

"Where should we focus our efforts next?" asked Ashley.

I could use your team's help with city construction, opined Ryan.

Emma nodded, "Very well. David, Ashley, and Anthony, you will join the city team. I would like to retain Violet, though. I need her assistance with smaller projects."

Something new? asked Ryan.

"A new weapon," said Emma. "Violet's metalworking artistry would be useful."

Violet shifted uncomfortably, "I would prefer to assist with the construction. My talents would be more useful there. Besides, Ryan is a better metalworker than I am."

"Your delicate touch and fine eye will be very helpful in this," declared Emma, her tone ending the discussion.

The rest of the meeting was routine and within half an hour they were finished. Emma dismissed them, but as they were leaving she called Abby back, "Stay. I would have a word with you in private."

Once the room had emptied Abby gave her a curious look, "Sister, what do you need?"

Emma didn't answer immediately. Rising from her chair, she smoothed her skirt gracefully before walking down the few short steps that elevated her seat above the table. She stopped when they were only a couple of feet apart. "The next time you have questions like that, come to me first." Her eyes were calm, but the tone was menacing.

Abby shrugged, "It seemed like a matter for everyone to discuss."

"So you could undermine me in front of the others?" snarled Emma.

"That was not my intention…"

"Don't play stupid with me Abbs! And don't for a minute make the mistake of thinking *I* am stupid. Test me again, and you'll regret it." Emma had lost her composure and there was fire in her eyes.

Abby held up her hands in a placating gesture, "We are on the same side, Em."

"We had better be," threatened Emma. "Next time, talk to me first. I like to be prepared fully before bringing something up with the others."

Abby nodded, but she wasn't done, "You've changed, Em. You're too angry. If you don't find some way to relax you're going to do yourself harm."

"My emotions are my own business," Emma said, rebuking her. "And don't even think of bringing Ryan into this."

"I wasn't," said Abby calmly. "He has already accepted what happened to him, but you bringing him up is telling. You have to let go of that and move on. You won't help him, or yourself, by becoming more bitter."

"I don't recall asking your opinion."

"Em, please...," began Abby.

"I'm not your friend any more Abigail. I'm not that person. I'm your superior, and I no longer have the luxury of having friends. It's time for you to leave."

Abby's face was a picture of sadness and compassion, "Emma, listen to me..."

"Get out," said Emma firmly. "Now."

Ryan sat at his desk, staring down at his arm that wasn't an arm.

Oh, it looked like an arm, but it was just dead metal. He was reminded of that by the fact that he could still feel his missing arm, his real arm. It wasn't there, of course, but he still felt it. His one good eye could confirm that, and his magesight definitely didn't show him anything where it had once been, but he could *feel it.*

And it hurt, almost constantly. At the moment it ached fiercely, as though the muscles had been kept tensed far too long. It was the mother of all charley horses.

Occasionally it got better, but it never vanished.

And that was just his arm.

His face didn't cause him pain, physically at least, but he couldn't bear to look at himself in a mirror. He had become used to blocking his magesight when it came to his own features. He didn't want to see what wasn't there anymore, or what was left either, for that matter.

Eating was a challenge, and drinking was worse. Without most of his jaw the mechanical aspects of keeping himself alive were more than embarrassing, they were humiliating, even when he was alone.

He survived solely because he was too stubborn to submit to his circumstances. He had always been focused, determined. He had derived pleasure from his work before, but now it was everything.

He had been grateful to Violet for the mask, but the arm was purely his own creation, and he was constantly improving it. He spent endless hours perfecting the joints, making them move smoothly, but that hadn't been enough. The metal was heavy, and smooth joints sometimes allowed it to move too freely and in ways that were unnatural.

The enchantments corrected most of those problems as well as endowing the artificial limb with its own strength. In the beginning he had been forced to maintain its position entirely with his own power and unwavering attention, but that was no longer necessary.

The combination of static enchantments and constant practice had allowed him to reach a point at which the prosthesis was almost as easy to control as his natural arm had once been. But it wasn't enough. If he was forced to wear pounds and pounds of heavy metal, it needed to be better than *almost* as good as his original limb.

He no longer strove to make it a better arm, now he sought to make it functional in ways his arm could never have been. Being large and composed of iron, it was an ideal medium to store power, and he could add far more enchantments to it than he ever could have done by tattooing the skin of a living arm.

It was a tool, and a weapon.

A knock at the door interrupted his thoughts. *Who could that be?* he wondered. He never had visitors, not this late, or for that matter, ever. He mingled with his family only during the course of his duties. Ryan had strongly discouraged his brothers and sisters from trying to be friendly, and they had taken the hint.

Only Emma had tried to get past his personal barriers, and she had finally given up months ago, much to his relief.

With a thought he lifted the mask to his face and settled it into place. The enchantment on it kept it in place and shielded the flesh beneath from scrutiny. The arm went on just as easily.

Crossing the room, he wished once more that he could speak. Speaking would have allowed him to question his visitor without opening the door. His privacy ward blocked mental communication, and he preferred to open the door than remove the barrier.

He swung the heavy wood aside to find Emma standing in the hall.

"May I come in?"

No.

"Too bad," she replied, slipping around him before he could block her path. Glancing back she added, "Close the door."

This is my room. I don't want visitors, he told her firmly.

"Who is in command here?" she asked suddenly.

You are.

"What is my title?"

First.

"And yours?" she continued.

Second, he answered.

"Then do as I say and shut the goddamn door," she concluded. "I need to speak with you, privately."

He did and then remained standing silently by it.

She watched him, overwhelmed by the feelings that rose in her heart whenever she saw his arm. The mask made it even worse, she couldn't simply avoid looking at the arm, for there was nothing but cold silver to fix her gaze on instead. He looked back, giving every impression of being the statue that he looked so much like.

"I have been told that I have become too angry, too distant. That I need to relax," she said at last.

This is true, he replied.

"What about you?"

I survive. My work is interesting, it sustains me.

Emma's jaw clenched, "And that is enough for you?"

He never moved, remaining as still as a pillar of stone. *It must be. I have accepted what is, something you would do well to consider.*

Her eyes lit with defiance, "No."

My arm will never grow back. You are being irrational.

"I don't give a fuck, and I don't give a damn about your stupid arm, or your face. You still have a body, a heart. The man I love is still there, in front of me. If you can accept being maimed then accepting my love should be easy." Her words were impassioned, but her eyes still dry. She had cried enough over the past months. She had no room left for sorrow.

That again? he responded, surprised. *We settled that long before this happened to me. You're still my sister.*

"How long do you think we'll live, Ryan? Do you think the world cares? We'll likely never live long enough for that to matter."

I care. I may be half a man, but I have principles.

"Do you love me?" she asked, her voice soft, vulnerable.

His right hand clenched, *Yes.*

"Then hold me."

Ryan's feet started to move on their own, but he restrained himself. *No.*

"That wasn't a request, *Second,*" said Emma. "It was an order." When he failed to respond, she added, "Don't make me tell you again."

He crossed the room in two long strides and crushed her against his chest.

"Oof," she said as the air went out of her. "Take that arm off, please."

I can't hug you very well with only one arm.

"I don't need it. I only need you," she said, burying her face against his neck.

A moment later a loud clank sounded as the arm fell to the floor. Emma looked up, but the mask was all she could see. "The mask too," she added.

Em, my face…

"I don't care!"

Ryan's hand trembled as he raised it to remove the metal that shielded his hideous visage from the world. What lay behind it was awful, but Emma could still see Ryan there, tears welling from his one good eye.

He saw the shiver of shock run through her when she looked on him, and he started to pull away. *Now you understand. This is all that's left.*

She held tightly to him, refusing to let go. "I want everything that's left, all of you. Now."

That's going too far, Em.

"Ask me if I care," she replied. Releasing him for a moment she pulled her dress over her head. It was all of one piece and when it was off there was nothing underneath. "Take off your pants."

It isn't that easy, he answered, hesitating.

255

"Do I have to order you?" she said, arching one brow.

No, I mean my arm. Give me a moment.

"Oh! Right. Let me help."

The next few minutes were awkward, clumsy, and frantic, but eventually the last obstacle was gone. Emma got what she wanted, and no orders were required.

CHAPTER 26

There weren't enough pillows. There were never enough pillows.

It was still dark, but Kate was awake. She couldn't get comfortable. Her belly was swollen with expectation, and no matter how she arranged herself in the bed she couldn't lie still. Of course, the kicking didn't help.

Her baby had no respect for the proper hours for sleeping.

Lyralliantha lay beside her, snoring so loudly it seemed to shake the foundations of the house. How such a delicate, graceful, and seemingly perfect face could issue such sounds was beyond Kate's comprehension.

She opened her eyes. Though it was dark, there was just enough light for her to see where her leg pillow had gone. Lyra had somehow wrestled it away while she was sleeping.

Kate watched her, jealous of her slumber. *She's so damn perfect, except for the snoring.* Lyra still looked as young as the day she had first seen her, while Kate was all too aware of her own aging. Her face was developing lines and the pregnancy had made her cheeks splotchy.

Lyra seemed to suffer none of that. Oh, she had had some morning sickness early on, but otherwise she weathered her pregnancy as though it were nothing unusual.

And she sleeps like a baby, thought Kate enviously. *I bet she won't even have stretch marks.*

At moments like that she wanted to hate the other woman, but she couldn't. Lyra was unfailingly kind to her.

Since Tyrion's disappearance the two of them had become almost inseparable.

A searing pain in her chest took Kate's breath away.

"Oh!" she exclaimed. That didn't feel normal. She had been having a lot of heartburn, but this was something new. A second wave followed, and she cried out despite herself.

The pain continued for several minutes while she tried to stifle her cries. Tears ran from her eyes and she kept hoping it would stop, but it didn't seem to be getting better.

Lyra's snoring stopped, "Kate?"

"Mmhmm," responded Kate in what was half an answer and half a moan.

"What's wrong? Is your leg cramping again?"

"No, it's my chest," said Kate with some difficulty. The pain, combined with the weight of the baby made it hard to breathe.

Lyra was sitting up now. Placing one hand over Kate's chest, she closed her eyes and concentrated, looking for anything amiss within her friend. "Your stomach is spilling acid into the tube that leads from your throat," she said after a moment.

Rising from the bed she returned a minute later carrying a pitcher of water and a wooden cup. "Drink," she ordered firmly.

Struggling to sit up, Kate did so. The water helped a bit, but not nearly enough. Then the pain began to fade. "Did you do something?" she asked.

"After the water passed I blocked the opening to your stomach. I don't think it's good to leave it that way, though it should help temporarily," answered Lyralliantha. Raising her hand, she created a globe of soft light in the air above them. Her features were marked with concern.

"Is that all that's wrong?"

Lyra wasn't sure how to answer. Kate's liver was swollen, and there were several tiny clots within the veins that fed from it. *And if I am seeing those, what else am I not seeing?* she wondered. Silently she worked to dissolve the clots she had found, but she feared that much more might be wrong. "I think so," she lied to avoid alarming her friend. She had learned much from her time among humans over the past few years. "You need sleep."

"I can't," complained Kate.

"Let me help," said Lyra softly.

"Wait, let me change positions. I don't want to wake up sore from lying in the bed funny."

"Of course."

A second later she added softly, "Can I have the extra pillow back?"

"Sure."

Kate arranged herself carefully on her side, using the pillow to support one leg. "Alright."

Lyra leaned over and kissed her softly on the cheek as she began to manipulate Kate's aythar, sending her gently into a deep slumber. She sat watching her for several minutes after that, wondering at the fate that had conspired to bring her to the place she was now in her life.

She couldn't imagine anything different. Her life had been empty before, cold and dark. Her heart swelled as she stared at her friend. *I couldn't bear to lose her.* That thought brought a wave of fear, making her heart clench.

A pressing need broke her train of thought. Sitting up put the weight of her own child directly on her bladder. With a sigh, Lyra got up and went to relieve herself.

The next day Kate felt somewhat better, but she couldn't shake the lingering malaise that had been affecting her over the past week. Her head was pounding, but she had learned to live with the headaches. She didn't remember her last two pregnancies being so difficult.

The knife she was holding slipped, and she nearly cut herself. Putting it down she shook her hands, trying to ease the numbness and tingling in them.

Lyra noticed immediately, "Your hands again? Let me have the carrots. We can trade jobs."

Kate looked at the She'Har woman and struggled to contain her tears. Nodding she moved to the other table and began working the dough that would make the crusts for the meat pies later in the day.

Ashley passed by the kitchen doorway, heading who knew where.

"Can you give us a hand?" called Kate.

The younger woman hardly paused, "Sorry, can't. Emma doesn't like to be kept waiting."

Kate ground her teeth together. They hardly spoke to her anymore, and no one listened, now that Daniel was gone. She was irrelevant. *Daniel, where are you? Are you even alive?* The thought was enough to ruin her self-control and tears of frustration, sorrow, and self-pity began to spill down her cheeks.

"Oh, Kate," said Lyralliantha, moving closer and embracing her. "It will be alright."

She didn't answer. In her heart, she knew the truth. *It will never be alright.*

"How can it be so big?" asked Alan Tennick, glancing at his granddaughter.

"Magic," said Brigid, running her fingers through Gwenny's soft fur. Over the past months she had inexplicably formed a close bond with the Tennick's herding dog.

"It must be over fifty feet tall now," observed Alan. "I still don't understand why Daniel planted it."

That was the story she had given them when they inevitably noticed the rapidly growing sapling in the northern pasture. "It is supposed to bear a fruit with special powers," she said, repeating her standard answer.

"It certainly doesn't look like any fruit tree I've ever seen," said the older man. "It looks like an elm, but the leaves aren't right."

Gwenny barked running forward to sniff at something on the ground. There was a small round object there and with her magesight Brigid could see something moving within it.

"Gwenny, no!" she shouted as the dog started to pick it up with her mouth. Moving forward quickly she shooed the canine away from what must be the krytek fruit.

A crack had already formed in the outer skin.

"Take her home, Grandfather," said Brigid.

"What's wrong?"

"The fruit has fallen. I don't want Gwenny to damage it. I'll see if there are anymore."

He narrowed his eyes suspiciously. "It sounded more like you were afraid for Gwenny. That thing is dangerous, isn't it?"

She ignored his question, "Take her home."

"There wasn't anything on the branches yesterday. How can there be fruit on the ground already?" he went on.

Brigid looked up slowly at him. She had worked hard to seem normal over the past months and while she hadn't fully succeeded she had at least made Alan and Helen comfortable with her presence. The expression on her face now was different.

Alan stared into the dark madness and felt his heart grow cold with fear. "Come on, Gwenny," he called to the dog, and without another word, he left.

Brigid brought out the two boxes she carried with her whenever she visited the tree and carefully slipped the fruit into one of them. Then she began searching the area. She found two more. Luckily they were small enough that she could fit both into the other stasis box. She relaxed only when she was sure that the dangerous fruit was secure.

Placing her hand against Tyrion's rough bark, she sent her thoughts outward, *Father, I have them.*

She had tried talking to him on many occasions, without much success. She felt a sense of recognition, perhaps an acknowledgement, but nothing more.

You can return now, she told him.

There was no answer.

CHAPTER 27

Tyrion drifted, at peace.

The world passed by, light and dark, sunshine and moonlight, while he dreamed of many things. His task was done, but he no longer felt good about it.

Sheer determination had lent him the focus to stay with the task, but over the months that passed like days he had discovered a new contentment. Something he had never really had in his previous life.

He daydreamed about his childhood, recounting the events of his life to himself, but there was no longer an urgency to the stories—or regret. Things happened, but the pain was something he had created himself. Blaming others was pointless.

He still felt the emotions, but they were no longer the same. Love, that was there, and sadness too, but the burning rage had died. Trees had no need for such feelings.

The sun and rain were enough, and he had an endless wealth of knowledge to study and contemplate.

For the barest instant, he heard Brigid's plea for him to return, but she was gone before it registered. *How silly,* he thought, *why would I want to give this up?*

The wind stroked his limbs, and he dreamed. Occasionally, he worried about what he had done, but whatever the result it hardly mattered. His gift to his past self would scour the world, but it would not touch him.

He didn't like that thought, but there was nothing to be done for it now. Returning was out of the question. Only pain awaited him if he became human again.

The sun felt good, and when it passed the rain was a balm for his soul.

Night had already fallen as everyone gathered in Tyrion's dining hall for the evening meal. Emma sat at the head of the table with Ryan to her right. Kate and Lyra sat opposite one another at the other end, while the rest of Tyrion's children spread out along either side. There were more than enough seats now and half of them were unoccupied, since the table had been built with guests in mind.

No one spoke for a minute when Brigid walked in and seated herself near the middle—and, although dinner had not started yet, she casually took a large bun from a platter in the center of the table, stuffing it into her mouth.

She gave no greeting to anyone, or any other sign that she thought her absence of many months was unusual.

Silence ruled as every ongoing conversation stopped abruptly. Faces ranged back and forth, as everyone glanced first at Brigid, and then at Emma or Kate.

"Did you get it?!" said Emma.

Simultaneously Kate blurted out, "Is he alive?"

"Mmmhmblerga," mumbled Brigid around a mouthful of fresh bread.

"What?!" asked Emma, raising her voice in annoyance.

Kate was already on her feet, however, "Where have you been? Where's Daniel?"

Brigid held up a hand to forestall them before stealing Blake's cup from where it sat in front of him. Swallowing and chewing she cleared her mouth, "I said, 'I'm starving'."

"Answer the question, Brigid!" ordered Emma.

"Whose question do I answer first?"

"Mine!" said both Kate and Emma at the same time.

Brigid glanced back and forth between the two, arching one brow. "Helen says it's rude to interrogate a traveler before you feed them."

Several of their siblings chuckled but neither Emma nor Kate found the answer amusing. Even Lyralliantha looked perplexed.

Brigid sighed and then glanced back and forth, "Yes and sort of."

Emma gave her a steely stare, "Please clarify that."

Brigid looked at her sister, "In answer to your question, yes I did get it." She addressed Kate next, "And he is alive, sort of."

Things got confusing after that as everyone began speaking at once, but Ryan broke through the chaotic din with a silent shout, *This is not the place. There are too many ears here.*

The reminder worked and the room got quiet quickly. Within minutes Emma and Tyrion's other adult children had left, taking Brigid with them, presumably to the more secure council chamber.

Kate and Lyra were left sitting alone at the table.

Kate's knuckles were white as she gripped the table edge in front of her. Lyra put a hand on her shoulder, "You need to stay calm. It won't do you or your baby any good if you let this upset you."

"You're alright with this?" Kate asked her in astonishment.

"He has been gone a long time," said Lyra. "Another hour or two is unlikely to make a difference. We should eat now." She ran her hand over her round belly to emphasize the point.

"I'm starving but I get full after two or three bites," complained Kate. "This anxiousness isn't helping either."

"Best to eat now," advised Lyra. "It may be more than anxiety once we learn what Brigid has to tell."

"That isn't helping!" declared Kate.

"It appears we won't have to worry about alternative plans after all," said Anthony. Brigid had finished sharing her information, though it took them more than an hour to pry it all out of her. She was remarkably reticent. "You're sure you know how to handle them?" he asked.

Emma nodded, "Father gave me very careful instructions."

"They sound incredibly dangerous," observed Abby.

"They are," agreed Emma. "One mistake and we're all dead, but we have a place prepared that should contain them if the worst should occur."

"Nothing is foolproof," said Abby.

"If it goes wrong they only have to be contained for a few months before they die on their own. They can't survive long without feeding," responded Emma. "It's only myself at risk once we get them in there."

"It shouldn't be you," suggested Violet.

"Why?"

"No one else can do what you do, Emma," said her sister. "Trust someone else to handle this. We can afford to lose one of us, but you're unique and we'll need your talents for the other part of his plan."

I will do it, offered Ryan. *I designed the containment chamber, and I'm crafting the protective gear. No one understands the risks better than I do.*

"No," said Emma.

I also have less to lose, he continued, holding up his metal arm.

"You're the only one who might salvage things afterward if there's a mistake," argued Emma. "It won't be you. Besides, that arm is a liability. Aythar makes them more active."

"Let me," said Blake with a half-smile. "There's nothing special about me."

"Ian would be better," suggested Sarah. "No one would miss him."

"Hey!" exclaimed Ian.

"That isn't fair, Sarah," said Ashley, breaking in. "Ian has feelings too. Besides, he's too stupid. He's bound to get himself killed."

"All the more reason to let him," retorted Sarah.

"You can all go fuck yourselves!" shouted Ian, standing and heading for the door. "I don't have to take this shit."

"That was hardly wise," said Abby after he had gone.

"It was true," said Sarah bluntly. "Would you miss him?"

Abby's mouth compressed into a firm line, but she didn't disagree.

"If he betrays us, the She'Har will put an end to all of this," said Anthony.

"Who would he talk to?" said Sarah dismissively. "The She'Har wouldn't make any exceptions for him even if he ratted us out. He'd be the first to suffer."

Anthony shook his head, "You think he's smart enough to know that?"

"Not to worry," said Emma. She smiled, but it didn't reach her eyes. "I have him under close watch. If he even thinks about betraying us he'll have something sharp between his ribs before he even realizes what's happened."

She let that information sink in for a moment. They had to be wondering, *who else does she have under watch?* A little paranoia would do them good.

"Let's get to work," she added a moment later.

CHAPTER 28

"I already told you where he is," said Brigid.

"You did?" Kate didn't recall anything like that.

"What was the first thing I said when I sat down?"

Lyralliantha interrupted, "I don't think Kate's in the mood for games. Please speak plainly. This isn't good for her nerves—or mine."

But Kate was already thinking, "Helen!"

Her younger sister nodded, "I've been staying with them while I waited. Can you imagine how bored I've been?"

"But why didn't he come back with you?" asked Kate.

"He's a tree."

Kate stared at her in shock, but Lyra was more reactive, "What did you say?"

"You heard me."

"How is this possible?" wondered the silver-haired She'Har.

Brigid shrugged.

I knew he had some power that was unique, thought Lyralliantha, *but this?*

"He has to come back," said Kate. "He can do that, can't he?"

"He said he wasn't sure if he could," said Brigid. "Maybe he likes it. I warned him, though. If he doesn't come back, I'll set fire to him."

Lyra stared at her in horror. "That had better be one of your human jokes." Then she exclaimed, "Kate?!"

The world was spinning and turning dark around Kate. She tried to catch herself but the floor came up and struck her before she could recover.

Kate's body felt cold. Opening her eyes she struggled to focus. She seemed to be in bed, with Lyra sitting propped up on pillows beside her. "What happened?"

"You passed out," said Lyra.

Her hand found a goose egg on her forehead. "How bad is it?"

"Your belly broke your fall, otherwise that stone floor might have split your skull," Lyra informed her.

"The baby!"

"Not to worry, she's fine," added Lyra quickly.

"She?"

Lyra put a hand over her mouth, "Oops."

"You were supposed to keep it a secret," said Kate ruefully. She started to sit up but a wave of dizziness swept over her.

"Just relax," said Lyra, pushing her back gently. "You aren't well."

"What's wrong?"

"I'm not really sure. I know next to nothing about pregnancy, but I can tell your body is under a lot of stress," said Lyra. "I think you should rest."

Kate could see the worry in her eyes. It was well hidden, but it was definitely there. *And given how hard she is to read normally, that means it's probably pretty bad,* thought Kate. "What aren't you telling me?"

Lyralliantha sighed, "I don't know. I want to bring Koralltis here to look at you."

"Who?"

"He's a lore-warden, from the Prathion Grove."

"What would he know about pregnancy?" protested Kate.

"The lore-wardens have a lot of human knowledge preserved in their minds, and he has the most experience as a healer. If anyone can help you, it would be him."

"Daniel was very firm about keeping my pregnancy a secret," said Kate. "Isn't there anyone from the Illeniel Grove?"

"He is the best," argued Lyra. "I won't risk you with anyone less skilled and I trust him. I don't want to lose you, Kate."

Were those tears in her eyes? *Surely not,* thought Kate, but the evidence was right in front of her. Lyra was frightened, *for her.* "Alright," she agreed at last.

Remember, cautioned Ryan for the tenth time, *no magic. None.*

"Yeah," responded Blake nervously, "You said that before."

It bears repeating.

"Wouldn't this protect me?" asked Blake holding up his hand. It was covered in a finely wrought chainmail glove, as was the rest of his body. Unlike the mail that men had made in the distant past, to protect themselves from slashing weapons and the like, this mail was delicate and light.

I can't be certain, he answered. Ryan had spent countless hours crafting it, first making the thin wire and rolling it and then using his will to weld the tiny rings. It was made from pure iron so it was dark in color, the metal having begun to oxidize even as the wire had first begun to cool.

Another significant difference from normal mail, this was all of a piece, the shirt, legs, feet, and hands were all joined. A long slit in the back offered the only access to the suit. It made donning the protective garment slow and difficult and once Blake was inside Violet and Ryan worked together to close up the opening, putting new rings in place and welding them.

Blake's head was still bare, but once they were finished with the back they slipped a mail coif over his hair and began joining it to the rest at his shoulders. A glass plate covered his face. There were tiny rings embedded in the edges, placed there when it was created so that it could be knitted together with the mail that covered his head.

When they were done, there were no openings left. Nothing larger than the tiny rings that covered him should be able to reach his body. Dressing Blake and closing the back and neck had taken them almost two hours.

"What if I need to take a piss?" asked Blake with a smile, his voice slightly muffled by the glass plate.

I wouldn't advise it, said Ryan.

Blake frowned, "No, seriously. I need to pee."

"That's not coming off until you finish," said Violet. "If you can't hold it you'll have to pee inside it."

"Damnitt, now I really have to go," groaned Blake.

Try not to think about it, or take Violet's advice.

"It would be a lot stronger if you had enchanted it," noted Blake.

The magic might make things worse.

"But enchantments don't bleed magic the way normal spells do."

"These things originally ate She'Har elders. Enchantments and spellweaves are fundamentally the same. There's every chance they could eat through it, just like normal magic," explained Violet. "Best not to risk it."

"Then why don't they destroy the stasis box?" asked Blake.

"They aren't immune to magic. So long as they're contained, they're stuck in time, just like anything else in one," she replied.

"So when I open this box what will happen?" he asked.

Probably nothing, said Ryan. *It was still dormant when it went in. Just put it in with the food, close the lid and get out.*

"Alright."

Together Ryan and Violet lifted the heavy stone sarcophagus that contained the krytek's first 'meal'. It was too heavy for hands, of course, so they used their aythar to levitate it before pushing it through the doorway into the stone cell.

The room's dimensions were only five feet by eight and there was only one entrance. It had been carved from solid bedrock and they were currently more than a hundred feet underground. Ryan was taking no chances. Even the outer chamber was sealed. Should the worst happen, only the three of them would be at risk.

Lifting the lid from the sarcophagus Ryan stared down at the meal. A heavyset man lay within, unconscious. A temporary spell kept him asleep and blocked all sensory input from his nerves. There was no need for him to suffer. It was a small mercy. What they were doing was fundamentally evil, but they weren't cruel.

"Poor bastard," said Blake. "Why couldn't we just have used a sheep or something?"

According to what Emma was told, they only consume human flesh. When the She'Har redesigned them they silenced the traits that allowed them to devour She'Har trees and added traits that enabled them to devour humans, explained Ryan. *He said he would reactivate their original dietary habits, but he didn't have time to remove the new ones. Besides, the She'Har children are human in most respects and we need to eliminate them as well if we are to succeed.*

"I still feel bad for him."

At least he won't feel it. He's the only one that will be that lucky.

Violet turned away, "Please stop talking about it."

She walked back into the outer chamber and Ryan followed her. Once there they used their power to slide the large stone slab door that closed the inner chamber into place. Then Ryan took an additional precaution. Removing a heavy roll of lead that had been shaped into something akin to a rope, he wedged it into the crack around the door and melted it into place.

The inner chamber was sealed.

"If anything goes wrong we won't be able to get him out quickly," noted Violet.

If anything goes wrong the last thing we want to do is open that door, corrected Ryan.

Inside the chamber Blake held one of Brigid's stasis boxes in shaking hands. He shouldn't be nervous. "This will be easy," he told himself.

Placing the small box inside the sarcophagus he took a deep breath and twisted the knob on top, deactivating the stasis and unlocking the box. Removing the small lid he shook the contents out on top of the comatose man and held still.

A small round, brown skinned fruit rolled out. It came to rest on one side and he could see the crack in its skin. He jumped involuntarily when he saw a hint of movement. A tiny wasp-like creature was worming its way free.

"Fuck!" He moved to the other side and began shoving the heavy stone lid back into place, but it was heavy and difficult to move. For a split second he started to use his aythar before he caught himself. "Shit." He shoved harder, adrenaline and fear giving him the strength he needed as he threw his shoulder against the lid.

With a groan it slid into place.

Blake spent several minutes checking himself, looking up and down his body to see if anything had escaped before he got the lid into place. Then he searched the floor and walls around the stone coffin, making doubly sure.

Moving to the door he shouted, "Alright, it's done. Let me out!" He wasn't certain if they could hear him through the thick stone, though. *Should I project a mental voice,* he wondered. *How much aythar does that release? Does it matter now that the lid is on?*

Of course, they had already agreed ahead of time to wait an hour before opening the door, but fear and a new sense of claustrophobia had changed Blake's mind on that account. A faint rustling sound came from the coffin and he turned to face it.

"Stay calm, deep breaths," he told himself. "Everything is fine."

Then he heard a muffled scream. The krytek must have destroyed the magic that kept their subject comatose.

"This was a stupid idea," said Blake. "Why did I volunteer? I'm never going to do that again."

The screaming grew louder, punctuated by solid thumps as the man inside began to jerk, or perhaps beat against the sides of his stony prison.

Blake wanted to vomit. He felt lightheaded. *Am I hyperventilating?* He made a conscious effort to slow his breathing. "Everything's fine. The lid is closed.

Everything's fine, the lid is closed," he chanted to himself.

"How many could be in there?" he wondered. It hadn't been long, five, ten minutes at the most. Surely they couldn't reproduce that quickly.

And then he found out.

With a shuddering thump the lid jumped and slid partly to one side as the occupant threw his body against it from the inside. And then the little wasps began to pour out, flying directly at Blake.

"No, no, no, no, no!"

They should have tied it shut, or put straps around it. Hell, he should at least have sat on top. In that moment of clarity Blake knew that. But they hadn't considered it. The lid was too heavy for someone to lift ordinarily, and the man had been comatose. None of them had known he would awaken, and how strong fear might make their victim.

They were all over him, crawling up and down his chest, on his shoulders, and walking across the glass in front of his face. The krytek were small, as small as a wheat kernel, but still too large to get through the rings of his mail.

But what do I do next? Blake realized then that no matter how effective his protective gear was, they couldn't open the door, not like this, not with the krytek swarming everywhere. He was trapped.

The glass in front of his face fogged up as he panicked.

I have to kill them, or they won't let me out, but how? His breathing came in shallow rapid gasps, and then he realized the answer. *Fire.*

The bugs crawling on him were becoming still, as though resting. Perhaps they were frustrated at being unable to reach their next meal. But then Blake activated his shield tattoos, to protect himself from the flames he was about to create. His personal shield pressed the mail outward, inflating it almost like a balloon. At the same time the krytek became frenzied as their tiny bodies absorbed some of the magic.

And then the pressure from his shield caused the fine mesh to tear.

The chamber was filled with a bloom of fire, and many of the krytek were incinerated, even as they absorbed the aythar that fed the flame. But some survived, and a few found their way through the tear in Blake's protective suit. They ate through his enchanted shield and then he felt them burrowing under his skin.

His screams lasted almost ten minutes before his lungs were too damaged to hold air.

Ryan and Violet watched in horror from the other side of the stone wall. For once, having magesight was not a blessing.

"What do we do?!" asked Violet frantically.

Ryan had slid down, his back against the stone door and his masked face down. *Nothing. We can do nothing. He's already dead.*

"I can still hear him!"

He put his hands, metal and living, over his ears to block the sounds, *He's dead.*

Sometime later, when the sounds had stopped and their hearts had slowed, when frantic terror had congealed into cold dread, Violet spoke, "What do we do now? It's ruined. We can't open the door. Blake's dead and we have a room full of monsters we can't access."

Ryan didn't answer, but after a moment he pointed along the wall. Her eyes followed along until they spotted a small metal plate mounted innocuously there. It was an identical match to the one that had been built into the end of the coffin.

"Is that what I think it is?" she asked.

He nodded. It was an access plate, designed to mount the apparatus he had built to extract and seal the krytek, one by one, into small glass stasis boxes. He had shown Violet how it worked already, using the one on the stone sarcophagus to demonstrate. *That's plan B,* he said solemnly. *The entire inner chamber is just like the coffin, only larger.*

She stared at it for a minute, before addressing him again, her voice accusing, "You thought of everything, didn't you?"

No, he replied sadly, *or Blake would still be alive.*

Violet's anger swelled, and then died. She was just as much to blame as he was. She cried for a while, and Ryan wished he could do the same. Finally, when her chest stopped heaving, she laughed morbidly, "Sarah was right."

About what? asked Ryan.

"We should have used Ian."

CHAPTER 29

"Her body is reacting to the child," said Koralltis.

Lyralliantha frowned, "Reacting, how?"

"The defensive part of her body, what the ancient humans called the 'immune system', sees the child as foreign. It is attacking the proteins that spill into her blood stream. The end-result is excessive clotting, and it creates problems for her organs. If it continues it will eventually kill her," he explained.

"But the pregnancy is almost over," said Lyra. "She only has three or four weeks left. Surely she can last that long."

"Doubtful," replied the Prathion lore-warden. "There is also the chance that the reaction will become severe enough to damage the child directly."

"What can be done?" asked Kate nervously. Most of the conversation was being held in Barion, for her benefit, but the two She'Har kept switching to Erollith for parts of it, so she was confused.

"We must remove the child," said Koralltis directing his words to her.

"No!"

"You will die otherwise, and probably your child as well," he countered.

"If there's any chance of saving her I want to continue carrying her," said Kate with deadly conviction.

The lore-warden's expression softened, "You misunderstand me. I believe I can save both of you by taking her out now."

"What?"

"Your child is more developed than you realize. With the proper care I can keep her alive. The biggest risk is that she may not be able to breathe effectively, but with some preparation I can handle that as well," he answered.

Kate turned her eyes to Lyra, "Is this true?"

"It is beyond my experience, but if Koralltis says it can be done then it can. He would not lie," said Lyralliantha reassuringly.

"Please be aware," added the Prathion, "I can make no guarantee. There are still things that can go wrong, but I believe your offspring will have a much better chance of survival this way."

Kate looked back and forth between the two of them fearfully, a question in her eyes, but finally Lyra met her gaze and nodded. Firming up her resolve Kate made her decision, "Then do what you can."

The Prathion She'Har nodded, "I will return home to prepare. Give me two days and then I will take you to the Prathion Grove."

The next morning Lyralliantha was surprised when she found Ryan at the bedroom door. She gave him a patient look, waiting for whatever he had to say.

The First would like to speak with you.

"Emma could easily have found me herself," replied Lyra mildly confused.

Alone, added Ryan. *If you will follow me.* He gestured toward the hallway, his metal arm flexing with almost perfect precision.

Lyra frowned, noting Anthony's presence outside the door. "I'm rather busy tending to Kate right now. She needs complete bedrest. It would be far easier if she could simply come here."

It would be better if you came immediately, responded Ryan.

Lyra set the empty pitcher she held aside and turned back to the room, "I'll be back shortly, Kate." When she stepped into the hall Ryan led the way and Anthony fell into step behind her.

It felt odd. Nothing about their mannerisms was normal, but she kept that observation to herself. When they reached the council chamber Ryan opened the door and held it for her, but did not enter after her. She walked in to find Emma sitting on the elevated seat, looking down on her. The doors closed behind her. They were alone.

"They were acting rather strangely," said Lyra casually to Emma.

Emma's lips formed a flat line as she watched her. After a moment she spoke, "You brought a She'Har lore-warden to Albamarl yesterday."

Since it was a simple statement with no question, Lyralliantha didn't reply. She watched Emma with calm eyes. The young woman looked tense, or perhaps angry. But why?

"I'm waiting for an explanation," said Emma.

"Oh. Forgive me, I still miss some of the unspoken elements of human dialogue," apologized Lyra. "He came to examine Kate. She's having difficulty with her pregnancy."

"Why didn't you bring this to my attention first?"

"You've been very busy, nor did I think you had any experience in this regard. Do you think you could help her?" asked Lyra.

"The pregnancy is not my concern," said Emma flatly. "I was referring to you bringing a lore-warden here without my permission."

Lyra's expression was quizzical, "I was not aware I needed your permission."

Emma's eyes hardened, "You know very well that Tyrion did not want your pregnancy or Kate's to be made known to your people."

"Koralltis is of the Prathion Grove," Lyra informed her. "He is not 'my people'."

"That makes it even worse," said Emma, spitting the words out as though they were distasteful. "Explain yourself."

Lyralliantha's stomach fluttered, whether from the baby moving or as a reaction to the tension in the room, she wasn't sure. The young woman in front of her felt dangerous. The aura of aythar around her was practically sputtering with her agitation. "Kate is in trouble. Her pregnancy is killing her. I sought Koralltis' advice because he is the most skillful healer among any of the She'Har groves. Was I wrong to do so?"

"You have endangered everything we are working for."

Lyra frowned, "I do not even know *what* you are doing. How could I know that?"

Emma stood, increasing her height advantage even more, "You know that Tyrion's intentions are antithetical to the She'Har. For reasons I still do not understand he trusted you, but I have serious doubts in that regard. Do not give me more."

"The Illeniel Grove, *my people*," stressed Lyralliantha, "have allied themselves with him. I have been told to give him any aid necessary. Furthermore, he is my kianthi, even if that were not the case, my loyalty to him comes first for me."

"You have already said that Koralltis is of the Prathion Grove," noted Emma angrily. "He cannot be trusted."

"He has never done me a disservice before," said Lyra, "and *his* people are allied with the Illeniel Grove. He would do nothing to harm us, unless he had good reason."

"If he were to learn too much, he might have such a reason," said Emma. "You will not invite him here again."

"He already plans to come back in a few days," said Lyralliantha.

"Then you need to discourage him from doing so," ordered Emma.

"Do you not care what happens to Kate, or her child?" challenged Lyra.

"That is not my concern," said Emma coldly.

"It is Tyrion's concern," she countered.

"*He* is not here. I am!" said Emma, her voice rising. "If you care about *your* child, you would be wise to take that into account."

A flush came to Lyralliantha's cheeks as the threat registered. A number of arguments rose to her mind but she held her tongue. Butting heads with Emma would accomplish nothing and might provoke the woman to violence. She felt a coldness in the pit of her stomach, a sensation that was unusual for her. Fear. In the past she had had little to provoke such a feeling, but now she had things she did not want to lose, Kate, her baby, *her family*.

Lowering her eyes, she answered submissively, "I will make certain he does not return. Is there anything else you wish of me?"

Emma stared at her, "That will suffice for now."

"Am I permitted to leave then? Kate needs me."

"You may leave," said Emma dismissively, but before the She'Har woman could reach the door she spoke again, "Lyra…"

"If you ever betray us, if I even *think* you have betrayed us, I'll make sure you die first. Do you understand me?"

Lyralliantha didn't answer, merely nodding faintly and continuing on her way. *I have been threatened before, and he was much better at it than you are.*

CHAPTER 30

Kate hadn't slept properly in days. If someone had asked her, she'd have said that she hadn't slept at all, but apparently that wasn't entirely true. The hand shaking her shoulder was unexpected.

"Mmmm, what?" she asked groggily.

"Wake up, Kate. We have to go," said Lyra urgently.

A sharp pain in her side woke her up more thoroughly than any amount of shaking would have. Gritting her teeth, she answered, "Go where?"

"I'm taking you to Koralltis."

"It's the middle of the night. Can't it wait until morning?" Kate's leg was cramping, and she was all too aware of her bladder now that she was awake. *I'll never get back to sleep now.*

A hand stroked her forehead, "No, it can't. Emma has decided that I'm a traitor for bringing a lore-warden here. She won't let him come again, and she won't let you leave to see him. We have to sneak out."

Kate tried to take a deep breath and had to settle for a shallow one. "We can go tomorrow. If she objects, I'll tell her that's just too bad."

"You underestimate her resolve," said Lyra. "She will kill me if she thinks we are endangering her secret plan. I don't know if that extends to you as well, but if you don't get help you'll die anyway."

It sounded ridiculous to Kate's ears, but she could hear the seriousness in Lyra's tone. The She'Har woman truly believed their lives were at risk. Her first instinct was to tell her not to bother then. Why should Lyra endanger herself and her baby? But Kate was carrying her own child, and that shifted her priorities, even above the wellbeing of her friend. She felt selfish as she replied, "Can you get us out unseen?"

"Possibly." Lyra had no real idea, but she doubted the Illeniel Elders had planned for her to die. Her own prescience was narrowly defined and didn't extend far enough to tell her, but she felt that the time had come. Somehow it would work out. "Let me help you up."

Standing was a chore. Dressing was a nightmare, but Lyra was extremely patient. Twenty minutes later they were almost ready, except for one thing. "I have to pee," said Kate.

The privies were out of the question, and the chamber pot was an extreme challenge in her condition, but Lyra solved the problem by creating a spellwoven chair that held the pot beneath her while she sat.

"Are you ready now?" asked Lyra.

"Until I need to go again in a few minutes," said Kate, attempting to put some humor in her tone. Lyra missed it.

"I'm having similar problems," she replied, "but we just have to make it to the Grove."

That was at least a half an hour walk, *if* they were unencumbered. Unencumbered was not an adjective that Kate would apply to either of them anymore, whether their hands were empty or not. Just the thought of that walk made her want to cry with frustration. Her legs were swollen to the point that her skin felt as if it might split. Putting on a confident air she didn't feel she answered, "We had better get started then."

They encountered their first problem as soon as they reached the front door.

"What about the guards on the wall?" asked Kate before they stepped outside.

"We walk past them," said Lyra.

"Won't they report us?"

"Maybe not until morning," suggested Lyra. "We aren't outsiders after all."

It was a valid point, and Kate was still considering it when a voice behind her nearly made her jump out of her skin. "They have orders to stop you if you try to leave."

"Layla!" yelped Kate. "Don't do that!"

The former warden had been invisible to them until a moment before. The expression on her face was far from humorous. "In fact, I've been ordered to keep a close watch on your movements as well."

"The obvious question, then," began Lyra, "is what do you intend to do concerning that order?"

"I would like to come with you," she answered immediately.

"But…," Kate started to protest.

"I know," said Layla reassuringly. "Someone has to take care of Inara for you, and I can't leave Eldin."

The two children were over a year old now, but they still required a lot of looking after, a burden that had fallen largely on Layla since Kate had become increasingly bedridden. The woman had never seemed particularly maternal before, but motherhood had changed her. She was still an odd parent from Kate's viewpoint, but she was fiercely protective.

"Perhaps you can get us past the watchers," suggested Lyra.

"That I can do," said the older woman, "but I need an explanation for letting you out of my sight. Otherwise Emma might decide that I'm a traitor as well."

"You followed us, but somehow we discovered you and overpowered you…" started Kate.

Layla shook her head negatively.

"They will know she hid us, else the watchers would have seen us leaving," Lyra explained.

"That, and no one will believe that you overpowered me," said the former warden with a wry grin.

Lyralliantha frowned, "I know many battle magics."

"That you have probably never used," finished Layla. "Have you even been in a fight before?"

"I am not afraid to fight," said Lyra calmly.

"I believe you," said Layla, "and that's a good start, but lack of experience is a big problem. You wouldn't stand a chance unless you took me completely by surprise."

"Maybe we should just bring the children too," suggested Kate. "Then Layla could come with us."

They considered their options for several minutes before deciding there was no other practical choice. Once they had resolved themselves, they moved quickly. It was tempting to pack things to take with them but Lyra assured Kate that the Prathions would have anything they might need.

Lyra carried Inara and Layla held Eldin, while Kate went empty handed. It was all she could do just to walk. Cloaked in a shield that made them invisible to sight, sound, and magesight, they left the house and picked their way carefully toward the gate that led beyond the wall around the compound.

They could still talk within the shield, but there was no light, and Kate nearly fell several times. Eventually she put her hands on Lyra's waist, letting the more surefooted woman lead her. She felt embarrassed to be so completely dependent on her friend, and even worse, she already needed to pee again.

"I think we are almost there," Layla notified them. "Let me look and see for certain. I'd rather walk through the gate than into one of the walls." Making a tiny hole for visible light, she peeked at their surroundings.

"There are two watchers atop the wall on either side. The gate is directly ahead, and it's still open."

Another twenty feet and they passed through the archway, and then everything began to go wrong.

"What was that?" asked Lyra suddenly.

Kate hadn't noticed anything, but apparently Layla had, for she replied, "We just crossed another veil. They're overlapping."

"Veil?" asked Kate.

"Another Prathion invisibility shield," clarified the former warden. "They're next to us, but we still can't see one another since they're only overlapping a little bit." Layla chewed her lip. "But they undoubtedly know we're here, just like I know they're there."

"What do we do?" said Kate, beginning to panic.

"We can't run," observed Lyra. "Drop the sound barrier, Layla."

"…the shield immediately, or I'll be forced to take matters into my own hands!" came the last half of Emma's command as Layla modified her shield.

"Take Inara," said Lyra, handing the small girl to Layla. "Then lower the veil, I'll talk to her. If it goes badly cloak yourself and Kate again. Perhaps I can distract them long enough for you to escape."

"That's stupid," complained Layla.

"Just do it."

A second later they were visible again. After the prolonged darkness, the moonlight seemed brilliant, almost dazzling. Emma and Ryan stood fifteen feet ahead of them, with one of the Prathion slave-mages beside them. Above and slightly behind them the two wall sentries watched silently.

Emma looked triumphant rather than angry, "I knew you'd show your true colors."

"Kate needs help," said Lyra. "If she doesn't get it she'll…"

"And I'll give her all the aid I can," interrupted Emma, "but we aren't bringing any outsiders into this."

"It won't be enough," protested Lyra. "Let me take them to…"

"They aren't leaving, and neither are you and that little abomination you have brewing in your belly."

Em, please… came Ryan's thought, carrying with it a feeling of concern.

"What are you saying?" shouted Kate angrily. "Lyra's baby is just as human as mine. They're both Tyrion's children. Why are you doing this Emma?"

"Go back to the house, Kate," said Emma flatly. She held something in her hands, and whatever it was cast glints of moonlight occasionally as she moved. "You don't need to be here for this."

"The hell I don't!" growled Kate. "Have you lost your mind? Is that why you came alone? I don't see any of the others. Is that because you know they wouldn't support you?"

"I didn't need to bring anyone," countered Emma. "Ryan is here as a witness."

Kate's temper got the better of her, "Oh, you brought your incestuous lap dog as a witness! How thoughtful of you. Get out of the way and let us go. You know Daniel wouldn't want you doing any of this, so why don't you stop being an idiot?"

Emma jerked as though she had been slapped, and then her body tensed.

Everything happened at once. Emma's face grew smooth, and her hands opened. A small array of small sharp objects fanned out on either side of her, triangular pieces of metal that looked very much like spear heads, except that they had no shaft attached.

At the same time, Lyra raised a spellwoven shield around the three of them and the two children. Layla dropped the two children and vanished.

Emma, no! Ryan's mental voice sounded like a shout as it echoed in their minds.

Something flashed, and Lyra jerked as her shield broke. Layla reappeared in front of her and slowly collapsed to the ground. The fluid running down her shirt looked black in the moonlight. One of the metallic weapons was buried in the center of her chest.

"Layla?" said Emma in shock. "Why did she do that?!"

Pandemonium ensued. Both Inara and Eldin were wailing at their sudden fall, and Ryan was pulling at Emma. Kate watched it all in silence, shocked and numb. She wanted to reach down to help Layla, but her belly made it nearly impossible, and her head was throbbing.

But Lyra didn't hesitate. Her hands were up, and something deadly was forming between them. There was a look of rage on her face that none of them had ever seen before. Her spellweave lashed out, lancing toward Emma—and then disintegrated as Brigid's chain cut through it.

She had arrived unnoticed, and now she faced Lyralliantha, "Don't give me an excuse." Brigid's chain hovered dangerously close to the She'Har woman. Then she turned to Emma, "Things seem to have gotten out of hand, Sister. You should have invited me if you were planning a party."

Emma shoved Ryan away and glared at her. "Your assistance is neither needed nor desired."

Brigid looked down at Layla. It was too late for her, the weapon had nicked her heart. Her eyes glazed over as the former warden feebly stretched out her hand, trying to reach her son. Something flickered across Brigid's features, an emotion perhaps, but it was gone too quickly for Kate to decide what it had been. The dark haired young woman turned her attention to the two children and gathered them up awkwardly.

It was clear that she hadn't had much experience holding toddlers. Inara squirmed awkwardly and Eldin somehow found himself upside down in her arms. "You should be more careful, *First*," she admonished her sister. "You wouldn't want to hurt the children."

Kate was still trying to absorb Layla's death, and she fell as she tried to get on her knees to examine her. Her vision was dim and the world seemed darker than ever. "Why?"

Lyra looked at Brigid, "Kate needs help. She will die if I am not allowed to take her to Koralltis."

"You would betray us!" snarled Emma.

Brigid ignored her, "Take her and go. The children will stay as a safeguard for your good behavior."

Kate looked up, observing the tension in the two young women's shoulders. Latent violence hung heavy in the air. "No, let me take them with me."

Lyra put her arms under her shoulders and using a combination of muscle and magic she helped get Kate upright. "We should go, while we can," she said softly.

"You're badly mistaken if you think I'm letting them leave," said Emma sternly as she faced Brigid. "I am the one in charge here."

"Accidents happen," said Brigid casually. "I'd hate for one to happen to you, *First*." The statement was spoiled slightly as Eldin slipped partway through her right arm, and she wound up holding him by one foot. The boy found it humorous apparently, for he stopped crying and began to laugh.

The metal points hovering around Emma quivered slightly as her anger grew, but Ryan stepped forward, "Don't threaten her, Brigid. She is the First."

"Only if she's alive," answered Brigid as she appraised him with her eyes. "Two against one, normally that's good odds. Would you like to chance it?" She let Eldin slide the rest of the way to the ground, headfirst, and then she bent casually and sat Inara beside him. There was a dangerous light in her eyes as she straightened up again.

Emma took a deep breath and closed her eyes for a second. "Go," she ordered at last.

Lyra wasted no time. Levitating Kate completely off the ground she began walking quickly in the direction of the grove.

"Don't think this is over," Emma warned Brigid. "I won't forget this."

Brigid smiled, "I wouldn't want you to."

Emma turned away, heading back toward the dormitory. Ryan started to gather up the children but she barked, "Leave them. If she wants hostages, she can take care of them herself."

Brigid's confidence vanished, and her face took on a look of appeal as she looked at Ryan, but he merely shrugged. She stared down at the two infants. They were much larger than they had once been, almost toddlers they were of a size that they were no longer easy to carry, but they weren't able to confidently walk yet.

Eldin promptly sat down and slapped the growing puddle of blood on the ground before crawling over to peer into his mother's face. He had no comprehension of what had happened to her. Brigid felt her insides twist uncomfortably, "Shit."

Kate floated through the dark. Lyralliantha was a pale ghost in the moonlight ahead of her. It was a surreal experience, or it should have been, but the night air brought an uncomfortable touch of reality, that and the numbness in her feet and lower legs.

It wasn't a numbness brought on by the cold but something that had been affecting her off and on for days. Sometimes it was her hands, and other times it would be her legs. But Kate wasn't paying attention to any of that at the moment. All of that was secondary to the vision in her head. All she could see was Layla's body, once a picture of strength and vitality, falling slowly to the ground.

The former warden had always seemed invincible to her, much like Tyrion. Layla had been a fact of life. True, she was strange, with odd tempers and a twisted worldview, but she had been a constant presence. The woman had been possessed of an almost unshakeable confidence that combined, at times almost comically, with her complete ignorance of what Kate had thought were basic human skills.

She couldn't be dead.

The flow of cold air around Kate lessened, and then she realized that Lyra had stopped. Shadowy movement alerted her to the fact that they were no longer alone. Several large forms stepped out of the darkness around them. Strange creatures that should have frightened her, but Kate was too tired to care.

It was the krytek.

Lyra spoke to them in that strange language that Kate had never managed to learn. The conversation was brief, and then she turned to Kate, "They will escort us to the Prathion Grove."

"Who are they?" asked Kate in confusion. They had barely left Albamarl. It was much too soon to be encountering the She'Har.

"Krytek, sent by my people."

"The She'Har?"

"The Illeniels," corrected Lyra.

"You asked them to meet you here?"

"No."

Kate's forehead wrinkled in confusion, "Then how?"

"My people are never surprised. The Elders sent them to ensure our safe arrival."

What about Layla? thought Kate. She wasn't safe. Why hadn't they met them sooner? Her friend might still be alive if they had. She had a million questions and somewhere deep down she felt the beginnings of an angry spark, but she was too tired to examine it yet.

The cold air increased in speed as Lyralliantha towed her along, moving constantly in the direction of the Prathion Grove.

CHAPTER 31

Emma wanted to die.

She was sitting in her room, staring at the wall. Inside her emotions were tearing at her, demanding that she get up, that she *do* something, anything, to alleviate the guilt she felt, but she was paralyzed. She had killed Layla.

She had never particularly liked the woman, but she hadn't hated her either. Many of her brothers and sisters had liked her, though, and she certainly hadn't deserved to die.

But I killed her.

The others had already begun to doubt her sanity. She had seen the looks. That had been going on for weeks now. Her latest blunder would only serve to confirm their fears. Even Ryan was beginning to distrust her.

They must hate me, she thought. Hell, she hated herself. Seeing Eldin and Inara crying while Layla died in front of her, that had shocked her to the core, but she couldn't afford to show any sign of weakness. The only thing that kept the others in line was their fear. If they knew she had her own doubts, that she hated herself just as much as they did, they would tear her apart.

And that would be the end of the dream.

The dream was all that mattered anymore. She had lost everything else already. She lost her quiet life when Tyrion came and took her from Colne, she lost her innocence when she had been forced to kill in the arena, and she had lost her hope when she had seen Ryan maimed. Ryan's love, right or wrong, had been the only thing she had left to live for, but now she could feel him pulling away from her.

As loathsome as his face had become, she was uglier still. *How did I get here?*

Tyrion was easy to blame. It was his weakness that had brought her into the world, but he wasn't the source. His mistakes had created her particular situation, but it was the She'Har who had ultimately brought this misery upon her, upon them. Even if she hadn't been born, even if she hadn't been cursed, *someone* would be suffering for their arrogance, cruelty, and selfishness.

She fingered her blades, feeling the cool strength present in the metal. They were designed in a similar manner to Brigid's chains. They would only respond to her aythar, and they made her particular skill at rapid fire ranged attacks far deadlier. She could have killed Brigid last night.

She almost *did.*

But then she would have lost everything. Ryan might have tried to stop her, and she couldn't allow that. In the end she probably would have killed everyone, and that would have been certain to cause her plans to unravel. The dream would have died there.

When it was all over, the world would be free. Humankind, the small portion of it left, would be able to start anew. All the suffering, all the evil done, by herself and by those who had forced her to it, would be given at least a tiny bit of meaning, if it meant the people of the future could find their own happiness.

She wouldn't get to enjoy it, of course. She didn't deserve to, her soul had been blackened just as surely as her father's. Only death could release her from her inner torment, but she wouldn't accept the call of the grave until she had made certain that she had finished his task.

"What does it matter if they hate me?" she asked aloud. "Most of them are going to die anyway." Practically everyone around her was a walking corpse. They were dead, they just didn't know it yet.

Eldin grabbed at the shiny metal of the chain again. He was fascinated by the way it moved through the air, but his fingers slid away from it whenever he tried to grasp it.

"Stop that," ordered Brigid, not that she expected him to obey. The little boy was a handful. While Inara sat quietly, playing with whatever was close at hand, he was constantly in motion. Everything needed to be touched, and whatever he touched needed to be put in his mouth. "Why can't you be more like her?" she asked him.

He looked up at her. "Baa!"

With a sigh she picked him up but regretted it immediately. As usual he grabbed at her breast and tried to suckle, but there was nothing there for him. It was also an unpleasant sensation for her. She pulled him away. "How did they put up with you?" She was giving serious thought to wearing shirts again, just to keep him away from her chest.

Feeding the two of them was a problem, but thankfully they were old enough to eat real food, if she chewed it for them. Goat's milk had been the first thing she had given them, but it held its own problems. They drank it greedily and usually vomited most of it up afterward.

As a result, they smelled of sour milk, among other things.

A knock at the door was a welcome relief. Brigid opened it to find Abby standing in the hall. She stared at her sister with a look of hope and desperation. "Have you come to take them away?"

Abby's nose wrinkled at the smell in the room, but she managed to smile anyway, "No. I just wanted to check on you."

"Oh," said Brigid, losing interest almost immediately.

Abby's eyes assessed the room and the state of the toddlers with a long sweeping glance. "They need a bath."

Brigid shrugged, "Why bother? They'll just crap on themselves as soon as they're clean, or spit milk all over themselves."

"You're letting them get too much," said Abby.

"It doesn't matter. A little or a lot, they spit it up most of the time anyway."

"Are you burping them afterward?" asked her sister.

"Huh?"

Abby spent the next half an hour showing her. When she put little Eldin across her shoulder and began gently patting him on the back, Brigid warned her, "He's just going to puke sooner if you beat on him."

"That's what the rag is for," explained Abby. "If you do it right he'll bring up the air and keep most of the milk."

Sure enough, the little boy burped after a couple of minutes. A little milk came up, but it was nothing like his usual explosive belches of sour foulness.

"You try it now. Inara is still waiting," suggested Abby.

Brigid did.

"Not so hard," cautioned her sister. "It doesn't take much. Be patient, and she'll burp when she's ready."

After a while Inara let out a small burp of air, but nothing else. Brigid stared at Abby in amazement. "How did you know all this?"

"I had several smaller siblings at home, before coming here," answered Abby.

For the first time, Brigid felt a pang of jealousy for Abby's calm knowledge. Handling the two small children was hard. "I don't know how they did it," she commented.

"Did what?"

"Took care of these two all day," Brigid clarified.

"There's more than one kind of strength," said Abby. "The most important kinds often go unnoticed."

Brigid stared at her for a long minute, thinking. "You should be the one to do this. I'm not suited for it."

Abby smiled, "That may be true, but you can learn. I have other things that need doing."

Her eyes narrowed, "Such as?"

"People have to eat."

"We just fed them."

"Not them," explained Abby, "everyone else. With Kate and Lyra gone there's no one to organize the meals."

"Let the *First* do it," said Brigid sarcastically. "She used to love to cook."

"Emma is in a bad place," said Abby. "I don't think she'll be cooking again for a long time, if ever."

"She killed Layla," said Brigid, "the bitch doesn't deserve to feel good about herself."

Abby flinched, but said nothing. After a moment she spoke, "Let me show you how to bathe them."

"You think she was right to do that?" said Brigid in a challenging tone.

Her sisters face was smooth as she looked directly into her eyes, "I think I am as much to blame for Layla's death as she is. I have supported her through all of this. I only hope she can hold herself together long enough to finish what he started."

"It's supposed to be *them* that we are killing," said Brigid. "Layla was one of us."

"Murder is wrong, Brigid," said Abby firmly. "Everything we are doing is wrong. We have given up any right to judge. Layla's death was an accident. I've given up trying to be good, or justify my actions, or hers. It doesn't matter if we're killing each other, or killing the She'Har. It's wrong."

Brigid was confused, "You think we should just make peace? You're crazier than Emma."

Abby shook her head, "No, I think we're wrong, but I've already committed myself. They have as much right to live as we do, but we can't have it both ways. If I have to choose, I'll choose our people over theirs."

"You're seriously fucked up," declared Brigid.

Abby nodded, "You're right. Now let me show you how to bathe them. I don't have long, I need to get to the kitchen soon, or we'll all be eating porridge for dinner."

CHAPTER 32

She could hear the sounds of people moving, and it annoyed her. Why didn't they realize she was trying to sleep? It seemed like it had been ages since she had had a proper night's rest, and now that she had finally gotten deeply asleep, there was a horde of people rummaging around in her room.

Kate opened her eyes, or she thought she did. They didn't seem to be operating normally. There was light, but everything was blurry. She squinted as the room slowly resolved itself. It never truly got into proper focus, but after a short time she could see that there was a man standing at the foot of her bed. A more slender figure stood to one side.

"Kate? Can you hear me?" It was Lyra's voice.

"Why won't you let me sleep?" she asked.

A warm hand was placed against her forehead. No, it wasn't just warm, it felt positively hot, as though the owner had a fever. It belonged to the slender figure, and Kate decided it must belong to Lyralliantha. *Is she sick?*

"She's cold," announced Lyra's voice. "Can't you keep her warm?"

A deeper male voice replied, "I'm bringing her temperature up gradually. She lost more blood than I expected during the procedure. She'll be weak and disoriented, but it's primarily a symptom of the blood loss."

Kate's mind flashed back to a vision of Layla, bleeding onto the ground. Had she been wounded as well? "Why blood?" she asked.

"Everything is alright, Kate," said Lyra reassuringly. "Your baby girl is fine. The procedure was a success. You just have to get better now."

"My baby? What happened? Where is Koralltis? Did we reach the grove?"

"I am here," said the male voice.

"Yes, Kate. We got here last night. Your daughter is safe. Would you like to see her?" asked Lyra.

"How? She hasn't been born yet." Kate struggled to rise but encountered only pain. Firm hands pressed her back down into the bed.

"Don't try to get up," cautioned Koralltis. "I've closed the skin and rejoined your muscles, but the wound is still new. I don't want you to start bleeding again."

"Why doesn't she remember?" asked Lyra with concern in her voice.

"She was very weak when we started," explained Koralltis. "Her brain isn't getting enough blood. Her confusion will pass, but some memory loss of the recent past is to be expected."

A cry sounded from somewhere in the room.

Kate turned her head, trying to track the sound, but her eyes still weren't cooperating. "Is that?"

"Yes," said Lyra. "She's beautiful. Would you like to hold her?"

"Her lungs are functioning, but she will need support or they may not last," said Koralltis. "There's also a risk of infection at this stage. I don't recommend it."

"She needs to see her," insisted Lyra. "Let me have her."

A moment later Kate felt something warm pressed against her on one side. She looked down, trying to see the infant there. Her vision was blurry but she could see well enough to tell she had dark hair. She was also small, almost too small. "She's tiny."

"She would have been bigger if you had been able to carry her full term," said Koralltis, "but she is not too small to survive.

Kate wanted to hold her, but her arms betrayed her with their weakness. In the end, she settled for resting one hand beside the babe's cheek. She was tired, so very tired. She decided to close her eyes, just for a moment, and the world faded away.

Lyra turned to Koralltis, worried. "Why did she lose so much blood?"

"Her system had been clotting abnormally for weeks before this. It exhausted the part of her blood responsible for clotting. That is why she bled so much, but her life is not in danger. She will need rest and good food. I believe she will be largely recovered within a few weeks."

"You believe?" said Lyra.

The Prathion lore-warden sighed, "There are no certainties in this world, not even for the Illeniels. Surely you are aware of this?"

Lyra fought down an irrational surge of anger at his remark. Her own fatigue was greater than she would have liked to admit, and she had been on her feet for far too long. "Yes, of course," she replied. "I need to rest." She rested her hands on her own swollen abdomen.

"Please do," agreed Koralltis. "We will take care of her. Return when you have seen to your needs."

"I would rather sleep here," said Lyra. "If that is permitted."

"There will be no problem. Allow me to make you a bed."

"I can do it myself," insisted Lyra, but as she started to use her aythar she felt a wave of dizziness sweep over her. She had pushed herself too far already. Embarrassed she looked at the Prathion, "Never mind. I would be grateful for your assistance."

Careful! warned Ryan. The glass sphere was loose where it attached to the wall plate. *You have to make sure the retaining ring is in place before you open the interior partition. If one of these things gets jarred loose we're all dead.*

"Oh, sorry," said Anthony sheepishly. "I thought that part was just used when you were done with it."

Ryan didn't reply, other than to give his half-brother a hard stare. Anthony was good-natured, but he was also entirely too easy going for the work they were doing. One accident would be too many while they were extracting and sealing the weaponized krytek.

"If these things are that dangerous, wouldn't it be good to put a blanket down on the floor?" asked Anthony, partly out of curiosity and partly because he couldn't stand long awkward silences.

Why?

"What if you drop one? They look really fragile."

The glass spheres appeared quite delicate. They were less than an inch in diameter, barely bigger than the end of a man's thumb, and the glass itself wasn't very thick. What Anthony was failing to appreciate were the intricate runes engraved on its surface. To answer his question Ryan picked up one of the unused glass containers and threw it at the hard stone beneath their feet. It struck with a dull clink, bounced twice, and rolled away. *The enchantment makes them more resilient than steel,* he added. *The big danger is the transfer. Pay attention while I show you again, unless you want to wind up like poor Blake.*

Anthony watched while Ryan secured the retaining ring and then, once the glass was firmly attached, he pulled the small lever that raised the small inner door, allowing the creatures in the other room a way to reach the container. Within seconds one of the small wasp-like krytek crawled in. Ryan reversed the lever, closing the door and then, using a small metal stylus he inscribed the final rune on the glass, activating the stasis enchantment before he removed it and sealed the top.

"We didn't have to wait long," noted Anthony. "What makes them want to get in here so badly?"

Us, said Ryan blandly. *They are attracted to any source of aythar, like a moth to a flame.*

"Does that include animals or other things?"

I believe so, but they can survive and reproduce using only two food sources. Humans and the She'Har Elders, explained Ryan. *I tested one earlier on a rabbit to be certain. They went to it, but lost interest as soon as they were close.*

"So if one of those things escaped…"

It would find the first available host and burrow in to lay its eggs. The life cycle is very rapid. Within a span of less than a quarter of an hour there would be hundreds, if not thousands. The cycle appears to run faster if the host has a large amount of aythar.

"And then…"

They would spread. What remains of humankind would almost certainly be eliminated, along with most of the She'Har.

"Only most?"

I do not think they could cross the oceans. Unlike most krytek they can multiply and reproduce, but once they run out of food they will stop. Three months after that they will die and the cycle will end.

Anthony frowned, "That's what you *think* anyway. How do we know for sure?"

Ryan pointed at the sealed chamber with a metal finger, *Even after we finish preparing the spheres there will be some left in there. Without the benefit of the stasis enchantment they should die. Emma doesn't intend to release them any sooner than that. We will have a firm answer by then.*

"You've put a lot of thought into this."

Ryan shook his head, once again glad that someone like his brother wasn't in charge of the project. *Wouldn't you, if the fate of the world rested on your decisions?*

Anthony chuckled, "If my life were left up to me I would probably find a plump wife in Colne or maybe Lincoln and settle down. I might even get two or three wives, then I'd spend my days making babies by the dozen."

Two or three? Anthony never ceased to amaze him with his ridiculous ideas. Then again, the world would probably be a quieter place if everyone was like him. *No one would let him marry more than one woman, though,* thought Ryan. *Then again, that obviously didn't stop Father.* Directing his mental voice outward he teased him, *Perhaps you and Ian have more in common than I realized.*

Anthony made a sour face, "Don't even joke about that. He's only interested in girls that say 'no'. I'm the exact opposite."

Ryan found himself remembering the test subjects, all carrying Ian's children now, and shuddered as a feeling of shame swept over him. He felt a lot of guilt about their situation, guilt for capturing them, and guilt for allowing Ian to play his part. It would have been better if someone, anyone else, had handled that part of things. *But I wasn't able.* Was he any better for not being able to commit the final sin, or worse for allowing a sadistic bastard like Ian to do it instead?

As he always did when confronted with uncomfortable thoughts or feelings, Ryan dragged his mind back into focus, putting it firmly on the task in front of him. It was something he had to do almost constantly these days. There was very little about his current life that didn't make him queasy.

Back to the spheres, he told Anthony. *There's one thing I'm surprised you haven't asked me.*

"We can't all be geniuses, Ryan," said Anthony dryly. "What did I miss?"

You haven't asked me how the krytek will be released when required.

Anthony decided to humor him, "Very well o' sage, how will they be released when the time of apocalypse has come?"

Look at the runes, here, Ryan said, pointing to one portion of the enchantment engraved on an as yet unfilled sphere. *This links it to a master enchantment. Whoever has that can release them all at the same time with nothing more than a command word.*

"They don't seem to make any sense," said Anthony, frowning.

That's because they aren't a regular rune structure, they're an identifier. One that links that particular place in space with another.

"I don't really understand," admitted his brother, "but it seems very clever."

It was, cleverer than anything Ryan had seen before, except perhaps the stasis enchantment itself. Unlike most of the enchantments they used, which were derived from She'Har spellweaves that Tyrion had studied or otherwise learned about, this one was based on an idea that Ryan had come up with himself.

I've tested it, and it works, Ryan told him, *but the implications of what could be done with it make me wish I could spend all my time on it.*

Anthony sighed, "I don't really care, but I know you're going to tell me anyway."

Don't you see? Said Ryan, warming to his subject. *This is probably the sort of magic that underpins the way the Mordan gift works.*

"Teleportation?"

Exactly. They do it subconsciously, but that doesn't mean it can't be done deliberately, with careful planning and preparation. Using special identifiers like this, it might be possible to link two places that are separated by any amount of distance, to create a portal that anyone could use to travel.

"If that were possible, why haven't the She'Har done it already?" countered Ryan.

Perhaps they have, suggested Ryan. *Or perhaps they haven't bothered. They have the Mordan to rely on after all. We know nothing about the extent of their experience and knowledge. Or it may never have even occurred to them. They aren't gods after all. I don't think there's anything that they can do that we can't. They aren't any smarter than we are.*

"Do you just sit around in your room at night, thinking this shit up?"

Ryan shrugged, *It beats thinking about what we're actually doing.*

Anthony smirked, "I figured you had something more important to do with your evenings."

His metal fist clenched reflexively, just as his original flesh and blood fist might have done. For a second Ryan wanted nothing more than to use it to knock the knowing smile right off his brother's face. Instead he took a deep breath, controlling his anger. *Mention that again and things will get unpleasant,* he warned.

Anthony had already realized his mistake, glancing at his feet he apologized, "Sorry, Ryan, I didn't mean that. I mean, I understand, and its none of my business…"

Let's get back to work.

"Yeah," replied Anthony. "That's a good idea. How many of these do we have to do anyway, a hundred?"

Ryan pointed at a large straw lined box in one corner, *Thousands.*

"Ugh."

CHAPTER 33

It had been a little more than two months since Kate's emergency visit to the Prathion Grove. She and Lyra had stayed there for several weeks, until Lyra had had her own child, a boy. Shortly after that, though, they had relocated to Lyra's old home within the Illeniel Grove.

Kate couldn't complain about the accommodations, despite their strangeness. She still experienced a bit of vertigo whenever she looked down from the edge of the platform, but she solved that problem by not looking down. What she couldn't get over, however, was her constant fear that one day her baby might crawl over the edge.

Little Layla was insatiably curious already, but she wasn't moving enough for that to be a problem, yet. Lyra assured her that an invisible barrier would prevent such a thing, but it was hard for Kate to believe. Her brain might agree, but her heart was still worried.

Lyralliantha's baby, Garlin, was named after Daniel's one time friend among the Prathion wardens. He had been born impossibly fat but as his body began growing he was soon merely chubby, and cute beyond belief. While he was a month younger than Layla, he was already bigger. In part because he had been born with more weight, and possibly because Layla was still playing catchup from her premature delivery.

Kate glanced over at Lyra, who was currently sitting down, nursing her young son, her long silver hair draped casually over one shoulder. She was the very picture of motherhood, beauty, grace, and love. She was everything that Kate was not, with her disheveled hair, worn face, and sagging skin.

She had recovered much of her strength, but this pregnancy had left her with many more souvenirs of her experience than her previous pregnancies. Her belly hung loosely in front of her, and she doubted it would ever return to its previous tone as it had after her first child. The marks on her skin made bright pink stripes around her middle.

Perhaps it is better that he is gone. Daniel would not recognize me now, she thought.

Lyra looked up from her son, catching Kate's eye. Why she looked up Kate couldn't be sure, perhaps she felt her eyes on her, or maybe she was able to sense the dark turn of her thoughts. Whatever the reason was, Lyra smiled and without any obvious purpose or cause said, "I love you, Kate."

Kate had been struggling with dark moods and that comment, immediately on the heels of her jealous thoughts, undid her. Tears began sliding down her cheeks.

Lyra's expression turned to worry, "I'm sorry Kate. Did I do something wrong?"

"No," said Kate, getting up and walking over to give the other woman an awkward hug. "It's not you, it's me."

"Do you still miss him?"

Kate nodded. That was the simple answer, so she left it at that. She did miss Daniel, but she also mourned for their lost home—and Layla. There were so many things to cry over, and yet crying had never been her way, at least not in the past. Since giving birth she had found herself prone to long bouts of sadness, and she didn't know how to fix whatever was wrong.

And in the midst of all that, I sit here being jealous of the one person who has been the kindest to me, she thought, chiding herself.

Lyra was like the sister she had always wanted. But in the dreams she had had as a girl that sister hadn't been smarter, more beautiful, and eternally youthful.

"Don't worry, Kate," said Lyra calmly. "We will go home soon."

"How? They'll kill you if we go back."

Lyra shook her head, "We just have to get Tyrion first. He can straighten things out."

Kate looked at her without saying a word. The question in her eyes was plain enough.

"We will talk to him. Convince him to return."

"You can do that?" asked Kate. "Brigid said he didn't respond to her."

"I have been talking to the elders my entire life," said Lyralliantha. "She probably did not wait long enough. Our words, our entire lives, are like flickers of light to them. To speak with them takes time and patience. I do not think Brigid is very good at that."

The Illeniel child has produced his offspring, said Ceylendor as he made his report to the Centyr Elders.

Then it was not a ruse, the Illeniels have truly betrayed us, responded one of the elders.

They are giving their gifts to the humans, said another. *How well placed are your spies in the human encampment?*

Not very, admitted Ceylendor. *Tyrion has kept them isolated, virtually imprisoned.*

How did you get this information then? asked another elder.

Someone had to feed them. His older children are well guarded, but some of their slaves were not as well protected, answered Ceylendor.

Can one of them eliminate the problem?

They might, responded the She'Har lore-warden, *but they are clumsy and weak. It would be foolish to risk our plan on one of them.*

We need better information.

Tyrion has vanished. It may be safe to try sending a reaver among them, suggested Ceylendor.

Only to gather better information, ordered the most senior among the Centyr Elders. *The Illeniel Grove will respond if we try to do more.*

Won't they know anyway?

They only know what they 'will' learn..., responded the First Elder. *...and what 'may' happen. Until we make a decision it will be too unclear for them.*

But they will respond then, commented the youngest elder.

We will take that chance, said another.

Isn't that their greatest strength, asked Ceylendor, *chance?*

Some types of chance, yes, responded the First. *The chaotic doings of living beings follow patterns and make little difference usually. Conscious decisions about important matters become very obvious to them. Their weakness is when great choices depend upon entirely random processes.*

How can you make such a thing happen? asked the youngest elder.

The humans have a saying that fits perfectly, explained the First, *we 'roll the dice'.*

I will send someone immediately then, said Ceylendor.

Who will you choose? asked one of the elders who hadn't spoken before.

Someone subtle, Serrelia, I think, answered the lore-warden.

"No," said Abby adamantly. "Someone else can do it."

Emma arched one brow, "Why not you?"

"I'm too busy. The kitchens have been a mess since Kate left," she responded, but the excuse sounded weak even in her own ears.

"You weren't too busy to deliver babies," observed Emma. "In fact, you proved yourself to be a very capable healer. I'd rather have you do this. I want to avoid leaving obvious scars on them."

"It shouldn't matter," countered Abby. "You're just planning to pop them in a box afterward until they're needed. Just like those poor women and their children…"

She had delivered dozens of newborns over the past month, with more still on the way. Tyrion's 'subjects' were bearing fruit now, nearly a year after he had started his project. There were more still to come but within a month or so more they should be done.

"Our children," reminded Emma. "Those *poor women* you mentioned were monsters, but Father found a way to use them to our advantage. They should be grateful. Those children are our nieces and nephews, and the beginning of a new age."

"We should have put them in the boxes before they delivered," groused Abby.

"And if we should die?" asked Emma. "We don't know for certain who will be left when this is over. Childbirth is a risky thing, and the She'Har have no experience with it. Safer to deliver them now and store both."

"Do you hear yourself, Em?" asked Abby. "There's no feeling in your words. *'Store them',* does that sound like something we should be saying about human beings?"

"The words don't matter one damn," said Emma, dismissing her remark. "And I have no room for feelings in this. If I did…" She stopped there, catching herself as her emotions began to rise.

"That's exactly why I won't do this," said Abby, coming full circle. "I just can't. Thinking about what will happen to them. I saw what happened to Blake, it's horrible."

"You couldn't have seen that. You weren't there, neither of us was."

"Violet showed me, mind to mind," said Abby.

Emma frowned, tapping her chin with one finger, "Why would she do that? Perhaps, I should have a word with her."

"Because she's *human,* Em," said Abby in exasperation. "Because she needed to talk to someone. What she saw nearly crippled her. How many people do you think see one of their own family members devoured, from the inside out? I don't think she'll ever get over it."

Emma's visage grew stern, "If *I* can keep going, so can she, and so will *you.* You will do this Abby."

"No."

"I'm not asking. You'll do it, or I'll apply pressure until you comply. Do you understand?" threatened her sister.

Abby straightened, "No, I don't think I do, *First.* Tell me exactly what you mean by that."

"If you're so worried about children, and their welfare, you'll do as I command. There are an awful lot of them around here now."

Abby was shocked, "You wouldn't dare!"

Emma lips formed a flat line.

"You need them, for your precious plan."

"Not those children, dullard," said Emma with an exaggerated sigh.

The only other possibilities were Inara and Eldin. Abby's grew round, "Your own brother and sister? You couldn't possibly…"

"Not Inara, of course," said Emma coldly. "But Eldin can't contribute to the future anyway. There's no need for him. He's a waste of food now that I think about it."

"Brigid would kill you. You're bluffing."

The First raised one brow, "Is it worth being stubborn, worth forcing someone else to do the job you would be best at, to find out?"

Emma had once been her favorite sister and despite all that had happened over the past year she had continued to be empathetic to her situation and the pressures that it involved, but for the first time she felt genuine hatred for her. "Fine, you win," responded Abby angrily. "You'll get exactly what you wanted."

Emma smiled, "You'll do it then?"

"I will, but that's not what I was referring to," said Abby. "You said before that you couldn't afford to have friends. I ignored you then, but you've made a believer of me. From this point on you can count on it, you have *no* friends anymore, not one."

The First remained still, though one eyelid twitched slightly. She gave no sign that Abby's words had affected her in any way. "You'll start tomorrow morning, then. You may go."

Abby left without a word, and in a move that was entirely uncharacteristic of her, she slammed the door as she left. Emma stared after her for several minutes before lifting her hand to look at it. It was shaking like a leaf in a storm. With an effort of will she reengaged the privacy ward around the room. Only when that was done did she let go. Her shoulders began to shake, and her eyes filled with tears. When she opened her mouth finally, the only sound that emerged was a strangled shriek of despair.

The pain in her chest was so great she almost wondered if she was having a heart attack. It was almost a

319

welcome thought. Looking down at her enchanted blades she wanted desperately to pick one up and thrust it into her own heart.

She couldn't, so instead she wept. The storm of her emotions was worse than any she could remember experiencing before. It seemed as though it might never stop. It was only when she realized that the building itself had begun to shake that she reined herself in. Somehow her feelings had been transmitted to the earth, and the entire city had started trembling.

Deep breaths, she told herself, working consciously to soothe the earth and make it be still once more.

CHAPTER 34

"You understand what is required?" asked Ceylendor.
Serrelia nodded, "Yes, and also that it is dangerous."

"Only if you mistrust yourself," said the lore-warden.
"That is why we so rarely allow this. Only a few have the
necessary inner balance to survive the experience."

"You did," noted the Centyr woman. "Shouldn't you
do this? Your knowledge is far greater than mine."

"I am already well known among the She'Har,"
said Ceylendor. "Too many know me, and even the
krytek are often trained to recognize me. A new player
is required. Your aythar will be much harder for them
to identify."

"I am honored to be chosen," replied Serrelia. "My
only fear is disappointing the Elders."

Ceylendor smiled benignly, "You will not disappoint
them. Choose your target carefully. All we need for now,
is information. If more is required, you will be given new
instructions. Remain vigilant."

She dipped her head obediently and turned to go, but
she paused before taking the first step.

"You have a question?" he asked tolerantly.

"When it is over, when I rejoin myself, will it be easy?
Do you have any advice?"

He wanted to laugh, but he cloaked the humor
beneath a veil of patience, "Nothing could be simpler.
Trust yourself, and all will go well." *And whichever of
your selves is stronger will return,* he added mentally. *No
matter which it is, the Centyr will be stronger.*

Ceylendor watched her leave. Within a matter of days she would pick her target, and a new reaver would be born.

A noise alerted her to the arrival of a visitor. Looking up, Kate was surprised to see the black-skinned man standing at what passed for an entrance onto Lyralliantha's not-so-private platform. His name was a strange one, but she had heard Daniel say it many times in the past, Thillmarius.

"May I help you?" she asked, trying to hide her nervousness. Her brief encounters with him had mostly been neutral, but she knew that Daniel hated him with a passion beyond any of his other hatreds.

He gave her an unnatural smile. While he was somewhat better at it than many of the She'Har, Thillmarius hadn't completely mastered the skill. "Actually, I thought I might bring you a gift."

Kate wished that Lyralliantha was present, but she had left earlier, leaving Kate with both newborns to manage. She currently had one on either side of her, nursing. She couldn't have felt more vulnerable.

"Lyralliantha is out right now," she informed him. "This isn't the best time. I'm sort of occupied."

"I promise I won't stay long," he assured her. "Or if you wish, I can just leave it here, but I wouldn't want it to get cold before you taste it."

"Cold?"

"I brought some fresh bread, and butter as well," explained the lore-warden. Gone was his artificial smile, replaced by an awkward and entirely genuine pride.

For a moment, he reminded her of a small boy, hoping to win his mother's praise with some accomplishment. She couldn't help but remember her son Aaron, and the first time he had come home with a shiny rock in his pocket. The image was so at odds with the normal distant nature of the She'Har lore-warden that she almost laughed.

She was also starving, and the thought of bread after the bland diet afforded by the Illeniels over the past month made her mouth water. "Forgive my hesitation," she told him. "Please come in."

He did, and after assessing her state for a second he asked, "Since your hands are full, would you like me to cut a piece for you?"

Kate nodded.

The lore-warden carved a delicate slice from the round loaf and then produced a small container and opened it. Using his aythar, he drew a large dollop of butter from it and spread it evenly across the warm bread before bringing it over to her.

She managed to lean back, balancing Garlin and Layla with her upper arms and using her now free right hand to accept the gift. Murmuring a quick word of thanks, she ate it in three large bites that were anything but ladylike. The bread was delicious, possibly some of the best she had ever had.

"Daniel told me you had taken up baking as a hobby, but I had trouble believing it," she told him, "until now."

"Daniel?" answered the Prathion, looking puzzled for a second, until he realized she was referring to Tyrion. "Yes, he gave me some good advice on the matter. Did you know that my bread has become a sensation among the She'Har? I don't know how it compares to yours, but my people had never experienced such a thing before."

"Really?"

He nodded, "In fact, some of them may well be angry with me for bringing you this. There's a waiting list to get a loaf."

Kate hid a frown, "Then why did you come?"

"I had several motives," said Thillmarius honestly. "I haven't been able to find Tyrion, and his children won't let me into Albamarl, but he had told me before that you were a good cook, so I wanted to see what your opinion was. I also wanted to repay some of my debt to him. But perhaps my biggest reason was curiosity."

Her fear and concern came back to the fore, but there was little she could do.

Thillmarius saw the change in her aythar, "Please, don't be worried. I mean you no harm. The Prathions and the Illeniels have been the closest of allies for many millennia. I simply wanted to see the truth of it."

"The truth?"

"Lyralliantha's baby," he clarified. "I knew you were having a child, but no Illeniel female has ever given birth before. It has raised a storm of rumors among the Prathion lore-wardens."

"People are talking about it?"

"Only our lore-wardens know," said Thillmarius. "Koralltis was very circumspect, and we will not share the information with the other groves. Do not fear. But this is a very unusual event."

His words made her even more apprehensive, but it also piqued her interest, "Why is it so unusual?"

"The Illeniel gift is more closely guarded than that of the other groves," said Thillmarius. "Speaking objectively, it's the main reason we still exist. Without it we wouldn't have survived in the past, or been able to traverse the dimensions to find this, our last sanctuary. That is why the Prathions are so closely tied to the Illeniels. Practically speaking, our gift, while useful, is the least powerful of any of the She'Har talents."

"Is that why you protect their secrets?"

"Most assuredly," answered Thillmarius. "Their assistance keeps us on a more even footing with the other groves. Outwardly, the She'Har may appear monolithic to you, despite the superficial differences in our skin coloring, but we operate purely according to our needs. The five groves would strive with one another for dominance if the Illeniel gift did not hold sway. They are the keystone to the balance of power that maintains our society."

"Daniel once told me that the Illeniel Grove is the smallest of the five," said Kate. "If they are so important, why would that be?"

"When you are powerful, you have little need for numbers, or a show of strength," replied the lore-warden.

She was shocked, not by what he had said directly, but more by the fact that the She'Har seemed to suffer from many of the same flaws that humans did. "I thought your people were naturally harmonious…"

"Harmony is born of necessity."

"Why are you telling me this?" she asked.

Thillmarius was silent for a moment, as though deep in thought. "I think perhaps it is because I owe your mate a debt, and your people, but there are practical reasons as well. If humanity should gain the Illeniel gift, then it may become an important power in the future. Obviously the Illeniels have some reason for what they are doing, and it involves your race. Helping you might induce your people to view mine in a more favorable light."

It was a statement of fact that a human might have kept hidden, but Kate still appreciated his honesty. She felt compelled to return the favor, "You know Tyrion distrusts you." She disliked calling Daniel by that name, but she decided that using it would simplify the conversation.

"Which is why I am giving you this warning," said Thillmarius. "Perhaps, if we find ourselves in need of support someday, you can convince him to give it."

"Warning?" While the conversation had been interesting, she hadn't thought it to be that ominous.

The lore-warden nodded, "Yes. If the other groves discover the fact of Lyralliantha's birth, they are unlikely to view it in the same light that my people do. They will see it as a betrayal. They would probably seek to undo it."

"Do you mean a war?" she asked.

"You might call it that," he agreed. "They would try to destroy the child."

"Wouldn't that start a war?"

He shook his head, "Not in the sense you mean. There would be struggle, to assassinate the boy. The Centyr and the Mordan make highly efficient killers. The Gaelyn would probably support them while the Illeniels and my people would try to protect him."

"That sounds an awful lot like a war."

He shrugged, "Only until the child was dead. Once the matter was decided, it would be pointless to continue fighting. All parties would cease fighting. Unlike your people, we do not hold grudges. That is also why we must keep the child a secret.

"Despite their power, the Illeniels couldn't win. Killing one person is an easy thing, and the Centyr and Mordan are uniquely gifted for such a task. They could attack knowing their victory would end the hostilities almost immediately, whereas the Illeniels would be forced to defend a weak point indefinitely. In fact, they might choose not to fight at all, unless they had a dire reason. Secrecy is your best, perhaps your only, defense."

Kate was horrified.

"I don't understand," said the young man.

His name was Allred, but Abby would have rather not known. It only made her job harder. Like most of her subjects, he was a Mordan mage, originally from Sabortrea. After taking a few of the slaves from the other camps Tyrion had directed them to focus their efforts on bringing most of their laborers from there. Now that she understood most of his plan, Abby knew why, and the thought made her shudder.

"I'm going to put you to sleep, and make certain that you don't feel any pain." At least that part was true.

"But what is this thing for?" he asked.

She held up the small glass bauble. "After I'm done you'll be put in a stasis box, possibly even one of the ones you made. It will be taken to where you will be needed, and when it's opened this device will enable us to send and receive word letting you know what is to be done," she lied. The only word he would receive would be the signal that ended his life.

"But what do they want me to do?" asked Allred anxiously.

Tad was watching from one side of the room, and he leaned over, "It will be easy. All you need to focus on is the fact that once you finish, we will remove those tattoos. You'll be free to do as you please then."

Allred nodded, and Abby put him to sleep, grateful to end the conversation. Once he was unconscious she blocked the nerves around the entry point, his bellybutton, and began guiding the glass sphere to its destination, a place deep within his chest, near the heart and lungs.

The placement was almost arbitrary, but it did have some practical benefits. The aythar was stronger there, which would speed the krytek up, and it would make the enchanted glass harder to spot, should someone manage to observe one of their subjects before they were activated. Abby also consoled herself that being near the heart it would probably kill the man faster and shorten his suffering.

She closed the opening as soon as the sphere was within and when she finished the only sign that she had done anything was a small drop of blood. Wiping that away she nodded at Tad, indicating he could take the man away.

"You alright, Abby?" asked her brother.

"No," she admitted.

Tad patted her on the back, "That's the twentieth one you've done today. Anyone would be tired. Another week at this rate, though, and we'll be done."

He was completely clueless, and the look she gave him should have conveyed that. "He's the twentieth one I've *killed* today. If it was just being tired, I wouldn't be this upset."

Tad's face changed, "I know it's awful, but it isn't *you* killing them Abby."

"Have you always been this stupid?" she asked him bitterly. He started to reply but she held up her hand, "Never mind, just shut up. I don't want to talk about it. I'm done for the day. If it makes you feel better, tell the First that I'm tired. I'll be in my room."

She left.

Back in her room she stared at the wall, too numb to even cry. This had been her life for the past two weeks. Every evening she dreamed of making a stand, refusing to continue, but she knew that in the morning she would get up and do what Emma required.

CHAPTER 35

The field around Tyrion's tree was awash with the late summer sun. It was one of the few times of year that the high pasture was truly warm, but it wouldn't remain that way for long. Another month and the cold autumn wind would return, and only a couple of months after that, the first snow might come. Winter always came early in the hills.

But today was warm, and that was all that mattered to Kate and Lyralliantha as they walked toward the only large patch of shade, the area sheltered beneath his tree.

By the standards of those who lived in Colne, it was a large tree, over sixty-five feet in height already, but to Kate's eyes now it looked small. In the deep forest the god-trees grew much larger, even the normal trees, oaks and elms that bordered it made this one look modest by comparison. Few trees grew this large in the hard soil of the hills.

"Where did this stream come from?" she asked. The trickle hardly deserved the name, rivulet would have been a better moniker.

"I haven't been here before," responded Lyra, "but I would guess that Brigid diverted a spring or something to help him grow, since the rain is sparse up here."

There had been a spring on the other side of the hill, one that trickled down to the river, but Kate couldn't imagine how one person could move such a thing. She had seen so many things that defied description, though, what was one more? "I wish we could have brought the babies," she said at last, changing the subject.

Garlin and Layla were with Helen, who had been delighted to see her newest grandchildren. Despite having so many she had been denied the opportunity to see most of them until they were nearly grown, aside from Inara and Eldin, of course.

Thinking of those two made Kate worry again. They were never far from her thoughts, and a large part of her hope today regarded them. If they could convince Daniel to return, if he *could* return, then they could go back to Albamarl.

"We will be here for quite some time," reminded Lyra. "And we won't be able to care for them while we wait."

"How many hours will it take?" asked Kate.

Lyralliantha's lip curled into a half smile, "A better question would be, 'how many days?'"

"That's too long," protested Kate.

"Do you not trust Helen with them?"

She shook her head, "No, it's not that, but someone has to feed them." Garlin and Layla were three months old, nowhere close to being ready to be weaned, and certainly not so suddenly.

Lyra frowned. There was a lot she still didn't understand about raising children. The thought of food hadn't occurred to her, she had just assumed that their grandmother would have some solution. "Perhaps you should do this then," she suggested. "Once I help you reach the proper state I can return to assist Helen."

"Can't we take turns?" She glanced at Lyra's somewhat smaller chest. Her friend had never been overly endowed, and she doubted she could keep up with the demand of two infants. She also knew that if she didn't feed them regularly, her own supply would dry up.

"That will complicate things," said Lyra, "but it is possible."

In the end, they agreed to twelve hour shifts, after Kate insisted that full days were too long. Lyra really had no understanding of how infants, or her own body worked, but Kate convinced her it was necessary.

Lyralliantha produced a complex spellweave and constructed an odd shelter beside the tree. It looked something like an odd cocoon, open to the bark on one side, and open to the weather on the other, but as soon as Kate stepped into it she could tell that it somehow kept stray breezes from entering through the exterior opening. The interior was warm without being suffocating, and it held two seats that would allow them to recline against the bark while still keeping them comfortable.

"Did you just think this up?" asked Kate.

"No," said Lyra, "I have done this many times." She gestured at one of the seats. "Sit. I will guide you into the proper state before I go."

"I'm supposed to just sit here for twelve hours?"

"It's a little like going to sleep. Your sense of time will change. It will seem like only minutes before I rouse you again to take your place."

Kate did as she was told, and then Lyra placed her hands on her temples before kissing her on the forehead. "Do not worry. I love you," said the She'Har woman. Kate started to reply but the world faded, or perhaps it was just her eyes closing. She was enfolded in a warm darkness.

And then she felt him.

Daniel?

It was Kate's voice. As always it warmed his heart, though he knew she was just a dream. *Yes, my love?* he responded.

You need to come back, she told him.

Usually she was more relaxed in his dream, content to relive the past, or occasionally to engage in an extended game of 'what if'. He had few regrets about his current condition, and generally his dream actors followed suit. *That would be unpleasant,* he told her. *The world can get on without me.*

And then she vanished, replaced a moment later by Lyralliantha. *Please return,* she said.

I like it here, he answered, but she was gone.

Kate was back, *You have two new children, Layla and Garlin.*

A good choice of names, he noted.

Layla is dead, Lyralliantha told him.

This is just a dream, now you're just making things up.

Then Kate returned, looking sad, *Emma is losing her mind. She's threatening Lyra.*

Lyra was there again, before he could even reply. The constant shifting was beginning to irritate him. *Stop it,* he ordered, *this is too chaotic.* He attempted to focus on her, to make her image remain.

This is no vision, Tyrion. I am here. Kate and I are taking turns, we have to feed...

She was gone again.

Our children need us, Daniel. They need you, added Kate.

Kate woke with Lyra looking down at her. "This isn't working," she said. "He still thinks we're a dream."

"He is still young," said Lyralliantha. "Most elders spend several decades dreaming before they begin to think more actively. It takes even longer for them to learn to speed their thoughts."

"Speed their thoughts?"

"Normally when we speak to them, it takes a long time," said Lyra, "but in times of crisis the elders, the mature ones at least, can increase their subjective time to the point of being able to converse with us in our perceptual time frame. They dislike doing it, but it is possible."

"How old is mature?" asked Kate.

"Several hundred years."

Kate sighed, "The children will be grown before we rouse him."

"We simply have to convince him," said Lyra. "Once he understands our message, his response could be rapid."

This is no dream, said Lyra. *There is danger.*

He ignored her.

Kate appeared, *Emma plans to destroy everything.*

As I taught her, he murmured.

Lyra returned, but before she spoke he felt something new. Fire. One of his limbs was burning. The world shifted, as the She'Har equivalent of a surge of adrenaline coursed through him. A bonfire had been built beside him and its flames were tall enough to reach his lower branches. Sending forth his will he quenched the blaze, and then he turned his attention to the tiny being that had been feeding the fire.

A woman, her aythar familiar, stood staring at the now defunct fire. He considered killing her, to prevent any further attempts. He examined her more closely first. Brigid had once threatened to set fire to him if he didn't return, but this wasn't her.

Is that Kate?

Lyra spoke, *Of course it is. She is desperate. We need your...*

She was gone, and Kate was back in his dream, *Please wake up.*

Did you try to set fire to me? he asked.

Yes she did, replied, Lyralliantha, replacing her.

I thought you were a memory.

Help me, Daniel, Kate begged.

She was really there. The knowledge produced a surge of feeling, and he wanted to hold her, but she faded as he tried to put his mental arms around her. Now she was Lyra again.

I love you, he told her. It was true no matter which of them heard him.

Wake up, said Lyralliantha, kissing him.

I love you, he repeated, and then Kate bit him.

Wake up! she insisted.

Tyrion moved. It felt similar to standing and shrugging your shoulders, flexing the muscles after a long night in bed. He gathered his will, and then he directed his thoughts outward. The sun wheeled across the sky above, and the earth embraced his roots below. He remembered his days as a man, and he let the vision fill him.

Opening his eyes, he saw her, reclining in a strange spellwoven shelter of some sort, her red hair falling chaotically around her as she lifted her head to look back at him.

Kate looked older, tired and worn. There were circles under her eyes, and her once cute freckles had become a riot on cheeks that were no longer quite as firm. As she stood he could see that her chest was larger, and it hung lower beneath her dress.

She looked like she had been through an ordeal, but she was still beautiful to him. Within her eyes he still saw the spark that had once made his heart jump, though it was almost hidden by her tired expression.

Kate could see him appraising her, and she looked away. Daniel looked the same as ever, possibly younger. His once restored ear was gone again, replaced by the mangled remnant he had had in his twenties, but otherwise he looked fit and healthy, the very picture of vitality. Of course, his naked skin was still covered by a multitude of garish tattoos. As she looked back she saw that Lyra was approaching them, walking up the gentle incline.

"Say something," Kate challenged.

He tilted his head, and finally, after a long pause, he replied, "I have lost the habit."

"Why did you leave me, leave us?" she asked.

Lyralliantha had stopped, standing some fifteen feet away, content to watch their reunion.

"I would not have survived," he responded. "Afterward—after I had changed, it was peaceful. I thought the world would be better without me."

Kate looked up at him, her eyes watering, "Selfish ass."

"I love you," he told her.

Watching them, Lyra felt a new emotion. She was overjoyed by his change, and she was happy, and yet, beneath it all, she felt something dark. As Tyrion and Kate looked at one another she felt something pass between them, something stronger than she had ever had, a bond that she would never fully be a part of. *Is this jealousy?* She pushed it aside.

Stepping forward, Lyra spoke, "Would you like to meet your children?"

CHAPTER 36

It was very late before most of them fell asleep, but Tyrion was wide awake.

He sat in his mother's rocker in front of the modest hearth, holding Layla. Alan was the only other person still awake, sitting nearby in his own chair with Garlin in his arms.

The two men sat quietly, rocking a little now and then, and enjoying the silence as they stared into the flames.

His mother had been the first to bed, exhausted by the shock of his return, she had gone into a frenzy of cooking and talking, but her old body was no longer able to sustain such energies for very long. Kate had followed her not long after, and Lyra had been next.

His return had been a cause for excitement, and everyone had been determined to fill his attention and his ears with all the news, with everything he had missed. It should have worn him out, but he still wasn't tired. Perhaps his time as a tree had counted for sleep.

Only his father had remained relatively subdued. Alan had given him a brief hug and then had seemed content merely to listen to the women talk as they attempted to describe every detail of the past months.

Tyrion and his father hadn't been close in many years, not since he had returned and taken his nearly grown children from Colne. Alan had taken to drinking at the time, and his last major confession had been to tell Tyrion that he wished he had never been born.

The emptiness still hung between them, cold and dry.

He didn't hate his father, or resent him. If anything he thought his father's words had been more than justified. In the grand scheme of things he had been a colossal disappointment as a son, as a human being.

"I didn't mean it."

The words fell into the silence. Strange and unexpected, they came from Alan.

"Yeah you did," said Tyrion. "And you were right."

"I still shouldn't have said it."

"You were drunk."

"Doesn't excuse it," said Alan. "Sober or drunk, I meant it—then. I've had a lot of time to reflect since."

"And now?"

Alan didn't look at him, "You're still the boy I raised and loved, whatever else you've become. You did some things I can't forgive, but everyone walks their own path. I can't judge you from the life I've lived."

Tyrion swallowed, trying to clear the lump that had risen in his throat, "Dad…"

"You still scare the shit out of me," interrupted his father.

"That's probably wise," said Tyrion, "but I would never hurt you, or mom."

"I'm not worried about that, son," said Alan, clarifying. "I'm too old to worry about myself. It's the young ones I fear for." He shifted his arms slightly, lifting Garlin to emphasize his point.

"I wouldn't hurt them either."

Alan glanced at him, his eyes catching the firelight, "Don't make promises you can't keep."

Tyrion looked down, letting his vision focus on Layla. His father was right, he couldn't even promise that. They sat in silence a while longer, though it was somehow more comfortable than before.

Eventually, Alan spoke again, "Ever gotten to hold a little one like this before?"

"Just Inara," said Tyrion. "And only for a few months, before I was forced to…"

"…become a tree?" finished his father.

"Yeah."

"You've given me more grandchildren than any old man has a right to expect," said Alan. "It's good to finally be able to hold one."

You got to raise one, thought Tyrion, thinking of Haley, but he held his tongue. Bringing up his dead daughter wouldn't improve the conversation. "Brigid stayed with you for a while, recently," he said instead.

Alan chuffed, "That girl's weirder than you, and scarier too, maybe."

"True."

Another quarter of an hour passed before his father spoke again, "What's it like, having two wives?"

The question caught him entirely off guard. "They aren't really both my wives, Lyra calls me her ki…"

"Don't talk around it, just tell me, son. I'm genuinely curious," said Alan.

"I didn't set out to wind up in this situation," said Tyrion, "but it isn't as strange as you might think."

"How do you decide who…," Alan let the question trail away.

"Mostly they decide that," answered Tyrion. "I suspect they think of me like a dog. They figure out between them who has to feed and water it from day to day."

Alan gave out a small laugh, "You are a chore. No question about it."

Tyrion appreciated the remark, then he stared down at Layla once more, fascinated anew as he watched her breathing.

"They change you, don't they?" said Alan. "One minute you're just you, the next you realize you have someone who depends on you for everything. Changes your priorities. As it should, I suppose."

Tyrion didn't answer, merely nodded. He wondered what his father would think of his old plan. It wouldn't be positive, he was sure.

"What are you going to do, when you go back?" asked Alan.

He had no real idea. "I think I need to find a new path," he said at last.

"You know they want us to move, right? Was that part of your plan?"

"Yes," he admitted. "One of the good parts maybe. I want to give people a chance to build a better future."

"I like where I live."

But I have to make sure you survive, thought Tyrion. *Unless…*

"Doesn't make sense trying to get shepherds and farmers to live in a city, no matter how grand it is," opined his father. "We need space, otherwise there'll be no wool, and no crops either."

"It would only be temporary," said Tyrion. A new idea was rising in him, "Maybe you won't have to move."

"Have to?" said Alan with a frown. "Nothing's been said about *having to*. A lot of us won't go at all."

"Bad choice of words," he lied. "I do need to change things when I go back, though. It isn't going to be easy."

"That's life for you," said Alan.

"I don't know how to do it," he admitted. "Everyone expects certain things, and there's a lot I can't control."

His father stood, carrying the infant in his arms over to one of the two cradles on one side of the room. Settling the babe carefully into his place, Alan straightened and looked toward his son. "The answer's right there, in your arms. I don't know what you're into, or how any of that magic stuff works, but I've lived long enough to know how to make decisions. There's no secret to it."

"Apparently, I've failed to learn something obvious then."

Alan put his hand on his shoulder, squeezing slightly before moving on toward his bedroom door. "It's easy. Just think about that child you're holding. Whatever you're doing, or going to do, think about how it will affect her. One way or another, that'll tell you what you should do.

"Night, son." And then Alan Tennick went to bed.

Tyrion didn't sleep that night. He sat up through the dark hours, staring into the fire as it burned down to embers.

The two men watching the gate at Albamarl didn't recognize him.

It was an unusual sensation for him. Tyrion had risen to great heights of notoriety among the slaves of the She'Har, and eventually among everyone else as well, human and She'Har alike. But that had been years ago, and while most knew his name and reputation, many of the newer slave mages who had come to Albamarl did not know him on sight.

These two stared at him nervously. "Please wait, sir. We will get someone to verify you are who you say you are first."

He fought the urge to smirk as he watched one run off, looking for someone with more authority, presumably one of his children. Neither of these two were very bright. The intensity of his aura was enough to tell them he was no ordinary person from the slave camps. That combined with his tattoos should have been enough to convince them.

Once, he might have killed them to make a point. Not simply as a blind response to being challenged, but also to maintain his reputation, to instill fear in those who served him.

He was not that man anymore, however. He had changed, and today would be the day he began teaching a new way to those around him.

My old way was just a reaction to what happened. I fought hard because I had been abused, but the fighting only made me more of a victim. Going forward he would make his choices based on something greater than his pain. The cycle of pain wouldn't be resolved by hurting his enemies, it was just the opposite.

Convincing the children who he had inflicted his madness on, would not be easy, though. He knew that, but if there was anyone in the world who could do it, it had to be him. No, it could only be him. They wouldn't listen to anyone else.

Anthony appeared, and the look of surprise on his face was clearly evident, "Father!?"

"Anthony," he said, nodding his head slightly. He moved forward, passing through the arch and ignoring the two guards.

"I didn't believe them," murmured his son. "After Brigid came back alone, I never thought you would return."

"Nothing ever works out the way we think it will."

"I told the guard it couldn't possibly be you when he found me," said the younger man. "Otherwise he'd be dead for trying to make you wait."

"I've gained some perspective since leaving. How are things here?"

Anthony glanced at the two guards who still hung close, listening. "Back to your posts!" he ordered. Walking toward the main house with his father, he replied,

"Everything has gone according to your plan, the First saw to that."

"First?"

"Emma."

The sound in his son's voice as he named her told him much. Emma was no longer popular among her siblings.

"She killed Layla," added Anthony in a more subdued voice. "She might have killed Lyra too if it hadn't been for Layla's intervention. Kate and Lyra have fled to the Prathion Grove."

"So I heard," said Tyrion. He touched his son's arm, indicating he should stop. "Before we go any farther, let me make this clear. I am not here to punish anyone."

The look in Anthony's eyes was one of disappointment, "Oh."

"We've all made mistakes. What is important is not what was done, but what we do from here forward. Where's Brigid?"

"Behind the main house," said Anthony. "She's been taking care of Eldin and Inara. I saw her out there earlier, playing with them."

Tyrion's brows went up, "Brigid?"

"She was put in charge of them after Kate left, and Layla…"

"An odd choice," noted Tyrion. "She's hardly the nurturing sort."

"Emma was angry with her for interfering. I think it was a punishment as much as anything else."

Tyrion felt a vague sense of unease at the thought of Brigid being the primary caretaker for anyone, much less his younger children. "I need to see this." His magesight was already focusing on the area in question.

As they approached he could see she was throwing the children around the yard, tossing them like balls into the air. It looked dangerously violent, and his stomach tightened involuntarily, but as they drew closer he could hear the two children giggling.

She would launch them, spinning and tumbling away from her in random directions, and at a casual glance it appeared as though they landed hard, but she was actually interfering in subtle ways. Their falls would slow before they struck the ground, cushioning them just enough to make what might have been a bruising landing into a thrilling but harmless stop.

As soon as they could get their feet under themselves they would try to stand, frequently falling over, dizzy and uncoordinated, before charging toward her as quickly as their little legs would carry them. She would let them get almost close enough to grab her before tossing them up and away again.

She was smiling.

Tyrion saw all this before he turned the corner. There were many people in the area with strong auras, so Brigid hadn't taken much note of him yet, but once he rounded the corner it was apparent that he was coming to see her. Her smile vanished as her attention focused on him, and he saw the chain lift itself from the ground beside her, moving to float in the air between her and the newcomer.

Her face remained still as she recognized him, concealing her shock.

"I'll be damned," said Tyrion.

Inara and Eldin finished running back to her, this time unhindered, and they clasped her legs as she stood, laughing with joy at their catch. They still hadn't noticed him, but when they did Eldin pointed, "Who?"

"Father," said Brigid softly, as much a greeting as an answer to Eldin's question.

"Fadder," repeated Inara.

"Nice dress," said Tyrion, noting the simple green shift that Brigid was wearing.

His daughter's face flushed with embarrassment in much the same way a normal person's would if they had been caught naked. "It keeps them from trying to latch on," she observed, pointing at her chest, "or it did. I got a little used to it."

The plain dress was dirty and rumpled, a stark contrast to the children themselves, who looked much cleaner than she did. Brigid had changed in unexpected ways. He wanted to ask her about everything, but a number of people were approaching, from several directions.

Word of his arrival had spread, and his children were coming to see the truth for themselves.

In ones and twos they came. Anthony and Violet were first, and then Piper appeared. They stared at him with something close to hope in their eyes, something he had never expected to see. Tad and Ashley were next, followed by David and Sarah, then Ian, each of them stopping some ten feet away, unconsciously arranging themselves around him in a semicircle. Abby looked the most relieved to see him as she strode up anxiously. A dozen questions rose from them, but before he could answer any of them they fell silent.

Emma and Ryan had arrived, the two he had been closest to, his most trusted, and now their leaders. The air was tense as his children waited to see the result of their reunion.

Tyrion studied Emma with a stern gaze. She was gaunt. She had lost weight, and there were dark circles beneath her haunted eyes. Her former serenity was gone, replaced by a hardness that reminded him of himself. The past year had transformed her.

The old Tyrion might have killed her for her action regarding Lyra and especially for Layla's death, but he felt something different now. Seeing her was like gazing at his own soul, or at least at the version of himself that had existed a year ago.

He had put her in charge knowing her heart had been poisoned by rage and hatred. He had given her the reins because she was the most like him. Some of her choices might be different than what his might have been, but they had been executed in the same relentless spirit, and for the same reasons he had once believe in.

Whatever she had done, he might as well have done himself.

And those decisions had nearly destroyed her.

She crossed the invisible line that the others had stopped at, some ten feet distant, and approached until she stood directly in front of him. Emma's back was straight and her neck unbowed. "You actually came back," she said.

He wanted to embrace her, to take away the pain, but he knew her, knew himself too well. That would never work. Instead he told her what must be lurking on the surface of her mind, "I heard about Layla. Kate and Lyra woke me, forced me to come back."

Someone snickered faintly as he said it. Ian, expectantly watching. Tyrion ignored it.

Emma looked him straight in the eyes, seeing the judgment there, and without warning, she knelt before him, turning her face down to the ground. "I did as I saw fit, but I will accept whatever resolution you seek."

Her aura became brighter, and Tyrion could almost sense the burden lifting from her shoulders. She wanted to die, and his return had given her hope that he would end her suffering. It made him want to cry for her, but he kept his face expressionless.

"Did you do as I said?" he asked firmly.

"Yes, Father," answered Emma.

He looked at Ryan, "Is the construction finished?"

The parts that are required were done months ago. All we do now is to add to the city that will never be used, to maintain appearances, responded his son silently.

"The slaves, the Mordan?"

"They are ready," answered Ian. "They need only be awakened."

They had done it. Emma had done it, driving them according to his wishes, until they were ready to unleash a doom that would destroy the world. All that remained was to gather the people of Colne and Lincoln, to put them in the places prepared to keep them safe.

A word from him and they would turn the world to dust and ashes. But he no longer wanted that. *What a cruel irony,* thought Tyrion. *They did it, but I no longer want it.*

He turned his eyes to the rest of his children, searching their faces, and then he spoke, "Some of you are hoping I will punish her for what happened to Layla. You will be disappointed.

"Everything Emma has done has been in my name, and she has done well. If any of you have a grudge against her, you may bring it up with me, otherwise you may as well forget it. What is past is done. Kate and Lyralliantha will be returning tomorrow. There will be no more dissension among us. Do you understand?"

Their voices answered firmly, a smattering of, 'Yes, Father's ringing out.

Bending down, he took Emma by the shoulders, lifting her to stand on her feet again, "Do you understand, Emma?"

"Yes, Father." There was a mixture of relief and shame in her eyes.

"You did well," he told her. "Rest for now, eat something. You've shouldered an unbearable burden for far too long. Let me carry the weight now."

Emma kept her back straight, but her eyes were watering.

"Shhh," he whispered, giving her a wink. "Don't let them see you cry. I'm proud of you, but you can't let them see your weakness, not after ruling them."

CHAPTER 37

The next two weeks were largely uneventful. Autumn progressed into the first snow of an early winter, and the people in Albamarl slowed down. The frenetic pace was gone. Tyrion's return had left them all wondering what would be next, but when he didn't appear ready to do anything in particular everyone gradually began to relax.

The quality of the food certainly improved with Kate's return.

Some things were awkward, of course. Kate made no attempt to speak to Emma, actively ignoring the woman who had killed her friend. It was the best she could do. Abby was much the same, refusing to speak to her sister unless absolutely necessary.

Emma for her part actively avoided Kate whenever possible.

Lyralliantha, true to form, acted as though nothing had happened.

Brigid continued to play with Inara and Eldin whenever she got the chance, having discovered that she had more in common with children than any of the adults around her.

Inara and Eldin had some difficulty adjusting to Kate's return, not being entirely sure who their mother was, but with time there was little doubt they would sort it out. In the main they seemed delighted to have so many people interested in them. Kate and Lyra both spent time with them and having Brigid for a devoted big sister meant they never lacked attention. They were a bit skeptical about the two infants that had replaced them as the absolute center of attention, but they would adapt to that as well, eventually.

Tyrion did nothing.

Nothing of note, anyway. He ate, slept, and enjoyed watching the others, but he made no attempt to change anything, or further his old goals. He let his old plans sit dormant, and when he did consider them, it was to wonder how he would eventually dismantle them.

He told no one of his change of heart, thinking that time would make it easier. So he decided he would merely stall things for a year, and then begin to make his new wishes known. Once his children got used to waking up each day without contemplating the end of the world, they might be more amenable to creating a more peaceful future.

Let them grow fat and complacent with hope for tomorrow, he thought to himself. *Eventually they will want tomorrow more than vengeance.*

When mid-winter drew close, he invited Thillmarius to join them for a feast to celebrate the winter solstice. After his time as a tree he discovered that his old fear of the She'Har trainer had diminished. The cold dread he had felt in the Prathion lore-warden's presence had faded almost completely.

He was a new man, and ready to make new beginnings.

Thillmarius brought a small cart laden with bread and fresh butter to the feast. The She'Har had been overenthusiastic in his baking, but no one complained. They ate roast pig and followed it with the surplus of side dishes that Kate and Lyra prepared. The bread was a perfect complement, even if there was too much to finish.

Albamarl was content, and while everyone wondered at the change, no one questioned it for fear of ending what they thought must be a temporary period of happiness.

Serrelia watched it all, puzzled by their behavior.

She had entered Albamarl only days before Tyrion's return, stealing the body of one of the slave mages to make it easy for her to move around without suspicion. Of course, she wasn't the *true* Serrelia, she knew that. She was a mind-twin, and she periodically reported her news to her progenitor who stayed well beyond the area around Albamarl.

The body she inhabited had belonged to a woman named Tracy. She kept her memories, although they weren't very useful, other than to further her disguise. The biggest difficulty she had was avoiding detection by those who had known the woman previously.

Tracy had been a Gaelyn, but since Serrelia had crushed her mind and stolen her body, she was no more, and neither was her gift. If anyone expected her to change form, it might arouse suspicion when she was unable to do so.

The simple solution was to twin herself again, taking the bodies of those closest to her, but she was loathe to do that. She dreaded the confrontation that would come when she eventually returned to her progenitor. The fewer of her that existed, the greater her chance would be of remaining the primary when the day of her reunion came.

So she contented herself with subverting all the slaves who knew her, gradually altering their minds and personalities without directly taking control. Over time they became devoted to her, and she was certain that if the need arose they would give their lives for her.

She considered trying to take one of Tyrion's children, but discarded the idea. It was far too risky. Their minds were far more complex than the emotionally stunted former slaves, and their aythar was blindingly strong. If she caught one by surprise, perhaps, but it would be a risky battle and likely to draw attention from the others.

The most frustrating thing was the lack of information.

She interrogated those she held sway over and picked at the surface thoughts of those she didn't, and yet she still found nothing noteworthy. Almost everyone in Albamarl was clueless as to what Tyrion's intentions were.

There were interesting details, though. Some of the slaves had been involved in crafting numerous stasis boxes, she felt sure that was important, but she had no idea how. The construction of the empty city was curious, but mundane.

Tyrion's children knew more, but she dared not reveal herself by attempting to inspect them directly.

Serrelia waited, reporting what she found and nothing more.

Tyrion has done nothing since his return. He appears to be waiting for something, said Ceylendor.

His youngest children are still there? asked one of the elders.

Yes.

We should act while we still can.

Agreed, said the First among the Centyr Elders. *You will begin rolling the dice Ceylendor. When the result is nine you must act without delay.*

As you wish, Elders, responded the lore-warden.

The dice in question were a set of two decahedrons grown by one of the elders. Various numbers covered each face, and when rolled they could be added together to produce a random number. Ceylendor rolled them as soon as he got back to his platform.

"Eleven," he murmured in disappointment. It would have to wait for another day.

The possibilities have begun diverging rapidly, warned one of the Illeniel Elders. *The Centyr will move soon, but it is impossible to know when.*

How is this possible? questioned one of the younger ones.

They use blind chance to confuse us.

Clever, responded another. *We should post guards.*

They would be noticed, and if the Centyr know of them they will plan for them.

Bring the child here then, they would not dare attack it within the grove itself.

They might discover which child is critical to our plan if we do that.

Bring them all then.

Tyrion will not allow that, we have tested the possibility already. We can bring only one, and it must be done in secret or they will discover our deception, stated the First Elder.

They have a spy there, how can it be done?

The Prathions will assist. Lyralliantha must be given instruction.

I am afraid.

Of what? asked the First.

Death.

We all must die, but by our actions our race will survive, someday.

Lyralliantha had been gone a week, and when she returned she had Thillmarius with her. She asked to speak to Tyrion and Kate privately. The three of them gathered in the bedroom that they shared.

"The elders want to meet your daughter," she began without preamble, looking at Kate.

"Why?" asked Kate, suddenly suspicious. "Why not your son? Layla has nothing to do with them."

Tyrion understood the reason immediately. "Layla is different. She may have inherited the loshti from me."

"So could Garlin," argued Kate. "Why do they want to see *my* daughter?"

He shook his head, "I believe they created it to pass only to the first child. Layla was conceived before Garlin."

"Garlin is the one that might have the special Illeniel gift of theirs, they should be more interested in him," she countered.

Lyra's brows went up, she had not expected Kate to be aware of that detail. It wasn't something she had tried to hide, but neither had she made a habit of discussing it. "They tell me that they wish to examine Layla's mind, to make sure the transfer of knowledge worked as intended. In adults…" she nodded toward Tyrion, "… there are sometimes problems."

"Then they can come here to see her," insisted Kate.

"They cannot travel," reminded Lyra. "I assure you that they mean no harm to your child."

Kate changed tactics, "Then they won't mind me coming with her."

"You would be able to do nothing," said Lyra. "Let me go. I can commune with them during the process. You can trust that I will not allow them to do anything more than observe her."

Tyrion remained silent.

"Don't you have anything to say in this?" Kate challenged him.

"They know the consequences if they betray me," he said simply.

"I will be leaving Garlin with you, Kate," said Lyra sincerely. "I trust no one in this world to love and care for him more than you. Layla means as much to me as he does. I will let no harm come to either of our children."

Kate bit her lip, "Fine. I don't like it, but I'll trust you, Lyra."

They let Thillmarius enter after that, and when the door opened again, only Kate emerged. The Prathion lore-warden used his gift to spirit Lyra, Tyrion, and little Layla away without anyone noticing.

They didn't intend to make the trip public knowledge. Some of his children might notice Lyra's absence, but it might be a while before they realized that Kate's daughter was gone too, especially if Kate kept to herself for a while. Ironically, Brigid was the most likely to wonder since she came to play with the children almost daily.

Tyrion had no worries about her talking. Brigid was the least talkative of them all.

CHAPTER 38

Seven days after Lyra left with Layla, Ceylendor looked down at the dice and smiled. The sum showing was nine.

He immediately notified the Mordan krytek that was waiting for his message, and it vanished. It made two stops, one to the Mordan Grove, and the second to Serrelia's hidden position, several miles from Albamarl.

And then things began to happen.

Sarah looked askance at the men and women who entered through the main door to Tyrion's house. They were all slaves, but there was no reason for them to enter the house.

"What are you doing in here?" she asked.

Their response was immediate, powerful, and completely unexpected. Two of them, Prathions, vanished. The other six attacked her.

Sarah didn't have her enchanted shield up, none of them did that, but she did have a small, more ordinary shield around herself. If their attacks had reached it before she reinforced it, she still would have died, though.

She wasn't the fastest or most powerful of Tyrion's children, but she was no slouch either. Sarah saw their aythar flare and in that instant she threw her power into the shield. Their combined assault struck her defense, and just barely, it held. With a word she activated her tattoos and their enchantments sprang to life.

A broad stroke of pure force sent her flying through the air. It wasn't an attempt to break her shield, merely to disorient her.

Sarah still remembered the two that had vanished, and even as she hurtled toward the wall she summoned an aythar filled mist to obscure the room. If she couldn't see all of them, then neither would they see her. She struck the wall hard, but her shield kept the impact from doing more than rattling her teeth. If one of her siblings had done that to her it would have probably been strong enough to knock her senseless. Her enemies were weaklings.

She snarled as adrenaline made her heart quicken. She would kill them all.

Regaining her feet, Sarah stalked forward through the mist, following the wall to her right. She bumped into one of them almost immediately. The woman's reflexes were fast, and her armblade made contact with Sarah's shield first. It didn't have the power necessary to penetrate, however.

Sarah's return strike cut the woman neatly in two.

Sounds on either side of her let her know that her scuffle had been noticed. They were trying to get to her before she could move again. With a brief effort of will she lifted one of the heavy wooden chairs nearby and sent it sweeping sideways. It made contact with someone as she darted in the other direction.

The man whose chest she ran into was much larger than she was. Ordinarily that wasn't a factor in a battle between mages, but he managed to get his arms inside hers and force her back, against the wall. With her arms forced outward she had no way to attack him and his physical strength was much greater than her own.

He was pressing the point of his own armblade into her chest, but so far the shield had resisted it.

A number of options passed through her mind in an instant. The instinctive one was to use a blast of raw aythar to send him flying backward, but then she'd still have to find and kill him afterward. A second possibility was to use her will to strengthen her muscles, she could probably overpower him then.

But then her eyes fell on the tattoo at his neck.

Uttering the command word, she watched him slump and fall dead at her feet. It wasn't a satisfactory way to win, but she was outnumbered, and she still had no idea what they were after. Stepping over the body she moved forward, seeking her next opponent.

It was too cold to have small children outside. That's what Brigid would have been told when she was little, but she had certain advantages her parents had never had.

There was snow on the ground, but Inara and Eldin never felt the chill of the air. She kept an envelope of warm air around each of them while they giggled and played with the snow. Of course, the warmth melted the snow much faster than simple gloves would have, but that was alright.

Eldin delighted in watching it melt away almost as soon as he could grab it up.

Even if he could have held it, he and his sister were far too small and uncoordinated to make it into anything recognizable, so Brigid took that task on for them. Using her aythar, she scooped the snow up and formed it into fantastic shapes. She didn't have Violet's artistic skill, but she satisfied them with crude snow horses and other simple animals before switching to geometric shapes, cubes, squares and ellipsoids.

Inara was particularly entranced, watching raptly while Eldin spent half his time trying to grab the snow with his own hands.

The man who walked toward them was big, larger than most, standing almost six and a half feet tall. Like many from the slave camps he was covered with scars, a testament to the battles he had endured before becoming a warden.

Because of his height, Brigid had noticed him before; she even remembered his name, Bolger. She nodded faintly at him as he walked closer, intent on her snow inspired games.

He seemed inclined to watch them, and she was willing to ignore him, until he stepped too close to Eldin. He was just beside the little boy, and that was too close for her taste.

"You need to move on, Bolger. Tyrion won't like you getting too close to his children," she warned.

He glanced at her calmly, "Never got a chance to see many kids when I was in Baratrea. I don't mean him no harm." Leaning over he patted Eldin gently, feeling the boy's soft hair.

Two more strangers approached from the other direction, and Brigid turned her attention to them for a second, identifying them as more of the slaves that worked in and around Albamarl. The cracking sound that found her ears sent a shiver of cold horror down her spine.

Bolger's hand was around Eldin's neck and the toddler's head hung loosely, drool falling from his lips as his eyes fluttered.

Brigid was stunned, unable to believe her eyes, but that didn't stop her from reacting. An inarticulate howl rose from her throat, the cry of an animal that has lost something dear to it. Bolger activated his tattoos, shielding himself and stalking toward Inara with one armblade extended.

Brigid's will lifted him from the ground, smashing him against the stone wall that formed the back of Tyrion's house. His shield held, but the force of the impact was so great that Bolger lost consciousness, blood running from his nose and ears. The shield vanished then, and the second time she slammed him against the wall broke his skull and most of the other large bones in his body.

A lance of power shot forth from one of the two newcomers, aimed not at her, but at Inara. It was deflected at the last moment by the enchanted chain that interposed itself.

The shock and surprise that had slowed her initially was gone now as Brigid faced them, two women with crude features and brown hair. She didn't recognize these two, they looked much like most of the women who came from Ellentrea, their noses bent and flattened from repeated breaks in the past. They were already shielded as they approached her.

It was a mistake to give them tattoos, thought Brigid, but it never occurred to her to use the lethal ones inscribed on their necks.

She stood between them and Inara, her own shield active and her chain moving closely around the girl to protect her. She wouldn't need it to kill them. Brigid glared at them, her eyes carrying a hatred so strong, it seemed to make the air smolder, "Burn!"

With that, the air around them ignited into incandescent flames. Their shields kept it out, but the heat was so intense it hardly mattered. Brigid was howling, and the fires she had created burned hotter with each passing second. She kept it up long after they collapsed, until they lost consciousness and their shields vanished. Then she incinerated the bodies. A greasy black cloud rose into the air, and there was nothing left but ash when she stopped.

The blast of fire that caught her from behind was much weaker than hers had been, it washed over her shield and did little to her, other than surprise her. There had been no one there.

A Prathion, stood ten feet away now, revealed by the failed ambush.

Brigid snarled, sending her chain outward, she cut the upstart into five pieces in less than a second.

Then she bent down to retrieve Inara, and saw what the fire had done. Unshielded, the girl had been blackened by the fire that had passed between the lengths of chain around her. Most of her skin was charred, and the damage to her lungs had left her unable to breathe. She writhed silently on the ground, dying even as Brigid watched, helpless.

Brigid's cry of anguish was a small thing, too small to contain the horror and despair. It was limited by the constraints of her mortal frame, but the fury in her soul would not be bound by such things. She stood motionless for several minutes, while the ground beneath her vibrated with the intensity of her barely contained aythar.

And then, she began to hunt, her chain following her like a hungry serpent.

Kate was nursing Garlin when she heard a noise outside the bedroom. She didn't think much of it until she felt the heavy thump against the wall. The house was constructed of thick stone, the only blows that could be felt like that were powerful ones.

Worried, but not yet fearful, she pulled Garlin from her breast and laid him in his crib. The crossbow Tyrion had given her years before still hung on the wall, along with the quarrel she had once used to kill one of the She'Har. Taking it down she tried to cock it but the strength in her arms wasn't enough. There was a stirrup on the front end of the bow to allow the user to brace it with a foot while drawing the string, but she knew that wouldn't be enough.

A belt hung on the wall, next to where the weapon had been. A hook attached to it was meant to attach to the string, allowing someone like herself to bend at the knees and then straighten up, using the strength of their legs to arm the bow.

Lock the door first, she told herself.

Still holding the crossbow, she marched toward the door, but she stopped before reaching it. It began to move as someone drew the latch from the other side. *Calm down, it's probably just Sarah, come to explain the noise.*

As the door opened, however, she saw no one, and a strange mist billowed in from the other room.

Adrenaline hit her like a bolt of lightning as the more primitive portion of her brain recognized an unnatural threat. Kate slammed the weapon against the floor, and in one fluid motion set her foot in the stirrup and drew it back easily; fear had given her the strength she lacked before. Setting the bolt in place she leveled it at the doorway and fired at the vaguely human outline revealed by the mist.

A man appeared, the quarrel buried deep in his chest. Gasping he toppled over, dying rapidly.

Close the door! she thought. Taking two steps she moved to shove the stranger out of the way so she could close the entry, but a faint draft made her aware of the second invader a second later. Kate's head turned to look back toward the crib when the woman appeared behind her, and then she felt a blinding pain as the stranger's armblade pushed through her lower back. It went through her kidney and emerged from her lower abdomen.

She was falling.

She never felt the impact. Time had become distorted and desperation had narrowed her focus to one all important goal, the baby. The woman's boots walked toward the crib, she was ignoring her now. Kate was dying.

Her legs weren't working, but Kate pulled herself across the floor with her arms. The dead man was close, and she managed to get her hand on the bolt standing out from his chest. It didn't move at her first tug, but the second ripped it free. Her heart was pounding, giving her strength.

The quarrel was ruined, the wooden shaft had splintered from the impact when it struck her target, and Kate knew she couldn't have cocked the crossbow again anyway. Lifting the heavy wooden weapon she threw it across the room at the woman who had stabbed her.

It flew low, hitting the woman in the legs and causing her to fall backward. She landed close, just within Kate's reach, and she slammed her fist, still holding the damaged crossbow bolt like a dagger, into the woman's shoulder.

The blow was poorly placed, however. The enchanted point went through her enemy's shield, but it failed to penetrate deeply. She was bleeding, but the wound wasn't serious.

The crib had been overturned, though. The invader had grabbed at it as she fell, sending poor Garlin tumbling across the floor, wailing in fear. He was near the bed.

Kate pushed him under it as she rolled, trying to put her body between him and the stranger. Pain blossomed in her back as the woman's armblade went through her once, twice, and then a third time. The world dimmed as Kate's eyesight failed, but her ears could still hear Garlin screaming as other woman dragged him roughly from under the bed by one leg.

Lyra, forgive me—our baby... and then she mercifully lost consciousness.

Sarah burst in only seconds later, roaring like a beast as she came, only to see the stranger fling Garlin's limp body to the floor. He was already dead.

The Prathion mage's shield was still down, the enchanted quarrel had broken it when Kate stabbed her. Sarah's attack hit her like a battering ram built of fire and unholy violence. It ripped the woman in half and left what remained of her body charred beyond recognition.

Silence reigned for a moment as Sarah stared at the wreckage that had been Tyrion and Kate's bedroom, her eyes taking in the bodies and the blood, absorbing the sight of things that could never be made whole again. Slowly she crumpled to the floor, keening with despair as her trembling fingers felt the savage cuts in Kate's body.

CHAPTER 39

Ryan was in the empty city, reconsidering the layout for an aqueduct, when he heard the screams. He ignored the first one, so focused was he on his thoughts, but then a chorus of unholy wails rose to join the first one.

Stepping out of the small workroom that served as his makeshift office, he glanced up and down the street. It was mostly empty, except for the work crew lifting massive blocks along one side. Twenty men and women, previously inhabitants of one of the She'Har slave camps, were using their aythar to transfer the blocks one at a time from a massive sled to the partially completed wall of a building.

They had stopped now, letting the stone settle where it was as they glanced at one another and then at him. Several shrugged, no one knew what the source of the screaming was.

Violet poked her head out of a doorway across the way, where she had been working on a stone relief showing an idyllic pasture with sheep grazing. "What's going on?" she asked when she saw Ryan.

I don't know, he replied, broadcasting his thoughts.

Seconds later his magesight spotted the first fugitives, two men and a woman, running down the street behind the building he had just emerged from. They couldn't run very fast, though, for all three of them were limping, but they hobbled along as fast as they could possibly manage. A flare of aythar at the edge of his range struck one, and the woman went down, unmoving.

The other two rounded the corner and came into view. One of them yelled a warning, "She's gone insane!" Both of them were bleeding from a profusion of cuts, particularly their legs.

Then Brigid came into range, her aythar blazing like a phoenix, her chain writhing in the air around her, restless and angry. She wasn't quite running, but her steps were quick, moving her at a pace her wounded prey couldn't hope to match.

"Who?!" shouted one of the workers.

"Brigid, the raven-haired bitch!" answered the other one. Neither stopped moving. "If you want to live, run!"

Ryan stepped out, trying to block their path. *Stop. Calm down and explain what's happening.*

They ignored him, panic on their faces as they split up to go around him. Brigid rounded the corner at that point, her eyes taking in the work crew. She fired two short blasts, killing the two she had been chasing. She had fresh targets, making the two she had been chasing obsolete.

Brigid stop! shouted Ryan mentally, but his psychotic sister ignored him.

The workers watched her approach in fear and confusion, uncertain what was going on and looking to Ryan and each other for support. Pandemonium erupted when her chain blurred forward and cut three of them in two without pause.

Ryan was stunned by the sudden violence, and Violet ducked back into the building she had been working in. The workers scattered. Some tried to run and others used their magic to lift the stones they had been using and hurl them at their unexpected antagonist.

Brigid's enchanted chained spun, cutting down most of those who had dared to stand in front of her, while simultaneously she used her aythar to catch the heavy stone blocks hurtling toward her. The stones slowed and then reversed course, smashing into the ones who had wisely decided to flee.

Less than five seconds had passed, and most of his work crew was dead or dying. The only two left on their feet began to run, and Brigid watched them with an expression not unlike that of a cat, considering a toy. Her chain raced forward, hamstringing one leg on each of them.

Then she slowed her pace to let them gain some ground.

It took all of Ryan's resolve to step in front of her, *Explain yourself, Brigid. Why are you doing this?*

If she recognized him, it didn't register on her face. The enchanted chain whipped toward his face, and if he hadn't interposed his metal hand, it would have taken his head from his shoulders. He managed to catch it as it pulled back for another strike, iron fingers clamping into place before it could slide away.

That surprised her, but her will surged, and then he was flying into the air, pulled along with the weapon. He hung there awkwardly for a second as she prepared to whip the chain around and smash him into the ground, when Brigid suddenly paused, blinking.

Brigid stop! I'm your brother!

She croaked something, but her voice was too hoarse for him to understand.

Violet peeked out from the doorway, "It's Ryan, Brigid. Don't hurt him!"

Brigid lowered him slowly to the ground, but he didn't release the chain. He felt it pull as she tugged at it with her will, and then she stalked toward him with dead eyes.

Tell me what's going on! he insisted.

She got close enough for him to understand her hoarse words, "Let go or I'll cut that arm off and use it for a club." The other end of her chain twisted around to menace him.

"What happened?" asked Violet, having finally emerged from her hiding place.

Brigid's face twisted into a rictus of rage and agony, "They killed the babies! They killed *my* babies!" She yelled as she answered, but her voice had been ruined by screaming already, so it was still difficult to understand her.

Ryan let go of the chain, and she began moving automatically, following the ones she had wounded.

Violet and Ryan stared at one another as she left. Neither made a move to stop her.

We need to return, to find out what happened, he told her.

"What about Brigid?" asked Violet, her eyes slightly wild.

Do you want to try to stop her?

"No," she replied immediately.

Me either. Despite the bravery he had just displayed his body was already trembling in reaction to what had happened. Death had stared directly into his eyes and for a moment he had been certain he was about to die.

Together the two of them began heading for the main house and dormitory, where they lived. It was a fifteen minute walk normally, so they jogged to speed up the journey. Halfway there they met Emma, Anthony, and Piper heading toward them.

"Brigid?" asked Emma.

She went that way, replied Ryan. *What happened back there?*

"Assassins. Some of the people from the slave camps killed the children," stated Emma flatly. Her voice was smooth, but he could see the emotional strain hidden behind her eyes.

"Which ones?" asked Violet.

"All of them," answered Piper, her voice strident.

"Eight entered the main house," added Emma. "Sarah killed most of them, but two got past her. Kate and Garlin were dead before she could get to them. Several others ambushed Brigid. They slew Inara and Eldin right in front of her."

Violet's eyes grew round, "No wonder…"

She is killing every one of the workers she can find, Ryan informed them. *There's no stopping her.*

"It doesn't make sense," said Emma. "They knew they wouldn't survive the attacks, but they did it anyway. Even those hardened by the slave camps have a care for their own lives."

"We haven't exactly treated them well," observed Violet.

"They still have it much better here. We don't force them to fight," said Anthony.

"If they knew about what is planned…" wondered Piper.

They don't, insisted Ryan. *And if they did, they wouldn't throw their lives away, or target the children specifically.*

Emma glanced knowingly at Ryan, then she said two words, "The Centyr."

It's possible, acknowledged Ryan. *Though we kept them entirely isolated.*

"We don't really understand their capabilities," said Emma, "and it's possible one could have snuck in, hidden amongst the newer slaves."

Anyone here could be an assassin then, concluded Ryan.

"Except us," said Anthony. "Right?"

"That's not an established fact," said Emma, "but we have to assume so. If they had turned one of us, they wouldn't need to settle for something like this. One of us could kill the others by surprise and then do whatever he or she wished."

"I hate to say it," Piper put in, "but Brigid might have the right idea."

"There are at least four thousand workers here," said Violet, horrified.

Emma nodded, "Brigid can't kill them all."

Violet was shaking her head, "You didn't see her a few minutes ago, she looked perfectly capable of taking on an army."

That's beside the point, offered Ryan. *If she charges around killing them she'll start a panic. They will be running in every direction. We can't track them down if they run away. Even if they don't realize it, the tattoos on them have a limited range.*

"Are you proposing what I think?" asked Emma.

Better if we put an end to them quickly, before they escape, or worse, before the next group of hidden assassins tries to kill someone else.

"You want us to spread out and activate the kill tattoos, one at a time? That will take forever, even if all of us do it," objected Anthony.

"The others are back at the main house, watching over Sarah. She was pretty distraught after finding Kate and Garlin," noted Emma. "One of us could go back and mobilize them. The sooner we start, the sooner we finish."

Just tell them to fan out and try to stop anyone from leaving, Ryan told them. He tapped one section of the runes engraved on his arm. *I created a set of master runes that can do the job more efficiently.*

"How?" asked Anthony.

They allow me to activate the lethal tattoos on any of the slaves within my range, simultaneously.

Emma looked at him in surprise, "What's the range?"

Roughly a half a mile, I think, said Ryan. *Obviously I've never wanted to test it before.* Turning away, he walked back in the direction Brigid had gone, where the largest concentration of workers would be found. *I'll walk a pattern through the city and then back to Albamarl. It should be finished in a few hours.*

Violet shivered at the thought, but Emma was more practical, "What about the ones we prepared?"

They're in stasis boxes. They'll be safe, Ryan assured her.

The others looked at Emma, still expecting orders from her. With Tyrion absent, she was the obvious choice. "Spread out, head for the edges of the settlement. Make sure none escape. I'll go back and get the others to help."

And then Ryan began his march, stretching out his senses. Whenever his magesight made contact, he touched the spot on his arm and sent out a pulse, massacring every one of the slaves that came within his reach.

Thousands died, and most never knew their deaths were coming before it was over. The only small mercy to be found that day was that he got to the majority of them before Brigid did.

It was late in the afternoon when he found Brigid. She had cornered a small group within one of the newly finished residential buildings.

Since he was still outside he couldn't see her with his eyes, but he could tell by the fluttering of her fading aythar that she was close to collapse. Her chain dragged the ground beside her, only animating briefly when she used it to kill.

Sending out another pulse, he slew the last of her prey. Then he went inside to find his sister.

Brigid stood uncertainly in the largest room, her eyes unfocused and tired as she stared around herself, wondering what had happened. When Ryan entered, her head jerked toward him. "What did you do?" she rasped.

They're all dead, Brigid. There's no one left to kill, he told her.

"You stole them from me," she accused.

It's over.

Her eyes glared daggers at him, but then her knees sagged, and she slumped to the floor. She was so fatigued she should have passed directly into unconsciousness, but her eyes remained open, staring blankly along the floor. As her anger faded tears began to run from them.

Ryan went to her and bent down, slipping his arms beneath her shoulders and knees. She flinched away from his touch, but she no longer had the strength or will to resist. Straightening his back and knees he lifted her, cradling her slender form against his chest.

Brigid cried openly for several minutes as he walked, but by the time he had carried her home she had fallen into a troubled slumber.

CHAPTER 40

Tyrion was bored.

It was a problem he was well acquainted with. During his days as a slave, boredom had been his constant companion, even later, when he had lived alone with Lyralliantha, it had been common, but the last few years had been full of activity.

He looked up with anticipation when Byovar appeared. "You look healthy," he said, greeting the Illeniel lore-warden in his native Erollith. Learning the language had been the way he had first spent his time with Byovar.

"And your accent is flawless now," complimented the Illeniel. "I fear that I have dark news to bring you."

Tyrion was already on his feet, "Is Layla alright?"

"It isn't your child, or Lyralliantha either," said Byovar, shaking his head. "Something has happened in the place where you live."

His anxiety grew. *What have they done?*

"We just received a message from your daughter, Emma. There's been an attack."

Tyrion's eyes narrowed, "A message? Why not tell me sooner? If something was about to happen, your elders would know it before any message reached us."

Byovar looked embarrassed, "The elders move slowly, and I am not told much. This is the first I have learned of it. Your wife and…"

"Kate?!"

"Your wife and three of your youngest children are dead," finished the lore-warden.

The words washed over him, and as they passed his ears the world seemed to turn grey, as if all the color had leeched from it. Byovar's voice came to him from a great distance, echoing through an empty void. Tyrion remained still while his mind calculated, *three youngest children, that would be Garlin, Inara, and Eldin—and Kate, never forget Kate.*

What would Lyra say when she learned the news? How could he face Kate with the death of her children? His mind stopped, *No, Kate's dead.*

Byovar was still talking, but he could no longer hear him. In one swift motion, Tyrion whipped his fist forward, putting his shoulder behind it. The Illeniel She'Har hit the wooden platform as he went down, completely unconscious.

"You evil bastards," said Tyrion, looking down on the insensible She'Har. "You fucking knew. That's why we're here, to protect their plan, and everything else be damned. What about Kate? What about Inara and Eldin? What about Garlin!?" He was gripped by an urge to kill Byovar, even as the man began to twitch, his eyes fluttering open, unfocused.

Tyrion restrained himself, drawing on some reserve he hadn't known existed. He felt strangely calm, considering what he had just heard. *I feel nothing.*

Byovar groaned.

"Where are Lyra and our baby?" he demanded.

It took the She'Har a moment to answer, but he finally managed the words, "They are on their way here."

"Did she know? Did Lyra know about this, before we came?" *Of course, she didn't know,* he told himself, but he had to ask. He had to be sure.

"No," said Byovar, "I didn't know. She didn't know. The Elders tell us little that isn't required." His words were slurred as they passed his swollen lips.

Tyrion stared into space, motionless and feeling for all the world exactly like a statue. He was utterly dead inside.

"You have to believe me, Tyrion," insisted the groggy lore-warden.

He answered him in monotone, "I do, or you would be dead already. In the days to come you may wish I had slain you here and now, though."

In the distance, he sensed Lyra's hurried approach. She was carrying Layla in her arms. He went to meet her.

"Have you heard?" he asked her.

She looked worried, "No. They told me something had happened, and to find you. What is it?"

How would she react? How could he tell her that her only child was dead?

Lyralliantha had always been cool, calm, and level headed, like all of her people, but she was also the first of her kind to fall in love, to have a family. Tyrion stared at her, numb and unable to formulate a sentence. Eventually his mouth opened, as if on its own, "They're dead."

Her features grew concerned, "Who? Who's dead?"

"Our baby, Garlin, Kate, Inara, and Eldin," he answered, the names tumbling from his mouth like hard stones, and with each one he saw her register the impact, as if someone were striking her in the stomach.

Lyra's eyelids fluttered, and tears spilled out. Her mouth opened and closed, "That's not true. Is it?" she said at last, her voice halting uncertainly over each phrase. "This is some strange joke. It can't be true."

He couldn't bear to look at her, so he cast his eyes downward, "Byovar just told me."

"No," insisted Lyra. "The Elders would have known. They wouldn't let this happen." Her arms tightened as she spoke, squeezing Layla uncomfortably. The baby began to cry.

"They saved the ones they needed," he rasped, finding it difficult to speak. "That's why we're here. They needed us, they need Layla. Everyone and everything else is expendable to them."

A growling noise rose from her throat, or perhaps it was a partly strangled scream, but it made Layla begin to cry even harder. Lyra stopped, visibly taking control of herself and stroking Layla's cheeks with her trembling hands. "Shhh, baby. It's alright. I didn't mean to frighten you."

"Perhaps I should hold her," he suggested.

"No," said Lyralliantha, more forcefully than necessary. "Let me. This is all that's keeping me together right now." She looked around, struggling to find something to rest her eyes upon. Eventually she gazed upward, letting the tears run down her cheeks and neck as she fought to keep from shaking too hard.

After a minute, she added, "We're going home now?"

"Yeah."

The walk back wasn't much more than an hour under normal circumstances, but they went slowly, and the trip wound up taking closer to two. When they arrived, Albamarl seemed strangely quiet.

The gate guards were gone. In fact, there was no one visible anywhere, though once they entered the house, they found Abby and Sarah sitting together in the front room. Both looked as though they had been crying, and Sarah in particular, seemed distraught.

"Where is she?" asked Tyrion.

Sarah choked on her reply, but Abby managed to answer, "In the bedroom."

They started for it, but Abby cautioned, "Don't go in there. You don't want to see it."

They ignored her warning. Lyra handed Layla to Abby, and then they went in anyway.

There was blood in the doorway, blood on the floor, and even a small amount on the bedding. It pooled on the floor beneath where Kate's body lay, as well as under one of the strangers. The second attacker had died a fiery death, and that body hadn't bled much.

At first, neither of them said a word as they silently took in the scene, but when Lyra picked up Garlin's tiny broken body, her restraint vanished. She cried in a way that Tyrion had never heard from her before, emitting loud sobbing cries as her chest heaved and her lungs fought for air.

Tyrion could do nothing for her. Kneeling he stroked the hair from Kate's cold face. *I feel nothing.* The words repeated themselves in his mind, and for once they seemed true. He was dead, through and through. Then his eyes spied something clutched in Kate's hand.

He pulled her hand over to examine it, immediately recognizing the enchanted crossbow bolt. She had used it to kill the man by the door, and she must have pulled it free to stab the other one.

Kate had fought with everything she had, trying vainly to protect Lyra's baby. *And it wasn't enough,* he thought, staring at the sadly inadequate enchanted quarrel. *I left her here, and this is all she had to use...*

And then the dam broke, releasing a tide of anguish and pain so great that it swallowed him. Tyrion cried, and his body shook.

Lyra came to him, still carrying her dead baby, and the two of them held each other as they wept.

Sometime later, when they had finally fallen silent again, Lyra asked him, "You're going to do something, aren't you?"

"Yeah."

"You're going to kill them?"

"Yeah."

"All of them?"

"Everyone that had anything to do with this," he replied.

"That includes the Illeniel Grove," she said matter-of-factly. "You know that, right?"

He looked up at her with red eyes, "I do."

"Good."

CHAPTER 41

"What do we know?" asked Tyrion.

They were gathered in the council hall, and for the first time since it had been finished, Tyrion was the one sitting in the seat that had been named for him. Everyone who remained, David, Ashley, Sarah, Abby, Ian, Violet, Piper, Tad, Anthony, Emma, Ryan, Brigid, Lyra, and even tiny Layla, was present.

They were the only ones left alive in Albamarl and its environs. Ryan and Brigid had slain all the mages who had come from the slave camps, with the exception of those already in 'storage' within stasis boxes.

Emma began, "With certainty, only that eleven of the slaves were turned against us. Eight entered the main house. Six of those distracted Sarah, while two others slew Kate and Garlin. The last three approached Brigid while she played with Inara and Eldin. The two children were slain while she faced them."

"No," interrupted Brigid. "Eldin died before I did anything. I should never have let him get so close..."

"What's done is done," said Tyrion. "I'm not interested in 'what ifs' and 'might have beens'. All that matters now is what we do from this point forward. Does anyone know why the assassins did what they did?"

"They threw away their lives," answered Emma. "The only reasonable explanation I can come up with is that a Centyr must have turned their heads inside out."

"Did our Centyr mages have any contact with them?" asked Tyrion.

Ian shook his head, "No. They were kept separate. The only people they were allowed contact with were Piper and myself."

"Where are they now?"

"Dead," announced Brigid. "I took care of them first."

"And the rest of the slaves?" asked Tyrion.

"Also dead," responded Ryan. "Brigid and I eliminated them."

Tyrion studied Brigid for a moment before asking, "Whose decision was it to kill all of them?"

Brigid's mouth started to open, but Emma spoke over her, "Mine. We couldn't be sure how many of them had been manipulated."

He looked at Brigid, "You were about to say something?"

"Only that I agreed with her, although I would have preferred to do the job alone," answered Brigid sullenly.

"It would have been helpful to have saved a few to interrogate," noted Tyrion.

"You think I made the wrong choice?" said Emma, her chin firm.

"I won't second guess you. Under the circumstances, I doubt I would have been sane. I might have run amok, killing everyone I could find," he glanced at Brigid knowingly for a second. "Having Ryan put a quicker end to things was probably a better choice."

We still don't know how they subverted our servants, put in Ryan.

Lyra spoke then, her voice soft to avoid disturbing the baby in her arms, "The Centyr might have sent an agent in among some of the newer slaves."

Abby broke her silence, "Ultimately, however, we have no proof of anything, and we have destroyed any witnesses that might have provided proof."

"We don't need proof," said Tyrion coldly. "This is no court of justice. Are those in stasis still secure?"

Ryan nodded, *Yes.*

"How many do we have?"

Ryan answered, *Seven-hundred-twenty-three, primed for the final phase. More than half of those are Mordan. All have been given instructions on what to do when they are awakened. Another five hundred were put in stasis before them, when we were short of living space. Those are not primed, but given the timing, it is unlikely that they were subverted by the Centyr.*

Tyrion nodded, "And how many Mordan do we have who can be used?"

Only five, said Ryan. *Of those, only Brangor knows the locations that you selected for Emma and yourself, since Jordan did not return.*

"Wake them," ordered Tyrion. "Brangor can show them the locations first. After that we can make use of them transporting the civilians."

Sarah broke in, "The people of Lincoln and Colne aren't ready."

"They will be," said Tyrion. "I've decided to change the planned sequence. When the sky gets dark and the air gets cold, they'll beg us for shelter."

"Is that safe?" questioned Abby, looking concerned. "You always intended to protect them first."

Tyrion's expression was grim, "No, it isn't. I don't know for certain how bad it will be. But I do know that the Centyr will be watching us closely. They need something better to focus on. If they see us transporting the entire civilian population immediately after what happened here, they might decide to do something else. I intend to take the initiative before they have the chance."

"Let me do the first one, Father," begged Emma, her face somber. "They started this on my watch."

Tyrion locked eyes with her. If anyone had been wronged the most, if anyone had the right, it was him. He wanted to do it, but the dark despair that he saw in her made him reconsider. A tense minute passed before he gave her his answer, "You know which one to do first?"

Emma's eyes flashed, "I do."

"Take Brangor and the other Mordan. Have him show them the other teleport sites first, then send them back," he told her. "Ryan, you and Brigid will go as well. You make sure Emma doesn't lose control. Brigid, you'll make sure they survive."

The three of them stood, "Yes, Father."

Tyrion stared directly at Brigid, "This isn't the day for your personal revenge. Kill no one unless it is necessary. Draw no attention to yourself or them."

She growled but nodded affirmatively.

"Take a Prathion with you as well," he said, addressing Emma.

She smiled, "I was going to do that anyway."

After everyone had left, Lyralliantha asked him, "What are they going to do?" She had never been privy to his plans before.

"Shake the foundations of the world," he told her.

Was she successful, asked one of the Centyr Elders.

I believe so, reported Ceylendor. *Serrelia's attack was sudden and unexpected. Three of his youngest children were almost certainly killed.*

Almost certainly?

Her servants died before they were able to relay the results to her, but judging by the response, they must have been successful. Tyrion's older children slaughtered every baratti in the area.

Was the correct child among the three? asked the First of the Centyr Elders.

Yes, responded Ceylendor. *The Illeniels took one child out before the attack. Lyralliantha was caring for it, but the child actually belonged to Tyrion's human mate. We think it was a ruse meant to confuse us.*

Then Lyralliantha's child was one of those slain?

Yes.

Serrelia has done well, noted the First. *Have her confirm the deaths before she re...*

What was that? asked a different Elder.

The ground had jumped, and then the earth shook again.

Brigid had been disappointed when they found no one at the hot springs near the Centyr Grove, but she kept her irritation in check. Things were finally happening. Whether it was today or another day, she knew she would soon get what she desired.

She had lost sight of that for a while, distracted by In—*don't think about that.* She reined her thought in sharply. She might lose control, if she let herself think about them.

Keep it together, Brigid, Ryan told her. *I can't watch both of you at the same time.*

"Don't worry about me," she responded. "I only wish I could do this instead of her." She waved her hand at where Emma was reclining, her eyes already closed.

Emma heard neither of them, her mind was already in another place. She had changed, and this time it was a relief. Her inner pain and torment had faded, becoming almost insignificant within the greater being that she was an integral part of.

Releasing the pressure, the molten magma and gas that was pent up in the earth near her would be easy. It was already unstable, and her touch upon it in the recent past had only made it more unstable, but it wasn't enough.

The Centyr Grove was close, but the Elders had not taken root in the caldera itself. They would be shaken, and some would be damaged, but she wanted something more, and that would require some finesse.

Moving carefully, she began rearranging herself, reinforcing some areas, those closest to where the humans were, and relaxing others. She guided the hotter parts of herself, shepherding the magma and pressure to older chambers which had been dormant for much longer. Areas that lay deep beneath parts of the Centyr Grove.

When that was done, she fractured her skin, breaking the restraints imposed by layers of ancient bedrock. Her body shook with something that was neither pleasure nor pain, but something greater. At long last, the earth's ancient heat was free, and the world exploded with her rage.

It was with great reluctance that she listened to the tiny human voice that was calling her, urging her to return.

When Emma finally collapsed into herself, she opened her eyes to darkness and confusion.

She was inside a small bubble, a shield of intense strength, formed by both Brigid and Ryan. The two of them were holding hands, their minds interlinked to allow them to focus their efforts. Brangor sat beside her.

The Mordan's voice was close to panic when he announced, "She's awake!"

Emma's magesight searched the area beyond the shield, but she found only chaos. They had somehow fallen, dropping hundreds of feet into the earth, far below the area where she had first closed her eyes and begun to listen. Beyond that the ground was shaking and heaving, for as far as her senses could explore.

Get us out of here, Ryan ordered.

The world beyond the shield vanished, replaced by blue skies and snow covered ground. They were standing in the street outside the council building. Abby was waiting for them as they walked up the steps. Emma and Ryan would be reporting to Tyrion immediately.

"How did it go?" Abby asked them as they passed.

Emma and Ryan shrugged without stopping, but Brigid paused, "It was the most beautiful thing I've ever seen."

"Beautiful?"

Brigid nodded, "I don't understand what she did, or how she did it, but the world seemed to just come apart. Everything I could see, everything I could sense, for as far as my range extended, was torn apart. The ground shook, and then it collapsed beneath us. The smoke was too dense to see through with your eyes, the air too toxic to breathe—and that was the part near *us.* I think it was worse, much worse, for the Centyr Grove." Her eyes were rapt with enthusiasm as she spoke.

Abby's tone was flat as she responded, "It sounds awful."

"Dangerous is the word," said Brigid. "We almost died. It took everything we had to keep ourselves alive. If we hadn't left when we did, we would have died from lack of air, or been cooked by the heat." It was rare for Brigid to talk much, or with such vivacity.

Abby was puzzled by her reaction, "You sound as if you enjoyed it."

Brigid smiled, "Just when I thought the world was empty of joy, I saw a miracle. How many more times do we get to do this?"

Her sister shuddered, "Six, I think."

CHAPTER 42

Thillmarius entered Albamarl with a heavy heart. He had heard the news about Tyrion's family, and worse, the latest reports regarding what had occurred at the Centyr Grove's most populous territory. It was a region almost on the other side of the world, so he didn't give much credence to the suppositions put forth by some, that Tyrion had somehow caused the eruption, but he also knew that his opinion wouldn't matter.

The Centyr would respond, whether it was true or not.

The lore-warden was worried by the lack of guards, the lack of anyone really. Tyrion's city was empty, and Albamarl was barely more occupied. The tiny number of humans he met, all of them Tyrion's direct descendants, wouldn't be able to put up even a token resistance when the inevitable retribution came.

One of the daughters met him when he drew near to the original house. She seemed apprehensive, but she offered to find her father for him. He recognized her face, but had never learned her name.

"Wait here," she told him, directing him to a chair in the front room of the house. "He's busy, but he will come as soon as he can."

"What is he doing today?" asked Thillmarius, but the young woman didn't answer, though she had clearly heard the question. She backed out of the room and closed the door.

A half hour passed before it opened again. When it did Tyrion was there, his face grim. He took the seat across from Thillmarius, but he did not speak.

"I have news for you," began the lore-warden.

Tyrion nodded, but said nothing.

"The Centyr Grove, the larger portion of it, that lies on the other continent, has suffered a disaster," Thillmarius informed him.

Tyrion gave no sign of surprise or pleasure.

"There was a volcanic event," continued the lore-warden, "on a scale that is hard to imagine. The ancient humans called them 'super volcanoes', and there was one that lay near to their grove there."

"How bad was it?" asked Tyrion.

"More than half the grove was destroyed," said Thillmarius. "The remaining half will suffer from the aftermath for years to come."

"A tragedy I am sure," observed Tyrion blandly.

The Prathion leaned forward, "Not just for them. An event that size will have far reaching consequences for the weather."

Which won't be a problem for us, thought Tyrion smugly. "Pardon me, Thillmarius, three of my children were murdered very recently. I have little energy left for compassion or to worry about a change in the wind."

"Your people rely on crops to feed themselves, do they not?" queried the lore-warden. "This winter may last much longer than usual, and the summer that follows could be stunted and brief."

Tyrion already knew that, but he didn't intend to give that fact away, "That would be a serious problem."

"I wanted to offer my help, should things become difficult. The Prathion Grove could help make up for the shortage, should your crops fail."

"Why do you care?" asked Tyrion bluntly. "So a few of us starve, that makes little difference to the She'Har, doesn't it?"

Thillmarius frowned, "I know you dislike me, but I still would try to make up for past wrongs. We have discussed this before. I care dearly for the future between our two races."

"Yet the Illeniels were not concerned enough to help protect my children two days ago," accused Tyrion. "Do you think I don't realize what they could have done?"

"I am not an Illeniel…"

"But your people are their closest allies. Doesn't that put an equal share of the blame on your shoulders?"

"We were not given that information, Tyrion. If we were, I would have acted on it," said the lore-warden emphatically. "I understand your bitterness, but you have to believe that. I don't know the plan of the Illeniels. We do support them, but they tell us little. If I had known, plan or no plan, I would have done something."

Tyrion leaned back in his chair, looking down his nose at the Prathion, "So what are you here for now? What can you do now? Offer us bread when our crops fail? That won't be enough."

"It isn't just that," insisted Thillmarius, growing exasperated. "The Centyr will suspect you of having something to do with the disaster."

"Since they murdered my wife and children?" suggested Tyrion. "Do I take your statement as a confirmation that they were behind it?"

Thillmarius blanched, "I have no proof of that, but…"

"But you know it to be true!" spat Tyrion, leaning forward suddenly. "And now that some natural disaster has spoiled their precious lands, you come to relieve some of your guilt by warning me? Do you think we can face an attack from them if we are forewarned? If they come to take the lives of the rest of my family, what can we do? How many krytek do you think they will send?"

"The Illeniels…"

"Will do exactly as they please!" barked Tyrion. "If it suits their plan, they will intervene, if it doesn't, then they'll happily watch us bleed and die. Whatever happens, it will be what they wished for, just as it has always been."

"There are other options," said Thillmarius. "Fighting would be foolish, I agree, but you could hide your family. Bring them to the Prathion Grove. No one finds a Prathion who does not wish to be found."

"No."

"Don't let stubborn pride be the death of your people," begged the lore-warden.

"If you truly wish to aid us, send your krytek here. Let them guard us. Better still, come yourself. Learn what it is to risk your own blood." Tyrion's eyes bored into the She'Har.

"Tyrion, this is foolish…"

"I will not leave my home."

Thillmarius tried one more time, "Surely you can see that this…"

Tyrion stood, "I am tired, lore-warden, and I have a long winter to prepare for. Thank you for your warning."

Bowing his head, Thillmarius left. Once he had gone, Emma entered the room. Tyrion had left the privacy ward down so that she could eavesdrop.

"Are you sure that was wise, Father?" she asked.

"What better guardians against a foe that might teleport in to strike at any point, than those who cannot be seen?" he replied.

"We don't know that the Mordan will assist them," she countered.

"They will, and it will be a delight to watch them kill one another."

"A pointless battle," she observed.

"I have few entertainments left. Besides, we can't move until the people of Colne and Lincoln have been safely stored. If Thillmarius is correct, the Centyr might respond sooner than we desire. Better to have a strong defense. Get plenty of rest tonight, we begin moving them tomorrow."

Most of Colne came voluntarily, if reluctantly. When Sarah had brought the news that they needed to relocate immediately they had balked, since her anxious command was nothing like the pleasant invitation they had received before.

Tyrion appeared the next day, alone, and walked the streets. He went from door to door, speaking to heads of family households and generally spreading his message. Move or he would move them.

He did nothing to couch his demand as a request or anything genteel. He didn't beg, plead, or debate.

He merely told them he would return in two days, and he expected them to be on the road when he did, if they hadn't arrived at the meeting point near Albamarl already.

Belongings were to be left behind. They were to bring only what they could carry.

Given his violent history in Colne, only two families refused to leave.

"How do we handle them?" asked Sarah during her report to him in the council chamber.

"Send Brigid and twenty of the newly awakened slaves," he replied.

Sarah was aghast, "Brigid?"

The look on his face was cold, "I consider that merciful. Would you rather I send Ian?"

She shuddered, "No."

"What of Lincoln?" he asked. "I have not seen any of them in the arrivals."

Sarah cast her eyes downward. She had been the one go to Lincoln and demand the move, "None of them have come."

"Did you check on them?"

"Yesterday," she answered. "They were very clear in their dismissal."

"Did you make an example of any of them?"

"No, sir."

Tyrion sighed, "Well, there's not enough time for that now. Send the rest of the slave mages to round them up. The five Mordan we have can begin teleporting them here in batches."

"That will cause a panic," Sarah protested.

"You should have considered that when you were being diplomatic," he said, his voice harsh.

She blanched, "There are more than ten thousand people living in or near Lincoln."

"Who will be dead soon if we don't hurry," he finished for her.

"Unless you delay," she suggested. "An extra week would enable us…"

Tyrion lifted a finger, silencing her with the gesture. There was violence in his aura. Gone was the newly gentle man who had returned a few months ago. This was the man who had kidnapped her once, years past. The man who had taught her to fight and kill.

The man who wouldn't hesitate to punish disobedience with pain so intense it made one wish for death.

"We will move them now." Dismissing her with his eyes, he looked toward Ian, who sat silently at the table. "You will be in charge of bringing them here. Use whatever methods you prefer, just make sure they get here alive."

Ian stood, smiling, "Certainly Father." He had been discarded and distrusted by his siblings for so long that he hadn't expected to receive any meaningful instructions ever again. "We only have a few hundred slaves to use, it may be difficult to accomplish without injuring some of them."

Most of his children kept their expressions carefully neutral, though Abby and Sarah didn't bother hiding their disgust.

Sarah swallowed, forcing her anger down, "I'll go with him." She could at least moderate her sadistic brother's behavior.

"You'll be needed here, keeping our voluntary evacuees calm while we separate and store them in groups," he told her.

Sarah glanced at Emma, hoping to find support from the only other person in the room who might have some authority, but her sister turned her eyes away.

CHAPTER 43

Serrelia watched and waited. Her spellbeasts brought her frequent reports, linking directly with her mind to show her what they had witnessed. Most of them were tiny, finch sized flying creatures that would be hard for even a mage to spot, so long as they stayed a few hundred yards distant.

The slaughter of Tyrion's baratti servants made her job much more difficult, and since he and his children weren't allowing anyone new into the area she couldn't insert a new spy, forcing her to use this cruder method of gathering information.

She had yet to see anything that suggested he might have been involved in what happened at the Centyr Grove, but the events of the past few days were highly suspicious. One of the Prathion lore-wardens had visited, and the day after he had begun transporting large numbers of wildlings.

But why? she wondered. The numbers were boggling. Thousands had arrived in one day, only to vanish into the city he had been building. But they weren't there now. Now there were more arriving, teleported to the same area in groups of twenty. New groups arrived every few minutes, only to enter some of the buildings and disappear.

What is he doing with them? Doing a rough calculation in her head she realized he had brought in somewhere between two and three thousand people that day already. And that was on top of the much larger group that had arrived under their own power the day before.

They were powerless and lacking any useful weapons. Even if they had been mages, they wouldn't have been a real threat. What could ten or twenty thousand helpless humans be used for? They would be useless as soldiers.

She continued to send her reports home. It wasn't her job to judge.

Another two days passed, and the number of people arriving slowed dramatically. Dutifully, she reported that as well, and then she got a response from Ceylendor.

Stretching out her hand she accepted the tiny spellbeast on her palm, and then began absorbing the information stored in its tiny mind. Her mentor's voice played silently for her, *There have been new volcanic eruptions. One on the southern continent in a desert region, and a second near the smaller portion of the Mordan Grove. There was no significant damage, but their combined effect will likely produce a drastic effect on the climate. The elders believe Tyrion's actions to be responsible. It is clear now that he is moving to shelter the wildlings. The ash from these events will darken the skies, possibly forcing some of the elders into a dormant state for a time.*

Even after the sunlight recovers, the gases released will trigger a vicious winter that may last years, stunting growth. The Elders fear what he may be planning to do during such a period. Their response will be swift and decisive. The baratti threat is to be eliminated tomorrow.

Serrelia's eyes widened as she processed the information. The last line of his message could mean only one thing. The krytek would arrive soon.

Tyrion stood in the square in front of the council building, watching. He felt a constant tension, a pressure, to be doing something, anything, to speed up the process. There was nothing for him to do, though, other than look menacing.

Everyone moved a little faster when they saw him.

But it wasn't a very satisfying job. He had grown tired of seeing fear in people when they looked at him years ago. He had just gotten used to it, and whenever things started happening, it turned out to be too useful to give up.

The sky dimmed for a moment, and he looked up, wondering for a moment if the ash had finally reached them. It was just a normal cloud, however, passing in front of the sun. Tyrion turned his eyes back to the people in the square, disappointed. The latest eruption had been the closest to them so far, but it had still been several hundred miles to the west. That was close enough they would probably see some of the ash fall, eventually, but he wasn't sure of the wind movement. Most of it might fall elsewhere.

Of course, it didn't matter if they saw any of the ash at all. That was merely an added benefit. The ash would be a nuisance to the areas it landed in, but it was the less noticeable gases from the eruptions that would do most of the damage.

What he had learned of volcanic eruptions and the weather was interesting, but he didn't really know how severe the consequences of his plan might turn out to be. The She'Har studies of weather were largely theoretical. The knowledge they had gained from the ancient humans had been far more practical, but he had no way to use that knowledge in a meaningful way.

He was operating purely on guesswork. Besides, no one had ever seen a volcanic eruption of the magnitude that Emma had caused, much less seven of them.

It might even trigger an ice age, he thought. He didn't think that likely, though. From what he had learned, the sulfur dioxide and other aerosols wouldn't stay in the atmosphere more than a few years.

But he didn't *know* for certain, what the long term effects might be. It was all a giant gamble, to *nearly* destroy the world. *Like the farmwife who burns down her own home to rid it of mice.*

A flash of aythar signaled the latest arrival. There had been so many over the last few days that he hardly noticed. His eyes were open, but long seconds passed before he registered what he was seeing. The group standing in the middle of the square wasn't another group of civilians.

Ian was the closest, since he was there to direct the arrivals. Only chance saved him, for he stumbled when the first blast of aythar ripped through the space above, where his head had just been.

Most of the other people close to the landing point were not so lucky. People screamed and fell as the krytek leveled everything near their location, using blasts of raw aythar. They followed those attacks with spellwoven battlemagics, long lethal vines of energy that could be manipulated at will. They stripped flesh from bone wherever they touched human bodies.

More flashes of aythar registered in Tyrion's mind as more krytek arrived, appearing in spots scattered across the once empty city.

Ian's situation was dire. Everyone within ten feet of the landing platform was already dead. He was just beginning to react, his mind still struggling to catch up to reality. He had activated his runes, shielding himself, but even that defense would be inadequate as the krytek turned to focus their efforts on him.

"Wake up, boy!" shouted someone in Ian's ear, and then he was pushed sideways, out of the path of several of the spellwoven vines that were now orienting on his position.

Tyrion went over him as he sprawled, leaping into the enemy like a hunting cat that had finally found its prey. His armblades cut away the disorganized tendrils that reached for him, and then he was among them.

It was too many to face alone, or at least that's what a rational mind would have advised, but Tyrion's mind had gone silent already, replaced by the coldly calculating battle mind that had been his constant companion during his years in the arena.

Being outnumbered was always a disadvantage, but in that early instant, he had seen that his foes were still crowded together, shoulder to shoulder on the platform they had teleported onto. Their movements were limited as a result, for they didn't want to hurt their allies, but Tyrion had no such compunctions limiting him.

His armblades tore through their shields and then through arms, legs, heads, and other appendages too strange to name. The krytek came in a wide variety of bizarre forms. Those that survived his initial onslaught tried to scatter, but a square shield appeared just beyond the edge of the platform and then, in the span of a heartbeat, it compressed inward violently, knocking them back toward Tyrion's waiting blades. Off balance, they were easy prey.

Tyrion dismissed the shield and looked around. All those nearest him were dead, but others had appeared all throughout the city. "Where's Anthony?" he asked.

Anthony had been standing on the other side of the platform. He spotted the young man's still form before Ian could say anything. He had died in the first blast, before any of them had been able to react.

"Find Violet," he ordered Ian, pointing toward the building she had been working in. "Get back to the main house with her."

"What about…," Ian's eyes were wide as he gestured around them with his arms. "…them?"

Tyrion didn't know if he was referring to the krytek or the civilians they were slaughtering, not that it mattered. "We've saved as many as we can. Don't go out of your way to fight them, you aren't good enough. Get Violet, get to the house!"

Ian started running, and Tyrion went in the opposite direction, looking for Tad and Brigid. They hadn't been far away. If they were still alive he'd know soon enough.

He ran two blocks and reached the other landing platform, but they weren't there. From the bodies around it, it appeared that most of the krytek that showed up at that platform were dead. More had appeared not far off though, and he could sense fighting in a nearby building.

They were inside, killing krytek as they attempted to enter the building, but the extended battle was drawing reinforcements from other areas. While Brigid fought the ones entering the front, Tad struggled to keep up with those coming through windows and the back door.

Tyrion fell on those entering from the front since they were the larger group. They were so intent on their attempt to enter that they failed to sense the threat coming from their rear. Half were dead before they realized he was among them, the other half died when they tried to retreat, Brigid's chain weaving a deadly path through them.

In the brief pause that followed he spoke, "Get Tad, we have to return to the house."

"The people?" she asked, arching one brow curiously.

"We've done all we can, these can no longer be saved."

"There are twenty in the building with us," she informed him.

They had been protecting them. *How noble,* he thought. He started to order her to abandon them, but then he realized they might be useful. "Circle around to the back. Give the ones back there something better to do. I'll get Tad and bring the others out. We'll take them with us."

She left without hesitation, her lean figure running gracefully, her chain circling her tightly as she went. Tyrion found Tad inside, and together they gathered up the group they were sheltering. Brigid was back at the front of the building by the time they emerged, smiling.

Tyrion's magesight found no evidence of anything living near the house, but by the smile on his daughter's face, he knew there wouldn't be. "We're running for my house in Albamarl. Stay together and don't fall behind." He pointed up the road in the direction he meant, since most of them were unfamiliar with the area. "Go!"

He put a hand on Brigid and Tad's shoulders, forcing them to pause before following. "Brigid, follow on the left. Tad you take the right and I'll stay center."

"We can't protect them from the rear," said Tad, puzzled.

Tyrion started jogging, and his children did likewise. "There are hundreds of krytek here already. We can't protect anyone. If anything starts killing them it will give us advance notice. We can counterattack if there aren't many, or change course if they run into something too big for us."

"But…," Tad started to protest.

"Shut up and run boy," ordered Tyrion. "If you want to live, you'll do as I say."

Tyrion was thinking as they ran. *Lyra and Abby are at the house. Ashley, David, Sarah, and Piper are at the four storage chambers, they should be safe, so long as the She'Har haven't discovered our plans.* Emma and Ryan were a big question, though. He wasn't sure where they were. Emma had earned a rest after her efforts, and Ryan might or might not be with her.

A black cloud, lit from within by red and orange flashes rolled out from the left side of the street, engulfing the first four people running ahead of them. Tyrion didn't recognize the technique, but it was definitely a spellweave of some sort. Those who were touched by it died almost instantly.

Focusing his magesight, he identified three krytek within the building. "Run left!" he yelled. The cloud was still moving, passing to their right, so moving left would make it easier for them to avoid it. It also sent them heading more directly toward their enemies.

Tyrion sent a tightly focused blast of pure force toward the building, aiming not for the krytek, but the supporting wall that faced the street. His second blast struck an interior wall, and the building shifted, collapsing inward and towards them.

It wasn't likely to hurt the krytek since they were using powerful shields, but it was hard for anyone to do much while a building fell on them. The now smaller band of fugitives ran around the collapsing building, circling it to continue on a different street.

He pointed at the shifting pile of rubble as they passed, "Brigid."

She grinned and nodded as she slowed her pace.

A finely focused beam of power lanced out from the rubble, aimed directly at her midsection, but the chain hovering in the air around her moved to deflect it. Seconds later the collapsed building exploded in two places, as its entombed occupants used their energies to blast their way free. The first of the krytek to emerge fell in three pieces as her chain lashed forward, slicing through it.

The second ducked back, retreating into the pocket within the rubble that it had occupied. Another cloud of roiling black and red emerged instead. The cloud of violent energies moved far faster than any normal cloud would have, perhaps as fast as a deer might run. Brigid wouldn't be able to escape it on foot, and she could already tell it would eat straight through any normal shield she placed in front of it.

Whether it could get through the rune shield around her body was another question, but she didn't intend to test it. Her chain sped forward, stretching out like some impossibly long arrow as it went through the cloud. It had no effect on the spellweave, but after it went through it went into the hole in the rubble, seeking the krytek and blurring into a whirlwind of sharp edges. It died almost instantly.

But the cloud didn't vanish.

Bending her knees, Brigid focused her power in her legs, then she straightened, releasing the tension in her body like a whip, and she shot skyward.

Tyrion watched, even as they continued herding their small group of refugees. Brigid's leap surprised him. Using aythar to empower the body wasn't that unusual, but his daughter had shifted her power almost instantly, and done so with perfect efficiency. Her leap took her almost a hundred feet into the air. He wondered how she intended to handle the landing.

She soared up, making a parabolic arc as she flew, but her chain never stopped moving. It found the third krytek as she reached the apex. The creature was already dead as she began her meteoric fall, black hair streaming behind her like the tail of a comet.

She sailed over the fallen building, and made no attempt to slow her descent. Instead, she landed hard, the empowered muscles in her legs and back absorbing the impact. Tyrion also spotted the telltale flash of aythar inside her body, as the enchantment she had crafted into her bones was forced into activity for a second.

Brigid had planned her leap, for she landed some fifty feet ahead of her father and the band of refugees. Straightening, she turned her head to look back at them, tossing the black mane of her hair over one shoulder and grinning ecstatically at Tyrion and Tad. She didn't wait, though, like a wild animal she darted off, running before them.

She ran far faster than any of those following, and soon she was lost to sight.

Tad angled his run to bring him closer as he shouted, "She's crazy!"

Tyrion nodded. He couldn't ever recall seeing Brigid looking so happy before.

The last ten minutes of their jog was uneventful. The only krytek they encountered on the way were dead and dismembered. Brigid's chain had been busy.

They found her crouched down a couple of hundred yards from the wall that surrounded the house and dormitory where they lived, the true Albamarl, as Tyrion's children thought of it. The wall had fallen in most places, only jagged remnants remained jutting upward at irregular intervals. Hundreds of krytek fought in the area around it, seemingly with one another.

Smoke was rising from the dormitory building.

Ian and Violet were with Brigid, though Ian was unconscious and one arm looked to be broken.

"What happened to him?" asked Tyrion. *Probably fell in a hole trying to hide,* he thought uncharitably.

"We were attacked before we got here," explained Violet. "He killed one and then nearly got himself squashed trying to keep a wall from falling on me."

Tyrion's brows went up in surprise, and he glanced at Brigid. She merely shrugged.

"I took out the last two and levitated his body," finished Violet. She could see the doubt in their faces, "I know, I know—I never expected he had it in him either."

Brigid had already turned her attention back to the battle raging some distance ahead of them. "Some of the krytek are Prathions," she announced. "They keep vanishing and reappearing."

"Thillmarius must have taken me seriously," observed Tyrion.

"How do we get through that?" asked Tad.

A good question, thought Tyrion. He looked at Violet, "Take my hand." Then he spoke to Brigid and Tad, "If they notice us before I finish, try to buy us some time."

Violet reached out hesitantly.

"Link with me," commanded Tyrion, grasping her hand firmly. His daughter's mind shied away from his instinctively for a moment, but then she forced herself to relax, and their thoughts began to mingle.

He wasted no time. His mind expanded, and his body dwindled to insignificance as his self grew to encompass the air around them. Albamarl shrank beneath him as he joined the clouds, filling them with his anger.

The sky darkened, and the wind picked up dramatically.

Tad and Violet watched as the weather changed from mild to frightening in the span of a few minutes. Even the warring krytek noticed, and some of the enemy peeled away from the battle, heading toward the small group of humans. Brigid tensed, preparing to meet them, but Tad put a hand on her shoulder.

"Don't. Let them come to us. Whatever he's doing is going to be bad. You don't want to be out there when it happens," Tad cautioned. "Let's try this instead." Holding up one hand, he bent his will and his strength forward, tearing at the ground between them and the enemy, pulling it up to create a makeshift barrier.

It wouldn't be enough to stop them, but it slowed their advance. Seeing what he was doing Brigid began to help, using her greater strength to good effect.

And then the sky exploded.

The light was so brilliant it blinded them, as lightning began falling in sheets so dense it seemed like some bizarre actinic rain. The thundering roar that accompanied it was deafening. The lightning seemed to devour everything in the space between their group, and the ruined wall of Albamarl.

Some of the krytek survived, those with strong spellwoven shields were merely stunned, but most of the battling She'Har had already been wounded. Those without perfect defenses were slain instantly, and smoke began to rise from their charred corpses.

The shower of lightning continued for a full minute before it finally stopped. They looked at Tyrion. His eyes were fluttering, but he still hadn't regained himself.

Violet gave the command, "He's done. Run for it!" Using her aythar she lifted Tyrion and Ian both and began the charge.

Brigid, Tad, and the seven frightened people from Lincoln who were still with them took the hint and followed her lead.

Brigid and Tad overtook Violet and got ahead, ranging to either side to kill any krytek that were still moving. Most weren't, though. They passed through the former battleground with almost no resistance, and a few minutes later they reached the wall. Climbing awkwardly over the rubble of a fallen section, they were inside.

CHAPTER 44

The first thing Tyrion noticed was an oddly ephemeral spellweave that hung over the entire interior region behind where the walls had been. He wasn't sure of its purpose, for it didn't block aythar or material things from passing through it. He hesitated at its border, along with his children, but the mundane citizens of Lincoln who were still with them ran blindly through, since apparently it was only visible to magesight.

They were unharmed, and Tyrion could see Ryan standing at the door of his home, motioning for them to enter. Taking a deep breath, he stepped through, feeling an odd chill pass down his spine as his body went through the alien magic.

But he wasn't hurt. Following his example, the others crossed over as well, and then they ran for the house.

Since the fighting on that side of Albamarl had effectively ceased, due to a lack of combatants, things were quiet at the moment. Ryan met them at the door.

We weren't sure you had survived, said Ryan.

Tyrion nodded, "It appears the worst of the attack came here. Are the others alright? Where is Lyra?"

Inside, responded Ryan, *with Emma, Abby and Thillmarius.*

"Thillmarius?"

He saved them. None of us would have survived the first minute, if he hadn't been waiting, explained Ryan.

"Is he responsible for this strange shield around everything?"

It prevents them from teleporting into the area, explained Ryan, *and yes, he did that. Otherwise, there would have been no way to organize a defense.*

Tyrion and the others went inside, while Ryan remained at the door, guarding against the almost inevitable next assault. As soon as Tyrion passed the threshold his senses found Lyra. She was in the dining room with everyone else. Being the largest room, it was the most obvious location for them to gather. He went to her immediately.

She was holding Kate's baby, her baby now, but her eyes had a wild look in them. Her expression gained some relief when she saw him, "Everything has come undone, my love."

He glanced from her to the others. Everyone was watching him. "What do you mean?"

"Your enemies moved too soon. Even with the Prathion's assistance we won't last long."

Emma's eyes were on him, her expression unreadable. Tyrion knew what she must be thinking. Brigid still looked energized by her recent combat, but the rest looked deeply worried.

Nothing had worked out exactly as he planned it, but somehow he felt more comfortable with the chaos and uncertainty than he had during the peace and planning of the past few years. He felt sure it was a sign of the madness bubbling even now at the back of his brain. Tossing back his head, he began to laugh. His plan might be disordered, but it hardly mattered.

None of it would change the end result.

His laughter did nothing to reassure the other people in the room. Some of them were already close to panic, so Tyrion did his best to suppress the paradoxical giggles that were bubbling up from the dark center of his being.

Forcing a serious expression, he turned to Emma, "Where is Brangor?"

Her eyes flicked toward Thillmarius for a second before she answered, "In the usual place, until he is needed again."

Tyrion nodded. That meant he was in stasis in the chamber nearest to Albamarl, where Tyrion's experiments had taken place. Then he addressed Thillmarius, "How much longer do you think your people can keep them out of here?"

The lore-warden's expression was dark, "Not much longer. Your arrival took out almost half of those attacking here, as well as half of the krytek that were defending. More of your enemies are arriving with each passing minute."

"Thank you, Thillmarius," said Tyrion. "I doubted you before, but I believe you now. You've done enough. Return home before you become another casualty."

"What will you do?" asked the Prathion, concerned.

"I have a way to hide us. Don't worry. Have your krytek protect this place for a few minutes more, then they can withdraw."

"Very well," agreed Thillmarius, sadly. "I will go and pass the word to them." He vanished, becoming invisible. The only further sign of him was the door opening and closing as he left the room.

Tyrion waited until he heard the front door open and close as well, before he continued, "Emma, take everyone to Brangor. Ian, Brigid, Violet, Tad, Abby, you will be taken to your assigned places. Tell the others, Ashley, David, Sarah, and Piper when you arrive, then tuck yourselves in for a long sleep. When you next awaken, the world will be a different place.

"After they are settled, Emma, you and Ryan will go to the next site and continue your work. Once you finish, go to your place and do the same. Make sure to deal with Brangor first, though. He's the only one who knows the locations of all the chambers."

Emma nodded, "Yes, Father."

Brigid stepped forward, "No."

Tyrion focused on her, "Pardon me?"

Her shoulders were square and her back straight, "I'm not going. I have no interest in a new world. Everything I want is here."

"You'll die," he told her. "Is that what you want?"

"I don't care," she admitted. "I want to be free and unfettered. If this is the end, it's my last chance."

"Fine. You'll stay with me, but be warned, I have no intention of dying. When I'm done, I'll put you in a box or tie you into a knot trying."

Brigid smiled, "I'd love to see you try."

Tyrion looked back at Lyra, "You and Layla will stay with me as well."

"You couldn't have sent me away without you anyway," answered Lyralliantha.

Emma led the others to Tyrion's bedroom and relaxing her mind slightly she spoke to the earth, opening the way down into the tunnel that led to Tyrion's experimental chamber. As they went down the steps he gave her one further command, "Close the way, but don't hide it. By the time they find it you'll be gone, but I need them to find something to prevent them from tearing the entire foundation up hunting for us."

She nodded, and soon after the stone closed once more over the opening, but this time the tunnel beneath remained visible to magesight.

Tyrion went back to the dining hall, and on impulse he hugged Lyra and then stroked Layla's soft cheek. He glanced at Brigid, unsure if she would welcome an embrace or not, but she took the initiative.

Stepping forward she put her arms around him, squeezing tightly for a brief moment. "You remember what I told you when you were dying?"

414

"Yeah."

"I still mean it."

After that he led them to the front entry. It had one door leading outside and doors on either side and one at the end leading to different parts of the house. Motioning for them to stand near the front door, he spoke to the earth and opened the way to his last remaining secret.

The floor shifted as the foundation began to flow, revealing a staircase that ended in a featureless stone wall. Once there, Tyrion put his hand on it, and the stone vanished, revealing another chamber beneath the house.

It was a circular chamber, twenty feet in diameter. At its center were three adult sized stone sarcophagi and four smaller ones. He had intended them originally for Kate, Lyra, and himself, with the smaller ones for Inara, Eldin, Layla and Garlin. His chest clenched briefly at the thought. Now Brigid would have to use Kate's, while most of those for the children would remain empty, save for Layla's.

Together he and Lyra put Layla gently into her stasis box, kissing her once more before he activated the enchantment. The infant's face became motionless as the magic took hold, and time stopped for her, then he closed the lid over her.

"What if we never awaken?" mused Lyra sadly.

"I'll make certain that doesn't happen," he told her. "I will have Abby take the first watch, once I'm done, and even if something happens to her, my box will have a finite time set. If it runs out I'll wake up automatically."

"Is this really necessary to save my people?" she asked him, her blue eyes dark in the dim light.

Tyrion shook his head, "I'm not going to save your people."

Her aura flashed angrily in his magesight, "*Not* the Illeniels, Tyrion. Layla, Brigid, you, and the rest of your children. You are my people now, you are my family."

"Oh, well yes, then," he told her. "This is the only way I can save your people. Rest here and I will return to release you—once it is safe again. I give you my word, I will return for you." He had never meant anything more in his life.

She lay down in the stone sarcophagus, and he activated the enchantment, finishing it by speaking the phrase that would be the key to releasing it one day. He had been thinking of Kate when he thought it up, but it applied equally well to Lyra, "Your husband waits for your return…"

That should have been it, but on impulse he added something else, "…and your forgiveness."

When he had finished he could feel Brigid's eyes on him. "Are you ready?" he asked her.

"You aren't putting me in one of those," she answered flatly. "Are you getting in one?"

"Not yet," he replied. "I need to give Emma an hour or two to finish her work before I unleash the krytek."

"Then I will wait with you," said Brigid firmly. "And if I don't get enough blood before you're ready, I won't be getting into any boxes. Not alive, anyway."

He nodded, "Let's go upstairs then. You can guard the house until it's time."

Together they walked up the steps. Brigid felt an errant breeze on her cheek as they went, almost as if someone had passed. She turned her head and focused her senses, but no one was there. "You should close this entry."

Tyrion disagreed. "Not until I'm ready. I'll close it when you go in to stay, or if they manage to fight their way past you."

Her visage was calm, "You will be waiting a long time then."

"Brigid, I'm serious. I don't intend to leave you to die here. Don't you want to see the new world? You could have a new life. Take a husband, have children of your own…"

She began to laugh, "I will never have a man to bed, not unless he has the strength to command my respect, or failing that, the power to bend me to his desire. Do you know of such a man?"

Reconsidering his words, he had to admit the thought seemed rather ridiculous, but he remembered the change that had occurred when she had been forced to care for Inara and Eldin. Yet he still found it sad. After all that he had wrought, all the evils he had done and still had to do, to think that Brigid would never have a chance at something better.

Glancing up, he saw she was still staring at him, a challenge in her eyes as she waited for his reply. With a sigh, he answered, "No, I don't."

She stepped up to him, "There is only one whom I respect, and I won't have him. There is only one strong enough to force me, and he would never do such a thing." Standing on her toes she kissed his cheek before turning away.

Emma leaned over Brangor's stasis box as he opened his eyes, "We have another task for you."

The Mordan mage sat up, counting the people around him. They seemed even more tense than usual, which was saying something. "Where do you want to go?"

"Several places," she answered promptly. "First, I want you to take Violet to chamber one, then return and take Abby and Ian to chamber two. After that Tad needs to go to chamber three, and then you'll take Ryan and me to the next target."

He knew better than to ask questions. He did as he was told, taking Violet first and leaving as she started talking to her sister Ashley, who was already at chamber one. He did the same with the others, until only Emma and Ryan were left.

As he put his hands out for them, Emma spoke again, "Actually, take us to chamber four before we go to the target. I need to talk to Piper." *Just in case we don't make it back, she needs to know it's time to find her rest.*

Abby stood on the opposite side of Brangor as he teleported her and Ian, and after they arrived she was glad to see David. The thought of being alone with her demented brother was unpleasant.

"No more citizens to put away?" asked David.

She shook her head, "The Centyr have attacked. Those left, are lost. Father wants us to find our boxes and get in them."

"Hard to believe we're really doing this," said David. "What will it be like when we open our eyes again, I wonder?"

"For me, not much different," said Abby. The enchantment on her stasis box was set with a timer included. She would waken after a year to make certain everything was as it should be. She would continue to rise periodically after that, checking on the state of the world.

Someone had to decide when it was safe for what was left of humanity to emerge.

"If you prefer, I could take your place, Abby," suggested Ian, with a wicked gleam in his eye.

She could only imagine what he might do, alone in a cavern full of helpless women. "That won't be necessary."

Ian laughed, "Still don't trust me? I am your brother, after all."

"Let's find our places," said David, tired of the conversation already.

"How about a hug before we part?" said Ian, mockingly. He didn't really expect either of them to accept his offer.

Abby glanced at David, meeting his eyes, and he nodded faintly back at her. Then she answered, "One hug, but make it brief."

Ian looked at her, confused, and then he smiled. Opening his arms, he embraced her, though she kept her own hands at her side. "There won't be many of us in this new world, right Abbs? We have to stick together." He slid one hand down to caress her hip.

And then he stiffened, his body jerking as though it had been struck by lightning as David's knife slid between the vertebrae in the middle of his back. His arms lost their strength, and Abby pulled them away before helping him down to the floor. Ian's eyes stared up at her while his mouth gaped. He was still conscious, but he couldn't draw breath to speak.

"You won't be there," said David, looking down. "And the world will be better for it."

Abby's expression was hard, "Before you die, you should know, this wasn't just our decision. We all agreed to it. Even Emma couldn't forget what your part in all this was, and no one wanted to see you trying to act as a father to all those children. They'll be better off this way."

Ian died, and when Abby stood back up her hands were trembling.

David looked at her with concern, Abby was the least suited for this sort of thing. She still had more compassion than any of them. "I'm sorry, Abby, but you know it was for the best." He started to embrace, her but she stepped back.

"No more hugs, David. Not now, not after—that," she told him. She wasn't sure she would ever be able to hug another person again, not without remembering.

"I'm sorry," he replied, looking down. "It isn't fair that this has fallen on you. You're the last person who should have to do this." Stretching out his hand, he offered her the dagger.

It was a short, ugly thing. A dark iron blade with no magic or enchantment on it at all. They had chosen it because it was the least likely weapon to be noticed by a mage. It would be useless against a shield of any type, strong or weak, enchanted or otherwise. It would only serve against a defenseless target, one who trusted the holder.

Whatever his sins had been, Ian had trusted David and Abby.

Abby accepted it, tucking it into the belt around her waist. "It has to be me. I couldn't forgive myself otherwise." *Nor can I forgive myself for the horrors I've already committed,* she added mentally.

David nodded, and then the two of them found their respective boxes and got inside. Activating the enchantment from within, they were frozen in time, and then they knew no more.

CHAPTER 45

The place where Emma and Ryan appeared was bitterly cold. Located near the southern pole, she wondered if it was even worth the effort, but Tyrion had been adamant. According to him the locations were irrelevant, it was the effect they would have on the weather afterward that was important.

A darker, colder world would be difficult for any She'Har who survived the plague, *if* any survived.

Emma settled in, making herself comfortable before beginning her task, and Ryan held her hand, raising a shield around the three of them and beginning his vigil.

Brangor simply waited. Each time he had taken them to one of their targets, the result had been frightening. Twice he had feared they wouldn't survive. He doubted today would be any different, especially without the wild girl here to reinforce the shield.

Soon the earth began to shake, not in a steady fashion, but with great hiccupping jerks followed by still pauses. A deep cracking sound issued from the distant horizon, and the sky in that direction grew dark.

A hot wind blew from that direction and Ryan reinforced the shield surrounding them, keeping whatever toxic fumes were in the air from reaching them. Bowing his head he seemed to be meditating and then, after a moment, Emma's eyes began to flutter.

It's time to go, he told Brangor.

Their next destination should have been a quiet one. It had been when they had scouted it months before. It lay dozens of miles from the border of the Gaelyn Grove. Today, though, the area was swarming with She'Har. They roamed the region, no more than a few hundred yards between one and the next.

Ryan's magesight identified them by their odd shapes, krytek.

They didn't have a Prathion with them to hide their presence this time, and apparently the She'Har had enough knowledge of geology to figure out where they would likely show up.

The krytek noticed their appearance just as quickly as Ryan identified them. All those within range began to circle in toward them, signaling those farther away to join them.

Take us back, ordered Ryan.

"No," said Emma. "We will finish this."

They'll kill us, Em. There are too many, he argued.

"Give me just a few minutes, then they'll be too busy dying to worry about us." The determination in her face wouldn't be denied.

He was still holding her since she had hardly had time to recover her senses after her last effort. Emma reached up with one hand and pulled his mask away. "Let me see you, one more time."

We don't have time for this, he protested, flinching as his face became visible. He knew how hideous he was.

Craning her neck, Emma kissed his scarred cheek. He no longer had lips to serve the purpose. "I know you think you're ugly, but you've always been beautiful to me," she said.

You're a fool, Em. With a thought he activated the runes on his arm, creating a powerful rune shield around them. Then he noticed that Brangor was gone. The Mordan mage had decided to take his chances with the kill tattoo rather than face a horde of krytek. *We're going to die. You know that.*

"Them first," she whispered, and then she relaxed, closing her eyes.

The first attacks hardly registered. The shield created by the enchantment on his arm was reinforced by the power he had stored in it. But the krytek around them grew in number with each passing minute, and the spellweaves that they used to tear at his defense grew more powerful as the krytek realized their enemy wasn't fighting back. They took their time, creating efficient weaves to cut into his magic.

Minutes passed as they strove to destroy the shield, and with each second the attacks grew stronger, and the aythar stored in his arm dwindled.

Ryan ignored them, focused wholeheartedly on his task and keeping his attention on Emma's peaceful face.

She could almost be asleep, he thought.

He felt it when the energy in his arm faded. The shield flickered, but he threw his own power into it, straining with all his might to keep it intact. The effort required was enormous, but he would not relent. Watching Emma, tears began to run from his one good eye, *I love you, Em. I've always loved you.*

She couldn't hear him, of course. Her mind was far away.

And then the strain overcame him. The shield collapsed and he sank into unconsciousness. It was a small mercy that he never felt the pain of the blast that severed his head from his shoulders.

Emma struggled in the darkness of the earth. Above she could see the tiny speck of flesh that had been her body, still cradled in the arms of the man she loved. It was hard to let go, to expand enough to accomplish her task. The rock was more stable here, it needed more convincing to release its bonds. Yet her attention kept returning to the two humans forms crouched on the surface.

Time was her enemy, and the distraction made it worse.

Whatever time was...

She was nearly there when she felt the man's death. The pain of it made her contract, losing her grip on what she had been doing. *Ryan!*

The name meant something to her, and with it came a torrent of emotion—and pain. Anger filled her, and at last she was able to release her hold on the flesh that tormented her. She expanded, leaving her pain behind and carrying the rage as her humanity faded.

The ground where Emma and Ryan's bodies lay exploded upward as thousands of tons of rock and soil erupted. It swirled for a moment and then coalesced, forming a massive giant of stone with eyes of red fire.

The krytek attacked immediately. They were not created to know fear, but their attacks did little to the monster in their midst.

The giant swept those nearest away, using her colossal stone fists, and then she gestured at the earth. Red hot magma shot forth in geysers around her. The earth shook as she sundered the foundations of the world with her will, with her anger.

The land shook for hundreds of miles in every direction, and the thing that had been Emma strode across it, killing every living thing that she found. Humanoids, animals, and trees she destroyed, but she hated the trees most of all.

Her wrath lasted for days, but none survived to tell of it. When it finally ended, she lay down and found her rest, surrendering her body of stone and rejoining the earth.

"I wonder why they haven't attacked," said Tyrion.

Brigid was pacing, frustrated. "You did too much when you came in. They probably think you'll call the lightning down again."

Tyrion grunted. "Maybe. The krytek aren't made to be cautious, but perhaps they don't want to lose the rest of their force."

The ground bucked beneath their feet, and then a distant roar rolled over them.

"Was that Emma's doing?" asked Brigid.

He shook his head, "She's too far away. None of the targets were close enough for us to feel anything. It was one of the decoy chambers." Poking his head out the doorway he looked in the direction of the city. A dark brown cloud rose above it. "They must have been using their time to search for the rest of the people we hid."

There were several such chambers in the city, hidden, but not hidden, they were meant to be found. Each had several hundred of the slave mages entombed in the stasis boxes they had created for themselves. The enchantments were traps, though. They held more aythar than necessary, and when tampered with they were made to deconstruct themselves with violent consequences.

Tyrion gave an evil chuckle. Once the enemy had tangled with a few of those, they would be more hesitant to look for the rest of the people he had sequestered. The chambers that held the citizens of Colne and Lincoln were located much farther away and much deeper in the earth. They were hidden using his and Emma's special talent.

While he was almost certain the She'Har couldn't find them, he had decided that the best way to stop the enemy from looking was to give them something to find. Making the decoy chambers into traps was just an added benefit.

Brigid went to the door, "It's been more than an hour, closer to two. I'm tired of waiting."

He sighed, "I can't release the krytek until you go downstairs and get in that box."

"I'm going to take my reward."

Tyrion frowned.

"What you promised me, years ago, Father. Blood."

"They'll just overwhelm you. You can't win, Brigid."

"I don't want to win," she replied. "That's your job. But, I *cannot* lose." She gave him a feral grin, the light of madness shining clearly in her eyes.

"You lose when they kill you."

Brigid pulled the dirty dress she wore over her head. It was the one she had taken to wearing while she cared for Inara and Eldin. "They *can't* kill me, Father. Only I can do that. Come, watch me. Watch me bleed and burn."

Tyrion's heart twisted suddenly. He had thought he was done with such emotions, but now that he knew what she meant to do, he found himself reluctant. *I don't want to lose her. I've lost too many already.* "Don't do this, please."

She ignored him, walking out the door.

"Damnitt," he swore. Running down the stairs, he removed the two tokens he needed from the chamber below, *I didn't want to survive this anyway.*

He noticed something odd before he left the chamber. A spellweave had been laid over Lyralliantha's stasis box.

426

"What?" he said, talking to himself in the dark. Examining the alien magic, he read the pattern. Since taking the loshti he had gotten much better at identifying their magics, just as he could now speak and read their language perfectly.

The spellweave was a lock, and a trap. It would have to be removed before the enchantment on her sarcophagus could be released, and if it were forced, the results would be lethal.

And he didn't know the key.

He stared at it, thinking hard. Only one person could be responsible. Thillmarius hadn't left when he had said he would. He had waited, and listened. *He discovered our betrayal,* thought Tyrion, *and then committed one of his own.*

Now he had an excellent reason to leave.

Listening to the stone for a moment, he closed the chamber and ran back up the stairs. Brigid was already outside, walking away from the house. He caught up to her. "Let's head for the Prathion Grove."

"As long as there's fighting," she answered. "What do you want to do there?"

"I need to find Thillmarius."

CHAPTER 46

Brigid got her wish almost immediately. Once they had left the area closest to Albamarl and begun walking toward the grove, the krytek took notice of them.

It started with several massive spellbeasts running at them. Tyrion used the tattoos on his right arm as a channel, directing a precise lance of power that tore through the heart of each beast. Spellbeasts were largely immune to most attacks; their bodies would simply reform after any injury, but he had faced enough of them during his years in the arena, that he had learned to spot the central nexus of the magic that sustained them.

Brigid gave him a harsh look.

"Don't worry, there will be more," he said reassuringly.

And there were. He and his daughter broke into a fast trot, covering ground and trying to keep their momentum going as a nightmarish assembly of bizarre krytek began appearing from different directions.

Tyrion's rune channeled blasts were sufficient to pierce their defenses and slay them at great distances until there were just too many to continue. His focused attacks took too long, and required precision to aim.

Emma wouldn't have had that problem, he thought with a smile, thinking of her with pride, before they fell on him.

He kept his armblades short and intense, ensuring that even glancing strikes would still have the power required to break the defenses of his foes, and he never, ever, stopped moving. They were everywhere and the close range meant that any attack that landed might have the necessary force to bring his journey to the Prathion Grove to an abrupt and fatal end.

Tyrion ducked and dodged, keeping his defense tight and strong, so that it shed the few blows that landed. He cut and he slew, but the number of times an unseen strike sent him reeling told him that part of his success was down to luck. If any of the attacks that found him had been strong enough, it would have been over.

Brigid was another matter entirely. She moved across the field as though it was what she had been born to do; dancing through her foes with a grace that was beautiful despite its grisly results. Though she was nearly as strong as her father, she wasted none of her power on defense, as if she believed that aythar spent to preserve her life rather than ending another's, was a waste.

The distance between them grew gradually greater as they fought. Neither of them was particularly adept at fighting as a team. But for Brigid it hardly mattered, she was a goddess of destruction and she had no need of allies.

Her chain was everywhere, soaring and flying away at one moment and then dipping back down to deflect attacks that she couldn't manage to dodge, but it wasn't her only weapon. Brigid's arms were sheathed in power, and she used them flawlessly, as though it cost her nothing in attention to control the chain that wove around her.

Inevitably, however, there were too many even for her to avoid or deflect all the attacks. A spellwoven tentacle slipped past her chain and ripped through the meaty part of her right thigh, opening the flesh to the bone before she destroyed it. She would not be running any farther.

Fifty yards away, Tyrion saw her stall and then stop, hobbling on her one good leg as she killed everything near her. Not being able to move was a fatal flaw, though. Her opponents no longer needed to avoid her advance, they only needed to stay out of the lethal zone around her. A circle began to form and Tyrion knew they would pick her apart with long range attacks.

Altering course, he ran toward her, nearly getting himself killed with foolish haste. Brigid was laughing as the blood coursed down her leg.

He was still twenty feet away when he sensed the change. The krytek had paused, coordinating themselves for a joint assault that she would be unable to block. Without thinking he relaxed his mind, and in an instant, he reached out to the earth. A wall of stone and earth ten feet thick shot up around the two of them, reaching thirty feet into the air. It also encompassed five or six krytek unfortunate enough to have been caught within it.

Brigid killed those in a heartbeat before giving her father a disappointed look, "What are you doing? Don't ruin this for me."

"You were about to get killed," he said rebuking her. "You can't go any farther with your leg like that."

She started laughing again, tipping her head back and letting the coarse laughter rise toward the heavens.

She's utterly mad, he thought.

But then she spoke a word and an ugly red light began to flow from where the bone in her right leg was exposed. It wasn't just that bone, however, it was all of them. That one was simply the only one that was visible to normal sight. With his magesight Tyrion could see the runes covering the rest of her frame flaring to life, burning with the aythar that she had carefully stored within them for so long.

Brigid straightened, putting her weight once more on her damaged leg. "You don't understand, Father. They *can't* kill me."

431

Every bone in her body was enchanted in a fashion very similar to that of her magical chain, allowing her to control them with her will alone.

She had gotten the idea years before, when she alone of all his children noticed that Tyrion had enchanted the bones in one of his legs to enable him to store an emergency reserve of power, but she had taken it several steps farther. Her entire body was a tool, one that she had used to store her power, and one that she would now use as a weapon to enact her bloody will on her enemies.

And using it will kill her, Tyrion realized. "Brigid stop. We still have alternatives. You don't need to do this."

"Open your barrier, Father, so I don't have to waste this power tearing my way free," she replied, walking forward once more.

He knew there was no stopping her. Lowering his head sadly, Tyrion opened the wall of earth ahead of them.

Brigid began to run, her mouth open again as she laughed madly, "Watch me, Father. Watch me bleed, watch me burn!"

The enemy were waiting when she emerged, and multiple lines of focused power converged on her as she ran out. She didn't bother trying to block any of them; they tore through her torso, arms, and legs, shredding and tearing through her flesh.

If she felt pain, she gave no sign. The chain flashed through the air and destroyed everything that moved within its reach, and Brigid kept running.

The krytek focused on her, almost ignoring the man who followed in her wake. Tyrion ran behind, killing those that approached from her rear. As she advanced the She'Har continued their attacks, attacks Brigid no longer wasted time avoiding. She ran, and she slew, and with every minute that passed there was less undamaged flesh left on her.

Her skeleton was showing in dozens of places, and fire seemed to flow from her wounds, limning her body in crimson flames, but Brigid would not die.

They had passed the boundary of the Illeniel Grove now, and they angled their path to take the shortest path through it to the Prathion Grove. There were fewer krytek here, other than the few survivors that chased them. The Illeniel children they crossed paths with offered no resistance, but Brigid killed them anyway.

When they reached the Prathion Grove, the She'Har there tried to fight, but they were far worse at it than the battle-bred krytek. She slaughtered any she found in her path, and when one of the elders roused itself enough to attack her with a massive bolt of viridian power she simply laughed.

The Prathion Elder's blast scoured most of the remaining flesh from her burning bones, but she still did not die. Making note of which tree had attacked, Brigid altered her course to return the favor. A powerful spellwoven shield appeared around the trunk, but she tore through it, using the burning bones in her hands as though they were claws, and then she placed one bony palm against it and sent out a pulse that shattered the massive trunk.

Brigid was running again before the tree had even begun to fall. Tyrion followed, and all he could do was watch as she spent her life in front of him. In truth, he knew she was already dead. Her heart and most of her vital organs had been destroyed almost as soon as she had left his protection. What ran in front of him now was what was left, a blazing symbol of hatred and vengeance, infused with Brigid's mind and will.

Two more of the Prathion Elders tried to stop her, with similar results. After that, if any of them were awake, they did nothing to provoke her. The children of the elders, the

Prathion She'Har began to appear in greater numbers. They fought with illusions and ambushes, appearing suddenly and vanishing, if they survived her violent reprisals, but they couldn't stop her.

Eventually they gave up. Though they didn't value their lives nearly as much as a human might, there was no point in letting her kill them. The Prathions vanished and remained hidden.

Brigid continued her run, heading for Ellentrea, and now that she had been deprived of prey, she began to kill every Prathion Elder that had the misfortune to find itself in her path. But with each trunk shattered, with every use of that devastating power, Brigid's flames dimmed.

Eventually her steps faltered, and soon after that she fell.

Tyrion stopped, kneeling beside her, his heart aching. He had no tears left, he had used them all up after losing Kate and his little ones, but he still felt a black despair as he watched her fading in front of him.

Brigid looked up at him, her burning skull almost completely bare, with only a small bit of scalp and hair still attached. There were flames where her eyes had been, but they were flickering, like candles in a strong wind. Without a throat or lungs, she couldn't speak, but her thoughts reached him, *Do you think they'll forgive me?*

"Who?"

Inara and Eldin, for failing them...

The lump in his throat almost made it impossible to answer, "I'm sure they are waiting for you. I bet Haley has been playing with them to keep them occupied until you get there." He had grown up thinking the She'Har Elders, the God-trees, were divine. Now that he knew they were merely sentient trees, he had no idea what to believe, or whether there was any sort of afterlife at all.

But as he watched his daughter's fire going out, he could only believe there must be something for her after death.

Haley, she whispered with her thoughts. *I did this for her, in the beginning. She told me to take care of you, Father. But I couldn't even do that.*

"She would have been proud of you," he muttered.

I love... Brigid's thought was never finished. The flames guttered out, and her bones collapsed into ash. All that was left of her now, was dust.

Tyrion sat there, staring at what remained, watching as the breeze picked up her ashes and began to scatter them. "It didn't have to be like this," he muttered. "I could have saved you. If only you had let me."

But that hadn't been what she wanted.

Looking around, he gauged his distance from Ellentrea. It was still at least half a mile away, and he had no guarantee that Thillmarius would be there, waiting to be found, if he got there. He could feel the eyes of the hidden Prathions on him, watching. Soon they would decide it was safe to attack.

Tyrion stood, straightening his back and feeling the soreness in his muscles. He was tired, so very tired. He still had the strength to fight, but he knew it wouldn't be enough. It had been a fools run, trying to reach Ellentrea.

It had served no purpose, other than to give Brigid her last wish. *"Watch me, Father. Watch me bleed, watch me burn!"*

He had, and now he was out of time. His final task had waited long enough. Emma had surely finished and found safety in her own stasis box by now. Reaching into the pouch at his waist Tyrion pulled out the small iron talisman that served as the key to particular stasis boxes, the ones that held his final gift to the She'Har. With a word he activated it, and several hundred stasis enchantments stopped working, releasing the slave mages that Abby had prepared.

The second item he removed from the pouch was one of the glass spheres that Ryan had created. They had all been identically made, with no master. If any of them was broken or released, all of them would be.

Tyrion waited, counting silently. *Give the Mordan time to find their destinations first...*

The first attack nearly caught him unprepared. Ducking, Tyrion felt the spellwoven tendril pass over him. His return stroke was raw and unfocused, but it sent the Prathion who had appeared, flying backward, stunned if unhurt.

Clenching his hands into fists, Tyrion gripped the air around him with his aythar, whipping it into a wind so tight and swift that it screamed as it circled him. Within seconds the tempest had become a deadly whirlwind that caught up leaves and dirt, sticks and small stones. It expanded around him, sweeping outward with deadly power, destroying everything it touched.

Tyrion poured his power into it, but he ignored its results. It was merely a distraction; in the back of his mind he continued counting.

His strength was coming to its end when he finished his count. "Five hundred," he intoned, letting the wind die down. Touching the glass sphere with one finger, he erased one rune and watched the magic that powered its tiny stasis field collapse. The glass cracked, and the small wasp-like krytek emerged, crawling up his arm.

It sat there for a moment, sniffing his skin, excited by the aythar in him. But it recognized its parent. Losing interest, it flew away, in a seemingly random direction.

It went almost a hundred feet before diving toward a section of empty earth, a place that had been scoured clean of leaves, plants, and debris. It vanished for a moment and then reappeared, having eaten its way through the veil of invisibility that hid a Prathion who had been sheltering there.

The She'Har stared at it, puzzled, and then it dove, piercing the spellwoven shield around the Prathion and burrowing into his skin.

Must not have been a lore-warden, thought Tyrion idly. *Otherwise he'd have known to kill it instead of staring at it.*

Not that it would have mattered. Hundreds of others just like it were finding their first meals in scattered locations around the world. If even half of them were killed by quick thinking She'Har, it wouldn't matter, only a few had to succeed to start a cascade that would eventually kill every human, She'Har child, and Elder who lived under the sun.

Tyrion watched the Prathion die, screaming, and then he smiled.

CHAPTER 47

The calm left behind after Tyrion's windstorm died down was short-lived. Only moments after the Prathion finished dying, his enemies renewed their attacks.

The Prathion krytek had arrived, probably called back by the elders, desperate to stop Brigid's one woman rampage through their grove. She was dead already, but that merely simplified their job, which now was reduced to getting rid of him.

The first appeared directly behind him, a monstrous beast that stood on four legs and was ten feet tall at the shoulder. Invisibility aside, it was hard to imagine how such a thing had moved quietly enough to get that close, but it had.

And its first spellweave was already prepared. A wide circle appeared in front of it, trapping Tyrion within its boundaries as it began to contract.

Tyrion was tired. He had fought long and hard, even while following in Brigid's wake, and the windstorm he had just used had drained him of what energy had been left. Adrenaline didn't help him either. A man can only fight for so long, facing death at every turn, before he finds himself numb. Tyrion's heart didn't even quicken as this latest threat materialized.

In the quiet void that was his heart and mind Tyrion wondered, *This must be it. I'll finally be able to rest.*

But his actions didn't reflect that silent sentiment. Too many years of struggling to survive had been ingrained in his soul, to accept death so easily. Activating the enchantment on the bones of his leg, he drew deeply on the power stored there and used it to leap high into the air.

His enchantment was nothing so serious as Brigid's, it merely kept a reserve of power for him to draw upon, it didn't make his bones unbreakable or anything as nuanced as turning him into an un-killable machine. As he sailed upward he used that power to recreate his rune shield, and then he turned his attention on the ground below.

Four more krytek had appeared and predictably, they were preparing to destroy him in mid-air. That was always the danger of leaping high, you couldn't alter your course again until your feet found solid ground again.

Taking the best aim he could manage while soaring skyward, he sent a rune channeled blast down his arm and slew one of them. The rest of his power he devoted to his defenses.

It almost wasn't enough.

Their return fire knocked him sideways and sent him rocketing into the trunk of one of the presumably dormant Prathion Elders. Stunned, he fell and after a brief drop of ten feet, the ground knocked the rest of the wind out of him. Dazed, he sat up. Hardly able to think straight he was still struggling to live. Old habits die hard.

Somehow his shield was still up, but if the krytek had followed up on their advantage then, he would have been finished. Oddly, though, they didn't fire, preferring to charge toward him. If he had been thinking clearly, he might have realized they didn't dare to damage the Elder he was sitting in front of.

The massive four-legged one reached him first, stomping down on him with a foot that he could now see was studded with large claws. Still sitting, he manage to lop it off with a drunken swing, and then the damned creature fell on him, crushing him beneath its multi-ton body.

Tyrion's shield encased body sank into the soft ground, until it pressed against one of the Elder's roots, trapping him there between the bulk of the thrashing krytek and the unyielding wood. He couldn't have been more helpless. His arms couldn't move, his torso was trapped, and he could only imagine his legs sticking awkwardly out of the ground on one side of his gargantuan oppressor.

What a stupid fucking way to die.

His immobility and the awkwardness of the krytek, still foundering as it worked to stand on its three good legs, on top of him, did give him a brief pause to think.

He remembered what he had once told Emma, *"We don't need power, we become the power we seek to wield."* It had been a good line, though he wasn't sure he was remembering it exactly as he had said it at the time. Either way, he knew what he needed to do.

Fighting his instincts, he let his mind slip free, expanding slightly and growing to encompass more of the world around him. The earth surged beneath his human body, pushing him upward. Simultaneously he tried to make the Elder's roots rise, to use as a weapon, but they ignored him. Their voice was different, as was that of the krytek. He hadn't noticed it before, but his ability was much more difficult to use with regard to the physical forms of other living creatures.

So, he focused on the earth, using it to create a swell of earth that separated him from his massive opponent before he raised it like a thick shield around himself.

The other krytek were close, but they never reached him; before they could attack his flimsy defense they found themselves sinking into the ground, mired by soil that had somehow come to life.

The fight that followed was surreal. Maneuvering his weakened human body and the ground around it simultaneously, he staggered to and fro, slashing at his opponents when they were close enough and using the ground to unbalance them whenever their attacks became too coordinated for him to handle.

It was like fighting in a boat, except that it only shifted and rolled beneath his enemies. Tyrion's body only staggered because of its exceptional exhaustion and fatigue.

He finished those four off and then noticed the horde that had grown around him. Hundreds more had found his position, but they were no longer paying any heed to him. A cloud of insects was in the air, and the Prathions danced and jerked as they tried to avoid being bitten. Some were already down, thrashing on the ground as they died.

Tyrion's gift had finally come to fruition.

Gouts of fire went up, along with other subtler uses of power, but while they killed some of his diminutive krytek, they couldn't kill them all. The Prathion krytek died, the She'Har with them died, and as the wasp burrowed into the bark of the elders, they began to die too.

The buzzing of tiny wings became a roar in his ears as the dark clouds of Tyrion's vengeance grew and filled the sky.

Tyrion's mind collapsed inward, until he was merely a man again, and he lay down, letting his tiredness have its way. Lying in the dry leaves and churned up soil, he watched the world die around him.

Many of his tiny children flew over to him, intrigued by his aythar, but once they had sampled it and recognized him, they flew away again. He watched the clouds pass by, white against the tiny blue spot visible through the canopy. Occasionally his view was obscured by the buzzing hordes, but that only made him smile. Drifting, he finally closed his eyes and fell asleep.

The She'Har could finish dying without him.

Thillmarius sat in the small room that had served him for many years while he oversaw the training of Prathion slaves. He could still remember clearly the first day he had seen Tyrion enter the room. It was not because the day had been special to him, it was a byproduct of being a lore-warden. The loshti granted perfect recall along with the knowledge of all the generations it had passed through before.

A loaf of bread sat on the table in front of him. He had never been sentimental, it wasn't a trait his people prized, but it held a world of meaning for him now. It embodied a failed dream, his attempt at rising above the wrongs done in the past, to find a way forward for both his people and those they had wronged.

The bread was perfect, lovely and light in its texture. It would have tasted wonderful, but he would never eat it. No one would.

He had thought it was just the Centyr that were being foolish, ignoring the accord and letting their paranoia and xenophobia spoil the accord, but today he had learned differently. Tyrion had never intended to honor it either.

He had planned all along to destroy the She'Har, he had admitted as much with his own words, and the hidden chamber that held Lyralliantha had been proof that he had not been making empty threats.

The Illeniels were no better. They had refused to help guard the humans, choosing instead to sit quietly in their grove, waiting for the destruction that they had engineered. It went without saying that they had some plan for survival, even if it came at great cost, but he doubted that their salvation extended to the Prathion Grove.

They were the ultimate betrayers, and Tyrion had been their tool, unwittingly at first, but willingly at the end. *But how will they do it?*

He didn't know. The Prathions were not in a good position no matter how he looked at it. Having put themselves at the forefront defending Tyrion and his people, they were now firmly in the sights of the Centyr and Mordan Groves, and probably the Gaelyn as well. Did the Illeniels plan to use them as scape goats?

Thillmarius shook his head, that didn't make sense. Whatever Tyrion was planning, even a civil war wouldn't be big enough to give him what he wanted, which apparently was the destruction of all the She'Har.

He had left his door open, and when a small insect flew in, buzzing as it homed in on him, his eyes spotted it immediately. He knew exactly what it was.

Throwing himself backward, he avoided its first zooming dive at his head. Panic almost robbed him of reason, but he managed to fry the tiny creature with a small burst of fire before it came back for a second try.

With a thought, he closed the door just as two more flew in. He fried them just as quickly. For the moment, he was safe. But for how long?

At last he understood Tyrion's plan, though how the man had accomplished it eluded him. Had the Illeniels created these forbidden krytek for him? If so, why? From the behavior of the wasps it seemed obvious that their original inclinations had been restored, which made them as great a danger to the Illeniels as it did to the other groves.

Why would they do such a thing?

A buzzing grew outside his door, and his magesight showed him an ever greater collection of the creatures gathering there.

They weren't content to wait. They were already burrowing into the wood of the building, which after all, was made from the extrusions of one of the Elder's roots. Most of them were digging into the door, though, weakening it as they sought to get to him.

His mind ran through a quick succession of defensive spellweaves, but none of them would be sufficient. From what he knew the creatures wouldeat through any magical defense he created, and the more aythar he used, the more they would be drawn to him.

He could kill some of them, but eventually he would lose.

A feeling of helplessness swept over him, followed soon after by anger. It wasn't right. It wasn't fair! *I tried to fix it.* But Tyrion hadn't cared. All the human wanted was revenge, narrow, short-sighted, revenge.

"Just like any other baratt, just like an animal," he intoned softly. "And now he's killed us all."

He had never been given to strong emotion, but his anger grew ever stronger. For the first time in his life, Thillmarius felt his anger burn hot. For the first time, Thillmarius hated.

And then he had an idea.

He would die, that was certain, but that didn't necessarily have to be the end. The kionthara were constructed using Centyr spellbeasts, and a spellweave that made them effectively immortal. He couldn't create a spellbeast, but he could do something similar, using his own mind as the substrate for the magic.

Of course, it was forbidden, and for good reason, but who would be left to gainsay his choices? He could already feel the building he occupied dying, along with the Elder that it was comprised of. The rest of the Elders were almost certainly suffering the same fate, and if the krytek plague was here, he was certain that Tyrion had made sure to spread it everywhere else as well.

He could already see holes appearing in the wooden door. Time was running out.

Drawing on the memories of his ancestors and feeding aythar to his spellmind, he quickly began knitting the necessary spellweave together. He felt a pain in his leg as the first wasp bit into his flesh, burrowing inward. It felt like a fiery ember tunneling through his body.

Ignoring the pain, he continued working. When the weave was finished, he swirled it around himself, letting it sink in over his shoulders like a shawl. The magic passed through his skin and went deeper, bringing with it a cold darkness.

The pain of the krytek in his leg faded, and then his heart shuddered. Everything went dark for a moment as oblivion overtook him. Thillmarius died, and his eyes closed.

But seconds later, they opened again.

Did I die? Am I still me? he wondered. He still felt like himself, but his rationale mind said otherwise. He knew that the true Thillmarius had to be dead. He was a replica, frozen in time by the spellweave, tied forever to a body that would never live again.

But he certainly felt real.

And he definitely felt hatred.

He remembered the krytek that had burrowed into his leg. What had happened to it? Examining himself, he found the entry hole, but the tiny krytek's body was dead. Using his aythar Thillmarius carefully worked it free, and then watched in amazement as his leg healed itself afterward. He hadn't known that would happen.

He also didn't understand what had killed the krytek. He hadn't been sure how it would react to his transformation. His first expectation had been that it would simply carry on eating him without being able to kill him, but that definitely wasn't the case.

More of the little creatures were buzzing around him now, but they showed no interest in him. Reaching out, he caught one with his hand and then watched with interest as it died in his hand. He felt a tiny surge of aythar as the krytek's life force was sucked out.

"Oh," he said simply. So that was how it worked. A slow smile spread across his face. Unable to die, no longer of interest to the weapon that Tyrion or the Illeniels created, he should have no difficulties now.

He had only one goal. To kill the man who had undone a civilization that had lasted for millennia.

CHAPTER 48

Tyrion woke to silence.

Something had tickled his nose, but his magesight detected no one nearby. Opening his eyes he saw snow falling. Reaching up, he wiped it away only to find a grey smear on his finger. Ash.

Emma did a good job, he thought, *for the ash to fall this far away.*

He sat up. The air was bitterly cold, which was one reason he had expected snow. Shivering, he took to his feet, staggering a little as he found his balance. If he hadn't woken when he did, he might never have woken at all. It was freezing.

With an almost unconscious effort of will he surrounded his body with a blanket of warm air. Having solved that problem, he stretched out his senses, letting his magesight explore the world within its reach.

He found nothing alive.

Well, that wasn't entirely true. There were animals, and small plants, even a few stunted trees that had somehow survived amid the tall Elders of the She'Har. But beyond those things, he found—nothing, no She'Har, no shining towers of aythar representing the elders, and no humans. The Prathion Grove was a graveyard, filled with the husks of dead trees and fallen bodies.

"Well, that's a nice change," he said aloud, mostly just to hear the sound of his own voice. It was deafeningly quiet. He had no idea what to do next.

Walking home was the obvious choice, so he did, but he had hardly taken two steps before he thought of the emptiness he would find there. The only people in the house were Lyralliantha and Layla, and he could talk to neither of them. He didn't dare. Awakening them now, before he was certain that the krytek he had created were gone, would be a death sentence.

"I've been alone before," he told himself. But never this alone. Even during his solitary confinement in Ellentrea there had been Amarah, coming several times a day to bring him food. At the moment, he was quite literally the last man left to walk the face of the earth.

He kept walking, filled simultaneously with lonely dread and a curious lightness. His burden was gone. His trials were over. He had succeeded, and now he had nothing left to do. An empty future stretched out before him.

It was when he finally entered his home in Albamarl that he remembered the spellweave over Lyralliantha's stasis box. He couldn't waken her, not in three months, when the krytek were gone, not in years, when the world began to recover, not ever. Not unless he discovered the key to disarming the spellweave that kept her trapped.

Unable to stop himself he opened the way to her chamber. He spent the rest of the evening simply staring at her and Layla. At least he could waken Layla, eventually. But how could he raise the child with no mother.

Thinking of Kate sent his thoughts into dark downward spirals that revolved around her and his lost children. He had gained exactly what he wanted and lost everything that he had ever had.

"Having second thoughts, baratt?" said a familiar voice over his shoulder.

His magesight told him no one was there, but he knew the voice. Thillmarius. Tyrion didn't move. *How did he survive?* The spellweave, that was the clue. The lore-warden hadn't just locked Lyra away from him; he must have hidden in the chamber.

Tyrion activated his defensive tattoos.

"Did I startle you, animal?" asked the lore-warden.

"I guess all your talk of humans being a sentient species was just for show, eh Thillmarius?" growled Tyrion in a low voice.

"Don't even begin to think to judge me, traitor!" spat the She'Har.

Tyrion turned slowly around, facing the empty space in which he knew Thillmarius must be standing. "Oh, but I do! You call me a traitor? You blame me for the death of your people? You started all of this, when you tortured me in the name of 'training'. When you forced my children to fight one another. When your people took a world that wasn't theirs and nearly wiped humanity from it."

"My only mistake was in thinking we could bridge the gap between our people. I acted in good faith, trying to forge a better future for your kind."

His voice was moving as he circled, trying to keep Tyrion from knowing exactly where he was. "You were a fool," taunted Tyrion.

The lore-warden appeared then, spellweavings flying from his hands to encircle Tyrion. He was standing five feet to his right. Tyrion leapt toward him, and before the magic could close around him, he thrust his right armblade completely through the She'Har's chest.

Which accomplished exactly nothing.

The Prathion never flinched, and his face showed no sign of pain. Tyrion might as well have been stabbing a straw dummy.

Now that the veil of invisibility was gone he could see something else as well. Thillmarius looked normal enough to his physical sight, but to his magesight the man was a black void, an emptiness where a living body should have been. Something was wrong.

Some kind of weird illusion?

The spellweave around him had tightened now, like a strange thorny vine, and its power tore at his shield. He kept it at bay by continuing to put more energy into his defensive tattoos, but he couldn't keep it up forever.

Shifting some of his power to his now trapped arms, he strengthened them, until he could force them down and out, slicing through the magic that held him. Then he ran.

The chamber that housed Lyra and Layla was no place for fighting.

Thillmarius followed him, laughing softly. "Do you think you can win, baratt? You only delay your defeat, and make it more enjoyable for me."

Up the stairs and through the front door, Tyrion ran into the yard. There was space there. When Thillmarius stepped through, he sent a blast of raw aythar, in the form of fire, to engulf his body. The lore-warden had been overconfident and hadn't bothered to create a defensive spellweave, and he would pay for it.

But the fire died the moment it touched him, the flames winking out as though they had never been. The aythar he had used to create them simply vanished, sucked into the void that was Thillmarius.

How is he doing that?

"Do you like fire, baratt? You use it like a child. Let me show you how it should be done." Magic flowed from the Prathion's fingers, weaving itself into a flame that seemed alive. It spiraled outward in ropes that grew and writhed around him, burning with intense heat—and then it converged on Tyrion.

His shield kept it at bay, but it was mere inches from his skin, and the heat radiated through, baking him within his protections. Tyrion didn't have long. Frantic, he spun, using his armblades in an attempt to destroy the spellweave, but the fire simply let them pass, reforming behind them as they passed.

Reverting to old tactics, Tyrion ripped the earth from beneath Thillmarius' feet, or tried to, but the moment the aythar he sent into the soil touched the lore-warden's feet, it vanished. A blast of wind failed as well, and his skin was beginning to blister inside his shield.

Desperate, and knowing he was only seconds from death, Tyrion lifted his arm and channeled a blast of force through the tattoos on his arm. This time he was rewarded, for the magic didn't die when it reached the lore-warden. It sent his opponent hurtling backward to smash into the stone wall of the house.

Tyrion heard bones snap when the She'Har impacted the wall. The flames around him vanished, and he knew he had found victory.

Thillmarius slumped to the ground and then, impossibly, he stood up again. Tyrion watched in astonishment as the lore-warden's upper arm straightened, the bones realigning. A large depression in the side of his skull swelled outward and then took its normal shape again.

And still the She'Har was a black blot of nothingness to his magesight.

"What have you done to yourself?" he asked.

Thillmarius laughed. "Wondering why I won't die? You already killed me, baratt. But I decided that I wouldn't let that stop me from returning the favor."

Tyrion couldn't help but think of Brigid's chain. It would have been an ideal weapon. He wondered how his foe would fare if he were cut into a dozen small pieces. The chain was in his bedroom, a memento he had brought back with him to remember Brigid, but he couldn't use it. No one could, it would respond only to her aythar.

But he knew his armblades still worked, even if stabbing wasn't the best attack. Slashing should work much better. And for some reason power channeled through the runes on his arms worked when raw aythar failed.

He started to level another channeled blast at the She'Har, but Thillmarius vanished, falling back on the talent of the Prathions again.

Tyrion created an aythar laced mist, to hide him from Thillmarius, but it died as soon as it contacted the skin of his already dead opponent. He couldn't tell where the contact had been. Changing tactics he sent a lacework of energy through the soil beneath his feet.

He had used the technique in the past, to discover where hidden enemies were standing. It would likely fail this time, but he would at least know where Thillmarius was when it contacted him.

The spell died almost instantly, Thillmarius was standing immediately beside him.

Before he could react a spellweave with the force of an avalanche struck. It was almost the same thing he had just done, seconds before. Except Tyrion's body couldn't recover as Thillmarius' had. He felt something crack deep in his chest when he struck the wall, and then the world went black.

Opening his eyes, he knew, somewhere in his fuzz laden brain that he must have lost consciousness. His shield was gone and Thillmarius was kneeling over him. He struggled to move as the lore-warden's hand reached for his throat, but his body was sluggish and reluctant to obey.

As their skin came into contact he felt a cold wind blow through his soul. The world dimmed and it felt as though he had ice in his veins. What little energy he had left quickly faded. Helpless, he stared into the eyes of the man he had hated and feared for so long.

He was going to die.

"After you're gone, I'll release Lyralliantha and remake this world," said Thillmarius. "I want you to know that. Whatever you think you accomplished, with all this meaningless destruction, it was for naught. You suffered, your family suffered, your children died, for nothing but your stupid animalistic pride. No one will mourn your passing, betrayer."

Tyrion gasped, his chest growing too weak to even draw breath.

"You lost before we even started, Tyrion," the She'Har informed him. "I *can't* die."

"Watch me, Father," Brigid had told him. *"Watch me bleed, watch me burn!"* In his mind's eye Tyrion saw her bones falling into dust once more, as her energy faded away. And then his eye noticed the flames on the ground behind Thillmarius. The dry grass there had caught fire when the She'Har's burning spellweave had been around him.

He can't die, thought Tyrion, *but that body can burn, and if there's nothing left...* The cold emptiness almost made it easier for him as he let his mind slip away, expanding and encompassing not the earth or wind, but the tiny flame burning a few feet away.

Tyrion became the flame, and the fire became his rage.

A pillar of fire blossomed, roaring skyward, and Thillmarius released his neck, turning around to see what had happened. Tyrion fell on him, and this time the fire didn't die, for this fire was not born of magic, of deliberately molded aythar.

This was a natural flame, imbued with the will and murderous rage of Tyrion Illeniel. It caught the unnatural body of the lore-warden within it, and then it began to burn ever brighter, becoming a scathing white column of incandescent fury.

Thillmarius screamed, a hideous cry of impotent despair as his body was reduced to ash. Then he was gone. Tyrion almost thought he could still see him, like a spirit left behind once his body was gone, but then even that faded away.

With nothing left to burn and no will to do more, the fire began to die, and Tyrion collapsed inward, until at last, he was just a man, cold and broken on the ground beside his home.

He could hardly move, something had broken, probably his collarbone, but he still felt a strange sense of contentment. He had been disappointed by his failure to reach Thillmarius before. As brutal as the fight had been, it gave him a sense of closure.

"I won, asshole," he whispered.

Tyrion managed, painfully, to drag himself into the house. Otherwise he would have frozen to death. He passed out after that, and whether it was one day or three before he woke again, he was never able to figure out. It didn't matter. He lived.

When he did come around, he spent a long time sorting out his injuries, fixing his broken collarbone and mending several other less serious fractures. The bruises he could do little about, and the blisters from his burns were hard to deal with as well.

Some things simply took time.

Eventually, he was able to walk, and after that he took care of his other needs. There was still food in the kitchen, and while his cooking was awful compared to Kate's, he wouldn't starve. After a week had passed he realized his food wouldn't last forever.

He hadn't planned well for this part. The townsfolk, frozen in stasis, didn't need to eat, but he did, and so would they when they were eventually brought back. The winter had turned bitterly cold and ice was everywhere.

The livestock in Colne were probably still alive, but when the winter failed to abate after a few months, most of the animals would die. Tyrion had nothing but time, though.

After a second week of recovering he went back to his parent's home. It was a relief to find them gone. He had never checked to make sure that they had relocated with the other villagers, and he had been afraid he might find their bodies there.

The sheep were alright, so he herded them slowly back to Albamarl. Over the following months he crafted new stasis boxes to keep them in, one by one, along with the horses and other animals he found in Colne. The people would need them when they returned.

He had worried about food, but the entire world had become a freezer. The food left behind in the abandoned homes of Colne was hard frozen when he recovered it for his larder. Some of it he stored, some of it he ate.

He spent the rest of the year slowly gathering everything of value, food, tools, and animals. What he didn't use for himself, he put into stasis.

Alone, he had nothing but time.

The year turned, but winter never faded. He had considered waking Lyra to keep him company; the threat of the krytek he had created was long past, but that was impossible. He decided not to bother waking any of his children either, since there was nothing for them. The world was dark, cold, and bleak.

Tyrion waited, and watched, eating food that had lost all flavor from being frozen too long. The entire world seemed a perfect reflection of his soul.

EPILOGUE

He was shocked when Abby walked into the house. He had been alone for so long he had begun to talk to himself, and he frequently thought that he heard his children's voices, but he knew they were just his imagination.

Tyrion stared at her carefully, trying to determine whether she was real or just a dream. He had lost track of time. Had it been a year? That was when she was supposed to awaken.

She stared back at him, a look of pity on her face. "You look terrible, Father."

He reached up, scratching his face through the long beard he had grown. "I've been worse," he replied. He jumped when a second figure stepped through the door, a man he didn't recognize. "Who's that?" he asked suspiciously.

"Relax," she said, holding out a hand placatingly. "This is Davor, one of the Mordan we preserved. I woke him to help me get here sooner. It would have taken a week on foot."

"Oh." He spotted the tattoos around the man's throat, it was one of the slave mages. "Are you hungry?" he asked. It was the only conversation he could think of.

Abby shook her head, "No. I ate not long before we went into stasis. It feels like I just left the kitchen. What do you have in there?"

"Some meat," he told her. "Beef I think, it's hard to remember. There are turnips and carrots too."

She walked into the kitchen to inspect his provisions, and what she saw appalled her. When she returned, she glared at him, "Have you been cooking any of it?" The vegetables were frozen and appeared to be partially gnawed. The beef was raw and it looked as though he had simply been tearing pieces from it when he got hungry. None of the dishes looked to have been used in recent history.

He had been alone so long that he felt like a child as he looked into her angry face. "No," he whispered, his voice cracking. And then he began to cry.

His reaction startled her, and her native compassion immediately rose to the fore. "Shhh, it's alright. What's wrong? What happened?" He flinched when she put her hand on his shoulders, and it took her several awkward minutes to finally get him to relax so she could hug him.

He cried brokenly for a while, and then he began to talk. He told her of Lyralliantha's predicament, and Brigid's end. He told her about Thillmarius, and then he talked of the winter. Through it all he ached, from his heart outward, because he knew that in a few days she would be gone again, back to stasis, while he remained, to watch and wait.

Abby listened without commenting much, and when he had finally run out of words, she rubbed her hands on her skirt and stood up. "Let me see what I can do about that kitchen. You need a hot meal."

She worked in there for several hours, lighting a fire in the long dead hearth and cleaning several pots. After she had located some vegetables in a stasis box that looked like they wouldn't turn to mush once they were thawed, she began to cook. She discarded the frozen lump of beef and recovered a fresh-looking piece of mutton from another stasis box. When she finished the pot was bubbling, and a heavenly aroma filled the house.

Tyrion stood in the doorway, his eyes red and his face pale. "What's that?"

"Mutton stew, one of your favorites," she replied. "Kate taught me to make it, and while it's probably not as good as hers, I think you'll find it an improvement over what you've been having."

They ate, and Tyrion couldn't have said if it was better or worse than Kate's. It had been so long that it tasted like heaven to him, and he ate so much that when he finally stopped his stomach began to churn. Rushing outside he vomited onto the frozen ground.

Abby stroked his back while he heaved, "You ate too much, too fast. Your body couldn't handle it."

He looked up at her, "I want some more."

So, he ate again, this time more modestly, and Abby began to give him her news.

"Emma and Ryan didn't make it back," she said bluntly. "Davor and I checked the sites she was supposed to go to. It appears they never got to the seventh one, I think they died at the sixth, the one near the Gaelyn Grove."

"Did you see any sign of the She'Har?" he asked. "Did any of the Elders survive?" He had never found one living during his wandering, but he wanted to be sure.

"Nothing but the dead," she answered. "Even the She'Har, the children, their bodies are all still out there, frozen."

He had seen as much in the areas of the Illeniel and Prathion Groves.

"Would you like to see where she died?" asked Abby. "Davor and I could take you."

There was an odd tone in her voice, but Tyrion's mind was too disorganized to take note of it. The warmth of the food in his belly, the warmth of her presence, the presence of another human being, it all made him dizzy. He couldn't bear the thought of her leaving again.

Anything to keep her with him a little longer. The loneliness was unbearable. He doubted he could survive it again. "Sure."

"We'll go in the morning," she decided. "Tonight you need a proper rest."

She made him sleep in Layla's room, after she had cleaned it. He had been sleeping in his own bedroom, wrapped in a blanket of magical warmth while Kate and Garlin's frozen corpses lay nearby, but Abby wouldn't allow that.

The air felt warmer there, despite the altitude. Perhaps it was because they were closer to the sun, or perhaps it was his imagination. The region where the Gaelyn Grove had been was drastically different.

Emma's handiwork had caused the land to sink, except for the mountain that had risen where they stood. The ocean had rushed in, filling the area around it to create a new sea. The site of Emma's fall was now a large rocky island with long slopes that stretched down to the water.

It seemed fitting.

Whatever had happened to her and Ryan's bodies, they never found them. They had probably been buried, or incinerated. Massive flows of hardened lava covered much of the island landscape, and some of it was still hot. *That might explain the warmer temperature here,* thought Tyrion.

Abby and Tyrion stood in a flat depression, high up on one side of the new mountain. They were alone, having left Davor to wait near the shoreline. Reaching out she took his hand.

"You did it, Father," she told him, "you and Emma."

"Yeah," he replied, his voice toneless and empty, "with your help too."

"I'm not proud of that," she answered. "I never really wanted this. All the death, it was too much."

"Too late to lament that now."

"What will you do now?" she asked.

"In a few years, or a decade, when this winter finally ends, we can wake everyone up," he said flatly.

"And then?"

"Then we raise the children, train them to fight, rebuild the world," he finished.

She raised an eyebrow, "Train them to fight? Like you did with us? Why? There are no enemies left."

How little she knew. The She'Har were gone, but they hadn't come from nowhere. Reality was much larger than the world that humanity knew. Someday others might come, crossing the void between dimensions, as the She'Har had. He intended to make certain that humankind was strong and ready, for when that day came.

"There is always a need for fighting," he told her, his voice gaining some of its former steel. "We will never be weak again. I won't allow it." His hand tightened until she pulled hers away to prevent him from crushing it. "Our race once had power almost too great to believe, and the She'Har crushed them. We were naïve. Now we have the power that the She'Har brought with them, and I have some of the knowledge our ancestors possessed.

"I will rebuild the world. We can resurrect our technology and perfect the power we have taken from the She'Har, build ourselves into a force too great for any enemy to ever challenge again," he finished with conviction.

Abby looked up at him, her face sad. A solitary tear tracked its way down one cheek. "You can't let it go, can you?"

"Let what go?" he asked, staring at her in confusion.

"Never mind," she said, wrapping her arms around him and burying her face against his chest.

Too late he noticed the blade in her hand. He had trusted her completely, and solitude had made his instincts dull. By the time his magesight took note of it, it had already started sliding into his back, finding its way neatly between two vertebrae and severing his spinal cord.

It went in high, between his shoulder blades, causing his arms and legs to jerk and then go limp instantly. Falling, he never felt the ground when he landed. Abby knelt over him, her face wet with tears, the bloody knife still in her hand.

"Why?" he mouthed, unable to exhale. His body could feel nothing, except the burning ember of fiery pain between his shoulders. Pressing outward, he tried to use his aythar, to push her away, but Abby fought back, measuring her power against his.

In the end, it wasn't enough, the pain was too great, and his body was weak from a year of solitude and bad food. She smothered his power with her own, pinning him down, trapping him within the only part of him that worked, his mind.

"I'm sorry, Father," she whispered, looking down on him, her face only inches away. "None of us want the world you dream of. We want a new beginning, a place where people can be happy. We can't do that by bringing the old hatreds with us. We can't bring *you* with us."

"Lyra," he gasped.

She nodded, "We'll try to free her. Someday we will figure out a way."

"Promise…"

Abby kissed his forehead, still crying. "I promise." Then she stood. Looking down she saw the light in his eyes had gone out, and the aythar that defined his existence had almost faded.

Dropping the knife she walked away, toward a sea that beat mercilessly against rocky shores.

She was too far away to notice the transformation. There was no flash of aythar when it happened, and she was keeping her magesight focused firmly on the world in front of her, rather than the patricide that lay behind. It was all she could do to keep walking.

A sapling grew where Tyrion's body had fallen, and in time it would become a mighty tree.

"She killed him?!" exclaimed Moira. "Her own father? That's awful!"

I nodded, "And it was probably for the best."

"That's the worst story I ever heard," she complained, disgust on her face.

"The problem is the word 'father'," I told her. "When you think of it, you think of me, Mordecai, the man who raised you, who loved you. That's not what Tyrion was to her."

"He was a monster!" declared Moira. Then she looked at Lynaralla, realizing she was speaking of her friend's actual parent. "Sorry Lynn, I shouldn't have said that."

Lynaralla shrugged, unaffected as usual, "I never knew him as a man. That's why they sent me here, to understand what being human is."

Matthew spoke then, "What I don't get is how did Mom got the other part of it?"

"The other part of what?" asked Moira.

"Well, the loshti, that was passed down, from Layla to one of her children and so on, until now, with Dad and me, but Mom has the other thing, the Illeniel gift, right?" He looked to Mordecai, hoping for an answer.

I nodded, "That's my theory. She's no wizard, but she must have inherited something to cause her to have her visions."

"But how? They killed Lyra's baby, Garlin," said Matthew.

I gave my son a sympathetic look, "I'm not sure. I suspect they did the same thing Tyrion did, creating a human child, and then hiding it away protected by a stasis weaving, but that information isn't within the scope of my knowledge, or yours. The Illeniels were playing the long game."

"And now it has come full circle," said Lynaralla, "with me."

It was an obvious conclusion, since she was the first true She'Har child to be born in two thousand years, the beginning of the rebirth of the Illeniel She'Har. But I wasn't so sure, looking at Matthew, I had a different suspicion, but I didn't voice it.

Penny stuck her head in through the doorway, "Enough dark stories, come eat!"

"What is it?" asked Matthew with sudden interest.

"If it's mutton stew I'm not eating it," stated Moira. "I don't think I could ever eat that again, not after what we just heard."

I laughed and hugged her, grateful that my relationship with my children was as close as it was. Reaching out, I tried to snag Matthew with my other arm, but he ducked away.

"Let's not get too touchy, old man," he said with a grin.

We went and found our dinner, and thankfully, it was not mutton stew.

Coming in 2017

Demonhome

Matthew Illeniel seeks the source of the intruders into his world, traveling across dimensions to find answers. He must unravel the mystery of the She'Har's great enemy but the bigger challenge may lie in discovering the secrets of humanity itself.

For more information about the MAGEBORN series check out the author's Facebook page:

https://www.facebook.com/MagebornAuthor

or visit the website:

http://www.magebornbooks.com/

Made in United States
Orlando, FL
13 November 2022

24511586R00261